BARON TRIGAULT'S
VENGEANCE

She eagerly snatched it up, unfolded it, and read
From a drawing by John Sloan

BARON TRIGAULT'S VENGEANCE

A Sequel to " The Count's Millions "

Translated from the French of

EMILE GABORIAU

Wildside Press: 2003

Published by:

Wildside Press
P.O. Box 301
Holicong, PA 18928-0301
www.wildsidepress.com

Baron Trigault's Vengeance

1.

VENGEANCE! that is the first, the only thought, when a man finds himself victimized, when his honor and fortune, his present and future, are wrecked by a vile conspiracy! The torment he endures under such circumstances can only be alleviated by the prospect of inflicting them a hundredfold upon his persecutors. And nothing seems impossible at the first moment, when hatred surges in the brain, and the foam of anger rises to the lips; no obstacle seems insurmountable, or, rather, none are perceived. But later, when the faculties have regained their equilibrium, one can measure the distance which separates the dream from reality, the project from execution. And on setting to work, how many discouragements arise! The fever of revolt passes by, and the victim wavers. He still breathes bitter vengeance, but he does not act. He despairs, and asks himself what would be the good of it? And in this way the success of villainy is once more assured.

Similar despondency attacked Pascal Ferailleur when he awoke for the first time in the abode where he had hidden himself under the name of Mauméjan. A frightful slander had crushed him to the earth—he could kill his slanderer, but afterward—? How was he to reach and stifle the slander itself? As well try to hold a handful of water; as well try to stay with extended arms the progress of the poisonous breeze which wafts an epidemic on its wings. So the hope that had momentarily lightened his heart faded away again. Since he had received that fatal letter from Madame Léon the evening before, he believed that Marguerite was lost to him forever, and in this case, it was useless to struggle against fate. What would be the use of victory even if he conquered? Marguerite lost to him —what did the rest matter? Ah! if he had been alone in the world. But he had his mother to think of;—he belonged to this brave-hearted woman, who had saved him from suicide already. " I will not yield, then; I will struggle on for her sake," he muttered, like a man who foresees the futility of his efforts.

He rose, and had nearly finished dressing, when he heard a rap at his chamber door. " It is I, my son," said Madame Ferailleur outside.

Pascal hastened to admit her. " I have come for you because the woman you spoke about last evening is already here, and before employing her, I want your advice."

" Then the woman doesn't please you, mother? "

" I want you to see her."

On entering the little parlor with his mother, Pascal found himself in the presence of a portly, pale-faced woman, with thin lips and restless eyes, who bowed obsequiously. It was indeed Madame Vantrasson, the landlady of the model lodging-house, who was seeking employment for the three or four hours which were at her disposal in the morning, she said. It certainly was not for pleasure that she had decided to go out to service again; her dignity suffered terribly by this fall— but then the stomach has to be cared for. Tenants were not numerous at the model lodging-house, in spite of its seductive title; and those who slept there occasionally, almost invariably succeeded in stealing something. Nor did the grocery store pay; the few halfpence which were left there occasionally in exchange for a glass of liquor were pocketed by Vantrasson, who spent them at some neighboring establishment; for it is a well-known fact that the wine a man drinks in his own shop is always bitter in flavor. So, having no credit at the butcher's or the baker's, Madame Vantrasson was sometimes reduced to living for days together upon the contents of the shop—mouldy figs or dry raisins—which she washed down with torrents of *ratafia,* her only consolation here below.

But this was not a satisfying diet, as she was forced to confess; so she decided to find some work, that would furnish her with food and a little money, which she vowed she would never allow her worthy husband to see.

"What would vou charge per month?" inquired Pascal.

She seemed to reflect, and after a great deal of counting on her fingers, she finally declared that she would be content with breakfast and fifteen francs a month, on condition she was allowed to do the marketing. The first question of French cooks, on presenting themselves for a situation, is almost invariably, "Shall I do the marketing?" which of course means, "Shall I have any opportunities for stealing?" Everybody knows this, and nobody is astonished at it.

"I shall do the marketing myself," declared Madame Ferailleur, boldly.

"Then I shall want thirty francs a month," replied Madame Vantrasson, promptly.

Pascal and his mother exchanged glances. They were both unfavorably impressed by this woman, and were equally determined to rid themselves of her, which

it was easy enough to do. "Too dear!" said Madame
Ferailleur; "I have never given over fifteen francs."

But Madame Vantrasson was not the woman to be
easily discouraged, especially as she knew that if she
failed to obtain this situation, she might have considerable difficulty in finding another one. She could only
hope to obtain employment from strangers and new-
comers, who were ignorant of the reputation of the
model lodging-house. So in view of softening the
hearts of Pascal and his mother, she began to relate the
history of her life, skilfully mingling the false with the
true, and representing herself as an unfortunate victim
of circumstances, and the inhuman cruelty of relatives.
For she belonged, like her husband, to a very respectable family, as the Maumejans might easily ascertain
by inquiry. Vantrasson's sister was the wife of a man
named Greloux, who had once been a bookbinder in
the Rue Saint-Denis, but who had now retired from
business with a competency. "Why had this Greloux
refused to save them from bankruptcy? Because one
could never hope for a favor from relatives," she
groaned; "they are jealous if you succeed; and if you
are unfortunate, they cast you off."

However, these doleful complaints, far from rendering Madame Vantrasson interesting, imparted a deceitful and most disagreeable expression to her countenance. "I told you that I could only give fifteen
francs," interrupted Madame Ferailleur—"take it or
leave it."

Madame Vantrasson protested. She expressed her
willingness to deduct five francs from the sum she had
named, but more—it was impossible! Would they
haggle over ten francs to secure such a treasure as
herself, an honest, settled woman, who was entirely

devoted to her employers? "Besides, I have been a
grand cook in my time," she added, "and I have not
lost all my skill. Monsieur and madame would be delighted with my cooking, for I have seen more than one
fine gentleman smack his lips over my sauces when I
was in the employment of the Count de Chalusse."

Pascal and his mother could not repress a start on
hearing this name; but it was in a tone of well-assumed
indifference that Madame Ferailleur repeated, "M. de
Chalusse?"

"Yes, madame—a count—and so rich that he didn't
know how much he was worth. If he were still alive
I shouldn't be compelled to go out to service again.
But he's dead and he's to be buried this very day."
And with an air of profound secrecy, she added: "On
going yesterday to the Hôtel de Chalusse to ask for a
little help, I heard of the great misfortune. Vantrasson, my husband, accompanied me, and while we were
talking with the concierge, a young woman passed
through the hall, and he recognized her as a person
who some time ago was—well—no better than she
should be. Now, however, she's a young lady as lofty
as the clouds, and the deceased count has been passing
her off as his daughter. Ah! this is a strange world."

Pascal had become whiter than the ceiling. His eyes
blazed; and Madame Ferailleur trembled. "Very well,"
she said, "I will give you twenty-five francs—but on
condition you come without complaining if I sometimes require your services of an evening. On these
occasions I will give you your dinner." And taking
five francs from her pocket she placed them in Madame
Vantrasson's hand, adding: "Here is your earnest
money."

The other quickly pocketed the coin, not a little surprised by this sudden decision which she had scarcely hoped for, and which she by no means understood. Still she was so delighted with this dénouement that she expressed her willingness to enter upon her duties at once; and to get rid of her Madame Ferailleur was obliged to send her out to purchase the necessary supplies for breakfast. Then, as soon as she was alone with her son, she turned to him and asked: " Well, Pascal? "

But the wretched man seemed turned to stone, and seeing that he neither spoke nor moved, she continued in a severe tone: " Is this the way you keep your resolutions and your oaths! You express your intention of accomplishing a task which requires inexhaustible patience and dissimulation, and at the very first unforeseen circumstance your coolness deserts you, and you lose your head completely. If it had not been for me you would have betrayed yourself in that woman's presence. You must renounce your revenge, and tamely submit to be conquered by the Marquis de Valorsay if your face is to be an open book in which any one may read your secret plans and thoughts."

Pascal shook his head dejectedly. " Didn't you hear, mother? " he faltered.

" Hear what? "

" What that vile woman said? This young lady whom she spoke of, whom her husband recognized, can be none other than Marguerite."

" I am sure of it."

He recoiled in horror. " You are sure of it! " he repeated; " and you can tell me this unmoved—coldly, as if it were a natural, a possible thing. Didn't you understand the shameful meaning of her insinuations? Didn't you see her hypocritical smile and the malice gleaming in her eyes?" He pressed his hands to his burning brow, and groaned: "And I did not crush the infamous wretch! I did not fell her to the ground!"

Ah! if she had obeyed the impulse of her heart, Madame Ferailleur would have thrown her arms round her son's neck, and have mingled her tears with his, but reason prevailed. The worthy woman's heart was pervaded with that lofty sentiment of duty which sustains the humble heroines of the fireside, and lends them even more courage than the reckless adventurers whose names are recorded by history could boast of. She felt that Pascal must not be consoled, but spurred on to fresh efforts; and so mustering all her courage, she said: "Are you acquainted with Mademoiselle Marguerite's past life? No. You only know that hers has been a life of great vicissitudes—and so it is not strange that she should be slandered."

"In that case, mother," said Pascal, "you were wrong to interrupt Madame Vantrasson. She would probably have told us many things."

"I interrupted her, it is true, and sent her away—and you know why. But she is in our service now; and when you are calm, when you have regained your senses, nothing will prevent you from questioning her. It may be useful for you to know who this man Vantrasson is, and how and where he met Mademoiselle Marguerite."

Shame, sorrow, and rage, brought tears to Pascal's eyes. "My God!" he exclaimed, "to be reduced to the unspeakable misery of hearing my mother doubt Marguerite!" He did not doubt her. *He* could have listened to the most infamous accusations against her without feeling a single doubt. However, Madame Ferailleur had sufficient self-control to shrug her shoul-

ders. "Ah, well! silence this slander," she exclaimed.
"I wish for nothing better; but don't forget that we
have ourselves to rehabilitate. To crush your enemies
will be far more profitable to Mademoiselle Marguerite
than vain threats and weak lamentations. It seemed to
me that you had sworn to act, not to complain."

This ironical thrust touched Pascal's sensitive mind
to the quick; he rose at once to his feet, and coldly
said, "That's true. I thank you for having recalled
me to myself."

She made no rejoinder, but mentally thanked God.
She had read her son's heart, and perceiving his hesitation and weakness she had supplied the stimulus he
needed. Now she saw him as she wished to see him.
Now he was ready to reproach himself for his lack of
courage and his weakness in displaying his feelings.
And as a test of his powers of endurance, he decided
not to question Madame Vantrasson till four or five
days had elapsed. If her suspicions had been aroused,
this delay would suffice to dispel them.

He said but little during breakfast; for he was now
eager to commence the struggle. He longed to act,
and yet he scarcely knew how to begin the campaign.
First of all, he must study the enemy's position—gain
some knowledge of the men he had to deal with, find
out exactly who the Marquis de Valorsay and the
Viscount de Coralth were. Where could he obtain information respecting these two men? Should he be
compelled to follow them and to gather up here and
there such scraps of intelligence as came in his way?
This method of proceeding would be slow and incon-
venient in the extreme. He was revolving the subject
in his mind when he suddenly remembered the man
who, on the morning that followed the scene at Madame

d'Argelès's house, had come to him in the Rue d'Ulm to give him a proof of his confidence. He remembered that this strange man had said: "If you ever need a helping hand, come to me." And at the recollection he made up his mind. "I am going to Baron Trigault's," he remarked to his mother; "if my presentiments don't deceive me, he will be of service to us."

In less than half an hour he was on his way. He had dressed himself in the oldest clothes he possessed; and this, with the change he had made by cutting off his hair and beard, had so altered his appearance that it was necessary to look at him several times, and most attentively, to recognize him. The visiting cards which he carried in his pocket bore the inscription: "P. Mauméjan, Business Agent, Route de la Révolte." His knowledge of Parisian life had induced him to choose the same profession as M. Fortunat followed—a profession which opens almost every door. "I will enter the nearest *café* and ask for a directory," he said to himself. "I shall certainly find Baron Trigault's address in it."

The baron lived in the Rue de la Ville-l'Evêque. His mansion was one of the largest and most magnificent in the opulent district of the Madeleine, and its aspect was perfectly in keeping with its owner's character as an expert financier, and a shrewd manufacturer, the possessor of valuable mines. The marvellous luxury so surprised Pascal, that he asked himself how the owner of this princely abode could find any pleasure at the gaming table of the Hôtel d'Argelès. Five or six footmen were lounging about the courtyard when he entered it. He walked straight up to one of them, and with his hat in his hand, asked: "Baron Trigault, if you please?"

If he had asked for the Grand Turk the valet would not have looked at him with greater astonishment. His surprise, indeed, seemed so profound that Pascal feared he had made some mistake and added: " Doesn't he live here? "

The servant laughed heartily. " This is certainly his house," he replied, " and strange to say, by some fortunate chance, he's here."

" I wish to speak with him on business."

The servant called one of his colleagues. " Eh! Florestan—is the baron receiving? "

" The baroness hasn't forbidden it."

This seemed to satisfy the footman; for, turning to Pascal he said: " In that case, you can follow me."

II.

THE sumptuous interior of the Trigault mansion was on a par with its external magnificence. Even the entrance bespoke the lavish millionaire, eager to conquer difficulties, jealous of achieving the impossible, and never haggling when his fancies were concerned. The spacious hall, paved with costly mosaics, had been transformed into a conservatory full of flowers, which were renewed every morning. Rare plants climbed the walls up gilded trellis work, or hung from the ceiling in vases of rare old china, while from among the depths of verdure peered forth exquisite statues, the work of sculptors of renown. On a rustic bench sat a couple of tall footmen, as bright in their gorgeous liveries as gold coins fresh from the mint; still, despite their splendor, they were stretching and yawning to such a degree, that it seemed as if they would ultimately dislocate their jaws and arms.

"Tell me," inquired the servant who was escorting Pascal, "can any one speak to the baron?"

"Why?"

"This gentleman has something to say to him."

The two valets eyed the unknown visitor, plainly considering him to be one of those persons who have no existence for the menials of fashionable establishments, and finally burst into a hearty laugh. "Upon my word!" exclaimed the eldest, "he's just in time. Announce him, and madame will be greatly obliged to you. She and monsieur have been quarrelling for a good half-hour. And, heavenly powers, isn't he tantalizing!"

The most intense curiosity gleamed in the eyes of Pascal's conductor, and with an airy of secrecy, he asked: "What is the cause of the rumpus? That Fernand, no doubt—or some one else?"

"No; this morning it's about M. Van Klopen."

"Madame's dressmaker?"

"The same. Monsieur and madame were breakfasting together—a most unusual thing—when M. Van Klopen made his appearance. I thought to myself, when I admitted him: 'Look out for storms!' I scented one in the air, and in fact the dressmaker hadn't been in the room five minutes before we heard the baron's voice rising higher and higher. I said to myself: 'Whew! the mantua-maker is presenting his bill!' Madame cried and went on like mad; but, pshaw! when the master really begins, there's no one like him. There isn't a cab-driver in Paris who's his equal for swearing."

"And M. Van Klopen?"

"Oh, he's used to such scenes! When gentlemen abuse him he does the same as dogs do when they come up out of the water; he just shakes his head and troubles himself no more about it. He has decidedly the best of the row. He has furnished the goods, and he'll have to be paid sooner or later——"

"What! hasn't he been paid then?"

"I don't know; he's still here."

A terrible crash of breaking china interrupted this edifying conversation. "There!" exclaimed one of the footmen, "that's monsieur; he has smashed two or three hundred francs' worth of dishes. He *must* be rich to pay such a price for his angry fits."

"Well," observed the other, "if I were in monsieur's place I should be angry too. Would you let your wife have her dresses fitted on by a man? I says that it's indecent. I'm only a servant, but——"

"Nonsense, it's the fashion. Besides, monsieur does not care about that. A man who——"

He stopped short; in fact, the others had motioned him to be silent. The baron was surrounded by exceptional servants, and the presence of a stranger acted as a restraint upon them. For this reason, one of them, after asking Pascal for his card, opened a door and ushered him into a small room, saying: "I will go and inform the baron. Please wait here."

"Here," as he called it, was a sort of smoking-room hung with cashmere of fantastic design and gorgeous hues, and encircled by a low, cushioned divan, covered with the same material. A profusion of rare and costly objects was to be seen on all sides, armor, statuary, pictures, and richly ornamented weapons. But Pascal, already amazed by the conversation of the servants, did not think of examining these objects of *virtu*. Through a partially open doorway, directly opposite the one he had entered by, came the sound of loud voices in excited conversation. Baron Trigault, the baroness, and the famous Van Klopen were evidently in the adjoining room. It was a woman, the baroness, who was speaking, and the quivering of her clear and somewhat shrill voice betrayed a violent irritation, which was only restrained with the greatest difficulty. " It is hard for the wife of one of the richest men in Paris to see a bill for absolute necessities disputed in this style," she was saying.

A man's voice, with a strong Teutonic accent, the voice of Van Klopen, the Hollander, caught up the refrain. " Yes, strict necessities, one can swear to that. And if, before flying into a passion, Monsieur le Baron had taken the trouble to glance over my little bill, he would have seen——"

" No more! You bore me to death. Besides I haven't time to listen to your nonsense; they are waiting for me to play a game of whist at the club."

This time it was the master of the house, Baron Trigault, who spoke, and Pascal recognized his voice instantly.

" If monsieur would only allow me to read the items. It will take but a moment," rejoined Van Klopen. And as if he had construed the oath that answered him as an exclamation of assent, he began: " In June, a Hungarian costume with jacket and sash, two train dresses with upper skirts and trimmings of lace, a Medicis polonaise, a jockey costume, a walking costume, a riding-habit, two morning-dresses, a Velléda costume, an evening dress."

" I was obliged to attend the races very frequently during the month of June," remarked the baroness.

But the illustrious adorner of female loveliness had already resumed his reading. " In July we have: two

morning-jackets, one promenade costume, one sailor
suit, one Watteau shepherdess costume, one ordinary
bathing-suit, with material for parasol and shoes to
match, one Pompadour bathing-suit, one dressing-gown,
one close-fitting Medicis mantle, two opera cloaks——"

"And I was certainly not the most elegantly attired
of the ladies at Trouville, where I spent the month of
July," interrupted the baroness.

"There are but few entries in the month of August,"
continued Van Klopen. "We have: a morning-dress,
a travelling-dress, with trimmings——" And he went
on and on, gasping for breath, rattling off the ridiculous
names which he gave to his "creations," and interrupted
every now and then by the blow of a clinched fist on
the table, or by a savage oath.

Pascal stood in the smoking-room, motionless with
astonishment. He did not know what surprised him
the most, Van Klopen's impudence in daring to read
such a bill, the foolishness of the woman who had ordered all these things, or the patience of the husband
who was undoubtedly going to pay for them. At last,
after what seemed an interminable enumeration, Van
Klopen exclaimed: "And that's all!"

"Yes, that's all," repeated the baroness, like an echo.

"That's all!" exclaimed the baron—"that's all!
That is to say, in four months, at least seven hundred
yards of silk, velvet, satin, and muslin, have been put
on this woman's back!"

"The dresses of the present day require a great deal
of material. Monsieur le Baron will understand that
flounces, puffs, and ruches——"

"Naturally! Total, twenty-seven thousand francs!"

"Excuse me! Twenty-seven thousand nine hundred
and thirty-three francs, ninety centimes."

"Call it twenty-eight thousand francs then.   Ah, well, M. Van Klopen, if you are ever paid for this rubbish it won't be by me."

If Van Klopen was expecting this dénouement, Pascal wasn't; in fact, he was so startled, that an exclamation escaped him which would have betrayed his presence under almost any other circumstances.   What amazed him most was the baron's perfect calmness, following, as it did, such a fit of furious passion, violent enough even to be heard in the vestibule.   " Either he has extraordinary control over himself or this scene conceals some mystery," thought Pascal.

Meanwhile, the man-milliner continued to urge his claims—but the baron, instead of replying, only whistled; and wounded by this breach of good manners, Van Klopen at last exclaimed: " I have had dealings with all the distinguished men in Europe, and never before did one of them refuse to pay me for his wife's toilettes."

" Very well—I don't pay for them—there's the difference.   Do you suppose that I, Baron Trigault, that I've worked like a negro for twenty years merely for the purpose of aiding your charming and useful branch of industry?   Gather up your papers, Mr. Ladies' Tailor.   There may be husbands who believe themselves responsible for their wives' follies—it's quite possible there are—but I'm not made of that kind of stuff.   I allow Madame Trigault eight thousand francs a month for her toilette—that is sufficient—and it is a matter for you and her to arrange together.   What did I tell you last year when I paid a bill of forty thousand francs?   That I would not be responsible for any more of my wife's debts.   And I not only said it, I formally notified you through my private secretary."

"I remember, indeed——"

"Then why do you come to me with your bill? It is with my wife that you have opened an account. Apply to her, and leave me in peace."

"Madame promised me——"

"Teach her to keep her promises."

"It costs a great deal to retain one's position as a leader of fashion; and many of the most distinguished ladies are obliged to run into debt," urged Van Klopen.

"That's their business. But my wife is not a fine lady. She is simply Madame Trigault, a baroness, thanks to her husband's gold and the condescension of a worthy German prince, who was in want of money. *She* is not a person of consequence—she has no rank to keep up."

The baroness must have attached immense importance to the satisfying of Van Klopen's demands, for concealing the anger this humiliating scene undoubtedly caused her, she condescended to try and explain, and even to entreat. "I have been a little extravagant, perhaps," she said; "but I will be more prudent in future. Pay, monsieur—pay just once more."

"No!"

"If not for my sake, for your own."

"Not a farthing."

By the baron's tone, Pascal realized that his wife would never shake his fixed determination. Such must also have been the opinion of the illustrious ruler of fashion, for he returned to the charge with an argument he had held in reserve. "If this is the case, I shall, to my great regret, be obliged to fail in the respect I owe to Monsieur le Baron, and to place this bill in the hands of a solicitor."

"Send him along—send him along."

"I cannot believe that monsieur wishes a law-suit."
"In that you are greatly mistaken. Nothing would
please me better. It would at last give me an opportunity to say what I think about your dealings. Do
you think that wives are to turn their husbands into
machines for supplying money? You draw the bow-
string too tightly, my dear fellow—it will break. I'll
proclaim on the house-top what others dare not say,
and we'll see if I don't succeed in organizing a little
crusade against you." And animated by the sound of
his own words, his anger came back to him, and in a
louder and ever louder voice he continued: "Ah! you
prate of the scandal that would be created by my resistance to your demands. That's your system; but,
with me, it won't succeed. You threaten me with a
law-suit; very good. I'll take it upon myself to enlighten Paris, for I know your secrets, Mr. Dressmaker. I know the goings on in your establishment.
It isn't always to talk about dress that ladies stop at
your place on returning from the Bois. You sell silks
and satins no doubt; but you sell Madeira, and excellent cigarettes as well, and there are some who don't
walk very straight on leaving your establishment, but
smell suspiciously of tobacco and absinthe. Oh, yes,
let us go to law, by all means! I shall have an advocate who will know how to explain the parts your
customers pay, and who will reveal how, with your
assistance, they obtain money from other sources than
their husband's cash-box."

When M. Van Klopen was addressed in this style,
he was not at all pleased. "And I!" he exclaimed, "I
will tell people that Baron Trigault, after losing all his
money at play, repays his creditors with curses."

The noise of an overturned chair told Pascal that the

baron had sprung up in a furious passion. "You may say what you like, you rascally fool! but not in my house," he shouted. "Leave—leave, or I will ring——"

"Monsieur——"

"Leave, leave, I tell you, or I sha'n't have the patience to wait for a servant!"

He must have joined action to word, and have seized Van Klopen by the collar to thrust him into the hall, for Pascal heard a sound of scuffling, a series of oaths worthy of a coal-heaver, two or three frightened cries from the baroness, and several guttural exclamations in German. Then a door closed with such violence that the whole house shook, and a magnificent clock, fixed to the wall of the smoking-room, fell on to the floor.

If Pascal had not heard this scene, he would have deemed it incredible. How could one suppose that a creditor would leave this princely mansion with his bill unpaid? But more and more clearly he understood that there must be some greater cause of difference between husband and wife than this bill of twenty-eight thousand francs. For what was this amount to a confirmed gambler who, without as much as a frown, gained or lost a fortune every evening of his life. Evidently there was some skeleton in this household—one of those terrible secrets which make a man and his wife enemies, and all the more bitter enemies as they are bound together by a chain which it is impossible to break. And undoubtedly, a good many of the insults which the baron had heaped upon Van Klopen must have been intended for the baroness. These thoughts darted through Pascal's mind with the rapidity of lightning, and showed him the horrible position in which he was placed. The baron, who had been so favorably disposed toward him, and from whom he was expecting a

great service, would undoubtedly hate him, undoubtedly
become his enemy, when he learned that he had been
a listener, although an involuntary one, to this conversation with Van Klopen. How did it happen that he had
been placed in this dangerous position? What had
become of the footman who had taken his card? These
were questions which he was unable to answer. And
what was he to do? If he could have retired noiselessly, if he could have reached the courtyard and have
made his escape without being observed he would not
have hesitated. But was this plan practicable? And
would not his card betray him? Would it not be discovered sooner or later that he had been in the smoking-
room while M. Van Klopen was in the dining-room?
In any case, delicacy of feeling as well as his own interest forbade him to remain any longer a listener to
the private conversation of the baron and his wife.

He therefore noisily moved a chair, and coughed in
that affected style which means in every country:
"Take care—I'm here!" But he did not succeed in
attracting attention. And yet the silence was profound;
he could distinctly hear the creaking of the baron's
boots, as he paced to and fro, and the sound of fingers
nervously beating a tattoo on the table. If he desired
to avoid hearing the confidential conversation, which
would no doubt ensue between the baron and his wife,
there was but one course for him to pursue, and that
was to reveal his presence at once. He was about to
do so, when some one opened a door which must have
led from the hall into the dining-room. He listened
attentively, but only heard a few confused words, to
which the baron replied: "Very well. That's sufficient.
I will see him in a moment."

Pascal breathed freely once more. "They have just

given him my card," he thought. " I can remain now ; he will come here in a moment."

The baron must really have started to leave the room, for his wife exclaimed : " One word more : have you quite decided ? "

" Oh, fully ! "

" You are resolved to leave me exposed to the persecutions of my dressmaker ? "

" Van Klopen is too charming and polite to cause you the least worry."

" You will brave the disgrace of a law-suit ? "

" Nonsense ! You know very well that he won't bring any action against me—unfortunately. And, besides, pray tell me where the disgrace would be ? I have a foolish wife—is that my fault ? I oppose her absurd extravagance—haven't I a right to do so ? If all husbands were as courageous, we should soon close the establishments of these artful men, who minister to your vanity, and use you ladies as puppets, or living advertisements, to display the absurd fashions which enrich them."

The baron took two or three more steps forward, as if about to leave the room, but his wife interposed : " The Baroness Trigault, whose husband has an income of seven or eight hundred thousand francs a year, can't go about clad like a simple woman of the middle classes."

" I should see nothing so very improper in that."

" Oh, I know. Only your ideas don't coincide with mine. I shall never consent to make myself ridiculous among the ladies of my set—among my friends."

" It would indeed be a pity to arouse the disapproval of your friends."

This sneering remark certainly irritated the baroness,

for it was with the greatest vehemence that she replied : " All my friends are ladies of the highest rank
in society—noble ladies ! "

The baron no doubt shrugged his shoulders, for in a
tone of crushing irony and scorn, he exclaimed : " Noble
ladies ! whom do you call noble ladies, pray ?   The
brainless fools who only think of displaying themselves
and making themselves notorious ?—the senseless idiots
who pique themselves on surpassing lewd women in
audacity, extravagance, and effrontery, who fleece their
husbands as cleverly as courtesans fleece their lovers ?
Noble ladies ! who drink, and smoke, and carouse, who
attend masked balls, and talk slang ! Noble ladies ! the
idiots who long for the applause of the crowd, and consider notoriety to be desirable and flattering.   A woman
is only noble by her virtues—and the chief of all virtues, modesty, is entirely wanting in your illustrious
friends——"

"Monsieur," interrupted the baroness, in a voice
husky with anger, " you forget yourself—you——"

But the baron was well under way. " If it is scandal
that crowns one a great lady, you *are* one—and one of
the greatest ; for you are notorious—almost as notorious as Jenny Fancy.   Can't I learn from the newspapers all your sayings and gestures, your amusements,
your occupations, and the toilettes you wear ? It is impossible to read of a first performance at a theatre, or
of a horse-race, without finding your name coupled with
that of Jenny Fancy, or Cora Pearl, or Ninette Simplon.
I should be a very strange husband indeed, if I wasn't
proud and delighted.   Ah ! you are a treasure to the
reporters.   On the day before yesterday the Baroness
Trigault skated in the Bois.   Yesterday she was driving
in her pony-carriage.   To-day she distinguished herself

by her skill at pigeon-shooting. To-morrow she wil
display herself half nude in some *tableaux vivants*. Or
the day after to-morrow she will inaugurate a new style
of hair-dressing, and take part in a comedy. It is al·
ways the Baroness Trigault who is the observed of al
observers at Vincennes. The Baroness Trigault has
lost five hundred louis in betting. The Baroness
Trigault uses her lorgnette with charming impertinence.
It is she who has declared it proper form to take a
'drop' on returning from the Bois. No one is so famed
for 'form,' as the baroness—and silk merchants have
bestowed her name upon a color. People rave of the
Trigault blue—what glory! There are also *costumes
Trigault,* for the witty, elegant baroness has a host of
admirers who follow her everywhere, and loudly sing
her praises. This is what I, a plain, honest man, read
every day in the newspapers. The whole world not
only knows how my wife dresses, but how she looks
en dishabille, and how she is formed; folks are aware
that she has an exquisite foot, a divinely-shaped leg,
and a perfect hand. No one is ignorant of the fact that
my wife's shoulders are of dazzling whiteness, and that
high on the left shoulder there is a most enticing little
mole. I had the satisfaction of reading this particular
last evening. It is charming, upon my word! and I am
truly a fortunate man!"

In the smoking-room, Pascal could hear the baroness
angrily stamp her foot, as she exclaimed: " It is an outrageous insult—your journalists are most impertinent."

" Why? Do they ever trouble honest women? "

" They wouldn't trouble me if I had a husband who
knew how to make them treat me with respect! "

The baron laughed a strident, nervous laugh, which
it was not pleasant to hear, and which revealed the fact

that intense suffering was hidden beneath all this banter. "Would you like me to fight a duel then? After twenty years has the idea of ridding yourself of me occurred to you again? I can scarcely believe it. You know too well that you would receive none of my money, that I have guarded against that. Besides, you would be inconsolable if the newspapers ceased talking about you for a single day. Respect yourself, and you will be respected. The publicity you complain of is the last anchor which prevents society from drifting one knows not where. Those who would not listen to the warning voice of honor and conscience are restrained by the fear of a little paragraph which might disclose their shame. Now that a woman no longer has a conscience, the newspapers act in place of it. And I think it quite right, for it is our only hope of salvation."

By the stir in the adjoining room, Pascal felt sure that the baroness had stationed herself before the door to prevent her husband from leaving her. "Ah! well, monsieur," she exclaimed, "I declare to you that I must have Van Klopen's twenty-eight thousand francs before this evening. I will have them, too; I am resolved to have them, and you will give them to me."

"Oh!" thundered the baron, "you *will* have them— you will——" He paused, and then, after a moment's reflection, he said: "Very well. So be it! I will give you this amount, but not just now. Still if, as you say, it is absolutely necessary that you should have it to-day, there is a means of procuring it. Pawn your diamonds for thirty thousand francs—I authorize you to do so; and I give you my word of honor that I will redeem them within a week. Say, will you do this?" And, as the baroness made no reply, he continued: "You don't answer! shall I tell you why? It is be-

cause your diamonds were long since sold and replaced
by imitation ones; it is because you are head over heels
in debt; it is because you have stooped so low as to
borrow your maid's savings; it is because you already
owe three thousand francs to one of my coachmen; it
is because our steward lends you money at the rate of
thirty or forty per cent."

"It is false!"

The baron sneered. "You certainly must think me
a much greater fool than I really am!" he replied.
"I'm not often at home, it's true—the sight of you
exasperates me; but I know what's going on. You
believe me your dupe, but you are altogether mistaken.
It is not twenty-seven thousand francs you owe Van
Klopen, but fifty or sixty thousand. However, he is
careful not to demand payment. If he brought me a
bill this morning, it was only because you had begged
him to do so, and because it had been agreed he should
give you the money back if I paid him. In short, if
you require twenty-eight thousand francs before to-
night, it is because M. Fernand de Coralth has demanded that sum, and because you have promised to
give it to him!"

Leaning against the wall of the smoking-room,
speechless and motionless, holding his breath, with his
hands pressed upon his heart, as if to stop its throbbings, Pascal Ferailleur listened. He no longer thought
of flying; he no longer thought of reproaching himself
for his enforced indiscretion. He had lost all consciousness of his position. The name of the Viscount
de Coralth, thus mentioned in the course of this frightful scene, came as a revelation to him. He now understood the meaning of the baron's conduct. His visit
to the Rue d'Ulm, and his promises of help were all

explained. "My mother was right," he thought; "the baron hates that miserable viscount mortally. He will do all in his power to assist me."

Meanwhile, the baroness energetically denied her husband's charges. She swore that she did not know what he meant. What had M. de Coralth to do with all this? She commanded her husband to speak more plainly—to explain his odious insinuations.

He allowed her to speak for a moment, and then suddenly, in a harsh, sarcastic voice, he interrupted her by saying: " Oh! enough! No more hypocrisy! Why do you try to defend yourself? What matters one crime more? I know only too well that what I say is true; and if you desire proofs, they shall be in your hands in less than half an hour. It is a long time since I was blind—full twenty years! Nothing concerning you has escaped my knowledge and observation since the cursed day when I discovered the depths of your disgrace and infamy—since the terrible evening when I heard you plan to murder me in cold blood. You had grown accustomed to freedom of action; while I, who had gone off with the first gold-seekers, was braving a thousand dangers in California, so as to win wealth and luxury for you more quickly. Fool that I was! No task seemed too hard or too distasteful when I thought of you—and I was always thinking of you. My mind was at peace—I had perfect faith in you. We had a daughter; and if a fear or a doubt entered my mind, I told myself that the sight of her cradle would drive all evil thoughts from your heart. The adultery of a childless wife may be forgiven or explained; but that of a mother, never! Fool! idiot! that I was! With what joyous pride, on my return after an absence of eighteen months, I showed you the treasures I had

brought back with me! I had two hundred thousand
francs! I said to you as I embraced you: ' It is yours,
my well-beloved, the source of all my happiness!' But
you did not care for me—I wearied you! You loved
another! And while you were deceiving me with your
caresses, you were, with fiendish skill, preparing a conspiracy which, if it had succeeded, would have resulted
in my death! I should consider myself amply revenged
if I could make you suffer for a single day all the tor-
ments that I endured for long months. For this was
not all! You had not even the excuse, if excuse it be,
of a powerful, all-absorbing passion. Convinced of
your treachery, I resolved to ascertain everything, and
I discovered that in my absence you had become a
mother. Why didn't I kill you? How did I have the
courage to remain silent and conceal what I knew?
Ah! it was because, by watching you, I hoped to discover the cursed bastard and your accomplice. It was
because I dreamed of a vengeance as terrible as the
offence. I said to myself that the day would come
when, at any risk, you would try to see your child
again, to embrace her, and provide for her future.
Fool! fool that I was! You had already forgotten her!
When you received news of my intended return, she
was sent to some foundling asylum, or left to die upon
some door-step. Have you ever thought of her? Have
you ever asked what has become of her? ever asked
yourself if she had needed bread while you have been
living in almost regal luxury? ever asked yourself into
what depths of vice she may have fallen?"

"Always the same ridiculous accusation!" exclaimed
the baroness.

"Yes, always!"

"You must know, however, that this story of a

child is only a vile slander. I told you so when you
spoke of it to me a dozen years afterward. I have repeated it a thousand times since."

The baron uttered a sigh that was very like a sob,
and without paying any heed to his wife's words, he
continued: "If I consented to allow you to remain
under my roof, it was only for the sake of our daughter. I trembled lest the scandal of a separation should
fall upon her. But it was useless suffering on my part.
She was as surely lost as you yourself were; and it
was your work, too!"

"What! you blame me for that?"

"Whom ought I to blame, then? Who took her to
balls, and theatres and races—to every place where a
young girl ought *not* to be taken? Who initiated her
into what you call high life? and who used her as a
discreet and easy chaperon? Who married her to a
wretch who is a disgrace to the title he bears, and who
has completed the work of demoralization you began?
And what is your daughter to-day? Her extravagance
has made her notorious even among the shameless
women who pretend to be leaders of society. She is
scarcely twenty-two, and there is not a single prejudice
left for her to brave! Her husband is the companion
of actresses and courtesans; her own companions are
no better—and in less than two years the million of
francs which I bestowed on her as a dowry has been
squandered, recklessly squandered—for there isn't a
penny of it left. And, at this very hour, my daughter
and my son-in-law are plotting to extort money from
me. On the day before yesterday—listen carefully to
this—my son-in-law came to ask me for a hundred
thousand francs, and when I refused them, he threatened if I did not give them to him that he would pub-

lish some letters written by my daughter—by his wife
—to some low scoundrel. I was horrified and gave
him what he asked. But that same evening I learned
that the husband and wife, my daughter and my son-
in-law, had concocted this vile conspiracy together.
Yes, I have positive proofs of it. Leaving here, and
not wishing to return home that day, he telegraphed the
good news to his wife. But in his delight he made a mistake in the address, and the telegram was brought here.
I opened it, and read: ' Papa has fallen into the trap,
my darling. I beat my drum, and he surrendered at
once.' Yes, that is what he dared to write, and sign
with his own name, and then send to his wife—my
daughter ! "

Pascal was absolutely terrified. He wondered if he
were not the victim of some absurd nightmare—if his
senses were not playing him false. He had little conception of the terrible dramas which are constantly en-
acted in these superb mansions, so admired and envied
by the passing crowd. He thought that the baroness
would be crushed—that she would fall on her knees
before her husband. What a mistake ! The tone of
her voice told him that, instead of yielding, she was
only bent on retaliation.

" Does your son-in-law do anything worse than
you ? " she exclaimed. " How dare you censure him—
you who drag your name through all the gambling dens
of Europe ? "

" Wretch ! " interrupted the baron, " wretch ! " But
quickly mastering himself, he remarked: " Yes, it's
true that I gamble. People say, ' That great Baron
Trigault is never without cards in his hands ! ' But
you know very well that I really hold gambling in horror—that I loathe it. But when I play, I sometimes

forget—for I must forget. I tried drink, but it
wouldn't drown thought, so I had recourse to cards;
and when the stakes are large, and my fortune is
imperilled, I sometimes lose consciousness of my
misery!"

The baroness gave vent to a cold, sneering laugh,
and, in a tone of mocking commiseration, she said:
"Poor baron! It is no doubt in the hope of forgetting
your sorrows that you spend all your time—when you
are not gambling—with a woman named Lia d'Argelès.
She's rather pretty. I have seen her several times in
the Bois——"

"Be silent!" exclaimed the baron, "be silent!
Don't insult an unfortunate woman who is a thousand
times better than yourself." And, feeling that he could
endure no more—that he could no longer restrain his
passion, he cried: "Out of my sight! Go! or I sha'n't
be responsible for my acts!"

Pascal heard a chair move, the floor creak, and a
moment afterward a lady passed quickly through the
smoking-room. How was it that she did not perceive
him? No doubt, because she was greatly agitated, in
spite of her bravado. And, besides, he was standing a
little back in the shade. But he saw her, and his brain
reeled. "Good Lord! what a likeness!" he murmured.

III.

IT was as if he had seen an apparition, and he was
vainly striving to drive away a terrible, mysterious
fear, when a heavy footfall made the floor of the dining-room creak anew. The noise restored him to consciousness of his position. "It is the baron!" he

thought; "he is coming this way! If he finds me here I am lost; he will never consent to help me. A man would never forgive another man for hearing what I have just heard."

Why should he not try to make his escape? The card, bearing the name of Mauméjan, would be no proof of his visit. He could see the baron somewhere else some other day—elsewhere than at his own house, so that he need not fear the recognition of the servants. These thoughts flashed through his mind, and he was about to fly, when a harsh cry held him spell-bound. Baron Trigault was standing on the threshold. His emotion, as is almost always the case with corpulent people, was evinced by a frightful distortion of his features. His face was transformed, his lips had become perfectly white, and his eyes seemed to be starting from their sockets. "How came you here?" he asked, in a husky voice.

"Your servants ushered me into this room."

"Who are you?"

"What! monsieur, don't you recognize me?" rejoined Pascal, who in his agitation forgot that the baron had seen him only twice before. He forgot the absence of his beard, his almost ragged clothing, and all the precautions he had taken to render recognition impossible.

"I have never met any person named Mauméjan," said the baron.

"Ah! monsieur, that's not my name. Have you forgotten the innocent man who was caught in that infamous snare set for him by the Viscount de Coralth?"

"Yes, yes," replied the baron, "I remember you now." And then recollecting the terrible scene that had just taken place in the adjoining room: "How long have you been here?" he asked.

Should Pascal tell a falsehood, or confess the truth? He hesitated, but his hesitation lasted scarcely the tenth part of a second. "I have been here about half an hour," he replied.

The baron's livid cheeks suddenly became purple, his eyes glittered, and it seemed by his threatening gesture as if he were strongly tempted to murder this man, who had discovered the terrible, disgraceful secrets of his domestic life. But it was a mere flash of energy. The terrible ordeal which he had just passed through had exhausted him mentally and physically, and it was in a faltering voice that he resumed: "Then you have not lost a word—a word of what was said in the other room?"

"Not a word."

The baron sank on to the divan. "So the knowledge of my disgrace is no longer confined to myself!" he exclaimed. "A stranger's eye has penetrated the depths of misery I have fallen into! The secret of my wretchedness and shame is mine no longer!"

"Oh, monsieur, monsieur!" interrupted Pascal. "Before I recross the threshold of your home, all shall have been forgotten. I swear it by all that is most sacred!"

He had raised his hand as if to take a solemn oath, when the baron caught hold of it, and, pressing it with sorrowful gratitude, exclaimed: "I believe you! You are a man of honor—I only needed to see your home to be convinced of that. You will not laugh at my misfortunes or my misery!" He must have been suffering frightfully, for big tears rolled slowly down his cheeks. "What have I done, my God! that I should

be so cruelly punished?" he continued. "I have always been generous and charitable, and ready to help
all who applied to me. I am utterly alone! I have a
wife and a daughter—but they hate me. They long for
my death, which would give them possession of my
wealth. What torture! For months together I dared
not eat a morsel of food, either in my own house, or
in the house of my son-in-law. I feared poison; and
I never partook of a dish until I had seen my daughter
or my wife do so. To prevent a crime, I was obliged
to resort to the strangest expedients. I made a will,
and left my property in such a way that if I die, my
family will not receive one penny. So, they now have
an interest in prolonging my life." As he spoke he
sprang up with an almost frenzied air, and, seizing
Pascal by the arm, again continued. "Nor is this all!
This woman—my wife—you know—you have heard
the extent of her shame and degradation. Ah, well!
I—love her!"

Pascal recoiled with an exclamation of mingled horror and consternation.

"This amazes you, eh?" rejoined the baron. "It is
indeed incomprehensible, monstrous—but it is the
truth. It is to gratify her desire for luxury that I
have toiled to amass millions. If I purchased a title,
which is absurd and ridiculous, it was only because I
wished to satisfy her vanity. Do what she may, I can
only see in her the chaste and beautiful wife of our
early married life. It is cowardly, absurd, ridiculous—
I realize it; but my love is stronger than my reason
or my will. I love her madly, passionately; I cannot
tear her from my heart!"

So speaking, he sank sobbing on to the divan again.
Was this, indeed, the frivolous and jovial Baron

Trigault whom Pascal had seen at Madame d'Argelès's house—the man of self-satisfied mien and superb assurance, the good-natured cynic, the frequenter of gambling-dens? Alas, yes! But the baron whom the world knew was only a comedian; this was the real man.

After a little while he succeeded in controlling his emotion, and in a comparatively calm voice he exclaimed: "But it is useless to distract one's mind with an incurable evil. Let us speak of yourself, M. Ferailleur. To what do I owe the honor of this visit?"

"To your own kind offer, monsieur, and the hope that you will help me in refuting this slander, and wreaking vengeance upon those who have ruined me."

"Oh! yes, I will help you in that to the full extent of my power," exclaimed the baron. But experience reminded him that confidential disclosures ought not to be made with the doors open, so he rose, shut them, and returning to Pascal, said: "Explain in what way I can be of service to you, monsieur."

It was not without many misgivings that Pascal had presented himself at the baron's house, but after what he had heard he felt no further hesitation; he could speak with perfect freedom. "It is quite unnecessary for me to tell you, Monsieur le Baron," he began, "that the cards which made me win were inserted in the pack by M. de Coralth—that is proven beyond question, and whatever the consequences may be, I shall have my revenge. But before striking him, I wish to reach the man whose instrument he was."

"What! you suppose——"

"I don't suppose—I am sure that M. de Coralth acted in obedience to the instructions of some other scoundrel whose courage does not equal his meanness."

" Perhaps so! I think he would shrink from nothing in the way of rascality. But who could have employed him in this vile work of dishonoring an honest man? "

" The Marquis de Valorsay."

On hearing this name, the baron bounded to his feet. " Impossible! " he exclaimed; " absolutely impossible! M. de Valorsay is incapable of the villainy you ascribe to him. What do I say?—he is even above suspicion. I have known him for years, and I have never met a more loyal, more honorable, or more courageous man. He is one of my few trusted friends; we see each other almost every day. I am expecting a visit from him even now."

" Still it was he who incited M. de Coralth to do the deed."

" But why? What could have been his object? "

" To win a young girl whom I love. She—loved me, and he saw that I was an obstacle. He put me out of the way more surely than if he had murdered me. If I died, she might mourn for me—dishonored, she would spurn me——"

" Is Valorsay so madly in love with the girl, then? "

" I think he cares but very little for her."

" Then why—— "

" She is the heiress of several millions."

It was evident that this explanation did not shake Baron Trigault's faith in his friend. " But the marquis has an income of a hundred and fifty or two hundred thousand francs," said he; " that is an all-sufficient justification. With his fortune and his name, he is in a position to choose his wife from among all the heiresses of France. Why should he address his attentions in particular to the woman you love? Ah! if he were poor—if his fortune were impaired—if he felt the need of regilding his escutcheon, like my son-in-law——"

He paused; there was a rap at the door. The baron called out: " Come in," and a valet appeared, and informed his master that the Marquis de Valorsay wished to speak with him.

It was the enemy! Pascal's features were distorted with rage; but he did not stir—he did not utter a word. " Ask the marquis into the next room," said the baron. " I will join him there at once." Then as the servant retired, the baron turned to Pascal and said: " Well, M. Ferailleur, do you divine my intentions? "

" I think so, monsieur. You probably intend me to hear the conversation you are going to have with M. de Valorsay."

" Exactly. I shall leave the door open, and you can listen."

This word, " listen," was uttered without bitterness, or even reproach; and yet Pascal could not help blushing and hanging his head. " I wish to prove to you that your suspicions are without foundation," pursued the baron. " Rest assured that I shall prove this conclusively. I will conduct the conversation in the form of a cross-examination, and after the marquis's departure, you will be obliged to confess that you were wrong."

" Or you, that I am right? "

" So be it. Any one is liable to be mistaken, and I am not obstinate."

He was about to leave the room, when Pascal detained him. " I scarcely know how to testify my gratitude even now, monsieur, and yet—if I dared—if I did not fear to abuse your kindness, I should ask one more favor."

" Speak, Monsieur Ferailleur."

" It is this, I do not know the Marquis de Valorsay;
and if, instead of leaving the door wide open, you
would partially close it, I should hear as distinctly, and
I could also see him."

" Agreed," replied the baron. And, opening the
door, he passed into the dining-room, with his right
hand cordially extended, and saying, in his most genial
tones: " Excuse me, my dear friend, for keeping you
waiting. I received your letter this morning, and I was
expecting you, but some unexpected business required
my attention just now. Are you quite well?"

As the baron entered the room, the marquis had
stepped quickly forward to meet him. Either he was
inspired with fresh hope, or else he had wonderful
powers of self-control, for never had he looked more
calm—never had his face evinced haughtier indifference, more complete satisfaction with himself, and
greater contempt for others. He was dressed with
even more than usual care, and in perfect taste as well;
moreover, his valet had surpassed himself in dressing
his hair—for one would have sworn that his locks were
still luxuriant. If he experienced any secret anxiety,
it only showed itself in a slightly increased stiffness of
his right leg—the limb broken in hunting. " I ought
rather to inquire concerning your own health," he remarked. " You seem greatly disturbed; your cravat is
untied." And, pointing to the broken china scattered
about the floor, he added: " On seeing this, I asked
myself if an accident had not happened."

" The baroness was taken suddenly ill at the breakfast table. Her fainting fit startled me a little. But
it was a mere trifle. She has quite recovered already,
and you may rely upon her applauding your victory at

Vincennes to-day. She has I don't know how many hundred louis staked upon your horses."

The marquis's countenance assumed an expression of cordial regret. "I am very sorry, upon my word!" he exclaimed. "But I sha'n't take part in the races at Vincennes. I have withdrawn my horses. And, in future, I shall have nothing to do with racing."

"Nonsense!"

"It is the truth, however. I have been led to this determination by the infamous slander which has been circulated respecting me."

This answer was a mere trifle, but it somewhat shook Baron Trigault's confidence. "You have been slandered!" he muttered.

"Abominably. Last Sunday the best horse in my stables, Domingo, came in third. He was the favorite in the ring. You can understand the rest. I have been accused of manœuvering to have my own horse beaten. People have declared that it was my interest he should be beaten, and that I had an understanding with my jockey to that effect. This is an every-day occurrence, I know very well; but, as regards myself, it is none the less an infamous lie!"

"Who has dared to circulate such a report?"

"Oh, how can I tell? It is a fact, however, that the story has been circulated everywhere, but in such a cautious manner that there is no way of calling the authors to account. They have even gone so far as to say that this piece of knavery brought me in an enormous sum, and that I used Rochecotte's, Kervaulieu's, and Coralth's names in betting against my own horse."

The baron's agitation was so great that M. de Valorsay observed it, though he did not understand the

cause. Living in the same society with the Baroness
Trigault, and knowing her story, he thought that
Coralth's name might, perhaps, have irritated the baron.
" And so," he quickly continued, " don't be surprised
if, during the coming week, you see the sale of my
horses announced."

" What! you are going to sell——"

" All my horses—yes, baron. I have nineteen; and
it will be very strange if I don't get eight or ten thousand louis for the lot. Domingo alone is worth more
than forty thousand francs."

To talk of selling—of realizing something you possess—rings ominously in people's ears. The person
who talks of selling proclaims his need of money—
and often his approaching ruin. " It will save you at
least a hundred and fifty or sixty thousand francs a
year," observed the baron.

" Double it and you won't come up to the mark.
Ah! my dear baron, you have yet to learn that there is
nothing so ruinous as a racing stable. It's worse than
gambling; and women, in comparison, are a real economy. Ninette costs me less than Domingo, with his
jockey, his trainer, and his grooms. My manager declares that the twenty-three thousand francs I won last
year, cost me at least fifty thousand."

Was he boasting, or was he speaking the truth?
The baron was engaged in a rapid calculation. " What
does Valorsay spend a year?" he was saying to himself. " Let us say two hundred and fifty thousand
francs for his stable; forty thousand francs for Ninette
Simplon; eighty thousand for his household expenses,
and at least thirty thousand for personal matters, trav-
elling, and play. All this amounts to something like
four hundred and thirty thousand francs a year.

Does his income equal that sum? Certainly not. Then he must have been living on the principal—he is ruined."

Meanwhile the marquis gayly continued: "You see, I'm going to make a change in my mode of life. Ah! it surprises you! But one must make an end of it, sooner or later. I begin to find a bachelor life not so very pleasant after all; there is rheumatism in prospect, and my digestion is becoming impaired—in short, I feel that it is time for marriage, baron; and—I am about to marry."

"You!"

"Yes, I. What, haven't you heard of it, yet? It has been talked of at the club for three days or more."

"No, this is the first intimation I have received of it. It is true, however, that I have not been to the club for three days. I have made a wager with Kami-Bey, you know—that rich Turk—and as our sittings are eight or ten hours long, we play in his apartments at the Grand Hôtel. And so you are to be married," the baron continued, after a slight pause. "Ah, well! I know one person who won't be pleased."

"Who, pray?"

"Ninette Simplon."

M. de Valorsay laughed heartily. "As if that would make any difference to me!" he exclaimed. And then in a most confidential manner he resumed: "She will soon be consoled. Ninette Simplon is a shrewd girl—a girl whom I have always suspected of having an account book in place of a heart. I know she has at least three hundred thousand francs safely invested; her furniture and diamonds are worth as much more. Why should she regret me? Add to this that I have promised her fifty thousand francs to dry her tears with on my wedding-day, and you will understand that she really longs to see me married."

"I understand," replied the baron; "Ninette Simplon won't trouble you. But I can't understand why you should talk of economy on the eve of a marriage which will no doubt double your fortune; for I'm sure you won't surrender your liberty without good and substantial reasons."

"You are mistaken."

"How mistaken?"

"Well, I won't hesitate to confess to you, my dear baron, that the girl I am about to marry hasn't a penny of her own. My future wife has no dowry save her black eyes—but they are certainly superb ones."

This assertion seemed to disprove Pascal's statements. "Can it really be you who are talking in this strain?" cried the baron. "You, a practical, worldly man, give way to such a burst of sentiment?"

"Well, yes."

The baron opened his eyes in astonishment. "Ah! then you adore your future bride!"

"Adore only feebly expresses my feelings."

"I must be dreaming."

Valorsay shrugged his shoulders with the air of a man who has made up his mind to accept the banter of his friends; and in a tone of mingled sentimentality and irony, he said: "I know that it's absurd, and that I shall be the laughing-stock of my acquaintances. Still it doesn't matter; I have never been coward enough to hide my feelings. I'm in love, my dear baron, as madly in love as a young collegian—sufficiently in love to watch my lady's house at night even when I have no possible hope of seeing her. I thought myself *blasé*, I boasted of being invulnerable. Well, one fine morning

I woke up with the heart of a youth of twenty beating in my breast—a heart which trembled at the slightest glance from the girl I love, and sent purple flushes to my face. Naturally I tried to reason with myself. I was ashamed of my weakness; but the more clearly I showed myself my folly, the more obstinate my heart became. And perhaps my folly is not such a great one after all. Such perfect beauty united with such modesty, grace, and nobility of soul, such passion, candor, and talent, cannot be met twice in a lifetime. I intend to leave Paris. We shall first of all go to Italy, my wife and I. After a while we shall return and install ourselves at Valorsay, like two turtle-doves. Upon my word, my imagination paints a charming picture of the calm and happy life we shall lead there! I don't deserve such good fortune. I must have been born under a lucky star! "

Had he been less engrossed in his narrative, he would have heard the sound of a stifled oath in the adjoining room; and had he been less absorbed in the part he was playing, he would have observed a cloud on his companion's brow. The baron was a keen observer, and he had detected a false ring in this apparently vehement outburst of passion. " I understand it now, my dear marquis," said he; "you have met the descendant of some illustrious but impoverished family."

" You are wrong. My future bride has no other name than her Christian name of Marguerite."

" It is a regular romance then! "

" You are quite right; it is a romance. Were you acquainted with the Count de Chalusse, who died a few days ago? "

" No; but I have often heard him spoken of."

" Well, it is his daughter whom I am about to marry —his illegitimate daughter."

The baron started. " Excuse me," said he; " M. de Chalusse was immensely rich, and he was a bachelor. How does it happen then that his daughter, even though she be his illegitimate child, should find herself penniless? "

" A mere chance—a fatality. M. de Chalusse died very suddenly; he had no time to make a will or to acknowledge his daughter."

" But why had he not taken some precautions? "

" A formal recognition of his daughter was attended by too many difficulties, and even dangers. Mademoiselle Marguerite had been abandoned by her mother when only five or six months old; it is only a few years since M. de Chalusse, after a thousand vain attempts, at last succeeded in finding her."

It was no longer on Pascal's account, but on his own, that Baron Trigault listened with breathless attention. " How very strange," he exclaimed, in default of something better to say. " How very strange! "

" Isn't it? It is as good as a novel."

" Would it be—indiscreet——"

" To inquire? Certainly not. The count told me the whole story, without entering into particulars—you understand. When he was quite young, M. de Chalusse became enamoured of a charming young lady, whose husband had gone to tempt fortune in America. Being an honest woman, she resisted the count's advances for awhile—a very little while; but in less than a year after her husband's departure, she gave birth to a pretty little daughter, Mademoiselle Marguerite. But then why had the husband gone to America? "

" Yes," faltered the baron; " why—why, indeed? "

"Everything was progressing finely, when M. de Chalusse was in his turn obliged to start for Germany, having been informed that a sister of his, who had fled from the paternal roof with nobody knows who, had been seen there. He had been absent some four months or so, when one morning the post brought him a letter from his pretty mistress, who wrote: 'We are lost! My husband is at Marseilles: he will be here to-morrow. Never attempt to see me again. Fear everything from him. Farewell.' On receiving this letter, M. de Chalusse flung himself into a postchaise, and returned to Paris. He was determined, absolutely determined, to have his daughter. But he arrived too late. On hearing of her husband's return, the young wife had lost her head. She had but one thought—to conceal her fault, at any cost; and one night, being completely disguised, she left her child on a doorstep in the vicinity of the central markets——"

The marquis suddenly paused in his story to exclaim: "Why, what is the matter with you, my dear baron? What is the matter? Are you ill? Shall I ring?"

The baron was as pale as if the last drop of blood had been drawn from his veins, and there were dark purple circles about his eyes. Still, on being questioned, he managed to answer in a choked voice, but not without a terrible effort: "Nothing! It is nothing. A mere trifle! It will be over in a moment. It *is* over!" Still his limbs trembled so much that he could not stand, and he sank on to a chair, murmuring: "I entreat you, marquis—continue. It is very interesting—very interesting indeed."

M. de Valorsay resumed his narrative. "The husband was incontestably an artless fellow; but he was

also, it appears, a man of remarkable energy and determination. Having somehow ascertained that his
wife had given birth to a child in his absence, he moved
heaven and earth not only to discover the child, but its
father also. He had sworn to kill them both; and he
was a man to keep his vow unmoved by a thought of
the guillotine. And if you require a proof of his
strength of character, here it is: He said nothing to
his wife on the subject, he did not utter a single reproach; he treated her exactly as he had done before
his absence. But he watched her, or employed others
to watch her, both day and night, convinced that she
would finally commit some act of imprudence which
would give him the clue he wanted. Fortunately, she
was very shrewd. She soon discovered that her husband knew everything, and she warned M. de Chalusse, thus saving his life."

It is not at all remarkable that the Marquis de Valorsay should have failed to see any connection between
his narrative and the baron's agitation. What possible
connection could there be between opulent Baron
Trigault and the poor devil who went to seek his fortune in America? What imaginable connection could
there be between the confirmed gambler, who was
Kami-Bey's companion, Lia d'Argelès's friend, and the
husband who for ten long years had pursued the man
who, by seducing his wife, had robbed him of all the
happiness of life? Another point that would have dispelled any suspicions on the marquis's part was that
he had found the baron greatly agitated on arriving,
and that he now seemed to be gradually regaining his
composure. So he continued his story in his customary
light, mocking tone. It is the perfection of good taste
and high breeding—" proper form," indeed, not to be

astonished or moved by anything, in fact to sneer at everything, and hold one's self quite above the emotions which disturb the minds of plebeians.

Thus the marquis continued: " I am necessarily compelled to omit many particulars, my dear baron. The count was not very explicit when he reached this part of his story; but, in spite of his reticence, I learned that he had been tricked in his turn, that certain papers had been stolen from him, and that he had been defrauded in many ways by his *inamorata*. I also know that M. de Chalusse's whole life was haunted by the thought of the husband he had wronged. He felt a presentiment that he would die by this man's hand. He saw danger on every side. If he went out alone in the evening, which was an exceedingly rare occurrence, he turned the street corners with infinite caution; it seemed to him that he could always see the gleam of a poniard or a pistol in the shade. I should never have believed in this constant terror on the part of a really brave man, if he had not confessed it to me with his own lips. Ten or twelve years passed before he dared to make the slightest attempt to find his daughter, so much did he fear to arouse his enemy's attention. It was not until he had discovered that the husband had become discouraged and had discontinued his search, that the count began his. It was a long and arduous one, but at last it succeeded, thanks to the assistance of a clever scoundrel named Fortunat."

The baron with difficulty repressed a movement of eager curiosity, and remarked: " What a peculiar name! "

" And his first name is Isidore. Ah! he's a smooth-tongued scoundrel, a rascal of the most dangerous kind, who richly deserves to be in jail. How it is that he is allowed to prosecute his dishonorable calling I can't understand; but it is none the less true that he does follow it, and without the slightest attempt at concealment, at an office he has on the Place de la Bourse."

This name and address were engraved upon the baron's memory, never to be effaced.

"However," resumed M. de Valorsay, "the poor count was fated to have no peace. The husband had scarcely ceased to torment him, he had scarcely begun to breathe freely, when the wife attacked him in her turn. She must have been one of those vile and despicable women who make a man hate the entire sex. Pretending that the count had turned her from the path of duty, and destroyed her life and happiness, she lost no opportunity of tormenting him. She would not allow M. de Chalusse to keep the child with him, nor would she consent to his adopting the girl. She declared it an act of imprudence, which would surely set her husband upon the track, sooner or later. And when the count announced his intention of legally adopting the child, in spite of her protests, she declared that, rather than allow it, she would confess everything to her husband."

"The count was a patient man," sneered the baron.

"Not so patient as you may suppose. His submission was due to some secret cause which he never confided to me. There must have been some great crime under all this. In any case, the poor count found it impossible to escape this terrible woman. He took refuge at Cannes; but she followed him. He travelled through Italy, for I don't know how many months under an assumed name, but all in vain. He was at last compelled to conceal his daughter in some provincial convent. During the last few months of his life he obtained peace—that is to say, he bought it. This lady's husband must either be very poor or exceedingly stingy; and as she was exceedingly fond of luxury, M. de Chalusse effected a compromise by giving her a large sum monthly, and also by paying her dressmaker's bills."

The baron sprang to his feet with a passionate exclamation. " The vile wretch ! " he said.

But he quickly reseated himself, and the exclamation astonished M. de Valorsay so little that he quietly concluded by saying: " And this is the reason, baron, why my beloved Marguerite, the future Marquise de Valorsay, has no dowry."

The baron cast a look of positive anguish at the door of the smoking-room. He had heard a slight movement there; and he trembled with fear lest Pascal, maddened with anger and jealousy, should rush in and throw himself upon the marquis. Plainly enough, this perilous situation could not last much longer. The baron's own powers of self-control and dissimulation were almost exhausted, and so postponing until another time the many questions he still wished to ask M. de Valorsay, he made haste to check these confidential disclosures. "Upon my word," he exclaimed, with a forced laugh, "I was expecting something quite different. This affair begins like a genuine romance, and ends, as everything ends nowadays, in money ! "

IV.

As a millionaire and a gambler, Baron Trigault enjoyed all sorts of privileges. He assumed the right to be brutal, ill-bred, cynical and bold; to be one of those persons who declare that folks must take them as they find them. But his rudeness now was so thoroughly offensive that under any other circumstances the marquis would have resented it. However, he had special reasons for preserving his temper, so he decided to laugh.

"Yes, these stories always end in the same way, baron," said he. "You haven't touched a card this morning, and I know your hands are itching. Excuse me for making you waste precious time, as you say; but what you have just heard was only a necessary preface."

"Only a preface?"

"Yes; but don't be discouraged. I have arrived at the object of my visit now."

As Baron Trigault was supposed to enjoy an income of at least eight hundred thousand francs a year, he received in the course of a twelvemonth at least a million applications for money or help, and for this reason he had not an equal for detecting a coming appeal. "Good heavens!" he thought, "Valorsay is going to ask me for money." In fact, he felt certain that the marquis's pretended carelessness concealed real embarrassment, and that it was difficult for him to find the words he wanted.

"So I am about to marry," M. de Valorsay resumed —"I wish to break off my former life, to turn over a new leaf. And now the wedding gifts, the two

fêtes that I propose giving, the repairs at Valorsay, and
the honeymoon with my wife—all these things will cost
a nice little sum."

" A nice little sum, indeed! "

" Ah, well! as I'm not going to wed an heiress, I
fear I shall run a trifle short. The matter was worry-
ing me a little, when I thought of you. I said to
myself: ' The baron, who always has money at his
disposal, will no doubt let me have the use of five
thousand louis for a year.' "

The baron's eyes were fixed upon his companion's
face. " Zounds! " he exclaimed in a half-grieved, half-
petulant tone; " I haven't the amount! "

It was not disappointment that showed itself on the
marquis's face; it was absolute despair, quickly concealed.

But the baron had detected it; and he realized his
applicant's urgent need. He felt certain that M. de
Valorsay was financially ruined—and yet, as it did not
suit his plans to refuse, he hastily added: " When I say
I haven't that amount, I mean that I haven't got it on
hand just at this moment. But I shall have it within
forty-eight hours; and if you are at home at this time
on the day after to-morrow, I will send you one
of my agents, who will arrange the matter with
you."

A moment before, the marquis had allowed his consternation to show itself; but this time he knew how to
conceal the joy that filled his soul. So it was in the
most indifferent manner, as if the affair were one of
trivial importance, that he thanked the baron for being
so obliging. Plainly enough, he now longed to make
his escape, and indeed, after rattling off a few commonplace remarks, he rose to his feet and took his

leave, exclaiming: "Till the day after to-morrow,
then!"

The baron sank into an arm-chair, completely overcome. A martyr to a passion that was stronger than
reason itself, the victim of a fatal love which he had
not been able to drive from his heart, Baron Trigault
had passed many terrible hours, but never had he been
so completely crushed as at this moment when chance
revealed the secret which he had vainly pursued for
years. The old wounds in his heart opened afresh,
and his sufferings were poignant beyond description.
All his efforts to save this woman whom he at once
loved and hated from the depths of degradation, had
proved unavailing. "And she has extorted money
from the Count de Chalusse," he thought; "she sold
him the right to adopt their own daughter." And so
strange are the workings of the human heart, that this
circumstance, trivial in comparison with many others,
drove the unfortunate baron almost frantic with rage.
What did it avail him that he had become one of the
richest men in Paris? He allowed his wife eight
thousand francs a month, almost one hundred thousand
francs a year, merely for her dresses and fancies. Not
a quarter-day passed, but what he paid her debts to a
large amount, and in spite of all this, she had sunk
so low as to extort money from a man who had once
loved her. "What can she do with it all?" muttered
the baron, overcome with sorrow and indignation.
"How can she succeed in spending the income of several millions?"

A name, the name of Ferdinand de Coralth, rose to
his lips; but he did not pronounce it. He saw Pascal
emerging from the smoking-room; and though he had
forgotten the young advocate's very existence, his ap-

pearance now restored him to a consciousness of reality. "Ah, well! M. Ferailleur?" he said, like a man suddenly aroused from some terrible nightmare. Pascal tried to make some reply, but he was unable to do so—such a flood of incoherent thoughts was seething and foaming in his brain. "Did you hear, M. de Valorsay?" continued the baron. "Now we know, beyond the possibility of doubt, who Mademoiselle Marguerite's mother is. What is to be done? What would you do in my place?"

"Ah, monsieur! how can I tell?"

"Wouldn't your first thought be of vengeance! It is mine. But upon whom can I wreak my vengeance? Upon the Count de Chalusse? He is dead. Upon my wife? Yes, I might do so; but I lack the courage—Mademoiselle Marguerite remains."

"But she is innocent, monsieur; she has never wronged you."

The baron did not seem to hear this exclamation. "And to make Mademoiselle Marguerite's life one long misery," said he, "I need only favor her marriage with the marquis. Ah, he would make her cruelly expiate the crime of her birth."

"But you won't do so!" cried Pascal, in a transport, "it would be shameful; I won't allow it. Never, I swear before high Heaven! never, while I live, shall Valorsay marry Marguerite. He may perhaps vanquish me in the coming struggle; he may lead her to the threshold of the church, but there he will find me —armed—and I will have justice—human justice in default of legal satisfaction. And, afterward, the law may take its course!"

The baron looked at him with deep emotion. "Ah, you know what it is to love!" he exclaimed; and in a hollow voice, he added: " and thus it was that I loved Marguerite's mother."

The breakfast-table had not been cleared, and a large decanter of water was still standing on it. The baron poured out two large glasses, which he drained with feverish avidity, and then he began to walk aimlessly about the room.

Pascal held his peace. It seemed to him that his own destiny was being decided in this man's mind, that his whole future depended upon the determination he arrived at. A prisoner awaiting the verdict of the jury could not have suffered more intense anxiety. At last, when a minute, which seemed a century, had elapsed, the baron paused. " Now as before, M. Ferailleur," he said, roughly, " I'm for you and with you. Give me your hand—that's right. Honest people ought to protect and assist one another when scoundrels assail them. We will reinstate you in public esteem, monsieur. We will unmask Coralth, and we will crush Valorsay if we find that he is really the instigator of the infamous plot that ruined you."

" What, monsieur! Can you doubt it after your conversation with him? "

The baron shook his head. " I've no doubt but what Valorsay is ruined financially," said he. " I am certain that my hundred thousand francs will be lost forever if I lend them to him. I would be willing to swear that he bet against his own horse and prevented the animal from winning, as he is accused of doing."

" You must see, then——"

" Excuse me—all this does *not* explain the great discrepancy between your allegations and his story. You assure me that he cares nothing whatever for Mademoiselle Marguerite; he pretends that he adores her."

" Yes, monsieur, yes—the scoundrel dared to say so. Ah! if I had not been deterred by a fear of losing my revenge!"

" I understand; but allow me to conclude. According to you, Mademoiselle Marguerite possesses several millions. According to him, she hasn't a penny of her own. Which is right? I believe he is. His desire to borrow a hundred thousand francs of me proves it; and, besides, he wouldn't have come this morning to tell me a falsehood, which would be discovered to-morrow. Still, if he is telling the truth, it is impossible to explain the foul conspiracy you have suffered by."

This objection had previously presented itself to Pascal's mind, and he had found an explanation which seemed to him a plausible one. " M. de Chalusse was not dead," said he, " when M. de Coralth and M. de Valorsay decided on this plan of ridding themselves of me. Consequently, Mademoiselle Marguerite was still an heiress."

" That's true; but the very day after the commission of the crime, the accomplices must have discovered that it could do them no good; so, why have they still persisted in their scheme? "

Pascal tried to find a satisfactory answer, but failed.

" There must be some iniquitous mystery in this affair, which neither you nor I suspect," remarked the baron.

" That is exactly what my mother told me."

" Ah! that's Madame Ferailleur's opinion? Then it is a good one. Come, let us reason a little. Mademoiselle Marguerite loved you, you say? "

" Yes."

" And she has suddenly broken off the engagement?"

"She wrote to me that the Count de Chalusse extorted from her a promise on his death-bed, that she would marry the Marquis de Valorsay."

The baron sprang to his feet. " Stop," he cried— "stop! We now have a clue to the truth, perhaps. Ah! so Mademoiselle Marguerite has written to you that M. de Chalusse commanded her to marry the marquis! Then the count must have been fully restored to consciousness before he breathed his last. On the other hand, Valorsay pretends that Mademoiselle Marguerite is left without resources, simply because the count died too suddenly to be able to write or to sign a couple of lines. Can you reconcile these two versions of the affair, M. Ferailleur? Certainly not. Then which version is false? We must ascertain that point. When shall you see Mademoiselle Marguerite again?"

"She has requested me *never* to try to see her again."

"Very well! She must be disobeyed. You must discover some way of seeing her without anyone's knowledge. She is undoubtedly watched, so don't write on any account." He reflected for a moment, and then added: "We shall, perhaps, become morally certain of Valorsay's and Coralth's guilt, but there's a wide difference between this and the establishment of their guilt by material proofs. Two scoundrels who league to ruin an honest man don't sign a contract to that effect before a notary. Proofs! Ah! where shall we find them? We must gain an intimate knowledge of Valorsay's private life. The best plan would be to find some man devoted to our interests who would watch him, and insinuate himself into his confidence."

Pascal interrupted the baron with an eager gesture.

Hope glittered in his eyes. "Yes!" he exclaimed, "yes; it is necessary that M. de Valorsay should be watched by a man of quick perception—a man clever enough to make himself useful to the marquis, and capable of rendering him an important service in case of need. I will be the man, monsieur, if you will allow me. The thought occurred to me just now while I was listening to you. You promised to send some one to Valorsay's house with money. I entreat you to allow me to take the place of the man you intended to send. The marquis doesn't know me, and I am sufficiently sure of myself to promise you that I will not betray my identity. I will present myself as your agent; he will give me his confidence. I shall take him money or fair promises, I shall be well received, and I have a plan——"

He was interrupted by a rap at the door. The next moment a footman entered, and informed his master that a messenger wished to speak to him on urgent business. "Let him come in," said the baron.

It was Job, Madame Lia d'Argelès's confidential servant, who entered the room. He bowed respectfully, and, with an air of profound mystery exclaimed: "I have been looking for the baron everywhere. I was ordered by madame not to return without him."

"Very well," said M. Trigault. "I will go with you at once."

V.

How was it that a clever man like M. Fortunat made such a blunder as to choose a Sunday, and a racing Sunday too, to call on M. Wilkie. His anxiety might explain the mistake, but it did not justify it. He felt certain, that under any other circumstances he would not have been dismissed so cavalierly. He would at least have been allowed to develop his proposals, and then who knows what might have happened?

But the races had interfered with his plans. M. Wilkie had been compelled to attend to Pompier de Nanterre, that famous steeplechaser, of which he owned one-third part, and he had, moreover, to give orders to the jockey, whose lord and master he was to an equal extent. These were sacred duties, since Wilkie's share in a race-horse constituted his only claim to a footing in fashionable society. But it was a strong claim—a claim that justified the display of whips and spurs that decorated his apartments in the Rue du Helder, and allowed him to aspire to the character of a sporting man. Wilkie really imagined that folks were waiting for him at Vincennes; and that the *fête* would not be complete without his presence.

Still, when he presented himself inside the enclosure, a cigar in his mouth, and his racing card dangling from his button-hole, he was obliged to confess that his entrance did not create much of a sensation. An astonishing bit of news had imparted unusual excitement to the ring. People were eagerly discussing the Marquis de Valorsay's sudden determination to pay forfeit and withdraw his horses from the contest; and the best informed declared that in the betting-rooms the evening before he had openly announced his intention of selling his racing stable. If the marquis had hoped that by adopting this course he would silence the suspicions which had been aroused, he was doomed to grievous disappointment. The rumor that he had secretly bet against his own horse, Domingo, on the previous Sunday, and that he had given orders not to let the animal win the race, was steadily gaining credence.

Large sums had been staked on Domingo's success. He had been the favorite in the betting ring and the losers were by no means pleased. Some declared that they had seen the jockey hold Domingo back; and they insisted that it was necessary to make an example, and disqualify both the marquis and his jockey. Still one weighty circumstance pleaded in M. de Valorsay's favor—his fortune, or, at least, the fortune he was supposed to possess. "Why should such a rich man stoop to cheat?" asked his defenders. "To put money into one's pocket in this way is even worse than to cheat at cards! Besides, it's impossible! Valorsay is above such contemptible charges. He is a perfect gentleman."

"Perhaps so," replied the skeptical bystanders. "But people said exactly the same of Croisenois, of the Duc de H., and Baron P., who were finally convicted of the same rascality that Valorsay is accused of."

"It's an infamous slander! If he had been inclined to cheat, he could have easily diverted suspicion. He would have let Domingo come in second, not third!"

"If he were not guilty, and afraid of detection, he wouldn't pay forfeit to-day nor sell his horses."

"He only retires from the turf because he's going to marry——"

"Nonsense! That's no reason whatever."

Like all gamblers, the frequenters of the turf are distrustful and inclined to be quarrelsome. No one is above their suspicions when they lose nor above their wrath when they are duped. And this Domingo affair united all the losers against Valorsay; they formed a little battalion of enemies who were no doubt powerless for the time being, but who were ready to take a startling revenge whenever a good opportunity presented itself. Naturally enough, M. Wilkie sided with the marquis, whom he had heard his friend, M. de Coralth, speak of on several occasions. "Accuse the dear marquis!" he exclaimed. "It's contemptible, outrageous. Why, only last evening he said to me, 'My good friend, Domingo's defeat cost me two thousand louis!'" M. de Valorsay had said nothing of the kind, for the very good reason that he did not even know Wilkie by sight; still, no one paid much heed to the assertion, whereat Wilkie felt vexed, and resolved to turn his attention to his jockey.

The latter was a lazy, worthless fellow, who had been dismissed from every stable he had previously served in, and who swindled and robbed the young gentlemen who employed him without either limit or shame. Although he made them pay him a very high salary— something like eight thousand francs a year—on the plea that it was most repugnant to his feelings to act as a groom, trainer, and jockey at the same time, he regularly every month presented them with fabulous bills from the grain merchant, the veterinary surgeon, and the harness-maker. In addition, he regularly sold Pompier's oats in order to obtain liquor, and in fact the poor animal was so nearly starved that he could scarcely stand on his legs. The jockey ascribed the

horse's extreme thinness to a system of rigorous training; and the owners did not question the statement in
the least. He had made them believe, and they in
turn had made many others believe, that Pompier de
Nanterre would certainly win such and such a race;
and, trusting in this fallacious promise, they risked their
money on the poor animal—and lost it.

In point of fact, this jockey would have been the
happiest mortal in the world if such things as steeple-
chases had never existed. In the first place, he judged,
with no little reason, that it was dangerous to leap
hurdles on such an animal as Pompier; and, secondly,
nothing irritated him so much as to be obliged to
promenade with his three employers in turn. But how
could he refuse, since he knew that if these young
men hired him, it was chiefly, or only in view of, displaying themselves in his company. It afforded them
untold satisfaction to walk to and fro along the course
in front of the grand stand, with their jockey in his
orange jacket with green sleeves. They were firmly
convinced that he reflected enormous credit upon them,
and their hearts swelled with joy at the thought of the
envy they no doubt inspired. This conviction gave rise
indeed to terrible quarrels, in which each of the three
owners was wont to accuse the others of monopolizing
the jockey.

On this occasion, M. Wilkie—being fortunate enough
to arrive the first—immediately repaired to Pompier de
Nanterre's stall. Never had circumstances been more
favorable for a display of the animal's speed. The day
was magnificent; the stands were crowded, and thousands of eager spectators were pushing and jostling
one another beyond the ropes which limited the course.
M. Wilkie seemed to be everywhere; he showed him-

self in a dozen different places at once, always followed by his jockey, whom he ordered about in a loud voice, with many excited gesticulations. And how great his delight was when, as he passed through the crowd, he heard people exclaim: " That gentleman has a racing stable. His horses are going to compete!" What bliss thrilled his heart when he overheard the admiring exclamation of some worthy shopkeeper who was greatly impressed by the gay silk jacket and the top-boots!

But, unfortunately, this happiness could not last forever. His partners arrived, and claimed the jockey in their turn. So M. Wilkie left the course and strolled about among the carriages, until at last he found an equipage which was occupied by the young ladies who had accepted his invitation to supper the evening before, and who were now making a profuse display of the very yellowest hair they possessed. This afforded him another opportunity of attracting public attention, and to giving proofs of his " form," for he had not filled the box of his carriage with champagne for nothing. At last the decisive moment came, and he made himself conspicuous by shouting. " Now! Now! Here he is! Look! Bravo, Pompier! One hundred on Pompier!"

But, alas! poor Pompier de Nanterre fell exhausted before half the distance was accomplished; and that evening Wilkie described his defeat, with a profusion of technical terms that inspired the uninitiated with the deepest awe. " What a disaster, my friends," he exclaimed. " Pompier de Nanterre, an incomparable steeplechaser, to break down in such a fashion! And beaten by whom? My Mustapha, an outsider, without any record whatever! The ring was intensely excited —and I was simply crazed."

However, his defeat did not affect him very deeply. It was forgotten at thought of the inheritance which his friend Coralth had spoken to him about. And to-morrow M. de Coralth would tell him the secret. He had only twenty hours longer to wait! "To-morrow! to-morrow!" he said to himself again and again, with a thrill of mingled joy and impatience. And what bright visions of future glory haunted him! He saw himself the possessor of a magnificent stud, of suffi-cient wealth to gratify every fancy; he would splash mud upon all the passers-by, and especially upon his former acquaintances, as he dashed past them in his superb equipage; the best tailor should invent astonish-ing garments for him; he would make himself con-spicuous at all the first performances in a stage-box, with the most notorious women in Paris; his *fêtes* would be described in the papers; he would be the con-tinual subject of comment; he would be credited with splendid, perfect " form."

It is true that M. de Coralth had promised him all this, without a word of explanation; but what did that matter? Should he doubt his friend's word? Never! The viscount was not merely his model, but his oracle as well. By the way in which he spoke of him, it might have been supposed that they had been friends from their childhood, or, at least, that they had known each other for years. Such was not the case, however. Their acquaintance dated only seven or eight months back, and their first meeting had apparently been the result of chance; though it is needless to say, perhaps, that this chance had been carefully prepared by M. de Coralth. Having discovered Madame Lia d'Argelès's secret, the viscount watched Wilkie, ascertained where he spent his evenings, contrived a way of introducing

himself into his society, and on their third meeting was
skilful enough to render him a service—in other words,
to lend him some money. From that moment the conquest was assured; for M. de Coralth possessed in an
eminent degree all the attributes that were likely to
dazzle and charm the gifted owner of Pompier de
Nanterre. First of all, there was his title, then his
impudent assurance and his apparent wealth, and last,
but by no means least, his numerous and fashionable
acquaintances. He was not long in discovering his
advantage, and in profiting by it. And without giving
M. Wilkie an inkling of the truth, he succeeded in obtaining from him as accurate a knowledge of his past
career as the young fellow himself possessed.

M. Wilkie did not know much concerning his origin
or his early life; and his history, so far as he was
acquainted with it, could be told in a few words. His
earliest recollection was of the ocean. He was sure,
perfectly sure, that he had made a very long sea
voyage when only a little child, and he looked upon
America as his birthplace. The French language was
certainly not the first he had learned, for he still remembered a limited number of English phrases. The
English word " father " was among those that lingered
in his memory; and now, after a lapse of twenty years,
he pronounced it without the least foreign accent. But
while he remembered the word perfectly well, no recollection remained to him of the person he had called by
that name. His first sensations were those of hunger,
weariness, and cold. He recollected, and very distinctly too, how on one long winter night, a woman
had dragged him after her through the streets of Paris,
in an icy rain. He could still see himself as he wandered on, crying with weariness, and begging for some-

thing to eat. And then the poor woman who held him by the hand lifted him in her arms and carried him on—on, until her own strength failed, and she was obliged to set him on the ground again. A vague portrait of this woman, who was most probably his mother, still lingered in his memory. According to his description, she was extremely handsome, tall, and very fair. He had been particularly impressed with the pale tint and profusion of her beautiful hair.

Their poverty had not lasted long. He remembered being installed with his mother in a very handsome suite of rooms. A man, who was still young, and whom he called "Monsieur Jacques," came every day, and brought him sweetmeats and playthings. He thought he must have been about four years old at that time. However, he had enjoyed this comfortable state of things scarcely a month, when one morning a stranger presented himself. The visitor held a long conference with his mother, or, at least, with the person whom he called by that name. He did not understand what they were talking about, but he was none the less very uneasy. The result of the interview must have justified his instinctive fear, for his mother took him on her lap, and embraced him with convulsive tenderness. She sobbed violently, and repeated again and again in a faltering voice: "Poor child! my beloved Wilkie! I shall never kiss you again—never, never! Alas! It must be so! Give me courage, my God!"

Those were the exact words; Wilkie was sure on that point. It seemed to him he could still hear that despairing farewell. For it was indeed a farewell. The stranger took him in his arms and carried him away, in spite of his cries and struggles to escape. This person to whose care he was confided was the master of a small boarding-school, and his wife was the kindest and most patient of women. However, this did not prevent Wilkie from crying and begging for his mother at first; but gradually he forgot her. He was not unhappy, for he was petted and indulged more than any of the other pupils, and he spent most of his time playing on the terrace or wandering about the garden. But this charming life could not last for ever. According to his calculation, he was just ten years old when, one Sunday, toward the end of October, a grave-looking, red-whiskered gentleman, clad in solemn black with a white necktie, presented himself at the school, and declared that he had been instructed by Wilkie's relatives to place him in a college to continue his education.

Young Wilkie's lamentations were long and loud; but they did not prevent M. Patterson—for that was the gentleman's name—from taking him to the college of Louis-the-Great, where he was entered as a boarder. As he did not study, and as he was only endowed with a small amount of intelligence, he learned scarcely anything during the years he remained there. Every Sunday and every *fête* day, M. Patterson made his appearance at ten o'clock precisely, took Wilkie for a walk in Paris or the environs, gave him his breakfast and dinner at some of the best restaurants, bought everything he expressed a desire to have, and at nine o'clock precisely took him back to the college again. During the holidays M. Patterson kept the boy with him, refusing him nothing in the way of pleasure, granting all his wishes, but never losing sight of him for a moment. And if Wilkie complained of this constant watchfulness, M. Patterson always replied, "I must obey orders;" and this answer invariably put an end to the discussion.

So things went on until it became time for Wilkie to take his degree. He presented himself for examination; and, of course, he failed. Fortunately, however, M. Patterson was not at a loss for an expedient. He placed his charge in a private school; and the following year, at a cost of five thousand francs, he beguiled a poor devil into running the risk of three years' imprisonment, by assuming M. Wilkie's name, and passing the examination in his place. In possession of the precious diploma which opens the door of every career, M. Wilkie now hoped that his pockets would be filled, and that he would then be set at liberty. But the hope was vain! M. Patterson placed him in the hands of an old tutor who had been engaged to travel with him through Europe; and as this tutor held the purse-strings, Wilkie was obliged to follow him through Germany, England, and Italy.

When he returned to Paris he was just twenty years old, and the very next day M. Patterson conducted him to the suite of rooms which he still occupied in the Rue du Helder. "You are now in your own home, M. Wilkie," said M. Patterson in his most impressive manner. "You are now old enough to be responsible for your own actions, and I hope you will conduct yourself like an honest man. From this moment you are your own master. Those who gave you your education desire you to study law. If I were in your place, I should obey them. If you wish to be somebody, and to acquire a fortune, work, for you have no property, nor anything to expect from any one. The allowance which is granted you, a far too liberal one in my opinion, may be cut off at any moment. I don't think it right to conceal this fact from you. But at all events until then, I am instructed to pay you five thousand francs quarterly.   Here is the amount for the first quarter, and in three months' time I shall send you a similar amount.   I say 'shall *send*,' because my business compels me to return to England, and take up my abode there.   Here is my London address; and if any serious trouble befalls you, write to me.   Now, my duty being fulfilled, farewell."

"Go to the devil, you old preacher!" growled Wilkie, as he saw the door close on the retreating figure of M. Patterson, who had acted as his guardian for ten years.   None of M. Patterson's wise advice lingered in the young fellow's mind.   To use a familiar expression, "It went in through one ear and came out through the other."   Only two facts had made an impression upon him: that he was to be his own master henceforth, and that he had a fortune at his command. There it lay upon the table, five thousand francs in glittering gold.

If M. Wilkie had taken the trouble to attentively examine the rooms which had suddenly become his own, he would perhaps have recognized the fact that a loving hand had prepared them for his reception. Countless details revealed the delicate taste of a woman, and the thoughtful tenderness of a mother. None of those little superfluities which delight a young man had been forgotten.   There was a box of choice cigars upon the table, and a jar of tobacco on the mantel-shelf.   But Wilkie did not take time to discover this.   He hastily slipped five hundred francs into his pocket, locked the rest of his money in a drawer, and went out with as lofty an air as if all Paris belonged to him, or as if he had enough money to purchase it.

He had resolved to give a *fête* in honor of his deliverance, and so he hurried off in search of some of his

old college chums.   He found two of them; and, although it was very wounding to his self-love, M.
Wilkie was obliged to confess to them that this was
his first taste of liberty, and that he scarcely knew what
to do with himself.   Of course his friends assured him
that they could quickly make him acquainted with the
only life that it was worth while living; and, to prove
it, they accepted the invitation to dinner which he immediately offered them.   It was a remarkable repast.
Other acquaintances dropped in, the wine flowed in
rivers; and after dinner they danced.   And at daybreak, having served his apprenticeship at *baccarat,* M.
Wilkie found himself without a penny in his pocket,
and face to face with a bill of four hundred francs, for
which amount he was obliged to go to his rooms, under
the escort of one of the waiters.   This first experiment
ought to have disgusted him, or at least have made him
reflect.   But no.   He felt quite in his element in the
society of dissipated young men and enamelled women.
He swore that he would win a place in their midst, and
an influential place too.   But it was easier to form this
plan than to carry it into execution, as he discovered
when, at the end of the month, he counted his money
to see what remained of the five thousand francs that
had been given him for his quarterly allowance.   He
had just three hundred francs left.

   Twenty thousand francs a year is what one chooses
to make it—wealth or poverty.   Twenty thousand
francs a year represents about sixty francs a day; but
what are sixty francs to a high liver, who breakfasts
and dines at the best restaurants, whose clothes are de-
signed by an illustrious tailor, who declines to make a
pair of trousers for less than a hundred francs?   What
are three louis a day to a man who hires a box for first

performances at the opera, to a man who gambles and
gives expensive suppers, to a man who drives out with
yellow-haired demoiselles, and who owns a race-horse?
Measuring his purse and his ambition, M. Wilkie discovered that he should never succeed in making both
ends meet. " How do other people manage? " he wondered. A puzzling question! Every evening a thousand gorgeously apparelled gentlemen, with a cigar in
their mouth and a flower in their button-hole, may be
seen promenading between the Chaussée d'Antin and
the Faubourg Montmartre. Everybody knows them,
and they know everybody, but how they exist is a
problem which it is impossible to solve. How do they
live, and what do they live on? Everybody knows that
they have no property; they do nothing, and yet they
are reckless in their expenditures, and rail at work and
jeer at economy. What source do they derive their
money from? What vile business are they engaged in?

However, M. Wilkie did not devote much time to
solving this question. " My relatives must wish me to
starve," he said to himself. " Not I—I'm not that sort
of a person, as I'll soon let them know." And thereupon he wrote to M. Patterson. By return of post that
gentleman sent him a cheque for one thousand francs—
a mere drop in the bucket. M. Wilkie felt indignant
and so he wrote again. This time he was obliged to
wait for a reply. Still at last it came. M. Patterson
sent him two thousand francs, and an interminable
epistle full of reproaches. The interesting young man
threw the letter into the fire, and went out to hire a
carriage by the month and a servant.

From that day forward, his life was spent in demanding money and waiting for it. He employed in
quick succession every pretext that could soften the

hearts of obdurate relatives, or find the way to the most closely guarded cash-box. He was ill—he had contracted a debt of honor—he had imprudently lent money to an unscrupulous friend—he was about to be arrested for debt. And in accordance with the favorable or unfavorable character of the replies his manner became humble or impertinent, so that his friends soon learned to judge very accurately of the condition of his purse by the way he wore his mustaches. He became wise with experience, however; and on adding all the sums he had received together, he decided that his family must be very rich to allow him so much money. And this thought made him anxious to fathom the mystery of his birth and his infancy. He finally persuaded himself that he was the son of a great English nobleman— a member of the House of Lords, who was twenty times a millionaire. And he more than half believed it when he told his creditors that his lordship, his father, would some day or other come to Paris and pay all his debts. Unfortunately it was not M. Wilkie's noble father that arrived, but a letter from M. Patterson, which was couched as follows:

"MY DEAR SIR, a considerable sum was placed in my hands to meet your unexpected requirements; and in compliance with your repeated appeals, I have remitted the entire amount to you. Not a penny remains in my possession—so that my instructions have been fulfilled. Spare yourself the trouble of making any fresh demands; they will meet with no reply. In future you will not receive a penny above your allowance, which in my opinion is already too large a one for a young man of your age."

This letter proved a terrible blow to Wilkie. What should he do? He felt that M. Patterson would not revoke his decision; and indeed he wrote him several imploring letters, in vain. Yet never had his need of money been so urgent. His creditors were becoming uneasy; bills actually rained in upon his concierge; his next quarterly allowance was not due for some time to come, and it was only through the pawnbroker that he could obtain money for his more pressing requirements. He had begun to consider himself ruined. He saw himself reduced to dismissing his carriage, to selling his third share of Pompier de Nanterre and losing the esteem of all his witty friends.

He was in the depths of despair, when one morning his servant woke him up with the announcement that the Viscount de Coralth was in the sitting-room and wished to speak with him on very important business. It was not usually an easy task to entice M. Wilkie from his bed, but the name his servant mentioned seemed to have a prodigious effect upon him. He bounded on to the floor, and as he hastily dressed himself, he muttered: " The viscount here, at this hour! It's astonishing! What if he's going to fight a duel and wishes me to be his second? That would be a piece of grand good luck and no mistake. It would assure my position at once. Certainly something must have happened! "

This last remark was by no means a proof of any remarkable perspicuity on M. Wilkie's part. As M. de Coralth never went to bed until two or three o'clock in the morning, he was by no means an early riser, and only some very powerful reason could explain the presence of his blue-lined brougham in the street before nine o'clock A.M. And the influence that had made him rise betimes in the present case had indeed been extremely powerful. Although the brilliant viscount had discovered Madame d'Argelès's secret, several months previously, he had so far disclosed it to no one. It was certainly not from any delicacy of feeling that he had held his peace; but only because it had not been for his interest to speak. Now, however, the sudden death of the Count de Chalusse changed the situation. He heard of the catastrophe at his club on the evening after the count's death, and his emotion was so great that he actually declined to take part in a game of *baccarat* that was just beginning. "The devil!" he exclaimed. "Let me think a moment. Madame d'Argelès is the heiress of all these millions—will she come forward and claim them? From what I know of her, I am inclined to think that she won't. Will she ever go to Wilkie and confess that she, Lia d'Argelès, is a Chalusse, and that he is her illegitimate son? Never! She would rather relinquish her millions, both for herself and for him, than take such a step. She is so ridiculously antiquated in her notions." And then he began to study what advantages he might derive from his knowledge of the situation.

M. de Coralth, like all persons whose present is more or less uncertain, had great misgivings concerning his future. Just now he was cunning enough to find a means of procuring the thirty or forty thousand francs a year that were indispensable to his comfort; but he had not a farthing laid by, and the vein of silver he was now working might fail him at any moment. The slightest indiscretion, the least blunder, might hurl him from his splendor into the mire. The perspiration started out on his forehead when he thought of his peril. He passionately longed for a more assured position—for a little capital that would insure him his bread until the end of his days, and rid him of the grim

phantom of poverty forever. And it was this desire
which inspired him with the same plan that M. Fortunat had formed. " Why shouldn't I inform Wilkie? "
he said to himself. " If I present him with a fortune,
the simpleton ought certainly to give me some reward."
But to carry this plan into execution it would be necessary to brave Madame d'Argelès's anger; and that was
attended by no little danger. If he knew something
about her, she on her side knew everything connected
with his past life. She had only to speak to ruin him
forever. Still, after weighing all the advantages and
all the dangers, he decided to act, convinced that
Madame d'Argelès might be kept ignorant of his treason, providing he only played his cards skilfully. And
his matutinal visit to M. Wilkie was caused by a fear
that he might not be the only person knowing the truth,
and that some one else might forestall him.

"You here, at sunrise, my friend!" exclaimed
Wilkie, as he entered the room where the viscount was
seated. " What has happened? "

" To me?—nothing," replied the viscount. " It was
solely on your account that I deviated from my usual
habits."

" What is it? You frighten me."

"Oh! don't be alarmed. I have only some good
news to communicate," and in a careless tone which
cleverly concealed his anxiety, the viscount added: " I
have come, my dear Wilkie, to ask you what you would
be willing to give the man who put you in possession
of a fortune of several millions? "

M. Wilkie's face turned from white to purple at least
three times in ten seconds; and it was in a strangely
altered voice that he replied: " Ah! that's good—very
good—excellent! " He tried his best to laugh, but he

was completely overcome; and, in fact, he had cherished so many extravagant hopes that nothing seemed impossible to him.

"Never in all my life have I spoken more seriously," insisted the viscount.

His companion at first made no reply. It was easy to divine the conflict that was raging in his mind, between the hope that the news was true and the fear of being made the victim of a practical joke. "Come, my friend," he said at last, "do you want to poke fun at me? That wouldn't be polite. A debtor is always sacred, and I owe you twenty-five louis. This is scarcely the time to talk of millions. My relatives have cut off my supplies; and my creditors are overwhelming me with their bills——"

But M. de Coralth checked him, saying gravely: "Upon my honor, I am not jesting. What would you give a man who——"

"I would give him half of the fortune he gave me."

"That's too much!"

"No, no!"

He was in earnest, certainly. What wouldn't a man promise in all sincerity of soul to a fellow mortal who gave him money when he had none—when he needed it urgently and must have it to save himself from ruin?

At such a moment no commission, however large, seems exorbitant. It is afterward, when the day of settlement comes, that people begin to find fault with the rate of interest.

"If I tell you that one-half is too much, it is because such is really the case. And I am the best judge of the matter, since I am the man who can put you in possession of this enormous fortune."

M. Wilkie started back in speechless amazement.

"This astonishes you!" said the viscount; "and why, pray? Is it because I ask for a commission?"

"Oh! not at all!"

"It is not perhaps a very gentlemanly proceeding, but it is a sensible one. Business is business. In the afternoon, when I am in a restaurant, at the club, or in a lady's boudoir, I am merely the viscount and the grand seigneur. All money questions sicken me. I am careless, liberal, and obliging to a fault. But in the morning I am simply Coralth, a man of the middle classes who doesn't pay his bills without examining them, and who watches his money, because he doesn't wish to be ruined and end his brilliant career as a common soldier in some foreign legion."

M. Wilkie did not allow him to continue. He believed, and his joy was wild—delirious. "Enough, enough!" he interrupted. "A difficulty between us! Never! I am yours without reserve! Do you understand me? How much must you have? Do you wish for it all?"

But the viscount was unmoved. "It is not fitting that I should fix upon the indemnity which is due to me. I will consult a man of business; and I will decide upon this point on the day after to-morrow, when I shall explain everything to you."

"On the day after to-morrow! You won't leave me in suspense for forty-eight hours?"

"It is unavoidable. I have still some important information to procure. I lost no time in coming to you, so that I might put you on your guard. If any scoundrel comes to you with proposals, be extremely careful. Some agents, when they obtain a hold on an estate, leave nothing for the rightful owner. So don't treat with any one."

"Oh, no! You may rest assured I won't."

"I should be quieter in mind if I had your promise in writing."

Without a word, Wilkie darted to a table, and wrote a short contract by which he bound himself to give M. Ferdinand de Coralth one-half of the inheritance which the aforesaid Coralth might prove him to be entitled to. The viscount read the document, placed it in his pocket, and then said, as he took up his hat:

"Very well. I will see you again on Monday."

But M. Wilkie's doubts were beginning to return. "Monday, so be it!" said he; "but swear that you are not deceiving me."

"What, do you still doubt me?"

M. Wilkie reflected for a moment; and suddenly a brilliant inspiration darted through his brain. "If you are speaking the truth, I shall soon be rich," said he. "But, in the meantime, life is hard. I haven't a penny, and it isn't a pleasant situation. I have a horse entered for the race to-morrow, Pompier de Nanterre. You know the animal very well. The chances are enormously in his favor. So, if it wouldn't inconvenience you to lend me fifty louis——"

"Certainly," interrupted the viscount, cordially. "Certainly; with the greatest pleasure."

And drawing a beautiful little notebook from his pocket he took from it not one, but two bank-notes of a thousand francs, and handed them to M. Wilkie, saying: "Monsieur believes me now, does he not?"

As will be readily believed, it was not for his own pleasure that M. de Coralth postponed his confidential disclosures for a couple of days. He knew Wilkie perfectly well, and felt that it was dangerous to let him roam about Paris with half of an important secret.

Postponement generally furnishes fate with weapons against oneself. But it was impossible for the viscount to act otherwise. He had not seen the Marquis de Valorsay since the Count de Chalusse's death and he dared not conclude the contract with Wilkie before he had conferred with him, for he was completely in the marquis's power. At the least suspicion of treason, M. de Valorsay would close his hand, and he, Coralth, would be crushed like an egg-shell. It was to the house of his formidable associate that he repaired on leaving M. Wilkie; and in a single breath he told the marquis all that he knew, and the plans that he had formed.

M. de Valorsay's astonishment must have been intense when he heard that Lia d'Argelès was a Chalusse, but he knew how to maintain his composure. He listened quietly, and when the viscount had completed his story, he asked: " Why did you wait so long before telling me all this? "

" I didn't see how it could interest you in the least."

The marquis looked at him keenly, and then calmly said: " In other words, you were waiting to see whether it would be most advantageous to you to be with me or against me."

" How can you think——"

" I don't think, I'm sure of it. As long as I was strong support for you, you were devoted to me. But now I am tottering, and you are ready to betray me."

" Excuse me! The step I am about to take——"

" What, haven't you taken it already? " interrupted the marquis, quickly. And shrugging his shoulders, he added: " Observe that I don't reproach you in the least. Only remember this: we survive or we perish together."

By the angry gleam in M. de Coralth's eyes, the
marquis must have realized that his companion was disposed to rebel; still this knowledge did not seem to
disquiet him, for it was in the same icy tone that he
continued: " Besides, your plans, far from conflicting
with mine, will be of service to me. Yes, Madame
d'Argelès must lay claim to the count's estate. If she
hesitates, her son will compel her to urge her claims,.
will he not?"

" Oh, you may rest assured of that."

" And when he becomes rich, will you be able to
retain your influence over him?"

" Rich or poor, I can mould him like wax."

" Very good. Marguerite was escaping me, but I
shall soon have her in my power. I have a plan.
The Fondèges think they can outwit me, but we shall
soon see about that." The viscount was watching his
companion stealthily; as the latter perceived, and so
in a tone of brusque cordiality, he resumed: " Excuse
me for not keeping you to breakfast, but I must go out
immediately—Baron Trigault is waiting for me at his
house. Let us part friends—*au revoir*—and, above all,
keep me well posted about matters in general."

M. de Coralth's temper was already somewhat ruffled
when he entered Valorsay's house; and he was in a
furious passion when he left it. " So we are to survive or perish together," he growled. " Thanks for
the preference you display for my society. Is it my
fault that the fool has squandered his fortune? I fancy
I've had enough of his threats and airs."

Still his wrath was not so violent as to make him forget his own interests. He at once went to inquire if
the agreement which M. Wilkie had just signed would
be binding. The lawyer whom he consulted replied

that, at all events, a reasonable compensation would most probably be granted by the courts, in case of any difficulty; and he suggested a little plan which was a *chef d'œuvre* in its way, at the same time advising his client to strike the iron while it was hot.

It was not yet noon, and the viscount determined to act upon the suggestion at once; he now bitterly regretted the delay he had specified. " I must find Wilkie at once," he said to himself. But he did not succeed in meeting him until the evening, when he found him at the Café Riche—and in what a condition too! The two bottles of wine which the young fool had drank at dinner had gone to his head, and he was enumerating, in a loud voice, the desires he meant to gratify as soon as he came into possession of his millions. " What a brute!" thought the enraged viscount. " If I leave him to himself, no one knows what foolish thing he may do or say. I must remain with him until he becomes sober again."

So he followed him to the theatre, and thence to Brébant's, where he was sitting feeling terribly bored, when M. Wilkie conceived the unfortunate idea of inviting Victor Chupin to come up and take some refreshment. The scene which followed greatly alarmed the viscount. Who could this young man be? He did not remember having ever seen him before, and yet the young scamp was evidently well acquainted with his past life, for he had cast the name of Paul in his face, as a deadly insult. Surely this was enough to make the viscount shudder! How did it happen that this young man had been just on the spot ready to pick up Wilkie's hat? Was it mere chance? Certainly not. He could not believe it. Then why was the fellow there? Evi-

dently to watch somebody. And whom? Why, him—
Coralth—undoubtedly.

In going through life as he had done, a man makes
enemies at every step; and he had an imposing number
of foes, whom he only held in check by his unbounded
impudence and his renown as a duellist. Thus it was
not strange if some one had set a snare for him; it was
rather a miracle that he had not fallen into one before.
The dangers that threatened him were so formidable
that he was almost tempted to relinquish his attack
on Madame d'Argelès. Was it prudent to incur the
risk of making this woman an enemy? All Sunday he
hesitated. It would be very easy to get out of the
scrape. He could concoct some story for Wilkie's
benefit, and that would be the end of it. But on the
other hand, there was the prospect of netting at least
five hundred thousand francs—a fortune—a competency, and the idea was too tempting to be re-
linquished.

So on Monday morning, at about ten o'clock, he presented himself at Wilkie's house, looking pale with
anxiety, and far more solemn in manner than usual.
"Let us say but little, and that to the point," he remarked on entering. "The secret I am about to reveal
to you will make you rich; but it might ruin me if it
were known that you obtained this information through
me. You will therefore swear, upon your honor as a
gentleman, never to betray me, under any circumstances, or for any reason."

M. Wilkie extended his hand and solemnly exclaimed:
"I swear!"

"Very well, then. Now my mind is at rest. It is
scarcely necessary for me to add that if you break your
oath you are a dead man. You know me. You know

how I handle a sword; and don't forget it." His manner was so threatening that Wilkie shuddered. "You
will certainly be questioned," continued M. de Coralth;
"but you must reply that you received the information
through one of Mr. Patterson's friends. Now let us
sign our formal contract in lieu of the temporary one
you gave me the other day."

It is needless to say that Wilkie signed it eagerly.
Not so the viscount; he read the document through
carefully, before appending his signature, and then exclaimed: "The estate that belongs to you is that of the
Count de Chalusse, your uncle. He leaves, I am informed, at least eight or ten millions of property."

By M. Wilkie's excited gestures, by the glitter in his
eyes, it might have been supposed that this wonderful
good fortune was too much for him, and that he was
going mad. "I knew that I belonged to a noble family," he began. "The Count de Chalusse my uncle! I
shall have a coronet on the corner of my visiting cards."

But with a gesture M. de Coralth silenced him.
"Wait a little before you rejoice," said he. "Yes, your
mother is the sister of the Count de Chalusse, and it
is through her that you are an heir to the estate. But—
don't grieve too much—there are similar misfortunes in
many of our most distinguished families—circumstances—the obstinacy of parents—a love more powerful than reason——" The viscount paused, certainly
he had no prejudices; but at the moment of telling this
interesting young man who his mother really was, he
hesitated.

"Go on," insisted M. Wilkie.

"Well—when your mother was a young girl, about
twenty, she fled from her paternal home with a man
she loved. Forsaken afterward, she found herself in

the depths of poverty. She was obliged to live. You were starving. So she changed her name, and now she is known as Lia d'Argelès."

M. Wilkie sprang to his feet. " Lia d'Argelès! " he exclaimed. Then, with a burst of laughter, he added: " Nevertheless, I think it a piece of grand good luck! "

VI.

" THIS man carries away your secret; you are lost." A sinister voice whispered these words in Madame Lia d'Argelès's heart when M. Isidore Fortunat, after being rudely dismissed, closed the door of her drawing-room behind him. This man had addressed her by the ancient and illustrious name of Chalusse which she had not heard for twenty years, and which she had forbidden her own lips to pronounce. This man knew that she, Lia d'Argelès, was really a Durtal de Chalusse.

This frightful certainty overwhelmed her. It is true this man Fortunat had declared that his visit was entirely disinterested. He had pretended that his regard for the Chalusse family, and the compassion aroused in his heart by the unfortunate plight of Mademoiselle Marguerite, were the only motives that has influenced him in taking this step. However, Madame d'Argelès's experience in life had left her but limited faith in apparent or pretended disinterestedness. This is a practical age; chivalrous sentiments are expensive—as she had learned conclusively. " If the man came here," she murmured, " it was only because he thought he might derive some benefit from the prosecution of my claim to my poor brother's estate. In refusing to listen to his entreaties, I have deprived him of this expected profit and so I have made him my enemy. Ah! I was foolish to send him away like that! I ought to have pretended to listen—I ought to have bound him by all sorts of promises."

She suddenly paused. It occurred to her that M. Fortunat could not have gone very far; so that, if she sent for him to come back, she might perhaps be able to repair her blunder. Without losing a second, she rushed downstairs, and ordered her concierge and a servant to run after the gentleman who had just left the house, and ask him to return; to tell him that she had reflected, and wished to speak to him again. They rushed out in pursuit, and she remained in the court-yard, her heart heavy with anxiety. Too late! About a quarter of an hour afterward her emissaries returned. They had made all possible haste in contrary directions, but they had seen no one in the street who at all resembled the person they were looking for. They had questioned the shopkeepers, but no one had seen him pass. "It doesn't matter," faltered Madame d'Argelès, in a tone that belied her words. And, anxious to escape the evident curiosity of her servants, she hastened back to the little boudoir where she usually spent her mornings.

M. Fortunat had left his card—that is to say, his address—and it would have been an easy matter to send a servant to his house. She was strongly tempted to do so; but she ultimately decided that it would be better to wait—that an hour more or less would make but little difference. She had sent her trusty servant, Job, for Baron Trigault; he would probably return with the baron at any moment; and the baron would advise her. He would know at once what was the best course for her to pursue. And so she waited for his coming in breathless anxiety; and the more she reflected, the more imminent her peril seemed, for she realized that M. Fortunat must be a very dangerous and cunning man. He had set a trap for her, and she had allowed herself to be caught. Perhaps he had only suspected the truth when he presented himself at the house. He had suddenly announced the death of the Count de Chalusse; she had betrayed herself; and any doubts he might have entertained were dispelled. " If I had only had sufficient presence of mind to deny it," she murmured. " If I had only been courageous enough to reply that I knew absolutely nothing about the person he spoke of. Ah! then he would have gone away convinced that he was mistaken."

But would the smooth-spoken visitor have declared that he knew everything, if he had not really penetrated the mystery of her life? It was scarcely probable. He had implored her to accept the property, if not for her own sake at least for the sake of another. And when she asked him whom he meant he had answered, " Mademoiselle Marguerite," but he was undoubtedly thinking of Wilkie. So this man, this Isidore Fortunat, knew that she had a son. Perhaps he was even acquainted with him personally. In his anger he would very likely hasten to Wilkie's rooms and tell him everything. This thought filled the wretched woman's heart with despair. What! Had she not yet expiated her fault? Must she suffer again?

For the first time a terrible doubt came over her. What she had formerly regarded as a most sublime effort of maternal love, was, perhaps, even a greater crime than the first she had committed. She had given her honor as the price of her son's happiness and prosperity. Had she a right to do so? Did not the money

she had lavished upon him contain every germ of corruption, misfortune, and shame? How terrible Wilkie's
grief and rage would be if he chanced to hear the truth!

Alas! he would certainly pay no heed to the exten-
uating circumstances; he would close his ears to all
attempts at justification. He would be pitiless. He
would have naught but hatred and scorn to bestow upon
a mother who had fallen from the highest rank in
society down to everlasting infamy. She fancied she
heard him saying in an indignant voice, " It would have
been better to have allowed me to die of starvation
than to have given me bread purchased at such a price!
Why have you dishonored me by your ill-gotten wealth?
Fallen, you might have raised yourself by honest toil.
You ought to have made me a laborer, and not a spoiled
idler, incapable of earning an honest livelihood. As the
son of a poor, betrayed, and deserted woman, with
whom I could have shared my scanty earnings, I might
have looked the world proudly in the face. But where
can the son of Lia d'Argelès hide his disgrace after
playing the gentleman for twenty years with Lia d'Argelès's money?" Yes, Wilkie would certainly say this
if he ever learned the truth; and he would learn it—she
felt sure of it. How could she hope to keep a secret
which was known to Baron Trigault, M. Patterson, the
Viscount de Coralth, and M. Fortunat—four persons!
She had confidence in the first two; she believed she
had a hold on the third, but the fourth—Fortunat!

The hours went by; and still Job did not return.
What was the meaning of this delay? Had he failed to
find the baron? At last the sound of carriage-wheels
in the courtyard made her start. " That's Job!" she
said to herself. " He brings the baron."

Alas! no. Job returned alone. And yet the honest

fellow had spared neither pains nor horseflesh. He had visited every place where there was the least probability of finding the baron, and he was everywhere told that Baron Trigault had not been seen for several days. " In that case, you ought to have gone to his house. Perhaps he is there," remarked Madame d'Argelès.

" Madame knows that the baron is never at home. I did go there, however, but in vain."

This chanced to be one of three consecutive days which Baron Trigault had spent with Kami-Bey, the Turkish ambassador. It had been agreed between them that they should play until one or the other had lost five hundred thousand francs; and, in order to prevent any waste of " precious time," as the baron was wont to remark, they neither of them stirred from the Grand Hôtel, where Kami-Bey had a suite of rooms. They ate and slept there. By some strange chance, Madame d'Argelès had not heard of this duel with bank-notes, although nothing else was talked of at the clubs; indeed, the *Figaro* had already published a minute description of the apartment where the contest was going on; and every evening it gave the results. According to the latest accounts, the baron had the advantage; he had won about two hundred and eighty thousand francs.

" I only returned to inform madame that I had so far been unsuccessful," said Job. " But I will recommence the search at once."

" That is unnecessary," replied Madame d'Argelès. " The baron will undoubtedly drop in this evening, after dinner, as usual."

She said this, and tried her best to believe it; but in her secret heart she felt that she could no longer depend upon the baron's assistance. " I wounded him this morning," she thought. "He went away more angry than I had ever seen him before. He is incensed with me; and who knows how long it will be before he comes again?"

Still she waited, with feverish anxiety, listening breathlessly to every sound in the street, and trembling each time she heard or fancied she heard a carriage stop at the door. However, at two o'clock in the morning the baron had not made his appearance. "It is too late —he won't come!" she murmured.

But now her sufferings were less intolerable, for excess of wretchedness had deadened her sensibility. Utter prostration paralyzed her energies and benumbed her mind. Ruin seemed so inevitable that she no longer thought of avoiding it; she awaited it with that blind resignation displayed by Spanish women, who, when they hear the roll of thunder, fall upon their knees, convinced that lightning is about to strike their defenceless heads. She tottered to her room, flung herself on, the bed, and instantly fell asleep. Yes, she slept the heavy, leaden slumber which always follows a great mental crisis, and which falls like God's blessing upon a tortured mind. On waking up, her first act was to ring for her maid, in order to send a message to Job, to go out again in search of the baron. But the faithful servant had divined his mistress's wishes, and had already started off of his own accord. It was past midday when he returned, but his face was radiant; and it was in a triumphant voice that he announced: "Monsieur le Baron Trigault."

Madame d'Argelès sprang up, and greeted the baron with a joyful exclamation. "Ah! how kind of you to come!" she exclaimed. "You are most welcome. If you knew how anxiously I have been waiting for you!"

He made no reply. " If you knew," continued Madame d'Argelès, " if you only knew——"

But she paused, for in spite of her own agitation, she was suddenly struck by the peculiar expression on her visitor's face. He was standing silent and motionless in the centre of the room, and his eyes were fixed upon her with a strange, persistent stare in which she could read all the contradictory feelings which were battling for mastery in his mind—anger, hatred, pity, and forgiveness. Madame d'Argelès shuddered. So her cup of sorrow was not yet full. A new misfortune was about to fall upon her. She had hoped that the baron would be able to alleviate her wretchedness, but it seemed as if he were fated to increase it. " Why do you look at me like that? " she asked, anxiously. " What have I done? "

" You, my poor Lia—nothing ! "

" Then—what is it? Oh, my God! you frighten me."

" What is it? Well, I am going to tell you," he said, as he stepped forward and took her hand in his own. " You know that I have been infamously duped and deceived, that the happiness of my life has been destroyed by a scoundrel who tempted the wife I so fondly loved to forget her duty, and trample her honor under foot. You have heard my vows of vengeance if I ever succeeded in discovering him. Ah, well, Lia, I have discovered him. The man who stole my share of earthly happiness was the Count de Chalusse, your brother."

With a sudden gesture Madame d'Argelès freed her hand from the baron's grasp, and recoiled as terrified as if she had seen a spectre rise up before her. Then with her hands extended as if to ward off the horrible apparition, she exclaimed : " O, my God ! "

A bitter smile curved the baron's lips. " What do

you fear?" he asked. "Isn't your brother dead? He
has defrauded me alike of happiness and vengeance!"

If her son's life had depended on a single word,
Madame d'Argelès could not have uttered it. She knew
what mental agony had urged the baron to a sort of
moral suicide, and led him to contract the vice in which
he wasted his life and squandered, or, at least risk, his
millions.

"Nor is this all," he continued. "Listen. As I have
often told you, I was sure that my wife became a
mother in my absence. I sought the child for years,
hoping that through the offspring I might discover the
father. Ah, well! I've found what I sought, at last.
The child is now a beautiful young girl. She lives at
the Hôtel de Chalusse as your brother's daughter. She
is known as Mademoiselle Marguerite."

Madame d'Argelès listened, leaning against the wall
for support, and trembling like a leaf. Her reason was
shaken by so many repeated blows, and her son, her
brother, Marguerite, Pascal Ferailleur, Coralth, Valorsay—all those whom she loved or feared, or hated—
rose like spectres before her troubled brain. The horror
of the truth exceeded her most frightful apprehensions.
The strangeness of the reality surpassed every flight of
fancy. And, moreover, the baron's calmness increased
her stupor. She so often had heard him give vent to
his rage and despair in terrible threats, that she could
not believe he would be thus resigned. But was his
calmness real? Was it not a mask, would not his fury
suddenly break forth?

However, he continued, "It is thus that destiny
makes us its sport—it is thus that it laughs at our plans.
Do you remember, Lia, the day when I met you wandering through the streets of Paris—with your child in

your arms—pale and half dead with fatigue, faint for
want of food, homeless and penniless? You saw no
refuge but in death, as you have since told me. How
could I imagine when I rescued you that I was saving
my greatest enemy's sister from suicide—the sister of
the man whom I was vainly pursuing? And yet this
might not be the end, if I chose to have it otherwise.
The count is dead, but I can still return him disgrace
for disgrace. He dishonored me. What prevents me
from casting ineffaceable opprobrium upon the great
name of Chalusse, of which he was so proud? He seduced my wife. To-day I can tell all Paris what his
sister has been and what she is to-day."

Ah! it was this—yes, it was this that Madame d'Argelès had dreaded. She fell upon her knees, and, with
clasped hands she entreated: " Pity!—oh! have pity—
forgive me! Have mercy! Have I not always been a
faithful and devoted friend to you? Think of the past
you have just invoked! Who helped you then to bear
your intolerable sufferings? Don't you remember the
day when you, yourself, had determined to die by your
own hand? There was a woman who persuaded you
to abandon the thought of suicide. It was I!"

He looked at her for a moment with a softer expression, tears came to his eyes, and rolled down his
cheeks. Then suddenly he raised her, and placed her
in an arm-chair, exclaiming: " Ah! you know very well
that I shall not do what I said. Don't you know me
better than that? Are you not sure of my affection, are
you not aware that you are sacred in my eyes? " He
was evidently striving hard to master his emotion. " Besides," he added, " I had already pardoned before coming here. It was foolish on my part, perhaps, and for
nothing in the world would I confess it to my acquaint-

ances, but it is none the less true. I shall have my
revenge in a certain fashion, however. I need only hold
my peace, and the daughter of M. de Chalusse and
Madame Trigault would become a lost woman. Is this
not so? Very well, I shall offer her my assistance. It
may, or may not, be another absurd and ridiculous fancy
added to the many I have been guilty of. But no
matter. I have promised. And why, indeed, should
this poor girl be held responsible for the sins of her
parents? I—I declare myself on her side against the
world!"

Madame d'Argelès rose, her face radiant with joy
and hope. "Then perhaps we are saved!" she exclaimed. "Ah! I knew when I sent for you that I
should not appeal to your heart in vain!"

She took hold of his hand as if to raise it to her lips;
but he gently withdrew it, and inquired, with an air
of astonishment: "What do you mean?"

"That I have been cruelly punished for not wishing
you to assist that unfortunate man who was dishonored
here the other evening."

"Pascal Ferailleur?"

"Yes, he is innocent. The Viscount de Coralth is
a scoundrel. It was he who slipped the cards which
made M. Ferailleur win, into the pack, and he did it
at the Marquis de Valorsay's instigation."

The baron looked at Madame d'Argelès with profound amazement. "What!" said he; "you knew this
and you allowed it? You were cruel enough to remain
silent when that innocent man entreated you to testify
on his behalf! You allowed this atrocious crime to be
executed under your own roof, and under your very
eyes?"

"I was then ignorant of Mademoiselle Marguerite's

existence. I did not know that the young man was beloved by my brother's daughter—I did not know—"

The baron interrupted her, and exclaimed, indignantly: "Ah! what does that matter? It was none the less an abominable action."

She hung her head, and in a scarcely audible voice replied: "I was not free. I submitted to a will that was stronger than my own. If you had heard M. de Coralth's threats you would not censure me so severely. He has discovered my secret; he knows Wilkie—I am in his power. Don't frown—I make no attempt to excuse myself—I am only explaining the position in which I was placed. My peril is imminent; I have only confidence in you—you alone can aid me; listen!"

Thereupon she hastily explained M. de Coralth's position respecting herself, what she had been able to ascertain concerning the Marquis de Valorsay's plans, the alarming visit she had received from M. Fortunat, his advice and insinuations, the dangers she apprehended, and her firm determination to deliver Mademoiselle Marguerite from the machinations of her enemies. Madame d'Argelès's disclosures formed, as it were, a sequel to the confidential revelations of Pascal Ferailleur, and the involuntary confession of the Marquis de Valorsay; and the baron could no longer doubt the existence of the shameful intrigue which had been planned in view of obtaining possession of the count's millions. And if he did not, at first, understand the motives, he at least began to discern what means had been employed. He now understood why Valorsay persisted in his plan of marrying Mademoiselle Marguerite, even without a fortune. "The wretch knows through Coralth that Madame d'Argelès is a Chalusse," he said to himself; "and when Mademoiselle Mar-

guerite has become his wife, he intends to oblige
Madame d'Argelès to accept her brother's estate and
share it with him."

At that same moment Madame d'Argelès finished
her narrative. " And now, what shall I do? " she added.

The baron was stroking his chin, as was his usual
habit when his mind was deeply exercised. " The first
thing to be done," he replied, " is to show Coralth in
his real colors, and prove M. Ferailleur's innocence. It
will probably cost me a hundred thousand francs to do
so, but I shall not grudge the money. I should probably spend as much or even more in play next summer;
and the amount had better be spent in a good cause
than in swelling the dividends of my friend Blanc, at
Baden."

" But M. de Coralth will speak out as soon as he finds
that I have revealed his shameful past."

" Let him speak."

Madame d'Argelès shuddered. " Then the name of
Chalusse will be disgraced," said she; " and Wilkie will
know who his mother is."

" No."

" But——"

" Ah! allow me to finish, my dear friend. I have my
plan, and it is as plain as daylight. This evening you
will write to your London correspondent. Request M.
Patterson to summon your son to England, under any
pretext whatever; let him pretend that he wishes to give
him some money, for instance. He will go there, of
course, and then we will keep him there. Coralth certainly won't run after him, and we shall have nothing
more to fear on that score."

" Great heavens! " murmured Madame d'Argelès,
" why did this idea never occur to me? "

The baron had now completely recovered his composure. "As regards yourself," said he, "the plan you ought to adopt is still more simple. What is your furniture worth? About a hundred thousand francs, isn't it? Very well, then. You will sign me notes, dated some time back, to the amount of a hundred thousand francs. On the day these notes fall due, on Monday, for instance, they will be presented for payment. You will refuse to pay them. A writ will be served, and an attachment placed upon your furniture; but you will offer no resistance. I don't know if I explain my meaning very clearly."

"Oh, very clearly!"

"So your property is seized. You make no opposition, and next week we shall have flaming posters on all the walls, telling Paris that the furniture, wardrobe, cashmeres, laces, and diamonds of Madame Lia d'Argelès will be sold without reserve, at public auction, in the Rue Drouot, with the view of satisfying the claims of her creditors. You can imagine the sensation this announcement will create. I can see your friends and the frequenters of your drawing-room meeting one another in the street, and saying: 'Ah, well! what's this about poor d'Argelès?' 'Pshaw!—no doubt it's a voluntary sale.' 'Not at all; she's really ruined. Everything is mortgaged above its value.' 'Indeed, I'm very sorry to hear it. She was a good creature.' 'Oh, excellent; a deal of amusement could be found at her house,—only between you and me——' 'Well?' 'Well, she was no longer young.' 'That's true. However, I shall attend the sale, and I think I shall bid.' And, in fact, your acquaintances won't fail to repair to the Hôtel Drouot, and maybe your most intimate friends will yield to their generous impulses sufficiently to offer

twenty sous for one of the dainty trifles on your
étagères."

Overcome with shame, Madame d'Argelès hung her
head. She had never before so keenly felt the disgrace
of her situation. She had never so clearly realized what
a deep abyss she had fallen into. And this crushing
humiliation came from whom? From the only friend
she possessed—from the man who was her only hope,
Baron Trigault.

And what made it all the more frightful was, that
he did not seem to be in the least degree conscious of
the cruelty of his words. Indeed, he continued, in a
tone of bitter irony: " Of course, you will have an exhibition before the sale, and you will see all the dolls
that hairdressers, milliners and fools call great ladies,
come running to the show. They will come to see how
a notorious woman lives, and to ascertain if there are
any good bargains to be had. This is the right form.
These great ladies would be delighted to display diamonds purchased at the sale of a woman of the *demi
monde*. Oh! don't fear—your exhibition will be visited
by my wife and daughter, by the Viscountess de Bois
d'Ardon, by Madame de Rochecote, her five daughters,
and a great many more. Then the papers will take up
the refrain; they will give an account of your financial
difficulties, and tell the public what you paid for your
pictures."

It was with a sort of terror-stricken curiosity that
Madame d'Argelès watched the baron. It had been
many years since she had seen him in such a frame of
mind—since she had heard him talk in such a cynical
fashion. " I am ready to follow your advice," said she,
" but afterward? "

" What, don't you understand the object I have in

view? Afterward you will disappear. I know five or six journalists; and it would be very strange if I could not convince one of them that you had died upon an hospital pallet. It will furnish the subject of a touching, and what is better, a moral article. The papers will say, ' Another star has disappeared. This is the miserable end of all the poor wretches whose passing luxury scandalizes honest women.' "

" And what will become of me? "

" A respected woman, Lia. You will go to England, install yourself in some pretty cottage near London, and create a new identity for yourself. The proceeds of your sale will supply your wants and Wilkie's for more than a year. Before that time has elapsed you will have succeeded in accumulating the necessary proofs of your identity, and then you can assert your claims and take possession of your brother's estate."

Madame d'Argelès sprang to her feet. " Never! never! " she exclaimed, vehemently.

The baron evidently thought he must have misunderstood her. "What! " he stammered; "you will relinquish the millions that are legally yours, to the government? "

" Yes—I am resolved—it must be so."

" Will you sacrifice your son's future in this style? "

" No, it isn't in my power to do that; but Wilkie will do so, later, on, I'm sure of it."

" But this is simply folly."

A feverish agitation had now succeeded Madame d'Argelès's torpor; there was an expression of scorn and anger on her rigid features, and her eyes, usually so dull and lifeless, fairly blazed. " It is not folly," she exclaimed, " but vengeance! " And as the astonished baron opened his lips to question her: " Let me finish," she said imperiously, " and then you shall judge

me. I have told you with perfect frankness everything
concerning my past life, save this—this—that I am
married, Monsieur le Baron, legally married. I am
bound by a chain that nothing can break, and my husband is a scoundrel. You would be frightened if you
knew half the extent of his villainy. Oh! do not shake
your head. I ought not to be suspected of exaggeration
when I speak in this style of a man whom I once loved
so devotedly. For I loved him, alas!—even to madness
—loved him so much that I forgot self, family, honor,
and all the most sacred duties. I loved him so madly
that I was willing to follow him, while his hands were
still wet with my brother's blood. Ah! chastisement
could not fail to come, and it was terrible, like the sin.
This man for whom I had abandoned everything—
whom I had made my idol—do you know what he said
to me the third day after my flight from home? ' You
must be more stupid than an owl to have forgotten to
take your jewels.' Yes, those were the very words he
said to me, with a furious air. And then I could measure the depths of the abyss into which I had plunged.
This man, with whom I had been so infatuated, did not
love me at all, he had never loved me. It had only
been cold calculation on his part. He had devoted
months to the task of winning my heart, just as he
would have devoted them to some business transaction.
He only saw in me the fortune that I was to inherit.
Oh! he didn't conceal it from me. ' If your parents
are not monsters,' he was always saying, ' they will
finally become reconciled to our marriage. They will
give you a handsome fortune and we will divide it. I will
give you back your liberty, and then we can each of us
be happy in our own way.' It was for this reason that
he wished to marry me. I consented on account of my

anborn child. My father and mother had died, and he
hoped to prevail upon me to claim my share of the
paternal fortune. As for claiming it himself, he dared
not. He was a coward, and he was afraid of my
brother. But I took a solemn oath that he should never
have a farthing of the wealth he coveted, and neither
threats nor *blows* could compel me to assert my claim.
God only knows how much I had suffered from his
brutality when I at last succeeded in making my escape
with Wilkie. He has sought us everywhere for fifteen
years, but he has not yet succeeded in finding a trace
of us. Still he has not ceased to watch my brother. I
am sure of that, my presentiments never deceive me.
So, if I followed your advice—if I claimed possession
of my brother's fortune—my husband would instantly
appear with our marriage contract in his hands, and
demand everything. Shall I enrich him? No, never,
never! I would rather die of want! I would rather
see Wilkie die of starvation before my very eyes!"

Madame d'Argelès spoke in that tone of concentrated
rage which betrays years of repressed passion and un-
flinching resolution. One could scarcely hope to modify her views even by the wisest and most practical
advice. The baron did not even think of attempting to
do so. He had known Madame d'Argelès for years;
he had seen so many proofs of her invincible energy and
determination. She possessed the distinguishing characteristic of her family in a remarkable degree—that
proverbial Chalusse obstinacy which Madame Vantrasson had alluded to in her conversation with M.
Fortunat.

She was silent for a moment, and then, in a firm
tone she said: " Still, I will follow your advice in part,
baron. This evening I will write to M. Patterson and

request him to send for Wilkie. In less than a fortnight I shall have sold my furniture and disappeared.
I shall remain poor. My fortune is not so large as
people suppose. No matter. My son is a man; he
must learn to earn his own living."

"My banking account is always at your disposal,
Lia."

"Thanks, my friend, thanks a thousand times; but it
will not be necessary for me to accept your kind offer.
When Wilkie was a child I did not refuse. But now I
would dig the ground with my own hands, rather than
give him a louis that came from you. You think me
full of contradictions! Perhaps I am. It is certain
that I am no longer what I was yesterday. This trouble
has torn away the bandage that covered my eyes. I
can see my conduct clearly now, and I condemn it.
I sinned for my son's sake, more than for my own.
But I might have rehabilitated myself through him,
and now he will perhaps be dishonored through me."
Her breathing came short and hard, and it was in a
choked voice that she continued: "Wilkie shall work
for me and for himself. If he is strong, he will save
us. If he is weak—ah, well! we shall perish. But
there has been cowardice and shame enough! It shall
never be said that I sacrificed the honor of a noble
name and the happiness of my brother's child to my
son. I see what my duty is, and I shall do it."

The baron nodded approvingly. "That's no doubt
right," said he. "Only allow me to tell you that all
is not lost yet. The code has a weapon for every just
cause. Perhaps there will be a way for you to obtain
and hold your fortune independent of your husband."

"Alas! I made inquiries on the subject years ago,
and I was told that it would be impossible. Still, you

might investigate the matter. I have confidence in you.
I know that you would not advise me rashly;—but don't
delay. The worst misfortune would be less intolerable
than this suspense."

" I will lose no time. M. Ferailleur is a very clever
lawyer, I am told. I will consult him."

" And what shall I do about this man Fortunat, who
called upon me? "

The baron reflected for a moment. " The safest thing
would be to take no action whatever at present," he replied. " If he has any evil designs, a visit or a letter
from you would only hasten them."

By the way Madame d'Argelès shook her head, it
was easy to see that she had very little hope. " All this
will end badly," she murmured.

The baron shared her opinion, but he did not think
it wise or kind to discourage her. " Nonsense! " he
said lightly, " luck is going to change; it is always
changing."

Then as he heard the clock strike, he sprang from
his arm-chair in dismay. " Two o'clock," he exclaimed,
" and Kami-Bey is waiting for me. I certainly haven't
been wasting time here, but I ought to have been at
the Grand Hôtel at noon. Kami is quite capable of
suspecting a man of any knavery. These Turks are
strange creatures. It's true that I am now a winner to
the tune of two hundred and eighty thousand francs."
He settled his hat firmly on his head, and opening the
door, he added: " Good-by, my dear madame, I will
soon see you again, and in the meantime don't deviate
in the least from your usual habits. Our success depends, in a great measure, upon the fancied security of
our enemies! "

Madame d'Argelès considered this advice so sensible

that half an hour later she went out for her daily drive
in the Bois, little suspecting that M. Fortunat's spy,
Victor Chupin, was dogging her carriage. It was most
imprudent on her part to have gone to Wilkie's house
on her return. She incurred such a risk of awakening
suspicion by wandering about near her son's home that
she seldom allowed herself that pleasure, but sometimes
her anxiety overpowered her reason. So, on this occasion, she ordered the coachman to stop near the Rue
du Helder, and she reached the street just in time to
betray her secret to Victor Chupin, and receive a foul
insult from M. Wilkie. The latter's cruel words stabbed
her to the heart, and yet she tried to construe them as
mere proofs of her son's honesty of feeling—as proof
of his scorn for the depraved creatures who haunt the
boulevards each evening. But though her energy was
indomitable, her physical strength was not equal to her
will. On returning home, she felt so ill that she was
obliged to go to bed. She shivered with cold, and yet
the blood that flowed in her veins seemed to her like
molten lead. The physician who was summoned declared that her illness was a mere trifle, but prescribed
rest and quiet. And as he was a very discerning man,
he added, not without a malicious smile, that any excess
is injurious—excess of pleasure as well as any other.
As it was Sunday, Madame d'Argelès was able to obey
the physician, and so she closed her doors against every
one, the baron excepted. Still, fearing that this seclu-
sion might seem a little strange, she ordered her concierge to tell any visitors that she had gone into the
country, and would not return until her usual reception-
day. She would then be compelled to open her doors
as usual. For what would the *habitués* of the house,
who had played there every Monday for years, say if

they found the doors closed? She was less her own mistress than an actress—she had no right to weep or suffer in solitude.

So, at about seven o'clock on Monday evening, although still grievously suffering both in mind and body, she arranged herself to receive her guests. From among all her dresses, she chose the same dark robe she had worn on the night when Pascal Ferailleur was ruined at her house; and as she was even paler than usual, she tried to conceal the fact by a prodigal use of *rouge*. At ten o'clock, when the first arrivals entered the brilliantly lighted rooms, they found her seated as usual on the sofa, near the fire, with the same eternal, unchangeable smile upon her lips. There were at least forty persons in the room, and the gambling had become quite animated when the baron entered. Madame d'Argelès read in his eyes that he was the bearer of good news. "Everything is going on well," he whispered, as he shook hands with her. "I have seen M. Ferailleur—I wouldn't give ten sous for Valorsay's and Coralth's chances."

This intelligence revived Madame d'Argelès's drooping spirits, and she received M. de Coralth with perfect composure when he came to pay his respects to her soon afterward. For he had the impudence to come, in order to dispel any suspicions that might have been aroused anent his complicity in the card-cheating affair. The hostess's calmness amazed him. Was she still ignorant of her brother's death and the complications arising from it, or was she only acting a part? He was so anxious and undecided, that instead of mingling with the groups of talkers, he at once took a seat at the card-table, whence he could watch the poor woman's every movement.

Both rooms were full, and almost everybody was engaged in play, when, shortly after midnight, a servant
entered the room, whispered a few words in his mistress's ear, and handed her a card. She took it, glanced
at it, and uttered so harsh, so terrible, so heart-broken
a cry, that several of the guests sprang to their feet.
"What is it? What is it?" they asked. She tried to
reply, but could not. Her lips parted, she opened her
mouth, but no sound came forth. She turned ghastly
white under her rouge, and a wild, unnatural light
gleamed in her eyes. One curious guest, without a
thought of harm, tried to take the card, which she still
held in her clinched hand; but she repulsed him with
such an imperious gesture that he recoiled in terror.
"What is it? What is the matter with her?" was the
astonished query on every side.

At last, with a terrible effort, she managed to reply,
"Nothing." And then, after clinging for a moment to
the mantel-shelf, in order to steady herself, she tottered
out of the room.

VII.

It was not enough to tell M. Wilkie the secret of his
birth. He must be taught how to utilize the knowledge.
The Viscount de Coralth devoted himself to this task,
and burdened Wilkie with such a host of injunctions,
that it was quite evident he had but a poor opinion of
his pupil's sagacity. "That woman d'Argelès," he
thought, "is as sharp as steel. She will deceive this
young idiot completely, if I don't warn him."

So he did warn him; and Wilkie was instructed exactly what to do and say, how to answer any questions,

and what position to take up according to circumstances.   Moreover, he was especially enjoined to distrust tears, and not to let himself be put out of countenance by haughty airs.   The viscount spent at least an
hour in giving explanations and advice, to the great
disgust of M. Wilkie, who, feeling that he was being
treated like a child, somewhat testily declared that he
was no fool, and that he knew how to take care of
himself as well as any one else.   Still, this did not
prevent M. de Coralth from persisting in his instructions until he was persuaded that he had prepared his
pupil for all possible emergencies.   He then rose to
depart.   "That's all, I think," he remarked, with
a   shade   of   uneasiness.   "I've   traced   the   plan
—you must execute it, and keep cool, or the game's
lost."

His companion rose proudly.   "If it fails, it won't
be from any fault of mine," he answered with unmistakable petulance.

"Lose no time."

"There's no danger of that."

"And understand, that whatever happens, my name
is not to be mentioned."

"Yes, yes."

"If there should be any new revelations, I will inform you."

"At the club?"

"Yes, but don't be uneasy; the affair is as good as
concluded."

"I hope so, indeed."

Wilkie gave a sigh of relief as he saw his visitor
depart.   He wished to be alone, so as to brood over the
delights that the future had in store for him.   He was
no longer to be limited to a paltry allowance of twenty

thousand francs! No more debts, no more ungratified
longings. He would have millions at his disposal! He
seemed to see them, to hold them, to feel them gliding
in golden waves between his fingers! What horses he
would have! what carriages! what mistresses! And a
gleam of envy that he had detected in M. de Coralth's
eyes put the finishing touch to his bliss. To be envied
by this brilliant viscount, his model and his ideal, what
happiness it was!

The reputation that Madame d'Argelès bore had at
first cast a shadow over his joy; but this shadow had
soon vanished. He was troubled by no foolish prejudices, and personally he cared little or nothing for his
mother's reputation. The prejudices of society must,
of course, be considered. But nonsense! society has no
prejudices nowadays when millionaires are concerned,
and asks no questions respecting their parents. Society
only requires passports of the indigent. Besides, no
matter what Madame d'Argelès might have done, she
was none the less a Chalusse, the descendant of one of
the most aristocratic families in France.

Such were Wilkie's meditations while he was engaged in dressing himself with more than usual care.
He had been quite shocked by the suggestion that
Madame d'Argelès might try to deny him, and he
wished to appear before her in the most advantageous
light. His toilette was consequently a lengthy operation. However, shortly after twelve o'clock he was
ready. He cast a last admiring glance at himself in
the mirror, twirled his mustaches, and departed on his
mission. He even went on foot, which was a concession
to what he considered M. de Coralth's absurd ideas.
The aspect of the Hôtel d'Argelès, in the Rue de Berry,
impressed him favorably, but, at the same time, it some-

what disturbed his superb assurance. " Everything is very stylish here," he muttered.

A couple of servants—the concierge and Job—were standing at the door engaged in conversation. M. Wilkie approached them, and in his most imposing manner, but not without a slight tremble in his voice, requested to see Madame d'Argelès. " Madame is in the country," replied the concierge; " she will not return before this evening. If monsieur will leave his card——"

" Oh! that's quite unnecessary. I shall be passing again."

This, too, was in obedience to the instructions of M. de Coralth, who had advised him not to send in his name, but to gain admission into Madame d'Argelès's presence as speedily as possible, without giving her time to prepare herself for the interview; and Wilkie had ultimately decided that these precautions might not prove as superfluous as he at first supposed. But this first mishap annoyed him extremely. What should he do? how should he kill time till the evening? A cab was passing. He hired it for a drive to the Bois, whence he returned to the boulevards, played a game of billiards with one of the co-proprietors of Pompier de Nanterre, and finally dined at the Café Riche, devoting as much time as possible to the operation. He was finishing his coffee when the clock struck eight. He caught up his hat, drew on his gloves, and hastened to the Hôtel d'Argelès again.

" Madame has not yet returned," said the concierge, who knew that his mistress had only just risen from her bed, " but I don't think it will be long. And if monsieur wishes——"

" No," replied M. Wilkie brusquely, and he was

going off in a furious passion, when, on crossing the street, he chanced to turn his head and notice that the reception rooms were brilliantly lighted up. "Ah! I think that a very shabby trick!" grumbled the intelligent youth. "They won't succeed in playing that game on me again. Why, she's there now!"

It occurred to him that Madame d'Argelès had perhaps described him to her servants, and had given them strict orders not to admit him. "I'll find out if that is the case, even if I have to wait here until to-morrow morning," he thought, angrily. However, he had not been on guard very long, when he saw a brougham stop in front of the mansion, whereupon the gate opened, as if by enchantment. The vehicle entered the courtyard, deposited its occupants, and drove away. A second carriage soon appeared, then a third, and then five or six in quick succession. "And does she think I'll wear out my shoe-leather here, while everybody else is allowed to enter?" he grumbled. "Never!—I've an idea." And, without giving himself time for further deliberation, he returned to his rooms, arrayed himself in evening-dress, and sent for his carriage. "You will drive to No. — in the Rue de Berry," he said. "There is a *soirée* there, and you can drive directly into the courtyard." The coachman obeyed, and M. Wilkie realized that his idea was really an excellent one.

As soon as he alighted, the doors were thrown open, and he ascended a handsome staircase, heavily carpeted, and adorned with flowers. Two liveried footmen were standing at the door of the drawing-room, and one of them advanced to relieve Wilkie of his overcoat, but his services were declined. "I don't wish to go in," said the young man roughly. "I wish to speak with

Madame d'Argelès in private.   She is expecting me—
inform her.   Here is my card."

The servant was hesitating, when Job, suspecting
some mystery perhaps, approached.   " Take in the gentleman's card," he said, with an air of authority; and,
opening the door of a small room on the left-hand side
of the staircase, he invited Wilkie to enter, saying, " If
monsieur will be kind enough to take a seat, I will summon madame at once."

M. Wilkie sank into an arm-chair, considerably overcome.   The air of luxury that pervaded the entire establishment, the liveried servants, the lights and flowers,
all impressed him much more deeply than he would
have been willing to confess.   And in spite of his
affected arrogance, he felt that the superb assurance
which was the dominant trait in his character was deserting him.   In his breast, moreover, in the place where
physiologists locate the heart, he felt certain extraordinary movements which strongly resembled palpitations.
For the first time it occurred to him that this woman,
whose peace he had come to destroy, was not only the
heiress of the Count de Chalusse's millions, but also his
mother, that is to say, the good fairy whose protection
had followed him everywhere since he entered the
world.   The thought that he was about to commit an
atrocious act entered his mind, but he drove it away.
It was too late now to draw back, or even to reflect.

Suddenly a door opposite the one by which he had
entered opened, and Madame d'Argelès appeared on the
threshold.   She was no longer the woman whose anguish and terror had alarmed her guests.   During the
brief moment of respite which fate had granted her,
she had summoned all her energy and courage, and
had mastered her despair.   She felt that her salvation

depended upon her calmness, and she had succeeded in appearing calm, haughty, and disdainful—as impassive as if she had been a statue. "Was it you, sir, who sent me this card?" she inquired.

Greatly disconcerted, M. Wilkie could only bow and stammer out an almost unintelligible answer. "Excuse me! I am much grieved, upon my word! I disturb you, perhaps——"

"You are Monsieur Wilkie!" interrupted Madame d'Argelès, in a tone of mingled irony and disdain.

"Yes," he replied, drawing out the name affectedly, "I am M. Wilkie."

"Did you desire to speak with me?" inquired Madame d'Argelès, dryly.

"In fact—yes. I should like——"

"Very well. I will listen to you, although your visit is most inopportune, for I have eighty guests or more in my drawing-room. Still, speak!"

It was very easy to say "speak," but unfortunately for M. Wilkie he could not articulate a syllable. His tongue was as stiff, and as dry, as if it had been paralyzed. He nervously passed and repassed his fingers between his neck and his collar, but although this gave full play to his cravat, his words did not leave his throat any more readily. For he had imagined that Madame d'Argelès would be like other women he had known, but not at all. He found her to be an extremely proud and awe-inspiring creature, who, to use his own vocabulary, *squelched* him completely. "I wished to say to you," he repeated, "I wished to say to you——"
But the words he was seeking would not come; and, so at last, angry with himself, he exclaimed: "Ah! you know as well as I, why I have come. Do you dare to pretend that you don't know?"

She looked at him with admirably feigned astonishment, glanced despairingly at the ceiling, shrugged her shoulders, and replied: "Most certainly I don't know—unless indeed it be a wager."

"A wager!" M. Wilkie wondered if he were not the victim of some practical joke, and if there were not a crowd of listeners hidden somewhere, who, after enjoying his discomfiture, would suddenly make their appearance, holding their sides. This fear restored his presence of mind. "Well, then," he replied, huskily, "this is my reason. I know nothing respecting my parents. This morning, a man with whom you are well acquainted, assured me that I was—your son. I was completely stunned at first, but after a while I recovered sufficiently to call here, and found that you had gone out."

He was interrupted by a nervous laugh from Madame d'Argelès. For she was heroic enough to laugh, although death was in her heart, and although the nails of her clinched hands were embedded deep in her quivering flesh. "And you believed him, monsieur?" she exclaimed. "Really, this is too absurd! I—your mother! Why, look at me——"

He was doing nothing else, he was watching her with all the powers of penetration he possessed. Madame d'Argelès's laugh had an unnatural ring that awakened his suspicions. All Coralth's recommendations buzzed confusedly in his ears, and he judged that the moment had come "to do the sentimental," as he would have expressed it. So he lowered his head, and in an aggrieved tone, exclaimed: "Ah! you think it very amusing, I don't. Do you realize how wretched it makes one to live as utterly alone as a leper, without a soul to love or care for you? Other young men have a mother,

sisters, relatives. I have no one! Ah! if—— But I
only have friends while my money lasts." He wiped
his eyes, dry as they were, with his handkerchief, and
in a still more pathetic tone, resumed: "Not that I
want for anything; I receive a very handsome allowance. But when my relatives have given me the where-
withal to keep me from starving, they imagine their
duty is fulfilled. I think this very hard. I didn't come
into the world at my own request, did I? I didn't ask
to be born. If I was such an annoyance to them when
I came into existence, why didn't they throw me into
the river? Then they would have been well rid of me,
and I should be out of my misery!"

He stopped short, struck dumb with amazement, for
Madame d'Argelès had thrown herself on her knees at
his feet. "Have mercy!" she faltered; "Wilkie, my
son, forgive me!" Alas! the unfortunate woman had
failed in playing a part which was too difficult for a
mother's heart. "You have suffered cruelly, my son,"
she continued; "but I—I—— Ah! you can't conceive
the frightful agony it costs a mother to separate from
her child! But you were not deserted, Wilkie; don't
say that. Have you not felt my love in the air around
you? *You* forgotten? Know, then, that for years and
years I have seen you every day, and that all my
thoughts and all my hopes are centered in you alone!
Wilkie!"

She dragged herself toward him with her hands
clasped in an agony of supplication, while he recoiled,
frightened by this outburst of passion, and utterly
amazed by his easily won victory. The poor woman
misunderstood this movement. "Great God!" she exclaimed, "he spurns me; he loathes me. Ah! I knew it
would be so. Oh! why did you come? What infamous

wretch sent you here? Name him, Wilkie! Do you
understand, now, why I concealed myself from you?
I dreaded the day when I should blush before you,
before my own son. And yet it was for your sake.
Death would have been a rest, a welcome release for
me. But your breath was ebbing away, your poor little
arms no longer had strength to clasp me round the
neck. And then I cried: 'Perish my soul and body, if
only my child can be saved!' I believed such a sacrifice permissible in a mother. I am punished for it as
if it were a crime. I thought you would be happy, my
Wilkie. I said to myself that you, my pride and joy,
would move freely and proudly far above me and my
shame. I accepted ignominy, so that your honor might
be preserved intact. I knew the horrors of abject poverty, and I wished to save my son from it. I would
have licked up the very mire in your pathway to save
you from a stain. I renounced all hope for myself, and
I consecrated all that was noble and generous in my
nature to you. Oh! I will discover the vile coward who
sent you here, who betrayed my secret. I will discover
him and I will have my revenge! You were never to
know this, Wilkie. In parting from you, I took a solemn oath never to see you again, and to die without
the supreme consolation of feeling your lips upon my
forehead."

She could not continue; sobs choked her utterance.
And for more than a minute the silence was so profound
that one could hear the sound of low conversation in
the hall outside, the exclamations of the players as they
greeted each unexpected turn of luck, and occasionally
a cry of "Banco!" or "I stake one hundred louis!"
Standing silent and motionless near the window, Wilkie
gazed with consternation at Madame d'Argelès, his

mother, who was crouching in the middle of the room with her face hidden in her hands, and sobbing as if her heart would break. He would willingly have given his third share in Pompier de Nanterre to have made his escape. The strangeness of the scene appalled him. It was not emotion that he felt, but an instinctive fear mingled with commiseration. And he was not only ill at ease, but he was angry with himself for what he secretly styled his weakness. "Women are incomprehensible," he thought. "It would be so easy to explain things quietly and properly, but they must always cry and have a sort of melodrama."

Suddenly the sound of footsteps near the door roused him from his stupor. He shuddered at the thought that some one might come in. He hated the very idea of ridicule. So summoning all his courage he went toward Madame d'Argelès, and, raising her from the floor, he exclaimed: "Don't cry so. You grieve me, upon my word! Pray get up. Some one is coming. Do you hear me? Some one is coming." Thereupon, as she offered no resistance, he half led, half carried her to an arm-chair, into which she sank heavily. "Now she is going to faint!" thought Wilkie, in despair. What should he do? Call for help? He dared not. However, necessity inspired him. He knelt at Madame d'Argelès's feet, and gently said: "Come, come, be reasonable! Why do you give way like this? I don't reproach you!"

Slowly, with an air of humility which was indescrib‧ ably touching, she took her hands from her face, and for the first time raised her tear-stained eyes to her son's. "Wilkie," she murmured.

"Madame!"

She heaved a deep sigh, and in a half-stifled voice:

"*Madame!*" she repeated.   "Will you not call me
mother?"

"Yes, of course—certainly.   But—only you know it
will take me some time to acquire the habit.   I shall do
so, of course; but I shall have to get used to it, you
know."

"True, very true!—but tell me it is not mere pity
that leads you to make this promise?   If you should
hate me—if you should curse me—how should I bear
it!   Ah! when a woman reaches the years of understanding one should never cease repeating to her: ' Take
care!   Your son will be twenty some day, and you will
have to meet his searching gaze.   You will have to render an account of your honor to him!'   My God!   If
women thought of this, they would never sin.   To be
reduced to such a state of abject misery that one dares
not lift one's head before one's own son!   Alas! Wilkie,
I know only too well that you cannot help despising
me."

"No, indeed.   Not at all!   What an idea!"

"Tell me that you forgive me!"

"I do, upon my word I do."

Poor woman, her face brightened.   She so longed to
believe him!   And her son was beside her, so near that
she felt his breath upon her cheek.   It was he indeed.
Had they ever been separated?   She almost doubted
it, she had lived so near him in thought.   It was with
a sort of ecstasy that she looked at him.   There was a
world of entreaty in her eyes; they seemed to be begging a caress; she raised her quivering lips to his, but
he did not observe it.   For a long time she hesitated,
fearing he might spurn her; but at last, yielding to a
supreme impulse, she threw her arms around his neck,
drew him toward her, and pressed him to her heart in

a close embrace. " My son! my son!" she repeated;
" to have you with me again, after all these years!"

Unfortunately, no whirlwind of passion was capable
of carrying M. Wilkie beyond himself. His emotion
was now spent and his mind had regained its usual indifference. He flattered himself that he was a man of
mettle—and he remained as cold as ice beneath his
mother's kisses. Indeed, he barely tolerated them; and
if he did allow her to embrace him, it was only because
he did not know how to refuse. " Will she never have
done?" he thought. "This is a pretty state of things!
I must be very attractive. How Costard and Serpillon
would laugh if they saw me now." Costard and Serpillon were his intimate friends, the co-proprietors of
the famous steeplechaser.

In her rapture, however, Madame d'Argelès did not
observe the peculiar expression on her son's face. She
had compelled him to take a chair opposite her, and,
with nervous volubility, she continued: " If I don't deny
myself the happiness of embracing you again, it is because I have not broken the vow I took never to make
myself known to you. When I entered this room, I
was firmly resolved to convince you, no matter how,
that you had been deceived. God knows that it was not
my fault if I did not succeed. There are some sacrifices
that are above human strength."

M. Wilkie deigned to smile. " Oh! yes, I saw your
little game," he said, with a knowing air. " But I had
been well posted, and besides, it is not very easy to fool
me."

Madame d'Argelès did not even hear him. " Perhaps destiny is weary of afflicting us," she continued;
" perhaps a new life is about to begin. Through you,
Wilkie, I can again be happy. I, who for years have

lived without even hope. But will you have courage to forget?"

"What?"

She hung her head, and in an almost inaudible voice replied, "The past, Wilkie."

But with an air of the greatest indifference, he snapped his fingers, and exclaimed: "Nonsense! What is past is past. Such things are soon forgotten. Paris has known many such cases. You are my mother; I care very little for public opinion. I begin by pleasing myself, and I consult other people afterward; and when they are dissatisfied, I tell them to mind their own business."

The poor woman listened to these words with a joy bordering on rapture. One might have supposed that the strangeness of her son's expressions would have surprised her—have enlightened her in regard to his true character—but no. She only saw and understood one thing—that he had no intention of casting her off, but was indeed ready to devote himself to her. "My God!" she faltered, "is this really true? Will you allow me to remain with you? Oh, don't reply rashly! Consider well, before you promise to make such a sacrifice. Think how much sorrow and pain it will cost you."

"I have considered. It is decided—mother."

She sprang up, wild with hope and enthusiasm. "Then we are saved!" she cried. "Blessed be he who betrayed my secret! And I doubted your courage, my Wilkie! At last I can escape from this hell! This very night we will fly from this house, without one backward glance. I will never set foot in these rooms again—the detested gamblers who are sitting here shall never see me again. From this moment Lia d'Argelès is dead."

M. Wilkie positively felt like a man who had just fallen from the clouds. " What, fly? " he stammered. " Where shall we go, then? "

" To a country where we are unknown, Wilkie—to a land where you will not have to blush for your mother." " But——"

" Trust yourself to me, my son. I know a pleasant village near London where we can find a refuge. My connections in England are such that you need not fear the obstacles one generally meets with among foreigners. M. Patterson, who manages a large manufacturing establishment, will, I know, be happy to be of service to us—but we shall not be indebted to any one for long, now that you have resolved to work."

On hearing these words, M. Wilkie sprang up in dismay. " Excuse me," he said, " I don't understand you. You propose to set me to work in M. Patterson's factory? Well, to tell the truth, that doesn't suit me at all."

It was impossible to mistake M. Wilkie's manner, his tone, or gesture. They revealed him in his true character. Madame d'Argelès saw her terrible mistake at once. The bandage fell from her eyes. She had taken her dreams for realities, and the desires of her own heart for those of her son. She rose, trembling with sorrow and with indignation. " Wilkie! " she exclaimed, " Wilkie, wretched boy! what did you dare to hope? "

And, without giving him time to reply, she continued: " Then it was only idle curiosity that brought you here. You wished to know the source of the money which you spend like water. Very well, you may see for yourself. This is a gambling house; one of those establishments frequented by distinguished personages, which the police ignore, or which they cannot suppress. The hubbub you hear is made by the players. Men are ruined here. Some poor wretches have blown their brains out on leaving the house; others have parted with the last vestige of honor here. And the business pays me well. One louis out of every hundred that change hands falls to my share. This is the source of your wealth, my son."

This anger, which succeeded such deep grief—this outburst of disdain, following such abject humility—considerably astonished M. Wilkie. "Allow me to ask——" he began.

But he was not allowed a hearing. "Fool!" continued Madame d'Argelès, "did nothing warn you that in coming here you would deprive yourself forever of the income you received? Did no inward voice tell you that all would be changed when you compelled me, Lia d'Argelès, to say, 'Well, yes, it is true; you are my son?' So long as you did not know who and what I was, I had a mother's right to watch over you. I could help you without disgracing you, without despising you. But now that you know me, and know what I am, I can do nothing more for you—nothing! I would rather let you starve than succor you, for I would rather see you dead than dishonored by my money."

"But——"

"What! would you still consent to receive the allowance I have made you, even if I consented to continue it?"

Had a viper raised its head in M. Wilkie's path he would not have recoiled more quickly. "Never!" he exclaimed. "Ah, no! What do you take me for?"

This repugnance was sincere; there could be no doubt of that, and it seemed to give Madame d'Argelès a ray of hope. " I have misjudged him," she thought. " Poor Wilkie! Evil advice has led him astray; but he is not bad at heart. In that case, my poor child," she said aloud, " you must see that a new life is about to commence for you. What do you intend to do? How will you gain a livelihood? People must have food, and clothes, and a roof to shelter them. These things cost money. And where will you obtain it—you who rebel at the very word work? Ah! if I had only listened to M. Patterson. He was not blind like myself. He was always telling me that I was spoiling you, and ruining your future by giving you so much money. Do you know that you have spent more than fifty thousand francs during the past two years? How have you squandered them? Have you been to the law-school a dozen times? No. But you can be seen at the races, at the opera, in the fashionable restaurants, and at every place of amusement where a young man can squander money. And who are your associates? Dissipated and heartless idlers, grooms, gamblers, and abandoned women."

A sneer from M. Wilkie interrupted her. To think that any one should dare to attack his friends, his tastes, and his pleasures. Such a thing was not to be tolerated. " This is astonishing—astonishing, upon my word!" said he. " You moralizing! that's really too good! I should like a few minutes to laugh; it is too ridiculous!"

Was he really conscious of the cruelty of his ironical words? The blow was so terrible that Madame d'Argelès staggered beneath it. She was prepared for anything and everything except this insult from her son. Still, she accepted it without rebellion, although it was in a tone of heart-broken anguish that she replied: " Perhaps I have no right to tell you the truth. I hope the future will prove that I am wrong. However, you are without resources, and you have no profession. Pray Heaven that you may never know what it is to be hungry and to have no bread."

For some time already the ingenious young man had shown unmistakable signs of impatience. This gloomy prediction irritated him beyond endurance.

"All this is empty talk," he interrupted. "I don't mean to work, for it's not at all in my line. Still, I don't expect to want for anything! That's plain enough, I hope."

Madame d'Argelès did not wince. "What do you mean to do then?" she asked, coldly. "I don't understand you."

He shrugged his shoulders impatiently. "Are we to keep up this farce for ever?" he petulantly exclaimed. "It doesn't take with me. You know what I mean as well as I do. Why do you talk to me about dying of starvation? What about the fortune?"

"What fortune?"

"Eh? why, my uncle's, of course! Your brother's, the Count de Chalusse."

Now M. Wilkie's visit, manner, assurance, wheedling, and contradictions were all explained. That maternal confidence which is so strong in the hearts of mothers vanished from Madame d'Argelès's for ever. The depths of selfishness and cunning she discerned in Wilkie's mind appalled her. She now understood why he had declared himself ready to brave public opinion— why he had proved willing to accept his share of the past ignominy. It was not his mother's, but the Count de Chalusse's estate that he claimed. "Ah! so you've heard of that," she said, in a tone of bitter irony. And then, remembering M. Isidore Fortunat, she asked:

"Some one has sold you this valuable secret. How much have you promised to pay him in case of success?"

Although Wilkie prided himself on being very clever, he did not pretend to be a diplomatist, and, indeed, he was greatly disconcerted by this question; still, recovering himself, he replied: "It doesn't matter how I obtained the information—whether I paid for it, or whether it cost me nothing—but I know that you are a Chalusse, and that you are the heiress of the count's property, which is valued at eight or ten millions of francs. Do you deny it?"

Madame d'Argelès sadly shook her head. "I deny nothing," she replied, "but I am about to tell you something which will destroy all your plans and extinguish your hopes. I am resolved, understand, and my resolution is irrevocable, never to assert my rights. To receive this fortune, I should be obliged to confess that Lia d'Argelès is a Chalusse—and that is a confession which no consideration whatever will wring from me."

She imagined that this declaration would silence and discomfit Wilkie, but she was mistaken. If he had been obliged to depend upon himself he would perhaps have been conquered by it; but he was armed with weapons which had been furnished by the cunning viscount. So he shrugged his shoulders, and coolly replied: "In that case we should remain poor, and the government would take possession of our millions. One moment. I have something to say in this matter. You may renounce your claim, but I shall not renounce mine. I am your son, and I shall claim the property."

"Even if I entreated you on my knees not to do so?"

"Yes."

Madame d'Argelès's eyes flashed. ".Very well. I

will show you that this estate can never be yours. By
what right will you lay claim to it? Because you are
my son? But I will deny that you are. I will declare
upon oath that you are nothing to me, and that I don't
even know you."

But even this did not daunt Wilkie. He drew from
his pocket a scrap of paper, and flourishing it triumphantly, he exclaimed: " It would be extremely cruel
on your part to deny me, but I foresaw such a con-
tingency, and here is my answer, copied from the civil
code: ' Article 341. Inquiry as to maternity allowed,
etc., etc.' "

What the exact bearing of Wilkie's threat might be
Madame d'Argelès did not know. But she felt that
this Article 341 would no doubt destroy her last hope;
for the person who had chosen this weapon from the
code to place it in Wilkie's hand must have chosen it
carefully. She understood the situation perfectly.
With her experience of life, she could not fail to understand the despicable part Wilkie was playing. And
though it was not her son who had conceived this
odious plot, it was more than enough to know that he
had consented to carry it into execution. Should she
try to persuade Wilkie to abandon this shameful
scheme? She might have done so if she had not been
so horrified by the utter want of principle which she
had discovered in his character. But, under the circumstances, she realized that any effort in this direction would prove unavailing. So it was purely from a
sense of duty and to prevent her conscience from reproaching her that she exclaimed: " So you will apply
to the courts in order to constrain me to acknowledge
you as my son? "

" If you are not reasonable——"

" That is to say, you care nothing for the scandal that will be created by such a course. In order to prove yourself a member of the Chalusse family you will begin by disgracing the name and dragging it through the mire."

Wilkie had no wish to prolong this discussion. So much talk about an affair, which, in his opinion, at least, was an extremely simple one, seemed to him utterly ridiculous, and irritated him beyond endurance. " It strikes me this is much ado about nothing," he remarked. " One would suppose, to hear you talk, that you were the greatest criminal in the world. Goodness is all very well in its way, but there is such a thing as having too much of it! Break loose from this life to-morrow, assume your rightful name, install yourself at the Hôtel de Chalusse, and in a week from now no one will remember that you were once known as Lia d'Argelès. I wager one hundred louis on it. Why, if people attempted to rake up the past life of their acquaintances, they should have far too much to do. Folks do not trouble themselves as to whether a person has done this or that; the essential thing is to have plenty of money. And if any fool speaks slightingly of you, you can reply: ' I have an income of five hundred thousand francs,' and he'll say no more."

Madame d'Argelès listened, speechless with horror and disgust. Was it really her son who was speaking in this style, and to her of all people in the world? M. Wilkie misunderstood her silence. He had an excellent opinion of himself, but he was rather surprised at the effect of his eloquence. " Besides, I'm tired of vegetating, and having only one name," he continued. " I want to be on the move. Even with the small allowance I've had, I have gained a very good position in society; and if I had plenty of money I should be the most stylish man in Paris. The count's estate belongs to me, and so I must have it—in fact, I will have it. So believe me when I tell you that it will be much better for you if you acknowledge me without any fuss! Now, will you do so? No? Once, twice, three times? Is it still no? Very well then; to-morrow, then, you may expect an official notice. I wish you good-evening."

He bowed; he was really going, for his hand was already on the door-knob. But Madame d'Argelès detained him with a gesture. "One word more," she said, in a voice hoarse with emotion.

He scarcely deigned to come back, and he made no attempt to conceal his impatience. "Well, what is it?" he asked, hastily.

"I wish to give you a bit of parting advice. The court will undoubtedly decide in your favor; I shall be placed in possession of my brother's estate; but neither you nor I will have the disposal of these millions."

"Why?"

"Because, though this fortune belongs to me, the control of it belongs to your father."

M. Wilkie was thunderstruck. "To my father?" he exclaimed. "Impossible!"

"It is so, however; and you would not have been ignorant of the fact, if your greed for money had not made you forget to question me. You believe yourself an illegitimate child. Wilkie, you are mistaken. You are my legitimate child. I am a married woman——"

"Bah!"

"And my husband—your father—is not dead. If he is not here now, threatening our safety, it is because I have succeeded in eluding him. He lost all trace of us eighteen years ago. Since then he has been constantly striving to discover us, but in vain. He is still watching, you may be sure of that; and as soon as there is any talk of a law-suit respecting the Chalusse property, you will see him appear, armed with his rights. He is the head of the family—your master and mine. Ah! this seems to disturb you. You will find him full of insatiable greed for wealth, a greed which has been whetted by twenty years' waiting. You may yet see the day when you will regret the paltry twenty thousand francs a year formerly given you by your poor mother."

Wilkie's face was whiter than his shirt. "You are deceiving me," he stammered.

"To-morrow I will show you my marriage certificate."

"Why not this evening?"

"Because it is locked up in a room which is now full of people."

"And what was my father's name?"

"Arthur Gordon—he is an American."

"Then my name is Wilkie Gordon?"

"Yes."

"And—is my father rich?" he inquired.

"No."

"What does he do?"

"Everything that a man can do when he has a taste for luxury and a horror for work."

This reply was so explicit in its brevity, and implied so many terrible accusations, that Wilkie was dismayed. "The devil!" he exclaimed, "and where does he live!"

"He lives at Baden or Homburg in the summer; in Paris or at Monaco in the winter."

"Oh! oh! oh!" ejaculated Wilkie, in three different tones. He knew what he had to expect from such a father as that. Anger now followed stupor—one of those terrible, white rages which stir the bile and not the blood. He saw his hopes and his cherished visions fade. Luxury and notoriety, high-stepping horses, yellow-haired mistresses, all vanished. He pictured himself reduced to a mere pittance, and held in check and domineered over by a brutal father. "Ah! I understand your game," he hissed through his set teeth. "If you would only quietly assert your rights, everything could be arranged privately, and I should have time to put the property out of my father's reach before he could claim it. Instead of doing that—as you hate me—you compel me to make the affair public, so that my father will hear of it and defraud me of everything. But you won't play this trick on me. You are going to write at once, and make known your claim to your brother's estate."

"No."

"Ah! you won't? You refuse——" He approached threateningly, and caught hold of her arm. "Take care!" he vociferated; "take care! Do not infuriate me beyond endurance——"

As cold and rigid as marble, Madame d'Argelès faced him with the undaunted glance of a martyr whose spirit no violence can subdue. "You will obtain nothing from me," she said, firmly; "nothing, nothing, nothing!"

Maddened with rage and disappointment, M. Wilkie dared to lift his hand as if about to strike her. But at this moment the door was flung open, and a man sprang upon him. It was Baron Trigault.

Like the other guests, the baron had seen the terrible effect produced upon Madame d'Argelès by a simple visiting card. But he had this advantage over the others: he thought he could divine and explain the reason of this sudden, seemingly incomprehensible terror. "The poor woman has been betrayed," he thought; "her son is here!" Still, while the other players crowded around their hostess, he did not leave the card-table. He was sitting opposite M. de Coralth, and he had seen the dashing viscount start and change color. His suspicions were instantly aroused, and he wished to verify them. He therefore pretended to be more than ever absorbed in the cards, and swore lustily at the deserters who had broken up the game. "Come back, gentleman, come back," he cried, angrily. "We are wasting precious time. While you have been trifling there, I might have gained—or lost—a hundred louis."

He was nevertheless greatly alarmed, and the prolonged absence of Madame d'Argelès increased his fears each moment. At the end of an hour he could restrain himself no longer. So taking advantage of a heavy loss, he rose from the table, swearing that the beastly turmoil of a few moments before had changed the luck. Then passing into the adjoining drawing-room, he managed to make his escape unobserved. "Where is madame?" he inquired of the first servant he met.

"In the little sitting-room."

"Alone?"

"No; a young gentleman is with her."

The baron no longer doubted the correctness of his conjectures, and his disquietude increased. Quickly, and as if he had been in his own house, he hastened to the door of the little sitting-room and listened. At that moment rage was imparting a truly frightful intonation to M. Wilkie's voice. The baron really felt alarmed. He stooped, applied his eye to the keyhole, and seeing

M. Wilkie with his hand-uplifted, he burst open the door and went in. He arrived only just in time to fell Wilkie to the floor, and save Madame d'Argelès from that most terrible of humiliations: the degradation of being struck by her own son. "Ah, you rascal!" cried the worthy baron, transported with indignation, "you beggarly rascal! you brigand! Is this the way you treat an unfortunate woman who has sacrificed herself for you—your mother? You try to strike your mother, when you ought to kiss her very footprints!"

As livid as if his blood had been suddenly turned to gall—with quivering lips and eyes starting from their sockets—M. Wilkie rose, with difficulty, to his feet, at the same time rubbing his left elbow which had struck against the corner of a piece of furniture, in his fall. "Scoundrel! You brutal scoundrel!" he growled, ferociously. And then, retreating a step: "Who gave you permission to come in here?" he added. "Who are you? By what right do you meddle with my affairs?"

"By the right that every honest man possesses to chastise a cowardly rascal."

M. Wilkie shook his fist at the baron. "You are a coward yourself," he retorted. "You had better learn who you are talking to! You must mend your manners a little, you old——"

The word he uttered was so vile that no man could fail to resent it, much less the baron, who was already frantic with passion. His faced turned as purple as if he were stricken with apoplexy, and such furious rage gleamed in his eyes that Madame d'Argelès was frightened. She feared she should see her son butchered before her very eyes, and she extended her arms as if to protect him. " Jacques," she said beseechingly, " Jacques!"

This was the name which was indelibly impressed upon Wilkie's memory—the name he had heard when he was but a child. Jacques—that was the name of the man who had brought him cakes and toys in the comfortable rooms where he had remained only a few days. He understood, or at least he thought he understood, everything. " Ah, ha!" he exclaimed, with a laugh that was at once both ferocious and idiotic. " This is very fine—monsieur is the lover. He has the say here—he——"

He did not have time to finish his sentence, for quick as thought the baron caught him by the collar, lifted him from the ground with irresistible strength, and flung him on his knees at Madame d'Argelès's feet, exclaiming: " Ask her pardon, you vile wretch! Ask her pardon, or——" " Or " meant the baron's clinched fist descending like a sledge-hammer on M. Wilkie's head.

The worthy youth was frightened—so terribly frightened that his teeth chattered. " Pardon!" he faltered.

" Louder—speak up better than that. Your mother must answer you!"

Alas! the poor woman could no longer hear. She had endured so much during the past hour that her strength was exhausted, and she had fallen back in her arm-chair in a deep swoon. The baron waited for a moment, and seeing that her eyes remained obstinately closed, he exclaimed: " This is your work, wretch!"

And lifting him again, as easily as if he had been a child, he set him on his feet, saying in a calmer tone, but in one that admitted of no reply: " Arrange your clothes and go."

This advice was not unnecessary. Baron Trigault had a powerful hand; and M. Wilkie's attire was decidedly the worse for the encounter. He had lost his cravat, his shirt-front was crumpled and torn, and his waistcoat—one of those that open to the waist and are fastened by a single button—hung down in the most dejected manner. He obeyed the baron's order without a word, but not without considerable difficulty, for his hands trembled like a leaf. When he had finished, the baron exclaimed: "Now be off; and never set foot here again—understand me—never set foot here again, never!"

M. Wilkie made no reply until he reached the door leading into the hall. But when he had opened it, he suddenly regained his powers of speech. "I'm not afraid of you," he cried, with frantic violence. "You have taken advantage of your superior strength—you are a coward. But this shall not end here. No!—you shall answer for it. I shall find your address, and to-morrow you will receive a visit from my friends M. Costard and M. Serpillon. I am the insulted party— and I choose swords!"

A frightful oath from the baron somewhat hastened M. Wilkie's exit. He went out into the hall, and holding the door open, in a way that would enable him to close it at the shortest notice, he shouted back, so as to be heard by all the servants: "Yes; I will have satisfaction. I will not stand such treatment. Is it any fault of mine that Madame d'Argelès is a Chalusse, and that she wishes to defraud me of my fortune. To-morrow, I call you all to witness, there will be a lawyer here. You don't frighten me. Here is my card!" And actually, before he closed the door, he threw one of his cards into the middle of the room.

The baron did not trouble himself to pick it up; his attention was devoted to Madame d'Argelès. She was lying back in her arm-chair, white, motionless and rigid, to all appearance dead. What should the baron do? He did not wish to call the servants; they had heard too much already—but he had almost decided to do so, when his eyes fell upon a tiny aquarium, in a corner of the room. He dipped his handkerchief in it; and alternately bathed Madame d'Argelès's temples and chafed her hands. It was not long before the cold water revived her. She trembled, a convulsive shudder shook her from head to foot, and at last she opened her eyes, murmuring: " Wilkie ! "

" I have sent him away," replied the baron.

Poor woman ! with returning life came the consciousness of the terrible reality. " He is my son ! " she moaned, " my son, my Wilkie ! " Then with a despairing gesture she pressed her hands to her forehead as if to calm its throbbings. " And I believed that my sin was expiated," she pursued. " I thought I had been sufficiently punished. Fool that I was ! This is my chastisement, Jacques. Ah ! women like me have no right to be mothers ! "

A burning tear coursed down the baron's cheek; but he concealed his emotion as well as he could, and said, in a tone of assumed gayety: " Nonsense ! Wilkie is young—he will mend his ways ! We were all ridiculous when we were twenty. We have all caused our mothers many anxious nights. Time will set everything to rights, and put some ballast in this young madcap's brains. Besides, your friend Patterson doesn't seem to me quite free from blame. In knowledge of books, he may have been unequalled; but as a guardian for youth, he must have been the worst of fools. After keeping

your son on a short allowance for years, he suddenly
gorges him with oats—or I should say, money—lets him
loose; and then seems surprised because the boy is
guilty of acts of folly. It would be a miracle if he were
not. So take courage, and hope for the best, my dear
Lia."

She shook her head despondingly. " Do you suppose
that my heart hasn't pleaded for him? " she said. " I
am his mother; I can never cease to love him, whatever
he may do. Even now I am ready to give a drop of
blood for each tear I can save him. But I am not blind;
I have read his nature. Wilkie has no heart."

" Ah! my dear friend, how do you know what shameful advice he may have received before coming to
you? "

Madame d'Argelès half rose, and said, in an agitated
voice: " What! you try to make me believe that? ' Advice!' Then he must have found a man who said to
him: ' Go to the house of this unfortunate woman who
gave you birth, and order her to publish her dishonor
and yours. If she refuses, insult and beat her!' You
know, even better than I, baron, that this is impossible.
In the vilest natures, and when every other honorable
feeling has been lost, love for one's mother survives.
Even convicts deprive themselves of their wine, and
sell their rations, in order to send a trifle now and then
to their mothers—while he——"

She paused, not because she shrunk from what she
was about to say, but because she was exhausted and
out of breath. She rested for a moment, and then resumed in a calmer tone: " Besides, the person who sent
him here had counselled coolness and prudence. I discovered this at once. It was only toward the close of
the interview, and after an unexpected revelation from

me, that he lost all control over himself. The thought that he would lose my brother's millions crazed him. Oh! that fatal and accursed money! Wilkie's adviser wished him to employ legal means to obtain an acknowledgment of his parentage; and he had copied from the Code a clause which is applicable to this case. By this one circumstance I am convinced that his adviser is a man of experience in such matters—in other words, the business agent——"

"What business agent?" inquired the baron.

"The person who called here the other day, M. Isidore Fortunat. Ah! why didn't I not bribe him to hold his peace?"

The baron had entirely forgotten the existence of Victor Chupin's honorable employer. "You are mistaken, Lia," he replied. "M. Fortunat has had no hand in this."

"Then who could have betrayed my secret?"

"Why, your former ally, the rascal for whose sake you allowed Pascal Ferailleur to be sacrificed—the Viscount de Coralth!"

The bare supposition of such treachery on the viscount's part brought a flush of indignant anger to Madame d'Argelès's cheek. "Ah! if I thought that!" she exclaimed. And then, remembering what reasons the baron had for hating M. de Coralth, she murmured: "No! Your animosity misleads you—he wouldn't dare!"

The baron read her thoughts. "So you are persuaded that it is personal vengeance that I am pursuing?" said he. "You think that fear of ridicule and public odium prevents me from striking M. de Coralth in my own name, and that I am endeavoring to find some other excuse to crush him. This might have been

so once; but it is not the case now. When I promised
M. Ferailleur to do all in my power to save the young
girl he loves, Mademoiselle Marguerite, my wife's
daughter, I renounced all thought of self, all my former
plans. And why should you doubt Coralth's treachery?
You, yourself, promised me to unmask *him*. If he has
betrayed *you*, my poor Lia, he has only been a little
in advance of you."

She hung her head and made no reply. She had forgotten this.

" Besides," continued the baron, " you ought to know
that when I make such a statement I have some better
foundation for it than mere conjecture. It was to some
purpose that I watched M. de Coralth during your
absence. When the servant handed you that card he
turned extremely pale. Why? Because he knew whose
card it was. After you left the room his hands trembled like leaves, and his mind was no longer occupied
with the game. He—who is usually such a cautious
player—risked his money recklessly. When the cards
came to him he did still worse; and though luck
favored him, he made the strangest blunders, and lost.
His agitation and preoccupation were so marked as to
attract attention; and one acquaintance laughingly inquired if he were ill, while another jestingly remarked
that he had dined and wined a little too much. The
traitor was evidently on coals of fire. I could see the
perspiration on his forehead, and each time the door
opened or shut, he changed color, as if he expected to
see you and Wilkie enter. A dozen times I surprised
him listening eagerly, as if by dint of attention, or by
the magnetic force of his will, he hoped to hear what
you and your son were saying. With a single word I
could have wrung a confession from him."

This explanation was so plausible that Madame d'Argelès felt half convinced. "Ah! if you had only spoken that word!" she murmured. The baron smiled a crafty and malicious smile, which would have chilled M. de Coralth's very blood if he had chanced to see it. "I am not so stupid!" he replied. "We mustn't frighten the fish till we are quite ready. Our net is the Chalusse estate, and Coralth and Valorsay will enter it of their own accord. It is not my plan, but M. Ferailleur's. There's a man for you! and if Mademoiselle Marguerite is worthy of him they will make a noble pair. Without suspecting it, your son has perhaps rendered us an important service this evening—"

"Alas!" faltered Madame d'Argelès, "I am none the less ruined—the name of Chalusse is none the less dishonored!"

She wanted to return to the drawing-room; but she was compelled to relinquish this idea. The expression of her face betrayed too plainly the terrible ordeal she had passed through. The servants had heard M. Wilkie's parting words; and news of this sort flies about with the rapidity of lightning. That very night, indeed, it was currently reported at the clubs that there would be no more card-playing at the d'Argelès establishment, as that lady was a Chalusse, and consequently the aunt of the beautiful young girl whom M. and Madame de Fondège had taken under their protection.

VIII.

UNUSUAL strength of character, unbounded confidence in one's own energy, with thorough contempt of danger, and an invincible determination to triumph or perish, are all required of the person who, like Mademoiselle Marguerite, intrusts herself to the care of strangers—worse yet, to the care of actual enemies. It is no small matter to place yourself in the power of smooth-tongued hypocrites and impostors, who are anxious for your ruin, and whom you know to be capable of anything. And the task is a mighty one— to brave unknown dangers, perilous seductions, perfidious counsels, and perhaps even violence, at the same time retaining a calm eye and smiling lips. Yet such was the heroism that Marguerite, although scarcely twenty, displayed when she left the Hôtel de Chalusse to accept the hospitality of the Fondège family. And, to crown all, she took Madame Léon with her— Madame Léon, whom she knew to be the Marquis de Valorsay's spy.

But, brave as she was, when the moment of departure came her heart almost failed her. There was despair in the parting glance she cast upon the princely mansion and the familiar faces of the servants. And there was no one to encourage or sustain her. Ah, yes! standing at a window on the second floor, with his forehead pressed close against the pane of glass, she saw the only friend she had in the world—the old magistrate who had defended, encouraged, and sustained her—the man who had promised her his assistance and advice, and prophesied ultimate success.

"Shall I be a coward?" she thought; "shall I be unworthy of Pascal?" And she resolutely entered the carriage, mentally exclaiming: "The die is cast!"

The General insisted that she should take a place beside Madame de Fondège on the back seat; while he found a place next to Madame Léon on the seat facing them. The drive was a silent and tedious one. The night was coming on; it was a time when all Paris was on the move, and the carriage was delayed at each street corner by a crowd of passing vehicles. The conversation was solely kept alive by the exertions of Madame de Fondège, whose shrill voice rose above the rumble of the wheels, as she chronicled the virtues of the late Count de Chalusse, and congratulated Mademoiselle Marguerite on the wisdom of her decision. Her remarks were of a commonplace description, and yet each word she uttered evinced intense satisfaction, almost delight, as if she had won some unexpected victory. Occasionally, the General leaned from the carriage window to see if the vehicle laden with Mademoiselle Marguerite's trunks was following them, but he said nothing.

At last they reached his residence in the Rue Pigalle. He alighted first, offered his hand successively to his wife, Mademoiselle Marguerite, and Madame Léon, and motioned the coachman to drive away.

But the man did not stir. "Pardon—excuse me, monsieur," he said, "but my employers bade—requested me——"

"What?"

"To ask you—you know, for the fare—thirty-five francs—not counting the little gratuity."

"Very well!—I will pay you to-morrow."

"Excuse me, monsieur; but if it is all the same to

you, would you do so this evening? My employer said that the bill had been standing a long time already."

" What, scoundrel! "

But Madame de Fondège, who was on the point of entering the house, suddenly stepped back, and drawing out her pocketbook, exclaimed: "That's enough! Here are thirty-five francs."

The man went to his carriage lamp to count the money, and seeing that he had the exact amount—

" And my gratuity? " he asked.

" I give none to insolent people," replied the General.

" You should take a cab if you haven't money enough to pay for coaches," replied the driver with an oath, " I'll be even with you yet."

Marguerite heard no more, for Madame de Fondège caught her by the arm and hurried her up the staircase, saying: " Quick! we must make haste. Your baggage is here already, and we must see if the rooms I intended for you—for you and your companion—suit you."

When Marguerite reached the second floor, Madame de Fondège hunted in her pocket for her latch-key. Not finding it, she rang. A tall man-servant of impudent appearance and arrayed in a glaring livery opened the door, carrying an old battered iron candlestick, in which a tiny scrap of candle was glaring and flickering.

" What! " exclaimed Madame de Fondège, " the reception-room not lighted yet? This is scandalous! What have you been doing in my absence? Come, make haste. Light the lamp. Tell the cook that I have some guests to dine with me. Call my maid. See that M. Gustave's room is in order. Go down and see if the General doesn't need your assistance about the baggage."

Finding it difficult to choose between so many contradictory orders, the servant did not choose at all.
He placed his rusty candlestick on one of the side-tables
in the reception-room, and gravely, without saying a
single word, went out into the passage leading to the
kitchen. " Evariste! " cried Madame de Fondège,
crimson with anger, " Evariste, you insolent fellow! "

As he deigned no reply, she rushed out in pursuit of
him. And soon the sound of a violent altercation
arose; the servant lavishing insults upon his mistress,
and she unable to find any response, save, " I dismiss
you; you are an insolent scamp—I dismiss you."

Madame Léon, who was standing near Mademoiselle
Marguerite in the reception-room, seemed greatly
amused. " This is a strange household," said she.
" A fine beginning, upon my word."

But the worthy housekeeper was the last person on
earth to whom Mademoiselle Marguerite wished to
reveal her thoughts. " Hush, Léon," she replied. " We
are the cause of all this disturbance, and I am very
sorry for it."

The retort that rose to the housekeeper's lips was
checked by the return of Madame de Fondège, followed
by a servant-girl with a turn-up nose, a pert manner,
and who carried a lighted candle in her hand.

" How can I apologize, madame," began Mademoiselle Marguerite, " for all the trouble I am giving
you? "

" Ah! my dear child, I've never been so happy.
Come, come, and see your room." And while they
crossed several scantily-furnished apartments, Madame
de Fondège continued: " It is I who ought to apologize
to you. I fear you will pine for the splendors of the
Hôtel de Chalusse. We are not millionaires like your

poor father. We have only a modest competence, no more. But here we are!"

The maid had opened a door, and Mademoiselle Marguerite entered a good-sized room lighted by two windows, hung with soiled wall paper, and adorned with chintz curtains, from which the sun had extracted most of the coloring. Everything was in disorder here, and, in fact, the whole room was extremely dirty. The bed was not made, the washstand was dirty, some woollen stockings were hanging over the side of the rumpled bed, and on the mantel-shelf stood an ancient clock, an empty beer bottle, and some glasses. On the floor, on the furniture, in the corners, everywhere in fact, stumps of cigars were scattered in profusion, as if they had positively rained down.

"What!" gasped Madame de Fondège, "you haven't put this room in order, Justine?"

"Indeed, madame, I haven't had time."

"But it's more than a month since M. Gustave slept here?"

"I know it; but madame must remember that I have been very much hurried this last month, having to do all the washing and ironing since the laundress——"

"That's sufficient," interrupted Madame de Fondège. And turning to Marguerite, she said: "You will, I am sure, excuse this disorder, my dear child. By this time to-morrow the room shall be transformed into one of those dainty nests of muslin and flowers which young girls delight in."

Connected with this apartment, which was known to the household as the lieutenant's room, there was a much smaller chamber lighted only by a single window, and originally intended for a dressing-room. It had two doors, one of them communicating with Mar-

guerite's room, and the other with the passage; and it
was now offered to Madame Léon, who on comparing
these quarters with the spacious suite of rooms she had
occupied at the Hôtel de Chalusse, had considerable
difficulty in repressing a grimace. Still she did not
hesitate nor even murmur. M. de Valorsay's orders
bound her to Marguerite, and she deemed it fortunate
that she was allowed to follow her. And whether the
marquis succeeded or not, he had promised her a sufficiently liberal reward to compensate for all personal
discomfort. So, in the sweetest of voices, and with a
feigned humility of manner, she declared this little
room to be even much too good for a poor widow whose
misfortunes had compelled her to abdicate her position
in society.

The attentions which M. and Madame de Fondège
showed her contributed not a little to her resignation.
Without knowing exactly what the General and his
wife expected from Mademoiselle Marguerite, she was
shrewd enough to divine that they hoped to gain some
important advantage. Now her " dear child " had declared her to be a trusted friend, who was indispensable
to her existence and comfort. " So these people will
pay assiduous court to me," she thought. And being
quite ready to play a double part as the spy of the
Marquis de Valorsay, and the Fondège family, and
quite willing to espouse the latter's cause should that
prove to be the more remunerative course, she saw a
long series of polite attentions and gifts before her.

That very evening her prophecies were realized; and
she received a proof of consideration which positively
delighted her. It was decided that she should take her
meals at the family table, a thing which had never
happened at the Hôtel de Chalusse. Mademoiselle

Marguerite raised a few objections, which Madame Léon answered with a venomous look, but Madame de Fondège insisted upon the arrangement, not understanding, she said, graciously, why they need deprive themselves of the society of such an agreeable and distinguished person. Madame Léon in no wise doubted but this favor was due to her merit alone, but Mademoiselle Marguerite, who was more discerning, saw that their hostess was really furious at the idea, but was compelled to submit to it by the imperious necessity of preventing Madame Léon from coming in contact with the servants, who might make some decidedly compromising disclosures. For there were evidently many little mysteries and make-shifts to be concealed in this household. For instance, while the servants were carrying the luggage upstairs, Marguerite discovered Madame de Fondège and her maid in close consultation, whispering with that volubility which betrays an unexpected and pressing perplexity. What were they talking about? She listened without any compunctions of conscience, and the words "a pair of sheets," repeated again and again, furnished her with abundant food for reflection. "Is it possible," she thought, "that they have no sheets to give us?"

It did not take her long to discover the maid's opinion of the establishment in which she served; for while she brandished her broom and duster, this girl, exasperated undoubtedly by the increase of work she saw in store for her, growled and cursed the old barrack where one was worked to death, where one never had enough to eat, and where the wages were always in arrears. Mademoiselle Marguerite was doing her best to aid the maid, who was greatly surprised to find this handsome, queenly young lady so obliging, when Evariste, the same who had received warning an hour before, made his appearance, and announced in an insolent tone that "Madame la Comtesse was served."

For Madame de Fondège exacted this title. She had improvised it, as her husband had improvised his title of General, and without much more difficulty. By a search in the family archives she had discovered—so she declared to her intimate friends—that she was the descendant of a noble family, and that one of her ancestors had held a most important position at the court of Francis I. or of Louis XII. Indeed, she sometimes confounded them. However, people who had not known her father, the wood merchant, saw nothing impossible in the statements.

Evariste was dressed as a butler should be dressed when he announces dinner to a person of rank. In the daytime when he discharged the duties of footman, he was gorgeous in gold lace; but in the evening, he arrayed himself in severe black, such as is appropriate to the butler of an aristocratic household. Immediately after his announcement everybody repaired to the sumptuous dining-room which, with its huge sideboards, loaded with silver and rare china, looked not unlike a museum. Such was the display, indeed, that when Mademoiselle Marguerite took a seat at the table, between the General and his wife, and opposite Madame Léon, she asked herself if she had not been the victim of that dangerous optical delusion known as prejudice. She noticed that the supply of knives and forks was rather scanty; but many economical housewives keep most of their silver under lock and key; besides the china was very handsome and marked with the General's monogram, surmounted by his wife's coronet.

However, the dinner was badly cooked and poorly served. One might have supposed it to be a scullery maid's first attempt. Still the General devoured it with delight. He partook ravenously of every dish, a flush rose to his cheeks, and an expression of profound satisfaction was visible upon his countenance. "From this," thought Mademoiselle Marguerite, "I must infer that he usually goes hungry, and that this seems a positive feast to him." In fact, he seemed bubbling over with contentment. He twirled his mustaches à la Victor Emmanuel, and rolled his "r," as he said, "Sacr-r-r-r-r-e bleu!" even more ferociously than usual. It was only by a powerful effort that he restrained himself from indulging in various witticisms which would have been most unseemly in the presence of a poor girl who had just lost her father and all her hopes of fortune. But he did forget himself so much as to say that the drive to the cemetery had whetted his appetite, and to address his wife as Madame Range-à-bord, a title which had been bestowed upon her by a sailor brother.

Crimson with anger to the very roots of her coarse, sandy hair—amazed to see her husband deport himself in this style, and almost suffocated by the necessity of restraining her wrath, Madame de Fondège was heroic enough to smile, though her eyes flashed ominously. But the General was not at all dismayed. On the contrary, he cared so little for his wife's displeasure that, when the dessert was served, he turned to the servant, and, with a wink that Mademoiselle Marguerite noticed, "Evariste," he ordered, "go to the wine-cellar, and bring me a bottle of old Bordeaux."

The valet, who had just received a week's notice, was only too glad of an opportunity for revenge. So

with a malicious smile, and in a drawling tone, he replied: " Then monsieur must give me the money. Monsieur knows very well that neither the grocer nor the
wine-merchant will trust him any longer."

M. de Fondège rose from the table, looking very
pale; but before he had time to utter a word, his wife
came to the rescue. " You know, my dear, that I
don't trust the key of my cellar to this lad. Evariste,
call Justine."

The pert-looking chambermaid appeared, and her
mistress told her where she would find the key of the
famous cellar. About a quarter of an hour afterward,
one of those bottles which grocers and wine-merchants
prepare for the benefit of credulous customers was
brought in—a bottle duly covered with dust and mould
to give it a venerable appearance, and festooned with
cobwebs, such as the urchins of Paris collect and sell
at from fifteen sous to two francs a pound, according
to quality. But the Bordeaux did not restore the General's equanimity. He was silent and subdued; and his
relief was evident when, after the coffee had been
served, his wife exclaimed: " We won't keep you from
your club, my dear. I want a chat with our dear
child."

Since she dismissed the General so unceremoniously,
Madame de Fondège evidently wished for a *tête-à-tête*
with Mademoiselle Marguerite. At least Madame
Léon thought so, or feigned to think so, and addressing
the young girl, she said: " I shall be obliged to leave
you for a couple of hours, my dear young lady. My
relatives would never forgive me if I did not inform
them of my change of residence."

This was the first time since she had been engaged
by the Count de Chalusse, that the estimable " com-

panion " had ever made any direct allusion to her relatives, and what is more, to relatives residing in Paris. She had previously only spoken of them in general terms, giving people to understand that her relatives had not been unfortunate like herself—that they still retained their exalted rank, though she had fallen, and that she found it difficult to decline the favors they longed to heap upon her.

However, Mademoiselle Marguerite evinced no surprise. " Go at once and inform your relatives, my dear Léon," she said, without a shade of sarcasm in her manner. " I hope they won't be offended by your devotion to me." But in her secret heart, she thought: " This hypocrite is going to report to the Marquis de Valorsay, and these relatives of hers will furnish her with excuses for future visits to him."

The General went off, the servants began to clear the table, and Mademoiselle Marguerite followed her hostess to the drawing-room. It was a lofty and spacious apartment, lighted by three windows, and even more sumptuous in its appointments than the dining-room. Furniture, carpets, and hangings, were all in rather poor taste, perhaps, but costly, very costly. As the evening was a cold one, Madame de Fondège ordered the fire to be lighted. She seated herself on a sofa near the mantelpiece, and when Mademoiselle Marguerite had taken a chair opposite her, she began, " Now, my dear child, let us have a quiet talk."

Mademoiselle Marguerite expected some important communication, so that she was not a little surprised when Madame de Fondège resumed: " Have you thought about your mourning? "

" About my mourning, madame? "

" Yes. I mean, have you decided what dresses you

will purchase? It is an important matter, my dear—
more important than you suppose. They are making
costumes entirely of *crêpe* now, puffed and plaited, and
extremely stylish. I saw one that would suit you well.
You may think that a costume for deep mourning made
with puffs would be a trifle *loud*, but that depends upon
tastes. The Duchess de Veljo wore one only eleven
days after her husband's death; and she allowed some
of her hair, which is superb, to fall over her shoulders,
à la pleureuse, and the effect was extremely touching."
Was Madame de Fondège speaking sincerely? There
could be no doubt of it. Her features, which had been
distorted with anger when the General took it into his
head to order the bottle of Bordeaux, had regained their
usual placidity of expression, and had even brightened
a little. "I am entirely at your service, my dear, if
you wish any shopping done," she continued. "And if
you are not quite pleased with your dressmaker, I will
take you to mine, who works like an angel. But how
absurd I am. You will of course employ Van Klopen.
I go to him occasionally myself, but only on great occasions. Between you and me, I think him a trifle too
high in his charges."

Mademoiselle Marguerite could scarcely repress a
smile. "I must confess, madame, that from my infancy I have been in the habit of making almost all
my dresses myself."

The General's wife raised her eyes to Heaven in real
or feigned astonishment. "Yourself!" she repeated
four or five times, as if to make sure that she had heard
aright. "Yourself! That is incomprehensible! You,
the daughter of a man who possessed an income of five
or six hundred thousand francs a year! Still I know
that poor M. de Chalusse, though unquestionably a very

worthy and excellent man, was peculiar in some of his ideas."

" Excuse me, madame. What I did, I did for my own pleasure."

But this assertion exceeded Madame de Fondège's powers of comprehension. " Impossible! " she murmured, " impossible! But, my poor child, what did you do for fashions—for patterns? "

The immense importance she attached to the matter was so manifest that Marguerite could not refrain from smiling. " I was probably not a very close follower of the fashions," she replied. " The dress that I am wearing now——."

" Is very pretty, my child, and it becomes you extremely; that's the truth. Only, to be frank, I must confess that this style is no longer worn—no—not at all. You must have your new dresses made in quite a different way."

" But I already have more dresses than I need, madame."

" What! black dresses? "

" I seldom wear anything but black."

Evidently her hostess had never heard anything like this before. " Oh! all right," said she, "these dresses will doubtless do very well for your first months of mourning—but afterward? Do you suppose, my poor dear, that I'm going to allow you to shut yourself up as you did at the Hôtel de Chalusse? Good heavens! how dull it must have been for you, alone in that big house, without society or friends."

A tear fell from Marguerite's long lashes. " I was very happy there, madame," she murmured.

" You think so; but you will change your mind. When one has never tasted real pleasure, one cannot realize how gloomy one's life really is. No doubt, you were very unhappy alone with M. de Chalusse."

"Oh! madame——"

"Tut! tut! my dear, I know what I am talking about. Wait until you have been introduced into society before you boast of the charms of solitude. Poor dear! I doubt if you have ever attended a ball in your whole life. No! I was sure of it, and you are twenty! Fortunately, I am here. I will take your mother's place, and we will make up for lost time! Beautiful as you are, my child—for you are divinely beautiful—you will reign as a queen wherever you appear. Doesn't that thought make that cold little heart of yours throb more quickly? Ah! *fêtes* and music, wonderful toilettes and the flashing of diamonds, the admiration of gentlemen, the envy of rivals, the consciousness of one's own beauty, are these delights not enough to fill any woman's life? It is intoxication, perhaps, but an intoxication which is happiness."

Was she sincere, or did she hope to dazzle this lonely girl, and then rule her through the tastes she might succeed in giving her? As is not unfrequently the case with callous natures, Madame de Fondège was a compound of frankness and cunning. What she was saying now she really meant; and as it was to her interest to say it, she urged her opinions boldly and even eloquently. Twenty-four hours earlier, proud and truthful Marguerite would have silenced her at once. She would have told her that such pleasures could never have any charm for her, and that she felt only scorn and disgust for such worthless aims and sordid desires. But having resolved to appear a dupe, she concealed her real feelings under an air of surprise, and was aston-

ished and even ashamed to find that she could dissemble
so well.

"Besides," continued Madame de Fondège, "a mar-
riageable young girl should never shut herself up like
a nun. She will never find a husband if she remains
at home—and she must marry. Indeed, marriage is a
sensible woman's only object in life, since it is her
emancipation."

Was Madame de Fondège going to plead her son's
cause? Mademoiselle Marguerite almost believed it—
but the lady was too shrewd for that. She took good
care not to mention as much as Lieutenant Gustave's
name.

"The season will certainly be unusually brilliant,"
she said, "and it will begin very early. On the fifth
of November, the Countess de Commarin will give a
superb *fête;* all Paris will be there. On the seventh,
there will be a ball at the house of the Viscountess de
Bois d'Ardon. On the eleventh, there will be a concert,
followed by a ball, at the superb mansion of the Baroness Trigault—you know—the wife of that strange
man who spends all his time in playing cards."

"This is the first time I ever heard the name mentioned."

"Really! and you have been living in Paris for years.
It seems incomprehensible. You must know then, my
dear little ignoramus, that the Baroness Trigault is one
of the most distinguished ladies in Paris, and certainly
the best dressed. I am sure her bill at Van Klopen's
is not less than a hundred thousand francs a year—
and that is saying enough, is it not?" And with genuine pride, she added: "The baroness is my friend. I
will introduce you to her."

Having once started on this theme, Madame de

Fondège was not easily silenced. It was evidently her
ambition to be considered a woman of the world, and
to be acquainted with all the leaders of fashionable
society; and, in fact, if one listened to her conversation for an hour one could learn all the gossip of the
day. Though she was unable to interest herself in this
tittle-tattle, Marguerite was pretending to listen to it
with profound attention when the drawing-room door
suddenly opened and Evariste appeared with an impudent smile on his face. "Madame Landoire, the milliner, is here, and desires to speak with Madame la
Comtesse," he said.

On hearing this name, Madame de Fondège started
as if she had been stung by a viper. "Let her wait,"
she said quickly. "I will see her in a moment."

The order was useless, for the visitor was already on
the threshold. She was a tall, dark-haired, ill-mannered
woman. "Ah! I've found you at last," she said, rudely,
"and I'm not sorry. This is the fourth time I've come
here with my bill."

Madame de Fondège pointed to Mademoiselle Marguerite, and exclaimed: "Wait, at least, until I am
alone before you speak to me on business."

Madame Landoire shrugged her shoulders. "As if
you were ever alone," she growled. "I wish to put
an end to this."

"Step into my room then, and we will put an end to
it, and at once."

This opportunity to escape from Madame de Fondège
must not be allowed to pass; so Marguerite asked permission to withdraw, declaring, what was really the
truth, that she felt completely tired out. After receiving a maternal kiss from her hostess, accompanied by a
"sleep well, my dear child," she retired to her own

room. Thanks to Madame Léon's absence, she found herself alone, and, drawing a blotting-pad from one of her trunks, she hastily wrote a note to M. Isidore Fortunat, telling him that she would call upon him on the following Tuesday. "I must be very awkward," she thought, "if to-morrow, on going to mass, I can't find an opportunity to throw this note into a letter-box without being observed."

It was fortunate that she had lost no time, for her writing-case was scarcely in its place again before Madame Léon entered, evidently out of sorts. "Well," asked Marguerite, "did you see your friends?"

"Don't speak of it, my dear young lady; they were all of them away from home—they had gone to the play."

"Ah?"

"So I shall go again early to-morrow morning; you must realize how important it is."

"Yes, I understand."

But Madame Léon, who was usually so loquacious, did not seem to be in a talkative mood that evening, and, after kissing her dear young lady, she went into her own room.

"She did not succeed in finding the Marquis de Valorsay," thought Marguerite, "and being in doubt as to the part she is to play, she feels furious."

The young girl tried to sum up the impressions of the evening, and to decide upon a plan of conduct, but she felt sad and very weary. She said to herself that rest would be more beneficial than anything else, and that her mind would be clearer on the morrow; so after a fervent prayer in which Pascal Ferailleur's name was mentioned several times, she prepared for bed. But before she fell asleep she was able to collect another bit of evidence. The sheets on her bed were new.

If Marguerite had been born in the Hôtel de Chalusse, if she had known a father's and a mother's tender care from her infancy, if she had always been protected by a large fortune from the stern realities of life, there would have been no hope for her now that she was left poor and alone—for how can a girl avoid dangers she is ignorant of? But from her earliest childhood Marguerite had studied the difficult science of real life under the best of teachers—misfortune. Cast upon her own resources at the age of thirteen, she had learned to look upon everybody and everything with distrust; and by relying only on herself, she had become strangely cautious and clear-sighted. She knew how to watch and how to listen, how to deliberate and how to act. Two men, the Marquis de Valorsay and M. de Fondège's son, coveted her hand; and one of the two, the marquis, so she believed, was capable of any crime. Still she felt no fears. She had been in danger once before when she was little more than a child, when the brother of her employer insulted her with his attentions, but she had escaped unharmed.

Deceit was certainly most repugnant to her truth-loving nature; but it was the only weapon of defence she possessed. And so on the following day she carefully studied the abode of her entertainers. And certainly the study was instructive. The General's household was truly Parisian in character; or, at least, it was what a Parisian household inevitably becomes when its inmates fall a prey to the constantly increasing passion for luxury and display, to the *furore* for aping the habits and expenditure of millionaires, and to the noble and elevated desire of humiliating and outshining their neighbors. Ease, health, and comfort had been unscrupulously sacrificed to show. The dining-room was magnificent, the drawing-room superb; but these were the only comfortably furnished apartments in the establishment. The other rooms were bare and desolate. It is true that Madame de Fondège had a handsome wardrobe with glass doors in her own room, but this was an article which the friend of the fashionable Baroness Trigault could not possibly dispense with. On the other hand, her bed had no curtains.

The aspect of the place fittingly explained the habits and manners of the inmates. What sinister fears must have haunted them! for how could this extreme destitution in one part of the establishment be reconciled with the luxury noticeable in the other, except by the fact that a desperate struggle to keep up appearances was constantly going on? And this constant anxiety made out-door noise, excitement, and gayety a necessity of their existence, and caused them to welcome anything that took them from the home where they had barely sufficient to deceive society, and not enough to impose upon their creditors. " And they keep three servants," thought Mademoiselle Marguerite—" three enemies who spend their time in ridiculing them, and torturing their vanity."

Thus, on the very first day after her arrival, she realized the real situation of the General and his wife. They were certainly on the verge of ruin when Mademoiselle Marguerite accepted their hospitality. Everything went to prove this: the coachman's insolent demand, the servants' impudence, the grocer's refusal to furnish a single bottle of wine on credit, the milliner's persistence, and, lastly, the new sheets on the visitors' beds. " Yes," thought Mademoiselle Marguerite to

herself, " the Fondèges were ruined when I came here.
They would never have sunk so low if they had not
been utterly destitute of resources. So, if they rise
again, if money and credit come back again, then the
old magistrate is right—they have obtained possession
of the Chalusse millions ! "

IX.

ON this side, at least, Mademoiselle Marguerite had no
very wide field of investigation to explore. Her common sense told her that her task would merely consist
in carefully watching the behavior of the General and
his wife, in noting their expenditure, and so on. It
was a matter of close attention, and of infinitesimal
trifles. Nor was she much encouraged by her first
success. It was, perhaps, important; and yet it might
be nothing. For she felt that the real difficulties would
not begin until she became morally certain that the
General had stolen the millions that were missing from
the count's escritoire. Even then it would remain for
her to discover how he had obtained possession of this
money. And when she had succeeded in doing this,
would her task be ended? Certainly not. She must
obtain sufficient evidence to give her the right of accusing the General openly, and in the face of every one.
She must have material and indisputable proofs before
she could say: "A robbery has been committed. I
was accused of it. I was innocent. Here is the
culprit ! "

What a long journey must be made before this goal
was reached! No matter ! Now that she had a positive and fixed point of departure, she felt that she pos-

sessed enough energy to sustain her in her endeavors
for years, if need be. What troubled her most was that
she could not logically explain the conduct of her
enemies from the time M. de Fondège had asked her
hand for his son up to the present moment. And first,
why had they been so audacious or so imprudent as to
bring her to their own home if they had really stolen
one of those immense amounts that are sure to betray
their possessors? "They are mad," she thought, "or
else they must deem me blind, deaf, and more stupid
than mortal ever was!" Secondly, why should they be
so anxious to marry her to their son, Lieutenant Gustave? This also was a puzzling question. However,
she was fully decided on one point: the suspicions of
the Fondège family must not be aroused. If they were
on their guard, it would be the easiest thing in the world
for them to pay their debts quietly, and increase their
expenditure so imperceptibly that she would not be
able to prove a sudden acquisition of wealth.

But the events of the next few days dispelled these
apprehensions. That very afternoon, although it was
Sunday, it became evident that a shower of gold had
fallen on the General's abode. The door-bell rang in-
cessantly for several hours, and an interminable pro-
cession of tradesmen entered. It looked very much as
if M. de Fondège had called a meeting of his creditors.
They came in haughty and arrogant, with their hats
upon their heads, and surly of speech, like people who
have made up their minds to accept their loss, but who
intend to pay themselves in rudeness. They were
ushered into the drawing-room where the General was
holding his *levée;* they remained there from five to ten
minutes, and then, bowing low with hat in hand, they
retired with radiant countenances, and an obsequious

smile on their lips. So they had been paid. And as if
to prove to Mademoiselle Marguerite that her suspicions were correct, she chanced to be present when
the livery stable-keeper presented his bill.

Madame de Fondège received him very haughtily.
" Ah! here you are! " she exclaimed, rudely, as soon as
he appeared. " So you are the man who teaches his
drivers to insult his customers? That is an excellent
way to gain patronage. What! I hire a one-horse carriage from you by the month, and because I happen to
wish for a two-horse vehicle for a single day, you make
me pay the difference. You should demand payment in
advance if you are so suspicious."

The stable-keeper, who had a bill for nearly four
thousand francs in his pocket, stood listening with the
air of a man who is meditating some crushing reply;
but she did not give him time to deliver it. " When I
have cause to complain of the people I employ, I dismiss them and replace them by others. Insolence is
one of those things that I never forgive. Give me your
bill."

The man, in whose face doubt, fear, and hope had
succeeded each other in swift succession, thereupon
drew an interminable bill from his pocket. And when
he saw the bank-notes, when he saw the bill paid without dispute or even examination, he was seized with a
wondering respect, and his voice became sweeter than
honey. They say the payment of a bad debt delights
a merchant a thousand times more than the settlement
of fifty good ones. The truth of this assertion became
apparent in the present case. Mademoiselle Marguerite
thought the man was going to beg " Madame la
Comtesse to do him the favor to withhold a portion of
the small amount." For the Parisian tradesman is so

constituted that very frequently it is not necessary to
pay him money, but only to show it.

However, this creditor's abnegation did not extend
so far; still he did entreat Madame la Comtesse not to
leave him on account of a blunder—for it was a blunder
—he swore it on his children's heads. His coachman
was only a fool and a drunkard, who had misunderstood
him entirely, and whom he should ignominiously dismiss on returning to his establishment. But "Madame
la Comtesse" was inflexible. She sent the man about
his business, saying, "I never place myself in a position
to be treated with disrespect a second time."

This probably accounted for the fact that Evariste,
the footman, who had been so wanting in respect the
previous evening, had been sent away that very morning. Mademoiselle Marguerite did not see him again.
Dinner was served by a new servant, who had been
sent by an Employment Office, and engaged without a
question, no doubt because Evariste's livery fitted him
like a glove. Had the cook also been replaced? Mademoiselle Marguerite thought so, though she had no
means of convincing herself on this point. It was certain, however, that the Sunday dinner was utterly unlike that of the evening before. Quality had replaced
quantity, and care, profusion. It was not necessary to
send to the cellar for a bottle of Château-Laroze; it
made its appearance at the proper moment, warmed to
the precise degree of temperature, and seemed quite to
the taste of excellent Madame Léon.

In twenty-four hours the Fondège family had been
raised to such affluence that they must have asked themselves if it were possible they had ever known the
agonies of that life of false appearances and sham
luxury which is a thousand times worse than an ex-

istence of abject poverty. "Is it possible that I am deceived?" Marguerite said to herself, on retiring to her room that evening. For it surprised her that a keen-sighted person like Madame Léon should not have remarked this revolution; but the worthy companion merely declared the General and his wife to be charming people, and did not cease to congratulate her dear young lady upon having accepted their hospitality. "I feel quite at home here," said she; "and though my room is a trifle small, I shall have nothing to wish for when it has been refurnished."

Mademoiselle Marguerite spent a restless and uncomfortable night. In spite of her reason, in spite of the convincing proofs she had seen, the most disturbing doubts returned. Might she not have judged the situation with a prejudiced mind? Had the Fondèges really been as reduced in circumstances as she supposed? Like every one who has been unfortunate, she feared illusions, and was extremely distrustful of everything that seemed to favor her hopes and wishes. The only thing that really encouraged her was the thought that she could consult the old magistrate, and that M. de Chalusse's former agent might succeed in finding Pascal Ferailleur. M. Fortunat must have received her letter by this time: he would undoubtedly expect her on Tuesday, and it only remained for her to invent some excuse which would give her a couple of hours' liberty without awakening suspicion.

She rose early the next morning, and had almost completed her toilette, when she heard some one in the passage outside rapping at the door of Madame Léon's room. "Who's there?" inquired that worthy lady.

It was Justine, Madame de Fondège's maid, who

answered in a pert voice, " Here is a letter, madame, which has just been sent up by the concierge. It is addressed to Madame Léon. That is your name, is it not?"

Marguerite staggered as if she had received a heavy blow. " My God! a letter from the Marquis de Valorsay!" she thought.

It was evident that the estimable lady was expecting this missive by the eagerness with which she sprang out of bed and opened the door. And Marguerite heard her say to the servant in her sweetest voice: " A thousand thanks, my child! Ah! this is a great relief. I have heard from my brother-in-law at last. I recognize his hand-writing." And then the door closed again.

Standing silent and motionless in the middle of her room, Marguerite listened with that feverish anxiety that excites the perceptive faculties to the utmost degree. An inward voice, stronger than reason, told her that this letter threatened her happiness, her future, perhaps her life! But how could she convince herself of the truth of this presentiment? If she had followed her first impulse, she would have rushed into Madame Léon's room and have snatched the letter from her hands. But if she did this, she would betray herself, and prove that she was not the dupe they supposed her to be, and this supposition on the part of her enemies constituted her only chance of salvation.

If she could only watch Madame Léon as she read the letter, and gain some information from the expression of her face; but this seemed impossible, for the keyhole was blocked up by the key, which had been left in the lock on the other side. Suddenly a crack in the partition attracted her attention, and finding that it extended through the wall, she realized she might watch what was passing in the adjoining room. So she approached the spot on tiptoe, and, with bated breath, stooped and looked in.

In her impatience to learn the contents of her letter, Madame Léon had not gone back to bed. She had broken the seal, and was reading the missive, standing barefooted in her night-dress, directly opposite the little crevice. She read line after line, and word after word, and her knitted brows and compressed lips suggested deep concentration of thought mingled with discontent. At last she shrugged her shoulders, muttered a few inaudible words, and laid the open letter upon the rickety chest of drawers, which, with two chairs and a bed, constituted the entire furniture of her apartment.

"My God!" exclaimed Marguerite, with bated breath, "if she would only forget it!"

But she did not forget it. She began to dress, and when she had finished she read the letter again, and then placed it carefully in one of the drawers, which she locked, putting the key in her pocket.

"I shall never know, then," thought Marguerite; "no, I shall never know. But I must know—and I will!" she added vehemently.

From that moment a firm determination to obtain that letter took possession of her mind; and so deeply was she occupied in seeking for some means to surmount the difficulties which stood in her way that she did not say a dozen words during breakfast. "I must be a fool if I can't find some way of gaining possession of that letter," she said to herself again and again. "I'm sure I could find in it the explanation of the abominable intrigue which Pascal and I are the victims of."

Happily, her preoccupation was not remarked. Each person present was too deeply engrossed in his or her own concerns to notice the behavior of the others. Madame Léon's mind was occupied with the news she had just received; and, besides, her attention was considerably attracted by some partridges garnished with truffles, and a bottle of Château-Laroze. For she was rather fond of good living, the dear lady, as she confessed herself, adding that no one is perfect. The General talked of nothing but a certain pair of horses which he was to look at that afternoon, and which he thought of buying—being quite disgusted with jobmasters, so he declared. Besides, he expected to get the animals at a bargain, as they were the property of a young gentleman who had been led to commit certain misdemeanors by his love of gambling and his passion for a notorious woman who was afflicted with an insatiable desire for jewelry.

As for Madame de Fondège, her head seemed to have been completely turned by the prospect of the approaching *fête* at the Countess de Commarin's. She had only a fortnight left to make her preparations. All the evening before, through part of the night, and ever since she had been awake that morning, she had been racking her brain to arrive at an effective combination of colors and materials. And at the cost of a terrible headache, she had at last conceived one of those *toilettes* which are sure to make a sensation, and which the newspaper reporters will mention as noticeable for its *"chic."* "Picture to yourself," she said, all ablaze with enthusiasm, " picture to yourself a robe of tea-flower silk, trimmed with bands of heavy holland-tinted satin, thickly embroidered with flowers. A wide flounce of Valenciennes at the bottom of the skirt. Over this, I shall wear a tunic of pearl-gray *crêpe*, edged with a fringe of the various shades in the dress, and forming a panier behind."

But how much trouble, time and labor must be expended before such an elaborate *chef-d'œuvre* could be completed! How many conferences with the dressmaker, with the florist, and the embroiderer! How many doubts, how many inevitable mistakes! Ah! there was not a moment to lose! Madame de Fondège, who was dressed to go out, and who had already sent for a carriage, insisted that Mademoiselle Marguerite should accompany her. And certainly, the General's wife deemed the proposal a seductive one. It is a very fashionable amusement to run from one shop to another, even when one cannot, or will not, buy. It is a custom, which some noble ladies have imported from America, to the despair of the poor shopkeepers. And thus every fine afternoon, the swell shops are filled to overflowing with richly-attired dames and damsels, who ask to see all the new goods. It is far more amusing than remaining at home. And when they return to dinner in the evening, after inspecting hundreds of yards of silk and satin, they are very well pleased with themselves, for they have not lost the day. Nor do the shrewdest always return from these expeditions empty-handed. A dozen gloves or a piece of lace can be hidden so easily in the folds of a mantle!

And yet, to Madame de Fondège's great surprise, Marguerite declined the invitation. "I have so many things to put in order," she added, feeling that an excuse was indispensable.

But Madame Léon, who had not the same reasons as her dear child for wishing to remain at home, kindly offered her services. She was acquainted with several of the best shops, she declared, particularly with the establishment of a dealer in laces, in the Rue de Mulhouse, and thanks to an introduction from her, Madame de Fondège could not fail to conclude a very advantageous bargain there. "Very well," replied Madame de Fondège, "I will take you with me, then; but make haste and dress while I put on my bonnet."

They left the breakfast-room at the same time, closely followed by Mademoiselle Marguerite, who was disturbed by a hope which she scarcely dared confess to herself. With her forehead resting against the wall, and her eye peering through the tiny crack, she watched her governess change her dress, throw a shawl over her shoulders, put on her best bonnet, and, after a glance at the looking-glass, rush from the room, exclaiming: "Here I am, my dear countess. I'm ready."

And a few moments afterward they left the house together.

As the outer door closed after them, Marguerite's brain whirled. If she were not deceived, Madame Léon had left the key of the drawers in the pocket of the dress she had just taken off. So it was with a wildly throbbing heart that she opened the communicating door and entered her "companion's" room. She hastily approached the bed on which the dress was lying, and, with a trembling hand, she began to search for the pocket. Fortune favored her! The key was there. The letter was within her reach. But she was about to do a deed against which her whole nature revolted. To steal a key, to force an article of furniture open, and violate the secret of a private correspondence, these were actions so repugnant to her sense of honor, and her pride, that for some time she stood irresolute. At last the instinct of self-preservation overpowered her scruples. Was not her honor, and Pascal's honor also, at stake—as well as their mutual love and happiness? "It would be folly to hesitate," she murmured. And with a firm hand she placed the key in the lock.

The latter was out of order and the drawer was only opened with difficulty. But there, on some clothes which Madame Léon had not yet found time to arrange, Marguerite saw the letter. She eagerly snatched it up, unfolded it, and read: "Dear Madame Léon—" "Dear me," she muttered, "here is the name in full. This is an indiscretion which will render denial difficult." And she resumed her perusal: "Your letter, which I have just received, confirms what my servants had already told me: that twice during my absence—on Saturday evening and Sunday morning—you called at my house to see me." So Mademoiselle Marguerite's penetration had served her well. All this talk about anxious relatives had only been an excuse invented by Madame Léon to enable her to absent herself whenever occasion required. "I regret," continued the letter, "that you did not find me at home, for I have instructions of the greatest importance to give you. We are approaching the decisive moment. I have formed a plan which will completely, and forever, efface all remembrance of that cursed P. F., in case any one condescended to think of him after the disgrace we fastened upon him the other evening at the house of Madame d'Argelès." P. F.— these initials of course meant Pascal Ferailleur. Then he was innocent, and she held an undeniable, irrefutable proof of his innocence in her hands. How coolly and impudently Valorsay confessed his atrocious crime! "A bold stroke is in contemplation which, if no unfortunate and well-nigh impossible accident occur, will throw the girl into my arms." Marguerite shuddered. "The girl" referred to her, of course. "Thanks to the assistance of one of my friends," added the letter, "I can place this proud damsel in a perilous, terribly perilous position, from which she cannot possibly extricate herself unaided. But, just as she gives herself up for lost, I shall interpose. I shall save her; and it will be strange if gratitude does not work the necessary miracle in my favor. The plan is certain to succeed. Still, it will be all the better if the physician who attended M. de C—— in his last moments, and whom you spoke to me about (Dr. Jodon, if I remember rightly), will consent to lend us a helping hand. What kind of a man is he? If he is accessible to the seductive influence of a few thousand francs, I shall consider the business as good as concluded. Your conduct up to the present time has been a *chef-d'œuvre,* for which you shall be amply compensated. You have cause to know that I am not ungrateful. Let the F's continue their intrigues, and even pretend to favor them. I am not afraid of these people. I understand their game perfectly, and know why they wish my little one to marry their son. But when they become troublesome, I shall crush them like glass. In spite of these explanations, which I have just given you for your guidance, it is very necessary that I should see you. I shall look for you on Tuesday afternoon, between three and four o'clock. Above all, don't fail to bring me the desired information respecting Dr. Jodon. I am, my dear madame, devotedly yours—V." Below ran a postscript which read as follows: "When you come on Tuesday bring this letter with you. We will burn it together. Don't imagine that I distrust you—but there is nothing so dangerous as letters."

For some time Marguerite stood, stunned and appalled by the Marquis de Valorsay's audacity, and by the language of this letter, which was at once so obscure and so clear, every line of it threatening her future.

The reality surpassed her worst apprehensions, but realizing the gravity of the situation, she shook off the torpor stealing over her. She felt that every second was precious, and that she must act, and act at once. But what should she do? Simply return the letter to its place, and continue to act the *rôle* of a dupe, as if nothing had happened? No; that must not be. It would be madness not to seize this flagrant proof of the Marquis de Valorsay's infamy. But on the other hand, if she kept the letter, Madame Léon would immediately discover its loss, and an explanation would be unavoidable. M. de Valorsay would be worsted, but not annihilated, and the plans which made the physician's intervention a necessity would never be revealed. She thought of hastening to her friend the old magistrate; but he lived a long way off, and time was pressing. Besides she might not find him at home. Then she thought of going to a notary, to a judge. She would show them the letter, and they could take a copy of it. But no—this would do no good—the marquis could still deny it. She was becoming desperate, and was accusing herself of stupidity, when a sudden inspiration illumined her mind, turning night into day, as it were. " Oh, Pascal, we are saved! " she exclaimed. And without pausing to deliberate any longer, she threw a mantle over her shoulders, hastily tied on her bonnet, and hurried from the house, without saying a word to any one.

Unfortunately she was not acquainted with this part of Paris, and on reaching the Rue Pigalle she was at a loss for her way. Unwilling to waste any more time, she hastily entered a grocer's shop at the corner of the Rue Pigalle and the Rue Notre Dame de Lorette, and anxiously inquired: " Do you know any photographer in this neighborhood, monsieur? "

Her agitation made this question seem so singular that the grocer looked at her closely for a moment, as if to make sure that she was not jesting. " You have only to go down the Rue Notre Dame de Lorette," he replied, " and on the left-hand side, at the foot of the hill, you will find the photographer Carjat."

" Thank you."

The grocer stepped to the door to watch her. " That girl is certainly light-headed," he thought.

Her demeanor was really so extraordinary that it attracted the attention of the passers-by. She saw this, and slackening her pace, tried to become more composed. At the spot the grocer had indicated, she perceived several show frames filled with photographs hanging on either side of a broad, open gateway, above which ran the name, " E. Carjat." She went in, and seeing a man standing at the door of an elegant pavilion on the right-hand side of a large courtyard, she approached him, and asked for his employer.

" He is here," replied the man. " Does madame come for a photograph? "

" Yes."

" Then will madame be so kind as to pass in. She will not be obliged to wait long. There are only four or five persons before her."

Four or five persons! How long would she be obliged to wait?—half an hour—two hours? She had not the slightest idea. But she *did* know that she had not a second to lose, that Madame Léon might return at any moment, and find the letter missing; and, to crown all, she remembered now that she had not even locked the drawer again. " I cannot wait," she said, imperiously. " I must speak to M. Carjat at once."

" But——"

" At once, I tell you. Go and tell him that he must come."

Her tone was so commanding, and there was so much authority in her glance, that the servant hesitated no longer. He ushered her into a little sitting-room, and said, " If madame will take a seat, I will call monsieur."

She sank on to a chair, for her limbs were failing her. She was beginning to realize the strangeness of the step she had taken—to fear the result it might lead to—and to be astonished at her own boldness. But she had no time to prepare what she wished to say, for a man of five-and-thirty, wearing a mustache and imperial, and clad in a velvet coat, entered the room, and bowing with an air of surprise, exclaimed: " You desire to speak with me, madame? "

" I have a great favor to ask of you, monsieur."

" Of me? "

She drew M. de Valorsay's letter from her pocket, and, showing it to the photographer, she said, " I have come to you, monsieur, to ask you to photograph this letter—but at once—before me—and quickly—very quickly. The honor of two persons is imperilled by each moment I lose here."

Mademoiselle Marguerite's embarrassment was extreme. Her cheeks were crimson, and she trembled like a leaf. Still her attitude was proud, generous enthusiasm glowed in her dark eyes, and her tone of voice revealed the serenity of a lofty soul ready to dare anything for a just and noble cause. This striking contrast—this struggle between girlish timidity and a lover's virgil energy, endowed her with a strange and powerful charm, which the photographer made no attempt to resist. Unusual as was the request, he did not hesitate. "I am ready to do what you desire, madame," he replied, bowing again.

"Oh! monsieur, how can I ever thank you?"

He did not stop to listen to her thanks. Not wishing to return to the reception-room, where five or six clients were impatiently awaiting their turn, he called one of his subordinates, and ordered him to bring the necessary apparatus at once. While he was speaking, Mademoiselle Marguerite paused; but, as soon as his instructions were concluded, she remarked: "Perhaps you are too hasty, sir. You have not allowed me to explain; and perhaps what I desire is impossible. I came on the impulse of the moment, without any knowledge on the subject. Before you set to work, I must know if what you can do will answer my purpose."

"Speak, madame."

"Will the copy you obtain be precisely like the original in every particular?"

"In every particular."

"The writing will be the same—exactly the same?"

"Absolutely the same."

"So like, that if one of your photographs should be presented to the person who wrote this letter——"

"He could no more deny his handwriting than he could if some one handed him the letter itself."

"And the operation will leave no trace on the original?"

"None."

A smile of triumph played upon Mademoiselle Marguerite's lips. It was as she had thought; the defensive plan which she had suddenly conceived was a good one. "One more question, sir," she resumed. "I am only a poor, ignorant girl; excuse me, and give me the

benefit of your knowledge. This letter will be returned
to its author to-morrow, and he will burn it. But afterward, in case of any difficulty—in case of a law-suit—
or in case it should be necessary for me to prove certain
things which one might establish by means of this
letter, would one of your photographs be admitted as
evidence?"

The photographer did not answer for a moment.
Now he understood Mademoiselle Marguerite's motive,
and the importance she attached to a fac-simile. But
this imparted an unexpected gravity to the service he
was called upon to perform. He therefore wished some
time for reflection, and he scrutinized Mademoiselle
Marguerite as if he were trying to read her very soul.
Was it possible that this young girl, with such a pure
and noble brow, and with such frank, honest eyes, could
be meditating any cowardly, dishonorable act? No, he
could not believe it. In whom, or in what, could he
trust if such a countenance deceived him? "My fac-
simile would certainly be admitted as evidence," he replied at last; "and this would not be the first time that
the decision of a court has depended on proofs which
have been photographed by me."

Meanwhile, his assistant had returned, bringing the
necessary apparatus with him. When all was ready,
the photographer asked her, "Will you give me the
letter, madame?"

She hesitated for a second—only for a second. The
man's honest, kindly face told her that he would not
betray her, that he would rather give her assistance. So
she handed him the Marquis de Valorsay's letter, saying, with melancholy dignity, "It is my happiness and
my future that I place in your hands—and I have no
fears."

He read her thoughts, and understood that she either dared not ask for a pledge of secrecy, or else that she thought it unnecessary. He took pity on her, and his last doubt fled. " I shall read this letter, madame," said he, " but I am the only person who will read it. I give you my word on that! No one but myself will see the proofs."

Greatly moved, she offered him her hand, and simply said, " Thanks; I am more than repaid."

To obtain an absolutely perfect fac-simile of a letter is a delicate and sometimes lengthy operation. However, at the end of about twenty minutes, the photographer possessed two negatives that promised him perfect proofs. He looked at them with a satisfied air; and then returning the letter to Mademoiselle Marguerite, he said, " In less than three days the fac-similes will be ready, madame; and if you will tell me to what address I ought to send them——"

She trembled on hearing these words, and quickly answered, " Don't send them, sir—keep them carefully. Great heavens! all would be lost if it came to the knowledge of any one. I will send for them, or come myself." And, feeling the extent of her obligation, she added, " But I will not go without introducing myself—I am Mademoiselle Marguerite de Chalusse." And, thereupon, she went off, leaving the photographer surprised at the adventure and dazzled by his strange visitor's beauty.

Rather more than an hour had elapsed since Marguerite left M. de Fondège's house. " How time flies ! " she murmured, quickening her pace as much as she could without exciting remark—" how time flies ! " But, hurried as she was, she stopped and spent five minutes at a shop in the Rue Notre Dame de Lorette, where

she purchased some black ribbon and a few other trifles.
How else could she explain and justify her absence, if
the servants, who had probably discovered she had gone
out, chanced to speak of it?

But her heart throbbed as if it would burst as she
ascended the General's staircase, and anxiety checked
her breathing as she rang the bell. "What if Madame
de Fondège and Madame Léon had returned, and the
abstraction of the letter been discovered!" Fortunately, Madame de Fondège required more than an
hour to purchase the materials for the elaborate toilette
she had dreamt of. The ladies were still out, and
Mademoiselle Marguerite found everything in the same
condition as she had left it. She carefully placed the
letter in the drawer again, locked it, and put the key
in the pocket of Madame Léon's dress. Then she
breathed freely once more; and, for the first time in six
days, she felt something very like joy in her heart.
Now she had no fear of the Marquis de Valorsay. She
had him in her power. He would destroy his letter the
next day, and think that he was annihilating all proofs
of his infamy. Not so. At the decisive moment, at the
very moment of his triumph, she would produce the
photograph of this letter, and crush him. And she—
only a young girl—had outwitted this consummate
scoundrel! "I have not been unworthy of Pascal," she
said to herself, with a flash of pride.

However, her nature was not one of those weak ones
which are become intoxicated by the first symptom of
success, and then relax in their efforts. When her excitement had abated a little, she was inclined to dis-
parage rather than to exaggerate the advantage she had
gained. What she desired was a complete, startling, in-
contestable victory. It was not enough to prove Val-

orsay's *guilt*—she was resolved to penetrate his designs, to discover why he pursued her so desperately. And, though she felt that she possessed a formidable weapon of defence, she could not drive away her gloomy forebodings when she thought of the threats contained in the marquis's letter. " Thanks to the assistance of one of my friends," he wrote, " I can place this proud girl in a perilous, terribly perilous, position, from which she cannot possibly extricate herself unaided."

These words persistently lingered in Mademoiselle Marguerite's mind. What was the danger hanging over her? whence would it come? and in what form? What abominable machination might she not expect from the villain who had deliberately dishonored Pascal? How would he attack her? Would he strive to ruin her reputation, or did he intend to forcibly abduct her? Would he attempt to decoy her into a trap where she would be subjected to the insults of the vilest wretches? A thousand frightful memories of the time when she was an apprentice drove her nearly frantic. " I will never go out unarmed," she thought, " and woe to the man who raises his hand against me! "

The vagueness of the threat increased her fears. No one is courageous enough to confront an unknown, mysterious, and always imminent danger without sometimes faltering. Nor was this all. The marquis was not her only enemy. She had the Fondège family to dread—these dangerous hypocrites, who had taken her to their home so that they might ruin her the more surely. M. de Valorsay wrote that he had no fears of the Fondèges—that he understood their little game. What was their little game? No doubt they were resolved that she should become their son's wife, even if they were obliged to use force to win her consent. At

this thought a sudden terror seized her soul, so full of
peace and hope an instant before. When she was attacked, would she have time to produce and use the fac-
simile of Valorsay's letter? " I must reveal my secret
to a friend—to a trusty friend—who will avenge me! "
she muttered.

Fortunately she had a friend in whom she could safely
confide—the old magistrate who had given her such
proofs of sympathy. She felt that she needed the advice of a riper experience than her own, and the
thought of consulting him at once occurred to her. She
was alone; she had no spy to fear; and it would be
folly not to profit by the few moments of liberty that
remained. So she drew her writing-case from her
trunk, and, after barricading her door to prevent a surprise, she wrote her friend an account of the events
which had taken place since their last interview. She
told him everything with rare precision and accuracy
of detail, sending him a copy of Valorsay's letter, and
informing him that, in case any misfortune befell her,
he could obtain the fac-similes from Carjat. She finished her letter, but did not seal it. " If anything should
happen before I have an opportunity to post it, I will
add a postscript," she said to herself.

She had made all possible haste, fearing that Madame
de Fondège and Madame Léon might return at any
moment. But this was truly a chimerical apprehension.
It was nearly six o'clock when the two shoppers made
their appearance, wearied with the labors of the day,
but in fine spirits. Besides purchasing every requisite
for that wonderful costume of hers, the General's wife
had found some laces of rare beauty, which she had
secured for the mere trifle of four thousand francs. " It
was one of those opportunities one ought always to

profit by," she said, as she displayed her purchase. "Besides, it is the same with lace as with diamonds, you should purchase them when you can—then you have them. It isn't an outlay—it's an investment." Subtle reasoning that has cost many a husband dear!

On her side, Madame Léon proudly showed her dear young lady a very pretty present which Madame de Fondège had given her. " So money is no longer lacking in this household," thought Mademoiselle Marguerite, all the more confirmed in her suspicions.

The General came in a little later, accompanied by a friend, and Marguerite soon discovered that the worthy man had spent the day as profitably as his wife. He too was quite tired out; and he had reason to be fatigued. First, he had purchased the horses belonging to the ruined spendthrift, and he had paid five thousand francs for them, a mere trifle for such animals. Less than an hour after the purchase he had refused almost double that amount from a celebrated *connoisseur* in horse-flesh, M. de Breulh-Faverlay. This excellent speculation had put him in such good humor that he had been unable to resist the temptation of purchasing a beautiful saddle-horse, which they let him have for a hundred louis. He had not been foolish, for he was sure that he could sell the animal again at an advance of a thousand francs whenever he wished to do so. " So," remarked his friend, " if you bought such a horse every day, you would make three hundred and sixty-five thousand francs a year."

Was this only a jest—one of those witticisms which people who boast of wonderful bargains must expect to parry, or had the remark a more serious meaning? Marguerite could not determine. One thing is certain, the General did not lose his temper, but gayly continued his account of the way in which he had spent his time. Having purchased the horses, his next task was to find a carriage, and he had heard of a barouche which a Russian prince had ordered but didn't take, so that the builder was willing to sell it at less than cost price; and to recoup this worthy man, the General had purchased a brougham as well. He had, moreover, hired stabling in the Rue Pigalle, only a few steps from the house, and he expected a coachman and a groom the following morning.

"And all this will cost us less than the miserable vehicle we have been hiring by the year," observed Madame de Fondège, gravely. "Oh, I know what I say. I've counted the cost. What with gratuities and extras, it costs us now fully a thousand francs a month, and three horses and a coachman won't cost you more. And what a difference! I shall no longer be obliged to blush for the skinny horses the stable-keeper sends me, nor to endure the insolence of his men. The first outlay frightened me a little; but that is made now, and I am delighted. We will save it in something else."

"In laces, no doubt," thought Mademoiselle Marguerite. She was intensely exasperated, and on regaining her chamber she said to herself, for the tenth time, "What do they take me for? Do they think me an idiot to flaunt the millions they have stolen from my father—that they have stolen from me—before my eyes in this fashion? A common thief would take care not to excite suspicion by a foolish expenditure of the fruits of his knavery, but they—they have lost their senses."

Madame Léon was already in bed, and when Mademoiselle Marguerite was satisfied that she was asleep, she took her letter from her trunk, and added this postscript: " P. S.—It is impossible to retain the shadow of a doubt, M. and Madame de Fondège have spent certainly twenty thousand francs to-day. This audacity must arise from a conviction that no proofs of the crime they have committed exist. Still they continue to talk to me about their son, Lieutenant Gustave. He will be presented to me to-morrow. To-morrow, also, between three and four, I shall be at the house of a man who can perhaps discover Pascal's hiding-place for me,— the house of M. Isidore Fortunat. I hope to make my escape easily enough, for at that same hour, Madame Léon has an appointment with the Marquis de Valorsay."

X.

THE old legend of Achilles's heel will be eternally true. A man may be humble or powerful, feeble or strong, but there are none of us without some weak spot in our armor, a spot vulnerable beyond all others, a certain place where wounds prove most dangerous and painful. M. Isidore Fortunat's weak place was his cash-box. To attack him there was to endanger his life—to wound him at a point where all his sensibility centred. For it was in this cash-box and not in his breast that his heart really throbbed. His safe made him happy or dejected. Happy when it was filled to overflowing by some brilliant operation, and dejected when he saw it become empty as some imprudent transaction failed.

This then explains his frenzy on that ill-fated Sunday, when, after being brutally dismissed by M. Wilkie, he returned to his rooms in the company of his clerk, Victor Chupin. This explains, too, the intensity of the hatred he now felt for the Marquis de Valorsay and the

Viscount de Coralth. The former, the marquis, had defrauded him of forty thousand francs in glittering gold. The other, the viscount, had suddenly sprung up out of the ground, and carried off from under his very nose that magnificent prize, the Chalusse inheritance, which he had considered as good as won. And he had not only been defrauded and swindled—such were his own expressions—but he had been tricked, deceived, duped, and outwitted, and by whom? By people who did not make it their profession to be shrewd, like he did himself. Just fancy, his business was to outwit others, and a couple of mere amateurs had outgeneraled him. He had not only suffered in pocket, he had been humiliated as well, and so he indulged in threats of such terrible import.

However, at the very moment when he was dreaming of wreaking vengeance on the Marquis de Valorsay and the Viscount de Coralth, his housekeeper, austere Madame Dodelin, handed him Mademoiselle Marguerite's letter. He read it with intense astonishment, rubbing his eyes as if to assure himself that he were really awake. " Tuesday," he repeated, " the day after to-morrow—at your house—between three and four o'clock—I must speak with you."

His manner was so strange, and his usually impassive face so disturbed by conflicting feelings, that Madame Dodelin's curiosity overcame her prudence, and she remained standing in front of him with open mouth, staring with all her eyes and listening with all her ears. He perceived this, and angrily exclaimed: "What are you doing here? You are watching me, I do believe. Get back to your kitchen, or——"

She fled in alarm, and he then entered his private office. His heart was leaping with joy, and he laughed wickedly at the hope of a speedy revenge. " She's on the scent," he muttered; " and she has luck in her favor. She has chanced to apply to me on the very day that I had resolved to defend and rehabilitate her lover, the honest fool who allowed himself to be dishonored by those unscrupulous blackguards. Just as I was thinking of going in search of her, she comes to me. As I was about to write to her, she writes to me. Who can deny the existence of Providence after this? " Like many other people, M. Fortunat piously believed in Providence when things went to his liking, but it is sad to add that in the contrary case he denied its existence. " If she has any courage," he resumed, " and she seems to have plenty of it, Valorsay and Coralth will be in a tight place soon. And if it takes ten thousand francs to put them there, and if neither Mademoiselle Marguerite nor M. Ferailleur has the amount—ah, well! I'll advance—well, at least five thousand—without charging them any commission. I'll even pay the expenses out of my own pocket, if necessary. Ah, my fine fellows, you've laughed too soon. In a week's time we'll see who laughs last."

He paused, for Victor Chupin, who had lingered behind to pay the driver, had just entered the room. " You gave me twenty francs, m'sieur," he remarked to his employer. " I paid the driver four francs and five sous, here's the change."

" Keep it yourself, Victor," said M. Fortunat.

What! keep fifteen francs and fifteen sous? Under any other circumstances such unusual generosity would have drawn a grimace of satisfaction from young Chupin. But to-day he did not even smile; he slipped the money carelessly into his pocket, and scarcely deigned to say " thanks," in the coldest possible tone.

Absorbed in thought, M. Fortunat did not remark this little circumstance. "We have them, Victor," he resumed. "I told you that Valorsay and Coralth should pay me for their treason. Vengeance is near. Read this letter." Victor read it slowly, and as soon as he had finished his employer ejaculated, "Well?"

But Chupin was not a person to give advice lightly. "Excuse me, m'sieur," said he, "but in order to answer you, I must have some knowledge of the affair. I only know what you've told me—which is little enough—and what I've guessed. In fact, I know nothing at all."

M. Fortunat reflected for a moment. "You are right, Victor," he said, at last. "So far the explanation I gave you was all that was necessary; but now that I expect more important services from you, I ought to tell you the whole truth, or at least all I know about the affair. This will prove my great confidence in you." Whereupon, he acquainted Chupin with everything he knew concerning the history of M. de Chalusse, the Marquis de Valorsay, and Mademoiselle Marguerite.

However, if he expected these disclosures to elevate him in his subordinate's estimation he was greatly mistaken. Chupin had sufficient experience and common sense to read his master's character and discern his motives. He saw plainly enough that this honest impulse on M. Fortunat's part came from disappointed avarice and wounded vanity, and that the agent would have allowed the Marquis de Valorsay to carry out his infamous scheme without any compunctions of conscience, providing he, himself, had not been injured by it. Still, the young fellow did not allow his real feelings to appear on his face. First, it was not his business to tell M. Fortunat his opinion of him; and in the second place, he did not deem it an opportune moment for a declaration of his sentiments. So, when his employer paused, he exclaimed: " Well, we must outwit these scoundrels—for I'll join you, m'sieur ; and I flatter myself that I can be very useful to you. Do you want the particulars of the viscount's past life? If so, I can furnish them. I know the brigand. He's married, as I told you before, and I'll find his wife for you in a few days. I don't know exactly where she lives, but she keeps a tobacco store, somewhere, and that's enough. She'll tell you how much he's a viscount. Ha! ha! Viscount just as much as I am—and no more. I can tell you the scrapes he has been in."

"No doubt; but the most important thing is to know how he's living now, and on what! "

" Not by honest work, I can tell you. But give me a little time, and I'll find out for sure. As soon as I can go home, change my clothes, and disguise myself, I'll start after him; and may I be hung, if I don't return with a complete report before Tuesday."

A smile of satisfaction appeared on M. Fortunat's face. " Good, Victor! " he said, approvingly, " very good! I see that you will serve me with your usual zeal and intelligence. Rest assured that you will be rewarded as you have never been rewarded before. As long as you are engaged in this affair, you shall have ten francs a day; and I'll pay your board, your cab-hire, and all your expenses."

This was a most liberal offer, and yet, far from seeming delighted, Chupin gravely shook his head. " You know how I value money, m'sieur," he began.

 " Too much, Victor, my boy, too much——"

" Excuse me, it's because I have responsibilities, m'sieur. You know my establishment"—he spoke this word with a grandiloquent air—"you have seen my good mother—my expenses are heavy——"

"In short, you don't think I offer you enough?"

"On the contrary, sir—but you don't allow me to finish. I love money, don't I? But no matter, I don't want to be paid for this business. I don't want either my board or my expenses, not a penny—nothing. I'll serve you, but for my own sake, for my own pleasure —gratis."

M. Fortunat could not restrain an exclamation of astonishment. Chupin, who was as eager for gain as an old usurer—Chupin, as grasping as avarice itself, refuse money! This was something which he had never seen before, and which he would no doubt never see again.

Victor had become very much excited; his usually pale cheeks were crimson, and in a harsh voice, he continued: "It's a fancy of mine—that's all. I have eight hundred francs hidden in my room, the fruit of years of work. I'll spend the last penny of it if need be; and if I can see Coralth in the mire, I shall say, 'My money has been well expended.' I'd rather see that day dawn than be the possessor of a hundred thousand francs. If a horrible vision haunted you every night, and prevented you from sleeping, wouldn't you give something to get rid of it? Very well! that brigand's my nightmare. There must be an end to it."

M. de Coralth, who was a man of wide experience, would certainly have felt alarmed if he had seen his unknown enemy at the present moment, for Victor's eyes, usually a pale and undecided blue, were glittering like steel, and his hands were clinched most threateningly. "For he was the cause of all my trouble," he continued, gloomily. "I've told you, sir, that I was guilty of an infamous deed once upon a time. If it hadn't been for a miracle I should have killed a man—the king of men. Ah, well! if Monsieur André had broken his back by falling from a fifth-floor window, my Coralth would be the Duc de Champdoce to-day. And shall he be allowed to ride about in his carriage, and deceive and ruin honest people? No—there are too many such villains at large for public safety. Wait a little, Coralth—I owe you something, and I always pay my debts. When M. André saved me, though I richly deserved to have my throat cut, he made no conditions. He only said, 'If you are not irredeemably bad you will be honest after this.' And he said these words as he was lying there as pale as death with his shoulder broken, and his body mangled from his fall. Great heavens! I felt smaller than—than nothing before him. But I swore that I would do honor to his teachings—and when evil thoughts enter my mind, and when I feel a thirst for liquor, I say to myself, 'Wait a bit, and—and M. André will take a glass with you.' And that quenches my thirst instantly. I have his portrait at home, and every night, before going to bed, I tell him the history of the day—and sometimes I fancy that he smiles at me. All this is very absurd, perhaps, but I'm not ashamed of it. M. André and my good mother, they are my supports, my crutches, and with them I'm not afraid of making a false step." Schebel, the German philosopher, who has written a treatise on Volition, in four volumes, was no greater a man than Chupin. " So you may keep your money, sir," he resumed. " I'm an honest fellow, and honest men ought to ask no reward for the performance of a duty. Coralth mustn't be allowed to triumph over the innocent chap he ruined. What did you call him?

Ferailleur? It's an odd name. Never mind—we'll get him out of this scrape; he shall marry his sweetheart after all; and I'll dance at the wedding."

As he finished speaking he laughed a shrill, dangerous laugh, which revealed his sharp teeth—but such invincible determination was apparent on his face, that M. Fortunat felt no misgivings. He was sure that this volunteer would be of more service than the highest-priced hireling. " So I can count on you, Victor? " he inquired.

" As upon yourself."

" And you hope to have some positive information by Tuesday? "

" Before then, I hope, if nothing goes amiss."

" Very well; I will devote my attention to Ferailleur then. As to Valorsay's affairs, I am better acquainted with them than he is himself. We must be prepared to enter upon the campaign when Mademoiselle Marguerite comes, and we will act in accordance with her instructions."

Chupin had already caught up his hat; but just as he was leaving the room, he paused abruptly. " How stupid! " he exclaimed. " I had forgotten the principal thing. Where does Coralth live? "

" Unfortunately, I don't know."

According to his habit when things did not go to his liking, Chupin began to scratch his head furiously. " That's bad," growled he. " Viscounts of his stamp don't parade their addresses in the directory. Still, I shall find him." However, although he expressed this conviction he went off decidedly out of temper.

" I shall lose the entire evening hunting up the rascal's address," he grumbled, as he hastened homeward. " And whom shall I ask for it?—Madame d'Argelès's concierge? Would he know it—M. Wilkie's servant? That would be dangerous." He thought of roaming round about M. de Valorsay's residence, and of bribing one of the valets; but while crossing the boulevard, the sight of Brebant's Restaurant put a new idea into his head. " I have it ! " he muttered; " my man's caught ! " And he darted into the nearest *café* where he ordered some beer and writing materials.

Under other circumstances, he would have hesitated to employ so hazardous an expedient as the one he was about to resort to, but the character of his adversaries justified any course; besides, time was passing, and he had no choice of resources. As soon as the waiter served him, he drained his glass of beer to give himself an inspiration, and then, in his finest hand, he wrote:

"MY DEAR VISCOUNT—Here's the amount—one hundred francs—that I lost to you last evening at *piquet*. When shall I have my revenge?   Your friend,
VALORSAY."

When he had finished this letter he read it over three or four times, asking himself if this were the style of composition that very fashionable folks employ in repaying their debts. To tell the truth, he doubted it. In the rough draft which he penned at first, he had written bezique, but in the copy he wrote *piquet*, which he deemed a more aristocratic game. " However," said he, " no one will examine it closely ! "

Then, as soon as the ink was dry, he folded the letter and slipped it into an envelope with a hundred franc-note which he drew from an old pocketbook. He next addressed the envelope as follows: " Monsieur le Vicomte de Coralth, En Ville," and having completed his preparations, he paid his score, and hastened to

Brebant's Two waiters were standing at the doorway,
and, showing them the letter, he politely asked: " Do
you happen to know this name? A gentleman dropped
this letter on leaving your place last evening. I
ran after him to return it; but I couldn't overtake
him."

The waiters examined the address. " Coralth! " they
replied. " We scarcely know him. He isn't a regular
customer, but he comes here occasionally."

" And where does he live? "

" Why do you wish to know? "

" So as to take him this letter, to be sure! "

The waiters shrugged their shoulders. " Let the letter go; it is not worth while to trouble yourself."

Chupin had foreseen this objection, and was prepared
for it. " But there's money in the letter," he remon-
strated. And opening the envelope, he showed the
bank-note which he had taken from his own pocketbook.

This changed the matter entirely. " That is quite a
different thing," remarked one of the waiters. " If you
find money, you are, of course, responsible for it. But
just leave it here at the desk, and the next time the
viscount comes in, the cashier will give it to him."

A cold chill crept over Chupin at the thought of
losing his bank-note in this way. " Ah! I don't fancy
that idea! " he exclaimed. " Leave it here? Never
in life! Who'd get the reward? A viscount is
always generous; it is quite likely he would give me
twenty francs as a reward for my honesty. And that's
why I want his address."

The argument was of a nature to touch the waiters;
they thought the young man quite right; but they did
not know M. de Coralth's address, and they saw no

way of procuring it. "Unless perhaps the porter knows," observed one of them.

The porter, on being called, remembered that he had once been sent to M. de Coralth's house for an overcoat. " I've forgotten his number," he declared; " but he lives in the Rue d'Anjou, near the corner of the Rue de la Ville l'Evéque."

This direction was not remarkable for its precision, but it was more than sufficient for a pure-blooded Parisian like Victor Chupin. " Many thanks for your kindness," he said to the porter. " A blind man, perhaps, might not be able to go straight to M. de Coralth's house from your directions, but I have eyes and a tongue as well. And, believe me, if there's any reward, you shall see that I know how to repay a good turn."

" And if you don't find the viscount," added the waiters, " bring the money here, and it will be returned to him."

" Naturally! " replied Chupin. And he strode hurriedly away. " Return! " he muttered; " not I! I thought for a moment they had their hands on my precious bank-note."

But he had already recovered from his fright, and as he turned his steps homeward he congratulated himself on the success of his stratagem. " For my viscount is caught," he said to himself. " The Rue d'Anjou Saint Honoré hasn't a hundred numbers in it, and even if I'm compelled to go from door to door, my task will soon be accomplished."

On reaching home he found his mother engaged in knitting, as usual. This was the only avocation that her almost complete blindness allowed her to pursue; and she followed it constantly. " Ah! here you are,

Toto," she exclaimed, joyously. " I didn't expect you so soon. Don't you scent a savory smell? As you must be greatly tired after being up all night, I'm making you a stew."

As customary when he returned, Chupin embraced the good woman with the respectful tenderness which had so surprised M. Fortunat. " You are always kind," said he, " but, unfortunately, I can't remain to dine with you."

" But you promised me."

" That's true, mamma; but business, you see—business."

The worthy woman shook her head. " Always business!" she exclaimed.

" Yes—when a fellow hasn't ten thousand francs a year."

" You have become a worker, Toto, and that makes me very happy; but you are too eager for money, and that frightens me."

" That's to say, you fear I shall do something dishonest. Ah! mother! do you think I can forget you and Monsieur André? "

His mother said no more, and he entered the tiny nook which he so pompously styled his chamber, and quickly changed the clothes he was wearing (his Sunday toggery) for an old pair of checked trousers, a black blouse, and a glazed cap. And when he had finished, and given a peculiar turn to his hair, no one would have recognized him. In place of M. Fortunat's respectable clerk, there appeared one of those vagabonds who hang about *cafés* and theatres from six in the evening till midnight, and spend the rest of their time playing cards in the low drinking dens near the *barrières*. It was the old Chupin come to life once more—Toto Chupin as he had appeared before his conversion. And as he took a last look in the little glass hanging over the table, he was himself astonished at the transformation. " Ah! " he muttered, " I was a sorry looking devil in those days."

Although he had cautiously avoided making any noise in dressing, his mother, with the wonderfully acute hearing of the blind, had followed each of his movements as surely as if she had been standing near watching him. " You have changed your clothes, Toto," she remarked.

" Yes, mother."

" But why have you put on your blouse, my son? "

Although accustomed to his mother's remarkable quickness of perception, he was amazed. Still he did not think of denying it. She would only have to extend her hand to prove that he was telling a falsehood. The blind woman's usually placid face had become stern. " So it is necessary to disguise yourself," she said, gravely.

" But, mother——"

" Hush, my son! When a man doesn't wish to be recognized, he's evidently doing something he's ashamed of. Ever since your employer came here, you have been concealing something from me. Take care, Toto! Since I heard that man's voice, I'm sure that he is quite as capable of urging you to commit a crime as others were in days gone by."

The blind woman was preaching to a convert; for during the past three days, M. Fortunat had shown himself in such a light that Chupin had secretly resolved to change his employer. " I promise you I'll leave him, mother," he declared, " so you may be quite easy in mind."

" Very well; but now, at this moment, where are you going? "

There was only one way of completely reassuring the good woman, and that was to tell her all. Chupin did so with absolute frankness. " Ah, well! " she said, when the narrative was finished. " You see now how easy it is to lead you astray! How could you be induced to play the part of a spy, when you know so well what it leads to? It's only God's protecting care that has saved you again from an act which you would have reproached yourself for all your life. Your employer's intentions are good now; but they *were* criminal when he ordered you to follow Madame d'Argelès. Poor woman! She had sacrificed herself for her son, she had concealed herself from him, and you were working to betray her. Poor creature! how she must have suffered, and how much I pity her! To be what she is, and to see herself denounced by her own son! I, who am only a poor plebeian, should die of shame under such circumstances."

Chupin blew his nose so loudly that the window-panes rattled; this was his way of repressing his emotion whenever it threatened to overcome him. " You speak like the good mother that you are," he exclaimed at last, " and I'm prouder of you than if you were the handsomest and richest lady in Paris, for you're certainly the most honest and virtuous; and I should be a thorough scoundrel if I caused you a moment's sorrow. And if ever I set my foot in such a mess again, I hope some one will cut it off. But for this once——"

" For this once, you may go, Toto; I give my consent."

He went off with a lighter heart; and on reaching the Rue d'Anjou he immediately began his investigations.

They were not successful at first. At every house where he made inquiries nobody had any knowledge of the Viscount de Coralth. He had visited half the buildings in the street, when he reached one of the handsomest houses, in front of which stood a cart laden with plants and flowers. An old man, who seemed to be the concierge, and a valet in a red waistcoat, were removing the plants from the vehicle and arranging them in a line under the *porte cochère*. As soon as the cart was emptied, it drove away, whereupon Chupin stepped forward, and addressing the concierge, asked: "Does the Viscount de Coralth live here?"

"Yes. What do you want with him?"

Having foreseen this question, Chupin had prepared a reply. "I certainly don't come to call on him," he answered. "My reason for inquiring is this: just now, as I passed near the Madeleine, a very elegant lady called me, and said: 'M. de Coralth lives in the Rue d'Anjou, but I've forgotten the number. I can't go about from door to door making inquiries, so if you'll go there and ascertain his address for me, I'll give you five francs for yourself,' so my money's made."

Profiting by his old Parisian experience, Chupin had chosen such a clever excuse that both his listeners heartily laughed. "Well, Father Moulinet," cried the servant in the red waistcoat, "what do you say to that? Are there any elegant ladies who give five francs for *your* address?"

"Is there any lady who's likely to send such flowers as these to *you?*" was the response.

Chupin was about to retire with a bow, when the concierge stopped him. "You accomplish your errands so well that perhaps you'd be willing to take these flower-pots up to the second floor, if we gave you a glass of wine!"

No proposal could have suited Chupin better. Although he was prone to exaggerate his own powers and the fecundity of his resources, he had not flattered himself with the hope that he should succeed in crossing the threshold of M. de Coralth's rooms. For, without any great mental effort, he had realized that the servant arrayed in the red waistcoat was in the viscount's employ, and these flowers were to be carried to his apartments. However any signs of satisfaction would have seemed singular under the circumstances, and so he sulkily replied: "A glass of wine! you had better say two."

"Well, I'll say a whole bottleful, my boy, if that suits you any better," replied the servant, with the charming good-nature so often displayed by people who are giving other folk's property away.

"Then I'm at your service!" exclaimed Chupin. And, loading himself with a host of flower-pots as skilfully as if he had been accustomed to handling them all his life, he added: "Now, lead the way."

The valet and the concierge preceded him with empty hands, of course; and, on reaching the second floor, they opened a door, and said: "This is the place. Come in."

Chupin had expected to find that M. de Coralth's apartments were handsomer than his own in the Faubourg Saint Denis; but he had scarcely imagined such luxury as pervaded this establishment. The chandeliers seemed marvels in his eyes; and the sumptuous chairs and couches eclipsed M. Fortunat's wonderful sofa completely. "So he no longer amuses himself with petty rascalities," thought Chupin, as he surveyed the rooms. "Monsieur's working on a grand scale now. Decidedly this mustn't be allowed to continue."

Thereupon he busied himself placing the flowers in the numerous jardinières scattered about the rooms, as well as in a tiny conservatory, cleverly contrived on the balcony, and adjoining a little apartment with silk hangings, that was used as a smoking-room. Under the surveillance of the concierge and the valet he was allowed to visit the whole apartments. He admired the drawing-room, filled to overflowing with costly trifles; the dining-room, furnished in old oak; the luxurious bed-room with its bed mounted upon a platform, as if it were a throne, and the library filled with richly bound volumes. Everything was beautiful, sumptuous and magnificent, and Chupin admired, though he did not envy, this luxury. He said to himself that, if ever he became rich, his establishment should be quite different. He would have preferred rather more simplicity, a trifle less satin, velvet, hangings, mirrors and gilding. Still this did not prevent him from going into ecstasies over each room he entered; and he expressed his admiration so artlessly that the valet, feeling as much flattered as if he were the owner of the place, took a sort of pride in exhibiting everything.

He showed Chupin the target which the viscount practised at with pistols for an hour every morning; for Monsieur le Vicomte was a capital marksman, and could lodge eight balls out of ten in the neck of a bottle at a distance of twenty paces. He also displayed his master's swords; for Monsieur le Vicomte handled side arms as adroitly as pistols. He took a lesson every day from one of the best fencing-masters in Paris; and his duels had always terminated fortunately. He also showed the viscount's blue velvet dressing-gown, his fur-trimmed slippers, and even his elaborately embroidered night-shirts. But it was the dressing-room that most astonished and stupefied Chupin. He stood gazing in open-mouthed wonder at the immense white marble table, with its water spigots and its basins, its sponges and boxes, its pots and vials and cups; and he counted the brushes by the dozen—brushes hard and soft, brushes for the hair, for the beard, for the hands, and the application of cosmetic to the mustaches and eyebrows. Never had he seen in one collection such a variety of steel and silver instruments, knives, pincers, scissors, and files. " One might think oneself in a chiropodist's, or a dentist's establishment," remarked Chupin to the servant. " Does your master use all these every day? "

" Certainly, or rather twice a day—morning and evening—at his toilette."

Chupin expressed his feelings with a grimace and an exclamation of mocking wonder. " Ah, well! he must have a clean skin," he said.

His listeners laughed heartily; and the concierge, after exchanging a significant glance with the valet, said *sotto voce*, " Zounds! it's his business to be a handsome fellow! " The mystery was solved.

While Chupin changed the contents of the jardinières, and remained upstairs in the intervals between the nine or ten journeys he made to the *porte-cochère* for more flowers, he listened attentively to the conversation between the concierge and the valet, and heard snatches of sentences that enlightened him wonderfully. Moreover, whenever a question arose as to placing a plant in one place rather than another, the valet stated as a conclusive argument that the baroness liked it in such or such a place, or that she would be better pleased with this or that arrangement, or that he must comply with the instructions she had given him. Chupin was therefore obliged to conclude that the flowers had been sent here by a baroness who possessed certain rights in the establishment. But who was she?

He was manœuvering cleverly in the hope of ascertaining this point, when a carriage was heard driving into the courtyard below. "Monsieur must have returned!" exclaimed the valet, darting to the window.

Chupin also ran to look out, and saw a very elegant blue-lined brougham, drawn by a superb horse, but he did not perceive the viscount. In point of fact, M. de Coralth was already climbing the stairs, four at a time, and, a moment later, he entered the room, angrily exclaiming, "Florent, what does this mean? Why have you left all the doors open?"

Florent was the servant in the red waistcoat. He slightly shrugged his shoulders like a servant who knows too many of his master's secrets to have anything to fear, and in the calmest possible tone replied, "If the doors are open, it is only because the baroness has just sent some flowers. On Sunday, too, what a funny idea! And I have been treating Father Moulinet and this worthy fellow" (pointing to Chupin) "to a glass of wine, to acknowledge their kindness in assisting me."

Fearing recognition, Chupin hid his face as much as possible; but M. de Coralth did not pay the slightest attention to him. There was a dark frown on his handsome, usually smiling countenance, and his hair was in great disorder. Evidently enough, something had greatly annoyed him. "I am going out again," he remarked to his valet, "but first of all I must write two letters which you must deliver immediately."

He passed into the drawing-room as he spoke, and Florent scarcely waited till the door was closed before uttering an oath. "May the devil take him!" he exclaimed. "Here he sets me on the go again. It is five o'clock, too, and I have an appointment in half an hour."

A sudden hope quickened the throbbings of Chupin's heart. He touched the valet's arm, and in his most persuasive tone remarked: "I've nothing to do, and as your wine was so good, I'll do your errands for you, if you'll pay me for the wear and tear of shoe-leather."

Chupin's appearance must have inspired confidence, for the servant replied:—"Well—I don't refuse—but we'll see."

The viscount did not spend much time in writing; he speedily reappeared holding two letters which he flung upon the table, saying: "One of these is for the baroness. You must deliver it into *her* hands or into the hands of her maid—there will be no answer. You will afterward take the other to the person it is addressed to, and you must wait for an answer which you will place on my writing-table—and make haste." So saying, the viscount went off as he had entered— on the run—and a moment later, his brougham was heard rolling out of the courtyard.

Florent was crimson with rage. "There," said he, addressing Chupin rather than the concierge, "what did I tell you? A letter to be placed in madame's own hands or in the hands of her maid, and to be concealed from the baron, who is on the watch, of course. Naturally no one can execute that commission but myself."

"That's true!" replied Chupin; "but how about the other?"

The valet had not yet examined the second letter. He now took it from the table, and glanced at the address. "Ah," said he, "I can confide this one to you, my good fellow, and it's very fortunate, for it is to be taken to a place on the other side of the river. Upon my word! masters are strange creatures! You manage your work so as to have a little leisure, and the moment you think yourself free, pouf!—they send you anywhere in creation without even asking if it suits your convenience. If it hadn't been for you, I should have missed a dinner with some very charming ladies. But, above all, don't loiter on the way. I don't mind paying your omnibus fare if you like. And you heard him say there would be an answer. You can give it to Moulinet, and in exchange, he'll give you fifteen sous for your trouble, and six sous for your omnibus fare. Besides, if you can extract anything from the party the letter's intended for, you are quite welcome to it."

"Agreed, sir! Grant me time enough to give an answer to the lady who is waiting at the Madeleine, and I'm on my way. Give me the letter."

"Here it is," said the valet, handing it to Chupin. But as the latter glanced at the address he turned deadly pale, and his eyes almost started from their sockets. For this is what he read: "Madame Paul. Dealer in Tobacco. Quai de la Seine." Great as was his self-control, his emotion was too evident to escape notice. "What's the matter with you?" asked the concierge and the valet in the same breath. "What has happened to you?"

A powerful effort of will restored this young fellow's coolness, and ready in an instant with an excuse for his blunder, he replied, "I have changed my mind. What! you'd only give me fifteen sous to measure such a distance as that! Why, it isn't a walk—it's a journey!"

His explanation was accepted without demur. His listeners thought he was only taking advantage of the need they had of his services—as was perfectly natural under the circumstances. "What! So you are dissatisfied!" cried the valet. "Very well! you shall have thirty sous—but be off!"

"So I will, at once," replied Chupin. And, imitating the whistle of a locomotive with wonderful perfection, he darted away at a pace which augured a speedy return.

However, when he was some twenty yards from the house he stopped short, glanced around him, and espying a dark corner slipped into it. "That fool in the red waistcoat will be coming out to take the letter to that famous baroness," he thought. "I'm here, and I'll watch him and see where he goes. I should like to find out the name of the kind and charitable lady who watches over his brigand of a master with such tender care."

The day and the hour were in his favor. Night was coming on, hastened by a thick fog; the street lamps were not yet lighted, and as it was Sunday most of the shops were closed. It grew dark so rapidly that Chupin was scarcely able to recognize Florent when he at last emerged from the house. It is true that he looked altogether unlike the servant in the red waistcoat. As he had the key to the wardrobe containing his master's clothes, he did not hesitate to use them whenever an opportunity offered. On this occasion he had appropriated a pair of those delicately tinted trousers which were M. de Coralth's specialty, with a handsome overcoat, a trifle too small for him, and a very elegant hat.

"Fine doings, indeed!" growled Chupin as he started in pursuit. "My servants sha'n't serve me in that way if I ever have any."

But he paused in his soliloquy, and prudently hid himself under a neighboring gateway. The gorgeous Florent was ringing at the door of one of the most magnificent mansions in the Rue de la Ville l'Evêque. The door was opened, and he went in. "Ah! ah!" thought Chupin, "he hadn't far to go. The viscount and the baroness are shrewd. When you have flowers to send to anybody it's convenient to be neighbors!"

He glanced round, and seeing an old man smoking his pipe on the threshold of a shop, he approached him and asked politely: "Can you tell me whom that big house belongs to?"

"To Baron Trigault," replied the man, without releasing his hold on his pipe.

"Thank you, monsieur," replied Chupin, gravely. "I inquired, because I think of buying a house——" And repeating the name of Trigault several times to impress it upon his memory he darted off on his errand.

It might be supposed that his unexpected success had delighted him, but, on the contrary, it rendered him even more exacting. The letter he carried burned his pocket like a red-hot iron. "Madame Paul," he muttered, "that must be the rascal's wife. First, Paul is his Christian name; secondly, I've been told that his wife keeps a tobacco shop—so the case is plain. But the strangest thing about it is that this husband and wife should write to each other, when I fancied them at dagger's ends." Chupin would have given a pint of his own blood to know the contents of the missive. The idea of opening it occurred to him, and it must be confessed that it was not a feeling of delicacy that prevented him. He was deterred by a large seal which had been carefully affixed, and which would plainly furnish evidence if the letter were tampered with. Thus Chupin was punished for Florent's faults, for this seal was the viscount's' invariable precaution against his servant's prying curiosity. So our enterprising youth could only read and re-read the superscription and smell the paper, which was strongly scented with verbena. He fancied that there was some mysterious connection between this letter intended for M. de Coralth's wife and the missive sent to the baroness. And why should it not be so? Had they not both been written under the influence of anger? Still he failed to perceive any possible connection between the rich baroness and the poor tobacco dealer, and his cogitations only made him more perplexed than ever. However, his efforts to solve the mystery did not interfere with the free use of his limbs, and he soon found himself on the Quai de la Seine. "Here I am," he muttered. "I've come more quickly than an omnibus."

The Quai de la Seine is a broad road, connecting the Rue de Flandres with the canal de l'Ourcq. On the left-hand side it is bordered with miserable shanties interspersed with some tiny shops, and several huge coal dépôts. On the right-hand side—that next to the canal—there are also a few provision stores. In the daytime there is no noisier nor livelier place than this same Quai; but nothing could be more gloomy at night-time when the shops are closed, when the few gas-lamps only increase the grimness of the shadows, and when the only sound that breaks the silence is the rippling of the water as its smooth surface is ruffled by some boatman propelling his skiff through the canal.

" The viscount must certainly have made a mistake,"
thought Chupin; "there is no such shop on the Quai."
He was wrong, however; for after passing the Rue de
Soissons he espied the red lantern of a tobacco-shop,
glimmering through the fog.

XI.

HAVING almost reached the goal, Chupin slackened his
pace. He approached the shop very cautiously and
peered inside, deeming it prudent to reconnoitre a little
before he went in. And certainly there was nothing to
prevent a prolonged scrutiny. The night was very
dark, the quay deserted. No one was to be seen; not
a sound broke the stillness. The darkness, the sur-
roundings, and the silence were sinister enough to make
even Chupin shudder, though he was usually as thoroughly at home in the loneliest and most dangerous by-
ways of Paris as an honest man of the middle classes
would be in the different apartments of his modest
household. " That scoundrel's wife must have less
than a hundred thousand a year if she takes up her
abode here! " thought Chupin.

And, in fact, nothing could be more repulsive than
the tenement in which Madame Paul had installed herself. It was but one story high, and built of clay,
and it had fallen to ruin to such an extent that it had
been found necessary to prop it up with timber, and
to nail some old boards over the yawning fissures in
the walls. " If I lived here, I certainly shouldn't feel
quite at ease on a windy day," continued Chupin, *sotto
voce*.

The shop itself was of a fair size, but most wretched

in its appointments, and disgustingly dirty. The floor
was covered with that black and glutinous coal-dust
which forms the soil of the Quai de la Seine. An
auctioneer would have sold the entire stock and fixtures
for a few shillings. Four stone jars, and a couple of
pairs of scales, a few odd tumblers, filled with pipes
and packets of cigarettes, some wine-glasses, and three
or four labelled bottles, five or six boxes of cigars,
and as many packages of musty tobacco, constituted the
entire stock in trade.

As Chupin compared this vile den with the viscount's
luxurious abode, his blood fairly boiled in his veins.
" He ought to be shot for this, if for nothing else," he
muttered through his set teeth. " To let his wife die
of starvation here!" For it was M. de Coralth's wife
who kept this shop. Chupin, who had seen her years
before, recognized her now as she sat behind her counter, although she was cruelly changed. " That's her,"
he murmured. " That's certainly Mademoiselle Flavie."

He had used her maiden name in speaking of her.
Poor woman! She was undoubtedly still young—but
sorrow, regret, and privations, days spent in hard work
to earn a miserable subsistence, and nights spent in
weeping, had made her old, haggard, and wrinkled
before her time. Of her once remarkable beauty
naught remained but her hair, which was still magnificent, though it was in wild disorder, and looked as if it
had not been touched by a comb for weeks; and her big
black eyes, which gleamed with the phosphorescent and
destructive brilliancy of fever. Everything about her
person bespoke terrible reverses, borne without dignity.
Even if she had struggled at first, it was easy to see
that she struggled no longer. Her attire—her torn and
soiled silk dress, and her dirty cap—revealed thorough

indolence, and that morbid indifference which at times follows great misfortunes with weak natures.

"Such is life," thought Chupin, philosophically. "Here's a girl who was brought up like a queen and allowed to have her own way in everything! If any one had predicted this in those days, how she would have sneered! I can see her now as she looked that day when I met her driving her gray ponies. If people didn't clear the road it was so much the worse for them! In those times Paris was like some great shop where she could select whatever she chose. She said: ' I want this,' and she got it. She saw a handsome young fellow and wanted him for her husband; her father, who could refuse her nothing, consented, and now behold the result! "

He had lingered longer at the window than he had meant to do, perhaps because he could see that the young woman was talking with some person in a back room, the door of which stood open. Chupin tried to find out who this person was, but he did not succeed; and he was about to go in when suddenly he saw Madame Paul rise from her seat and say a few words with an air of displeasure. And this time her eyes, instead of turning to the open door, were fixed on a part of the shop directly opposite her. " Is there some one there as well, then? " Chupin wondered.

He changed his post of observation, and, by standing on tiptoe, he succeeded in distinguishing a puny little boy, some three or four years old, and clad in rags, who was playing with the remnants of a toy-horse. The sight of this child increased Chupin's indignation. " So there's a child? " he growled. " The rascal not only deserts his wife, but he leaves his child to starve! We may as well make a note of that: and when we settle up our accounts, he shall pay dearly for his villainy." With this threat he brusquely entered the shop.

"What do you wish, sir?" asked the woman.

"Nothing; I bring you a letter, madame."

"A letter for me! You must be mistaken."

"Excuse me; aren't you Madame Paul?"

"Yes."

"Then this is for you." And he handed her the missive which Florent had confided to his care.

Madame Paul took hold of it with some hesitation, eying the messenger suspiciously meanwhile; but, on seeing the handwriting, she uttered a cry of surprise. And, turning toward the open door, she called, "M. Mouchon! M. Mouchon! It's from him—it's from my husband; from Paul. Come, come!"

A bald-headed, corpulent man, who looked some fifty years of age, now timidly emerged from the room behind the shop with a cap in his hand. "Ah, well! my dear child," he said, in an oily voice, "what was I telling you just now? Everything comes to those who know how to wait."

However she had already broken the seal, and she was now reading the letter eagerly, clapping her hands with delight as she finished its perusal. "He consents!" she exclaimed. "He's frightened—he begs me to wait a little—look—read!"

But M. Mouchon could not read without his spectacles, and he lost at least two minutes in searching his pockets before he found them. And when they were adjusted, the light was so dim that it took him at least three minutes more to decipher the missive. Chupin had spent this time in scrutinizing—in appraising the man, as it were. "What is this venerable gentleman doing here?" he thought. "He's a middle class man, that's evident from his linen. He's married— there's a wedding-ring on his finger; he has a daughter, for the ends of his necktie are embroidered. He lives in the neighborhood, for, well dressed as he is, he wears a cap. But what was he doing there in that back room in the dark?"

Meanwhile M. Mouchon had finished reading the letter. "What did I tell you?" he said complacently.

"Yes, you were right!" answered Madame Paul as she took up the letter and read it again with her eyes sparkling with joy. "And now what shall I do?" she asked. "Wait, shall I not?"

"No, no!" exclaimed the elderly gentleman, in evident dismay. "You must strike the iron while it's hot."

"But he promises me——"

"To promise and to keep one's promises are two different things."

"He wants a reply."

"Tell him——" But he stopped short, calling her attention with a gesture to the messenger, whose eyes were glittering with intense curiosity.

She understood. So filling a glass with some liquor, she placed it before Chupin, and offered him a cigar, saying: "Take a seat—here's something to keep you from feeling impatient while you wait here." Thereupon she followed the old gentleman into the adjoining room, and closed the door.

Even if Chupin had not possessed the precocious penetration he owed to his life of adventure, the young woman and the old gentleman had said enough to enable him to form a correct estimate of the situation. He was certain now that he knew the contents of the letter as perfectly as if he had read it. M. de Coralth's

anger, and his order to make haste, were both explained. Moreover, Chupin distinctly saw what connection there was between the letter to the baroness
and the letter to Madame Paul. He understood that
one was the natural consequence of the other. Deserted
by her husband, Madame Paul had at last become weary
of poverty and privations. She had instituted a search
for her husband, and, having found him, she had written to him in this style: "I consent to abstain from
interfering with you, but only on conditions that you
provide means of subsistence for me, your lawfully
wedded wife, and for your child. If you refuse, I shall
urge my claims, and ruin you. The scandal won't be
of much use to me, it's true, but at least I shall no
longer be obliged to endure the torture of knowing
that you are surrounded by every luxury while I am
dying of starvation."

Yes, she had evidently written that. It might not be
the precise text; but no doubt it was the purport of her
letter. On receiving it, Coralth had become alarmed.
He knew only too well that if his wife made herself
known and revealed his past, it would be all over with
him. But he had no money. Charming young men
like the Viscount de Coralth never have any money on
hand. So, in this emergency, the dashing young fellow
had written to his wife imploring her to have patience,
and to the baroness, entreating, or rather commanding
her to advance him a certain sum at once.

This was no doubt the case, and yet there was one
circumstance which puzzled Chupin exceedingly. In
former years, he had heard it asserted that Mademoiselle Flavie was the very personification of pride,
and that she adored her husband even to madness. Had
this great love vanished? Had poverty and sorrow

broken her spirit to such a degree that she was willing to stoop to such shameful concessions! If she were acquainted with her husband's present life, how did it happen that she did not prefer starvation, or the alms-house and a pauper's grave to his assistance? Chupin could understand how, in a moment of passion, she might be driven to denounce her husband in the pres-ence of his fashionable acquaintances, how she might be impelled to ruin him so as to avenge herself; but he could not possibly understand how she could consent to profit by the ignominy of the man she loved. "The plan isn't hers," said Chupin to himself, after a mo-ment's reflection. "It's probably the work of that stout old gentleman."

There was a means of verifying his suspicions, for on returning into the adjoining room, Madame Paul had not taken her son with her. He was still sitting on the muddy floor of the shop, playing with his dilap-idated horse. Chupin called him. "Come here, my little fellow," said he.

The child rose, and timidly approached, his eyes dilat-ing with distrust and astonishment. The poor boy's repulsive uncleanliness was a terrible charge against the mother. Did she no longer love her own off-spring? The untidiness of sorrow and poverty has its bounds. A long time must have passed since the child's face and hands had been washed, and his soiled clothes were literally falling to rags. Still, he was a handsome little fellow, and seemed fairly intelligent, in spite of his bashfulness. He was very light-haired, and in feat-ures he was extremely like M. de Coralth. Chupin took him on his knees, and, after looking to see if the door communicating with the inner room were securely closed, he asked: "What's your name, little chap?"

" Paul."

" Do you know your father? "

" No."

" Doesn't your mother ever talk to you about him? "

" Oh, yes! "

" And what does she say? "

" That he's rich—very rich."

" And what else? "

The child did not reply; perhaps his mother had forbidden him to say anything on the subject—perhaps that instinct which precedes intelligence, just as the dawn precedes daylight, warned him to be prudent with a stranger. " Doesn't your papa ever come to see you? " insisted Chupin.

" Never."

" Why? "

" Mamma is very poor."

" And wouldn't you like to go and see him? "

" I don't know. But he'll come some day, and take us away with him to a large house. We shall be all right, then; and he will give us a deal of money and pretty dresses, and I shall have plenty of toys."

Satisfied on this point, Chupin, pushed his investigations farther. " And do you know this old gentleman who is with your mamma in the other room? "

" Oh, yes!—that's Mouchon."

" And who's Mouchon? "

" He's the gentleman who owns that beautiful garden at the corner of the Rue Riquet, where there are such splendid grapes. I'm going with him to get some."

" Does he often come to see you? "

" Every evening. He always has goodies in his pocket for mamma and me."

"Why does he sit in that back room without any light?"

"Oh, he says that the customers mustn't see him."

It would have been an abominable act to continue this examination, and make this child the innocent accuser of his own mother. Chupin felt conscience-smitten even now. So he kissed the cleanest spot he could find on the boy's face, and set him on the floor again, saying, "Go and play."

The child had revealed his mother's character with cruel precision. What had she told him about his father? That he was rich, and that, in case he returned, he would give them plenty of money and fine clothes. The woman's nature stood revealed in all its deformity. Chupin had good cause to feel proud of his discernment—all his suppositions had been confirmed. He had read Mouchon's character at a glance. He had recognized him as one of those wily evil-minded men who employ their leisure to the profit of their depravity—one of those patient, cold-blooded hypocrites who make poverty their purveyor, and whose passion is prodigal only in advice. "So he's paying his court to Madame Paul," thought Chupin. "Isn't it shameful? The old villain! he might at least give her enough to eat!"

So far his preoccupation had made him forget his wine and his cigar. He emptied the glass at a single draught, but it proved far more difficult to light the cigar. "Zounds! this is a non-combustible," he growled. "When I arrive at smoking ten sous cigars, I sha'n't come here to buy them."

However, with the help of several matches and a great deal of drawing, he had almost succeeded, when the door opened, and Madame Paul reappeared with a letter in her hand. She seemed greatly agitated; her anxiety was unmistakable. "I can't decide," she was saying to Mouchon, whose figure Chupin could only dimly distinguish in the darkness. "No, I can't. If I send this letter, I must forever renounce all hope of my husband's return. Whatever happens, he will never forgive me."

"He can't treat you worse than he does now, at all events," replied the old gentleman. "Besides, a gloved cat has never caught a mouse yet."

"He'll hate me."

"The man who wants his dog to love him, beats it; and, besides, when the wine is drawn, one must drink it."

This singular logic seemed to decide her. She handed the letter to Chupin, and drawing a franc from her pocket she offered it to him. "This is for your trouble," she said.

He involuntarily held out his hand to take the money, but quickly withdrew it, exclaiming: "No, thank you; keep it. I've been paid already." And, thereupon, he left the shop.

Chupin's mother—his poor good mother, as he called her—would certainly have felt proud and delighted at her son's disinterestedness. That very morning, he had refused the ten francs a day that M. Fortunat had offered him, and this evening he declined the twenty sous proffered him by Madame Paul. This was apparently a trifle, and yet in reality it was something marvellous, unprecedented, on the part of this poor lad, who, having neither trade nor profession, was obliged to earn his daily bread through the medium of those chance opportunities which the lower classes of Paris are continually seeking. As he returned to the Rue

de Flaudres, hc muttered: "Take twenty sous from
that poor creature, who hasn't had enough to satisfy
her hunger for heaven knows how long! That would
be altogether unworthy of a man."

It is only just to say that money had never given
him a feeling of satisfaction at all comparable with that
which he now experienced. He was impressed, too,
with a sense of vastly-increased importance on thinking
that all the faculties, and all the energy he had once
employed in the service of evil, were now consecrated
to the service of good. By becoming the instrument
of Pascal Ferailleur's salvation he would, in some
measure, atone for the crime he had committed years
before.

Chupin's mind was so busily occupied with these
thoughts that he reached the Rue d'Anjou and M. de
Coralth's house almost before he was aware of it. To
his great surprise, the concierge and his wife were not
alone. Florent was there, taking coffee with them.
The valet had divested himself of his borrowed finery,
and had donned his red waistcoat again. He seemed to
be in a savage humor; and his anger was not at all
strange under the circumstances. There was but a step
from M. de Coralth's house to the baroness's residence,
but fatalities may attend even a step! The baroness,
on receiving the letter from her maid, had sent a message to Florent requesting him to wait, as she desired
to speak with him! and she had been so inconsiderate as
to keep him waiting for more than an hour, so that he
had missed his appointment with the charming ladies
he had spoken of. In his despair he had returned
home to seek consolation in the society of his friend
the concierge. "Have you the answer?" he asked.

"Yes, here it is," replied Chupin, and Florent had

just slipped the letter into his pocket, and was engaged in counting out the thirty sous which he had promised his messenger, when the familiar cry, " Open, please," was heard outside.

M. de Coralth had returned. He sprang to the ground as soon as the carriage entered the courtyard, and on perceiving his servant, he exclaimed: " Have you executed my commissions? "

" They have been executed, monsieur."

" Did you see the baroness? "

" She made me wait two hours to tell me that the viscount need not be worried in the least; that she would certainly be able to comply with his request to-morrow."

M. de Coralth seemed to breathe more freely. " And the other party? " he inquired.

" Gave me this for monsieur."

The viscount seized the missive, with an eager hand, tore it open, read it at one glance, and flew into such a paroxysm of passion that he quite forgot those around him, and began to tear the letter, and utter a string of oaths which would have astonished a cab-driver. But suddenly realizing his imprudence, he mastered his rage, and exclaimed, with a forced laugh: " Ah! these women! they are enough to drive one mad! " And deeming this a sufficient explanation, he added, addressing Florent. " Come and undress me; I must be up early to-morrow morning."

This remark was not lost upon Chupin, and at seven o'clock the next morning he mounted guard at M. de Coralth's door. All through the day he followed the viscount about, first to the Marquis de Valorsay's, then to the office of a business agent, then to M. Wilkie's, then, in the afternoon, to Baroness Trigault's, and finally, in the evening, to the house of Madame d'Argelès. Here, by making himself useful to the servants, by his zeal in opening and shutting the doors of the carriages that left the house, he succeeded in gathering some information concerning the frightful scene which had taken place between the mother and the son. He perceived M. Wilkie leave the house with his clothes in disorder, and subsequently he saw the viscount emerge. He followed him, first to the house of the Marquis de Valorsay, and afterward to M. Wilkie's rooms, where he remained till nearly daybreak.

Thus, when Chupin presented himself in M. Fortunat's office at two o'clock on the Tuesday afternoon, he felt that he held every possible clue to the shameful intrigue which would ruin the viscount as soon as it was made public.

M. Fortunat knew that his agent was shrewd, but he had not done justice to his abilities; and it was, indeed, with something very like envy that he listened to Chupin's clear and circumstantial report. " I have not been as successful," he remarked, when Chupin's story was ended. But he had not time to explain how or why, for just as he was about to do so, Madame Dodelin appeared, and announced that the young lady he expected was there. " Let her come in! " exclaimed M. Fortunat, eagerly—" let her come in! "

Mademoiselle Marguerite had not been compelled to resort to any subterfuge to make her escape from Madame de Fondège's house. The General had decamped early in the morning to try his horses and his carriages, announcing, moreover, that he would breakfast at the club. And as soon as her breakfast was concluded, Madame de Fondège had hurried off to her dressmaker's, warning the household that she would not return before dinner-time. A little while later, Madame Léon had suddenly remembered that her noble relative would certainly be expecting a visit from her, and so she dressed herself in haste, and went off, first to Dr. Jodon's and thence to the Marquis de Valorsay's.

Thus, Mademoiselle Marguerite had been able to make her escape without attracting any one's attention, and she would be able to remain away as many hours as she chose, since the servants would not know how long she had been absent even if they saw her when she returned. An empty cab was passing as she left the house, so she hailed it and got in. The step she was about to take cost her a terrible effort. It was a difficult task for her, a girl naturally so reserved, to confide in a stranger, and open to him her maidenly heart, filled with love for Pascal Ferailleur! Still, she was much calmer than she had been on the previous evening, when she called on the photographer for a fac-simile of M. de Valorsay's letter. Several circumstances combined to reassure her. M. Fortunat knew her already, since he was the agent whom the Count de Chalusse had employed to carry on the investigations which had resulted in her discovery at the foundling asylum. A vague presentiment told her that this man was better acquainted with her past life than she was herself, and that he could, if he chose, tell her her mother's name—the name of the woman whom the count so dreaded, and who had so pitilessly deserted her. However, her heart beat more quickly, and she felt that she was turning pale when, at Madame Dodelin's invitation, she at last entered M. Fortunat's private office. She took in the room and its occupants with a single glance. The handsome appointments of the office surprised her, for she had expected to see a den. The agent's polite manner and rather elegant appearance disconcerted her, for she had expected to meet a coarse and illiterate boor; and finally, Victor Chupin, who was standing twisting his cap near the fireplace, attired in a blouse and a pair of ragged trousers, fairly alarmed her. Still, no sign of her agitation was perceptible on her countenance. Not a muscle of her beautiful, proud face moved—her glance remained clear and haughty, and she exclaimed in a ringing voice: " I am the late Count de Chalusse's ward, Mademoiselle Marguerite. You have received my letter, I suppose? "

M. Fortunat bowed with all the grace of manner he was wont to display in the circles where he went wife-hunting, and with a somewhat pretentious gesture he advanced an arm-chair, and asked his visitor to sit down. "Your letter reached me, mademoiselle," he replied, " and I was expecting you—flattered and honored beyond expression by your confidence. My door, indeed, was closed to any one but you."

Marguerite took the proffered seat, and there was a moment's silence. M. Fortunat found it difficult to believe that this beautiful, imposing young girl could be the poor little apprentice whom he had seen in the book-bindery, years before, clad in a coarse serge frock, with dishevelled hair covered with scraps of paper. In the meantime, Marguerite was regretting the necessity of confiding in this man, for the more she looked at him, the more she was convinced that he was not an honest, straightforward person; and she would infinitely have preferred a cynical scoundrel to this plausible and polite gentleman, whom she strongly suspected of being a hypocrite. She remained silent, waiting for M. Fortunat to dismiss the young man in the blouse, whose presence she could not explain, and who stood in a sort of mute ecstasy, staring at her with eyes expressive of the most intense surprise and the liveliest admiration. But weary at last of this fruitless delay, she exclaimed: " I have come, monsieur, to confer with you respecting certain matters which require the most profound secrecy."

Chupin understood her, for he blushed to the tips of his ears, and started as if to leave the room. But his employer detained him with a gesture.

" Remain, Victor," he said kindly, and, turning to Mademoiselle Marguerite, he added: " You have no indiscretion to fear from this worthy fellow, mademoiselle. He knows everything, and he has already been actively at work—and with the best result—on your behalf."

" I don't understand you, sir," replied the girl.

M. Fortunat smiled sweetly. " I have already taken your business in hand, mademoiselle," said he. " An hour after the receipt of your letter I began the campaign."

" But I had not told you——"

" What you wished of me—that's true. But I allowed myself to suspect——"

" Ah ! "

" I fancied I might conclude that you wished the help of my experience and poor ability in clearing an innocent man who has been vilely slandered, M. Pascal Ferailleur."

Marguerite sprang to her feet, at once agitated and alarmed. " How did you know this ? " she exclaimed.

M. Fortunat had left his arm-chair, and was now leaning against the mantel-shelf, in what he considered a most becoming and awe-inspiring attitude, with his thumb in the armhole of his waistcoat. "Ah! nothing could be more simple," he answered, in much the same tone as a conqueror might assume to explain his feat. "It is part of my profession to penetrate the intentions of persons who deign to honor me with their confidence. So my surmises are correct; at least you have not said the contrary?"

She had said nothing. When her first surprise was over, she vainly endeavored to find a plausible explanation of M. Fortunat's acquaintance with her affairs, for she was not at all deceived by his pretended perspicacity. Meanwhile, delighted by the supposed effect he had produced, he recklessly continued: "Reserve your amazement for what I am about to disclose, for I have made several important discoveries. It must have been your good angel who inspired you with the idea of coming to me. You would have shuddered if you had realized the dangers that threatened you. But now you have nothing to fear; I am watching. I am here, and I hold in my hand all the threads of the abominable intrigue for ruining you. For it is you, your person, and your fortune that are imperilled. It was solely on your account that M. Ferailleur was attacked. And I can tell you the names of the scoundrels who ruined him. The crime originated with the person who had the most powerful interest in the matter—the Marquis de Valorsay. His agent was a scoundrel who is generally known as the Viscount de Coralth; but Chupin here can tell you his real name and his shameful past. You preferred M. Ferailleur, hence it was necessary to put him out of the way. M. de Chalusse had promised your hand to the Marquis de Valorsay. This marriage was Valorsay's only resource—the plank that might save the drowning man. People fancy he is rich; but he is ruined. Yes, ruined completely, irretrievably. He was in such desperate straits that he had almost determined to blow his brains out before the hope of marrying you entered his mind."

"Ah!" thought Chupin, "my employer is well under way."

This was indeed the case. The name of Valorsay was quite sufficient to set all M. Fortunat's bile in motion. All thought of his ex-client irritated him beyond endurance. Unfortunately for him, however, his anger in the present instance had ruined his plans. He had intended to take Mademoiselle Marguerite by surprise, to work upon her imagination, to make her talk without saying anything himself, and to remain master of the situation. But on the contrary he had revealed everything; and he did not discover this until it was too late to retrieve his blunder. "How the Marquis de Valorsay has kept his head above water is a wonder to me," he continued. "His creditors have been threatening to sue him for more than six months. How he has been able to keep them quiet since M. de Chalusse's death, I cannot understand. However, this much is certain, mademoiselle: the marquis has not renounced his intention of becoming your husband; and to attain that object he won't hesitate to employ any means that may promise to prove effectual."

Completely mistress of herself, Mademoiselle Marguerite listened with an impassive face. "I know all this," she replied, in a frigid tone.

"What! you know——"

"Yes; but there is one thing that baffles my powers of comprehension. My dowry was the only temptation to M. de Valorsay, was it not? Why does he still wish to marry me, now that I have no fortune?"

M. Fortunat had gradually lost all his advantage.
"I have asked myself the same question," he replied,
"and I think I have found an answer. I believe that
the marquis has in his possession a letter, or a will, or
a document of some sort, written by M. de Chalusse—
in fact an instrument in which the count acknowledges
you as his daughter, and which consequently establishes
your right to his property."

"And the marquis could urge this claim if he became my husband?"

"Certainly he could."

M. Fortunat explained M. de Valorsay's conduct exactly as the old magistrate had done. However, Mademoiselle Marguerite discreetly refrained from committing herself. The great interest that M. Fortunat
seemed to take in her affairs aroused her distrust; and
she decided to do what he had attempted in vain—that
is, allow him to do all the talking, and to conceal all
that she knew herself. "Perhaps you are right," she
remarked, "but it is necessary to prove the truth of
your assertion."

"I can prove that Valorsay hasn't a shilling, and that
he has lived for a year by expedients which render him
liable to arrest and prosecution at any time. I can
prove that he deceived M. de Chalusse as to his financial position. I can prove that he conspired with M.
de Coralth to ruin your lover. Wouldn't this be
something?"

She smiled in a way that was exceedingly irritating
to his vanity, and in a tone of good-natured incredulity,
she remarked: "It is easy to *say* these things."

"And to do them," rejoined M. Fortunat, quickly.
"I never promise what I cannot perform. A man
should never touch a pen when he is meditating any

evil act. Of course, no one is fool enough to write down his infamy in detail. But a man cannot always be on the *qui vive*. There will be a word in one letter, a sentence in another, an allusion in a third. And by combining these words, phrases, and allusions, one may finally discover the truth."

He suddenly checked himself, warned of his fresh imprudence by the expression on Mademoiselle Marguerite's face. She drew back, and looking him full in the eyes, she exclaimed: " Then you have been in M. de Valorsay's confidence, sir? Would you be willing to swear that you never helped him in his designs?"

A silent and ignored witness of this scene, Victor Chupin was secretly delighted. " Hit!" he thought— "hit just in the bull's-eye. Zounds! there's a woman for you! She has beaten the guv'nor on every point."

M. Fortunat was so taken by surprise that he made no attempt to deny his guilt. " I confess that I acted as M. de Valorsay's adviser for some time," he replied, "and he frequently spoke to me of his intention of marrying a rich wife in order to retrieve his shattered fortunes. Upon my word, I see nothing so very bad about that! It is not a strictly honest proceeding, perhaps, but it is done every day. What is marriage in this age? Merely a business transaction, is it not? Perhaps it would be more correct to say that it is a transaction in which one person tries to cheat the other. The fathers-in-law are deceived, or the husband, or the wife, and sometimes all of them together. But when I discovered this scheme for ruining M. Ferailleur, I cried 'halt!' My conscience revolted at that. Dishonor an innocent man! It was base, cowardly, outrageous! And not being able to prevent this infamous act, I swore that I would avenge it."

Would Mademoiselle Marguerite accept this explanation? Chupin feared so, and accordingly turning quickly to his employer, he remarked: " To say nothing of the fact that this fine gentleman has swindled you outrageously, shrewd as you are—cheating you out of the forty thousand francs you lent him, and which he was to pay you eighty thousand for."

M. Fortunat cast a withering look at his clerk, but the mischief was done: denial was useless. He seemed fated to blunder in this affair. " Well, yes," he declared, " it's true. Valorsay *has* defrauded me, and I have sworn to have my revenge. I won't rest until I see him ruined."

Mademoiselle Marguerite was partially reassured, for she understood his zeal now. Her scorn for the man was only increased; but she was convinced that he would serve her faithfully. " I like this much better," said she. " It is better to have no concealment. You desire M. de Valorsay's ruin. I desire the rehabilitation of M. Ferailleur. So our interests are in common. But before acting in this matter, we must know M. Ferailleur's wishes."

" They cannot be considered."

" And why? "

" Because no one knows what has become of him. When the desire for revenge first took possession of me, I at once thought of him. I procured his address, and went to the Rue d'Ulm. But he had gone away. The very day after his misfortune, M. Ferailleur sold his furniture and went away with his mother."

" I am aware of that, and I have come to ask you to search for him. To discover his hiding-place will be only child's play to you."

" Do you suppose I haven't thought of this? " re-

plied M. Fortunat. " Why, I spent all day yesterday
searching for him. By questioning the people in the
neighborhood I finally succeeded in ascertaining that
Madame Ferailleur left her home in a cab several hours
after her son, and took a very large quantity of baggage with her. Well, do you know where she drove?
To the Western railway station. I am sure of this,
and I know she told a porter there that her destination
was London. M. Ferailleur is now *en route* for America, and we shall never hear of him again ! "

Mademoiselle Marguerite shook her head. " You
are mistaken, sir," said she.

" There can be no mistake about what I have just
told you."

" I don't question the result of your investigations,
but appearances are deceitful. I thoroughly understand
M. Ferailleur's character, and he is not the man to be
crushed by an infamous calumny. He may seem to fly,
he may disappear, he may conceal himself for a time,
but it is only to make his vengeance more certain.
What ! Pascal, who is energy itself, who possesses an
iron will, and invincible determination, would he renounce his honor, his future, and the woman he loves
without a struggle? If he had felt that his case was
hopeless, he would have destroyed himself, and as he
has not done so, he is not without hope. He has not
left Paris; I am sure of it."

M. Fortunat was not convinced. In his opinion this
was only sentiment and rubbish. Still there was one
person present who was deeply impressed by the confidence of this young girl, who was the most beautiful
creature he had ever seen, and whose devotion and
energy filled his heart with admiration, and this person
was Chupin. He stepped forward with his eyes spark-

ling with enthusiasm, and in a feeling voice he exclaimed: "I understand your idea! Yes, M. Ferailleur
is in Paris. And I shall be unworthy of the name of
Chupin, if I don't find him for you in less than a
fortnight!"

XII.

MADEMOISELLE MARGUERITE knew Pascal Ferailleur.
Suddenly struck down in the full sunlight of happiness by a terrible misfortune, he, of course, experienced moments of frenzy and terrible depression; but
he was incapable of the cowardice which M. Fortunat
had accused him of.

Mademoiselle Marguerite only did him justice when
she said that the sole condition on which he could consent to live was that of consecrating his life, and all
his strength, intelligence and will to confounding this
infamous calumny. And still she did not know the
extent of Pascal's misfortune. How could she suppose
that he believed himself deserted by her? How could
she know the doubts and fears and the anguish that had
been roused in his heart by the note which Madame
Léon had given him at the garden gate? What did
she know of the poignant suspicions that had rent his
mind, after listening to Madame Vantrasson's disparaging insinuations?

It must be admitted that he was indebted to his
mother alone for his escape from suicide—that grim
madness that seizes hold of so many desperate, despairing men. And it was still to his mother—the incomparable guardian of his honor—that he owed his reso-

lution on the morning he applied to Baron Trigault.
And his courage met with its first reward.

He was no longer the same man when he left the
princely mansion which he had entered with his heart
so full of anguish. He was still somewhat bewildered
with the strange scenes which he had involuntarily witnessed, the secrets he had overheard, and the revelations
which had been made to him; but a light gleamed on
the horizon—a fitful and uncertain light, it is true,
but nevertheless a hopeful gleam. At least, he would
no longer have to struggle alone. An honest and experienced man, powerful by reason of his reputation,
his connections and his fortune, had promised him his
help. Thanks to this man whom misfortune had made
a truer friend than years could have done, he would
have access to the wretch who had deprived him both
of his honor and of the woman he loved. He knew the
weak spot in the marquis's armor now; he knew where
and how to strike, and he felt sure that he should succeed in winning Valorsay's confidence, and in obtaining
irrefutable proofs of his villainy.

Pascal was eager to inform his mother of the fortunate result of his visit, but certain arrangements
which were needful for the success of his plans required
his attention, and it was nearly five o'clock when he
reached the Route de la Révolte. Madame Ferailleur
was just returning home when he arrived, which surprised him considerably, for he had not known that she
had intended going out. The cab she had used was
still standing before the door, and she had not had time
to take off her shawl and bonnet when he entered the
house. She uttered a joyful cry on perceiving her son.
She was so accustomed to read his secret thoughts on
his face, that it was unnecessary for him to say a

word; before he had even opened his lips, she cried:
" So you have succeeded? "

" Yes, mother, beyond my hopes."

" I was not deceived, then, in the worthy man who
came to offer us his assistance? "

" No, certainly not. Do what I may, I can never
repay him for his generosity and self-denial. If you
knew, my dear mother, if you only knew——"

" What? "

He kissed her as if he wished to apologize for what
he was about to say, and then he quickly replied:
" Marguerite is the daughter of Baroness Trigault."

Madame Ferailleur started back, as if she had seen
a reptile spring up in her pathway. " The daughter of
the baroness! " she faltered. " Great Heavens! "

" It is the truth, mother; listen to me." And in a
voice that trembled with emotion, he rapidly related all
he had learned by his visit to the baron, softening the
truth as much as he could without concealing it. But
prevarication was useless. Madame Ferailleur's indignation and disgust were none the less evident. " That
woman is a shameless creature," she said, coldly, when
her son's narrative was concluded.

Pascal made no reply. He knew only too well that
his mother was right, and yet it wounded him cruelly
to hear her speak in this style. For the baroness was
Marguerite's mother after all.

" So," continued Madame Ferailleur, with increasing
indignation, " creatures do exist who are destitute even
of the maternal instincts of animals. I am an honest
woman myself; I don't say it in self-glorification, it's
no credit to me; my mother was a saint, and I loved
my husband; what some people call duty was my
happiness, so I may be allowed to speak on this subject.

I don't excuse infidelity, but I can understand how such a thing is possible. Yes, I can understand how a beautiful young woman, who is left alone in a city like Paris, may lose her senses, and forget the worthy man who has exiled himself for her sake, and who is braving a thousand dangers to win a fortune for her. The husband who exposes his honor and happiness to such terrible risk, is an imprudent man. But when this woman has erred, when she has given birth to a child, how she can abandon it, how she can cast it off as if it were a dog, I cannot comprehend. I could imagine infanticide more easily. No, such a woman has no heart, no bowels of compassion. There is nothing human in her! For how could she live, how could she sleep with the thought that somewhere in the world her own child, the flesh of her flesh, was exposed to all the temptations of poverty, and the horrors of shame and vice? And she, the possessor of millions, she, the inmate of a palace, thinking only of dress and pleasure! How was it that she didn't ask herself every minute, 'Where is my daughter now, and what is she doing? What is she living on? Has she shelter, clothes and food? To what depths of degradation she may have sunk? Perhaps she has so far lived by honest toil, and perhaps at this very moment this support fails her, and she is abandoning herself to a life of infamy.' Great God! how does this woman dare to step out of doors? On seeing the poor wretches who have been driven to vice by want, how can she fail to say to herself: 'That, perhaps, is my daughter!'"

Pascal turned pale, moved to the depths of his soul by his mother's extraordinary vehemence. He trembled lest she should say: "And you, my son, would you marry the child of such a mother?" For he knew his mother's prejudices, and the great importance she attached to a spotless reputation transmitted from parent to child, from generation to generation. " The baroness knew that her husband adored her, and hearing of his return she became terrified; she lost her senses," he ventured to say in extenuation.

" Would you try to defend her? " exclaimed Madame Ferailleur. " Do you really think one can atone for a fault by a crime? "

" No, certainly not, but——"

" Perhaps you would censure the baroness more severely if you knew what her daughter has suffered— if you knew the perils and miseries she has been exposed to from the moment her mother left her on a door-step, near the central markets, till the day when her father found her. It is a miracle that she did not perish."

Where had Madame Ferailleur learned these particulars? Pascal asked himself this question without being able to answer it. " I don't understand you, mother," he faltered.

" Then you know nothing of Mademoiselle Marguerite's past life. Is it possible she never told you anything about it? "

" I only know that she has been very unhappy."

" Has she never alluded to the time when she was an apprentice? "

" She has only told me that she earned her living with her own hands at one time of her life."

' Well, I am better informed on the subject."

Pascal's amazement was changed to terror. " You, mother, you! "

" Yes; I—I have been to the asylum where she was received and educated. I have had a conversation with

two Sisters of Charity who remember her, and it is
scarcely an hour since I left the people to whom she
was formerly bound as an apprentice."

Standing opposite his mother with one hand con-
vulsively clutching the back of the chair he was leaning
on, Pascal tried to nerve himself for some terrible blow.
For was not his life at stake? Did not his whole
future depend upon the revelations Madame Ferailleur
was about to make? "So this was your object in
going out, mother?" he faltered.

"Yes."

"And you went without warning me?"

"Was it necessary? What! you love a young girl,
you swear in my presence that she shall be your wife,
and you think it strange that I should try to ascertain
whether she is worthy of you or not? It would be very
strange if I did not do so."

"This idea occurred to you so suddenly!"

Madame Ferailleur gave an almost imperceptible
shrug of the shoulders, as if she were astonished to
have to answer such puerile objections. "Have you
already forgotten the disparaging remarks made by our
new servant, Madame Vantrasson?"

"Good Heavens!"

"I understood her base insinuations as well as you
did, and after your departure I questioned her, or
rather I allowed her to tell her story, and I ascertained that Mademoiselle Marguerite had once been
an apprentice of Vantrasson's brother-in-law, a man
named Greloux, who was formerly a bookbinder in the
Rue Saint-Denis, but who has now retired from business. It was there that Vantrasson met Mademoiselle
Marguerite, and this is why he was so greatly surprised
to see her doing the mistress at the Hôtel de Chalusse."

It seemed to Pascal that the throbbing of his heart stopped his breath.

"By a little tact I obtained the Greloux's address from Madame Vantrasson," resumed his mother. "Then I sent for a cab and drove there at once."

"And you saw them?"

"Yes; thanks to a falsehood which doesn't trouble my conscience much, I succeeded in effecting an entrance, and had an hour's conversation with them." His mother's icy tones frightened Pascal. Her slowness tortured him, and still he dared not press her. "The Greloux family," she continued, "seem to be what are called worthy people, that is, incapable of committing any crime that is punishable by the code, and very proud of their income of seven thousand francs a year. They must have been very much attached to Mademoiselle Marguerite, for they were lavish in their protestations of affection when I mentioned her name. The husband in particular seemed to regard her with a feeling of something like gratitude."

"Ah! you see, mother, you see!"

"As for the wife, it was easy to see that she had sincerely regretted the loss of the best apprentice, the most honest servant, and the best worker she had ever seen in her life. And yet, from her own story, I should be willing to swear that she had abused the poor child, and had made a slave of her." Tears glittered in Pascal's eyes, but he breathed freely once more. "As for Vantrasson," resumed Madame Ferailleur, "it is certain that he took a violent fancy to his sister's apprentice. This man, who has since become an infamous scoundrel, was then only a rake, an unprincipled drunkard and libertine. He fancied the poor little apprentice

—she was then but thirteen years old—would be only too glad to become the mistress of her employer's brother; but she scornfully repulsed him, and his vanity was so deeply wounded that he persecuted the poor girl to such an extent that she was obliged to complain, first to Madame Greloux, who—to her shame be it said—treated these insults as mere nonsense; and afterward to Greloux himself, who was probably delighted to have an opportunity of ridding himself of his indolent brother-in-law, for he turned him out of the house."

The thought that so vile a rascal as this man Vantrasson should have dared to insult Marguerite made Pascal frantic with indignation. "The wretch!" he exclaimed; "the wretch!" But without seeming to notice her son's anger, Madame Ferailleur continued: "They pretended they had not seen their former apprentice since she had been living in grandeur, as they expressed it. But in this they lied to me. For they saw her at least once, and that was on the day she brought them twenty thousand francs, which proved the nucleus of their fortune. They did not mention this fact, however."

"Dear Marguerite!" murmured Pascal, "dear Marguerite!" And then aloud: "But where did you learn these last details, mother?" he inquired.

"At the asylum where Mademoiselle Marguerite was brought up, and there, too, I only heard words of praise. 'Never,' said the superior, 'have I had a more gifted, sweeter-tempered or more attractive charge.' They had reproached her sometimes for being too reserved, and her self-respect had often been mistaken for inordinate pride; but she had not forgotten the asylum any more than she had forgotten her former patrons. On one occasion the superior received from her the sum of twenty-five thousand francs, and a year ago she presented the institution with one hundred thousand francs, the yearly income of which is to constitute the marriage dowry of some deserving orphan."

Pascal was greatly elated. "Well, mother!" he exclaimed, "well, is it strange that I love her?" Madame Ferailleur made no reply, and a sorrowful apprehension seized hold of him. "You are silent," said he, "and why? When the blessed day that will allow me to wed Marguerite arrives, you surely won't oppose our marriage?"

"No, my son, nothing that I have learned gives me the right to do so."

"The right! Ah, you are unjust, mother."

"Unjust! Haven't I faithfully reported all that was told me, although I knew it would only increase your passion?"

"That's true, but——"

Madame Ferailleur sadly shook her head. "Do you think," she interrupted, "that I can, without sorrow, see you choose a girl of no family, a girl who is outside the pale of social recognition? Don't you understand my disquietude when I think that the girl that you will marry is the daughter of such a woman as Baroness Trigault, an unfortunate girl whom her mother cannot even recognize, since her mother is a married woman——"

"Ah! mother, is that Marguerite's fault?"

"Did I say it was her fault? No—I only pray God that you may never have to repent of choosing a wife whose past life must ever remain an impenetrable mystery!"

Pascal had become very pale. " Mother! " he said in a quivering voice, " mother ! "

" I mean that you will only know so much of Mademoiselle Marguerite's past life as she may choose to tell you," continued the obdurate old lady. " You heard Madame Vantrasson's ignoble allegations. It has been said that she was the mistress, not the daughter, of the Count de Chalusse. Who knows what vile accusations you may be forced to meet? And what is your refuge, if doubts should ever assail you? Mademoiselle Marguerite's word! Will this be sufficient? It is now, perhaps; but will it suffice in years to come? I would have my son's wife above suspicion; and she —why, there is not a single episode in her life that does not expose her to the most atrocious calumny."

" What does calumny matter? it will never shake my faith in her. The misfortunes which you reproach Marguerite for sanctify her in my eyes."

" Pascal ! "

" What! Am I to scorn her because she has been unfortunate? Am I to regard her birth as a crime? Am I to despise her because her *mother* is a despicable woman? No—God be praised! the day when illegitimate children, the innocent victims of their mother's faults, were branded as outcasts, is past."

But Madame Ferailleur's prejudices were too deeply rooted to be shaken by these arguments. " I won't discuss this question, my son," she interrupted, " but take care. By declaring children irresponsible for their mother's faults, you will break the strongest tie that binds a woman to duty. If the son of a pure and virtuous wife, and the son of an adulterous woman meet upon equal ground, those who are held in check only by the thought of their children will finally say to themselves, what does it matter?"

It was the first time that a cloud had ever arisen between mother and son. On hearing his dearest hopes thus attacked, Pascal was tempted to rebel, and a flood of bitter words rose to his lips. However he had strength enough to control himself. " Marguerite alone can triumph over these implacable prejudices," he thought; "when my mother knows her, she will feel how unjust they are!"

And as he found it difficult to remain master of himself, he stammered some excuse, and abruptly retired to his own room, where he threw himself on his bed. He felt that it was not his place to reproach his mother or censure her for her opinions. What mother had ever been so devoted as she had been? And who knows?—it was, perhaps, from these same rigid prejudices that this simple-minded and heroic woman had derived her energy, her enthusiastic love of God, her hatred of evil, and that virility of spirit which misfortune had been powerless to daunt. Besides, had she not promised to offer no opposition to his marriage! And was not this a great concession, a sacrifice which must have cost her a severe struggle? And where can one find the mother who does not count as one of the sublime joys of maternity the task of seeking a wife for her son, of choosing from among all others the young girl who will be the companion of his life, the angel of his dark and of his prosperous days? His mind was occupied with these thoughts when his door suddenly opened, and he sprang up, exclaiming: " Who is it?"

It was Madame Vantrasson, who came to announce that dinner was ready—a dinner which she had herself prepared, for on going out Madame Ferailleur had left her in charge of the household. On seeing this woman, Pascal was overcome with rage and indignation, and felt a wild desire to annihilate her. He knew that she was only a vile slanderer, but she might meet other beings as vile as herself who would be only too glad to believe her falsehoods. And to think that he was powerless to punish her! He now realized the suffering his mother had spoken of—the most atrocious suffering which the lover can endure—powerlessness to protect the object of his affections, when she is assailed. Engrossed in these gloomy thoughts, Pascal preserved a sullen silence during the repast. He ate because his mother filled his plate; but if he had been questioned, he could scarcely have told what he was eating. And yet, the modest dinner was excellent. Madame Vantrasson was really a good cook, and in this first effort in her new situation she had surpassed herself. Her vanity as a *cordon-bleu* was piqued because she did not receive the compliments she expected, and which she felt she deserved. Four or five times she asked impatiently, "Isn't that good?" and as the only reply was a scarcely enthusiastic "Very good," she vowed she would never again waste so much care and talent upon such unappreciative people.

Madame Ferailleur was as silent as her son, and seemed equally anxious to finish with the repast. She evidently wanted to get rid of Madame Vantrasson, and in fact as soon as the simple dessert had been placed on the table, she turned to her, and said: "You may go home now. I will attend to the rest."

Irritated by the taciturnity of these strange folks, the landlady of the Model Lodging House withdrew, and they soon heard the street door close behind her with

a loud bang as she left the house.   Pascal drew a long
breath as if relieved of a heavy weight.   While Madame
Vantrasson had been in the room he had scarcely dared
to raise his eyes, so great was his dread of encounter-
ing the gaze of this woman, whose malignity was but
poorly veiled by her smooth-tongued hypocrisy.   He
really feared he should not be able to resist his desire
to strangle her.   However, Madame Ferailleur must
have understood her son's agitation, for as soon as they
were alone, she said: " So you have not forgiven me
for my plain speaking ? "
    " How can I be angry with you, mother, when I
know that you are thinking only of my happiness? But
how sorry I shall be if your prejudices——"
    Madame Ferailleur checked him with a gesture.
" Let us say no more on the subject," she remarked.
" Mademoiselle Marguerite will be the innocent cause
of one of the greatest disappointments of my life; but
I have no reason to hate her—and I have always been
able to show justice even to the persons I loved
the least.   I have done so in this instance, and I
am going perhaps to give you a convincing proof of
it."
    " A proof ? "
    " Yes."
    She reflected for a moment and then she asked:
" Did you not tell me, my son, that Mademoiselle Marguerite's education has not suffered on account of her
neglected childhood ? "
    " And it's quite true, mother."
    " She worked diligently, you said, so as to improve
herself ? "
    " Marguerite knows all that an unusually talented
girl can learn in four years, when she finds herself very

unhappy, and study proves her only refuge and consolation."

"If she wrote you a note would it be written grammatically, and be free from any mistakes in spelling?"

"Oh, certainly!" exclaimed Pascal, and a sudden inspiration made him pause abruptly. He darted to his own room, and a minute later he returned with a package of letters, which he laid on the table, saying: "Here, mother, read and see for yourself."

Madame Ferailleur drew her spectacles from their case, and, after adjusting them, she began to read.

With his elbows on the table, and his head resting upon his hands, Pascal eagerly watched his mother, anxious to read her impressions on her face. She was evidently astonished. She had not expected these letters would express such nobility of sentiment, an energy no whit inferior to her own, and even an echo of her own prejudices. For this strange young girl shared Madame Ferailleur's rather bigoted opinions. Again and again she asked herself if her birth and past had not created an impassable abyss between Pascal and herself. And she had not felt satisfied on this point until the day when the gray-haired magistrate, after hearing her story, said: "If I had a son, I should be proud to have him beloved by you!"

It soon became apparent that Madame Ferailleur was deeply moved, and once she even raised her glasses to wipe away a furtive tear which made Pascal's heart leap with very joy. "These letters are admirable," she said at last; "and no young girl, reared by a virtuous mother, could have given better expression to nobler sentiments; but——" She paused, not wishing to wound her son's feelings, and as he insisted, she added:

"But, these letters have the irreparable fault of being addressed to you, Pascal!"

This, however, was the expiring cry of her intractable obstinacy. "Now," she resumed, "wait before you censure your mother." So saying, she rose, opened a drawer, and taking from it a torn and crumpled scrap of paper, she handed it to her son, exclaiming: "Read this attentively."

This proved to be the note in pencil which Madame Léon had given to Pascal, and which he had divined rather than read by the light of the street-lamp; he had handed it to his mother on his return, and she had kept it. He had scarcely been in his right mind the evening he received it, but now he was enjoying the free exercise of all his faculties. He no sooner glanced at the note than he sprang up, and in an excited voice, exclaimed, "Marguerite never wrote this!"

The strange discovery seemed to stupefy him. "I was mad, raving mad!" he muttered. "The fraud is palpable, unmistakable. How could I have failed to discover it?" And as if he felt the need of convincing himself that he was not deceived, he continued, speaking to himself rather than to his mother: "The handwriting is not unlike Marguerite's, it's true; but it's only a clever counterfeit. And who doesn't know that all writings in pencil resemble each other more or less? Besides, it's certain that Marguerite, who is simplicity itself, would not have made use of such pretentious melodramatic phrases. How could I have been so stupid as to believe that she ever thought or wrote this: 'One cannot break a promise made to the dying; I shall keep mine even though my heart break.' And again: 'Forget, therefore, the girl who has loved you so much; she is now the betrothed of another, and

honor requires she should forget even your name!'"
He read these passages with an extravagant emphasis,
which heightened their absurdity. "And what shall
I say of these mistakes in spelling?" he resumed. "You
noticed them, of course, mother?—command is written
with a single 'm,' and supplicate with one 'p.' These
are certainly not mistakes that we can attribute to
haste! Ignorance is proved since the blunder is always
the same. The forger is evidently in the habit of omitting one of the double letters."

Madame Ferailleur listened with an impassive face.
"And these mistakes are all the more inexcusable since
this letter is only a copy," she observed, quietly.

"What?"

"Yes; a verbatim copy. Yesterday evening, while I
was examining it for the twentieth time, it occurred to
me that I had read some portions of it before. Where,
and under what circumstances? It was a puzzle which
kept me awake most of the night. But this morning
I suddenly remembered a book which I had seen in the
hands of the workmen at the factory, and which I had
often laughed over. So, while I was out this morning I entered a book-shop, and purchased the volume.
That's it, there on the corner of the mantel-shelf. Take
it and see."

Pascal obeyed, and noticed with surprise that the
work was entitled, "The Indispensable and Complete
Letter-writer, for Both Sexes, in Every Condition of
Life."

"Now turn to the page I have marked," said
Madame Ferailleur.

He did so, and read: "(*Model* 198). Letter from
a young lady who has promised her dying father to
renounce the man she loves, and to bestow her hand

upon another." Doubt was no longer possible. Line for line and word for word, the mistakes in spelling excepted, the note was an exact copy of the stilted prose of the "Indispensable Letter-writer."

It seemed to Pascal as if the scales had suddenly fallen from his eyes, and that he could now understand the whole intrigue which had been planned to separate him from Marguerite. His enemies had dishonored him in the hope that she would reject and scorn him, and, disappointed in their expectations, they had planned this pretended rupture of the engagement to prevent him from making any attempt at self-justification. So, in spite of some short-lived doubts, his love had been more clear-sighted than reason, and stronger than appearances. He had been quite right, then, in saying to his mother: "I can never believe that Marguerite deserts me at a moment when I am so wretched —that she condemns me unheard, and has no greater confidence in me than in my accusers. Appearances may indicate the contrary, but I am right." Certain circumstances, which had previously seemed contradictory, now strengthened this belief. "How is it," he said to himself, "that Marguerite writes to me that her father, on his death-bed, made her promise to renounce me, while Valorsay declares the Count de Chalusse died so suddenly, that he had not even time to acknowledge his daughter or to bequeath her his immense fortune? One of these stories must be false; and which of them? The one in this note most probably. As for the letter itself, it must have been the work of Madame Léon."

If he had not already possessed irrefutable proofs of this, the "Indispensable Letter-writer" would have shown it. The housekeeper's perturbation when she met him at the garden gate was now explained. She was shuddering at the thought that she might be followed and watched, and that Marguerite might appear at any moment, and discover everything.

"I think it would be a good plan to let this poor young girl know that her companion is Valorsay's spy," remarked Madame Ferailleur.

Pascal was about to approve this suggestion, when a sudden thought deterred him. "They must be watching Marguerite very closely," he replied, "and if I attempt to see her, if I even venture to write to her, our enemies would undoubtedly discover it. And then, farewell to the success of my plans."

"Then you prefer to leave her exposed to these dangers?"

"Yes, even admitting there is danger, which is by no means certain. Owing to her past life, Marguerite's experience is far in advance of her years, and if some one told me that she had fathomed Madame Léon's character, I should not be at all surprised."

It was necessary to ascertain what had become of Marguerite; and Pascal was puzzling his brain to discover how this might be done, when suddenly he exclaimed: "Madame Vantrasson! We have her; let us make use of her. It will be easy to find some excuse for sending her to the Hôtel de Chalusse: she will gossip with the servants there, and in that way we can discover the changes that have taken place."

This was a heroic resolution on Pascal's part, and one which he would have recoiled from the evening before. But it is easy to be brave when one is hopeful; and he saw his chances of success increase so rapidly that he no longer feared the obstacles that had once seemed almost insurmountable. Even his mother's opposition had ceased to alarm him. For why should he fear after the surprising proof she had given him of her love of justice, proving that the pretended letter from Mademoiselle Marguerite was really a forgery?

He slept but little that night and did not stir from the house on the following day. He was busily engaged in perfecting his plan of attack against the marquis. His advantages were considerable, thanks to Baron Trigault, who had placed a hundred thousand francs at his disposal; but the essential point was to use this amount in such a way as to win Valorsay's confidence, and induce him to betray himself. Pascal's hours of meditation were not spent in vain, and when it became time for him to repair to his enemy's house, he said to his mother: " I've found a plan; and if the baron will let me follow it out, Valorsay is mine! "

XIII.

IT was pure childishness on Pascal's part to doubt Baron Trigault's willingness to agree even with closed eyes to any measures he might propose. He ought to have recollected that their interests were identical, that they hated the same men with equal hatred, and that they were equally resolved upon vengeance. And certainly the events which had occurred since their last interview had not been of a nature to modify the baron's intentions. However, misfortune had rendered Pascal timid and suspicious, and it was not until he reached the baron's house that his fears vanished. The manner in which the servants received him proved that the baron greatly esteemed him: for the man must be stupid indeed who does not know that the greeting of the servants is ever in harmony with the feelings of the master of the house. "Will you be kind enough to follow me?" said the servant to whom he handed his card. "The baron is very busy, but that doesn't matter. He gave orders that monsieur should be shown up as soon as he arrived."

Pascal followed without a word. The elegance of this princely abode never varied. The same careless, prodigal, regal luxury was apparent everywhere. The servants—whose name was legion—were always passing noiselessly to and fro. A pair of horses, worth at least a thousand louis, and harnessed to the baroness's brougham, were stamping and neighing in the courtyard; and the hall was, as usual, fragrant with the perfume of rare flowers, renewed every morning.

On his first visit Pascal had only seen the apartments on the ground floor. This time his guide remarked that he would take him upstairs to the baron's private room. He was slowly ascending the broad marble staircase and admiring the bronze balustrade, the rich carpet, the magnificent frescoes, and the costly statuary, when a rustle of silk resounded near him. He had only time to step aside, and a lady passed him rapidly, without turning her head, or even deigning to look at him. She did not appear more than forty, and she was still very beautiful, with her golden hair dressed high on the back of her head. Her costume, brilliant enough in hue to frighten a cab horse, was extremely eccentric in cut; but it certainly set off her peculiar style of beauty to admirable advantage.

"That's the baroness," whispered the servant, after she had passed.

Pascal did not need to be told this. He had seen her but once, and then only for a second; but it had been

under such circumstances that he should never forget
her so long as he lived. And now he understood the
strange and terrible impression which had been produced upon him when he saw her first. Mademoiselle
Marguerite was the living prototype of this lady, save
as regards the color of her hair. And there would
have been no difference in this respect had the baroness
allowed her locks to retain their natural tint. Her hair
had been black, like Marguerite's, and black it had
remained until she was thirty-five, when she bleached
it to the fashionable color of the time. And every
fourth day even now her hairdresser came to apply a
certain compound to her head, after which she remained
in the bright sunlight for several hours, so as to
impart a livelier shade of gold to her dyed locks.

Pascal had scarcely regained his composure, when
the servant opened the door of an immense apartment
as large as a handsome *suite* of rooms, and magnifi-
cently furnished. Here sat the baron, surrounded by
several clerks, who were busily engaged in putting a
pile of papers and documents in order.

But as soon as Pascal entered, the baron rose, and
cordially holding out his hand, exclaimed, " Ah! here
you are at last, Monsieur Mauméjan! "

So he had not forgotten the name which Pascal had
assumed. This was a favorable omen. " I called,
monsieur——" began the young man.

"Yes—I know—I know!" interrupted the baron.
" Come, we must have a talk."

And, taking Pascal's arm, he led him into his private
sanctum, separated from the large apartment by fold-
ing-doors, which had been removed, and replaced by
hangings. Once there he indicated by a gesture that they
could be heard in the adjoining room, and that it was

necessary to speak in a low tone. "You have no doubt
come," said he, "for the money I promised that dear
Marquis de Valorsay—I have it all ready for you;
here it is." So saying, he opened an escritoire, and
took out a large roll of bank-notes, which he handed to
Pascal. "Here, count it," he added, "and see if the
amount is correct."

But Pascal, whose face had suddenly become as red
as fire, did not utter a word in reply. On receiving
this money a new but quite natural thought had entered his mind for the first time. "What is the matter?" inquired the baron, surprised by this sudden
embarrassment. "What has happened to you?"

"Nothing, monsieur, nothing! Only I was asking
myself—if I ought—if I can accept this money."

"Bah! and why not?"

"Because if you lend it to M. de Valorsay, it is perhaps lost."

"*Perhaps!* You are polite——"

"Yes, monsieur, you are right. I ought to have said
that it is sure to be lost; and hence my embarrassment.
Is it not solely on my account that you sacrifice a sum
which would be a fortune to many men? Yes. Very
well, then. I am asking myself if it is right for me to
accept such a sacrifice, when it is by no means certain
that I shall ever be able to requite it. Shall I ever
have a hundred thousand francs to repay you?"

"But isn't this money absolutely necessary to enable
you to win Valorsay's confidence?"

"Yes, and if it belonged to me I should not hesitate."

Though the baron had formed a high estimate of
Pascal's character, he was astonished and deeply
touched by these scruples, and this excessive delicacy
of feeling. Like most opulent men, he knew few poor

people who wore their poverty with grace and dignity, and who did not snatch at a twenty-franc piece wherever they chanced to find it. " Ah, well, my dear Ferailleur," he said, kindly, " don't trouble yourself on this score. It's not at your request nor solely on your account that I make this sacrifice."

" Oh ! "

" No; I give you my word of honor it isn't. Leaving you quite out of the question, I should still have lent Valorsay this money; and if you do not wish to take it to him, I shall send it by some one else."

After that, Pascal could not demur any further. He took the baron's proffered hand and pressed it warmly, uttering only this one word, made more eloquent than any protestations by the fervor with which it was spoken : " Thanks ! "

The baron shrugged his shoulders good-naturedly, like a man who fails to see that he has done anything at all meritorious, or even worthy of the slightest acknowledgment. " And you must understand, my dear sir," he resumed, " that you can employ this sum as you choose, in advancing your interests, which are identical with mine. You can give the money to Valorsay at such a time and under such conditions as will best serve your plans. Give it to him in an hour or in a month, all at once or in fifty different instalments, as you please. Only use it like the rope one ties round a dog's neck before drowning him."

The keenest penetration was concealed beneath the baron's careless good-nature. Pascal knew this, and feeling that his protector understood him, he said : " You overpower me with kindness."

" Nonsense ! "

" You offer me just what I came to ask for."

"So much the better."

"But you will allow me to explain my intentions?"

"It is quite unnecessary, my dear sir."

"Excuse me; if I follow my present plan, I shall be obliged to ascribe certain sentiments, words, and even acts, to you, which you might perhaps disavow, and—"

With a careless toss of the head, accompanied by a disdainful snap of the fingers, the baron interrupted him. "Set to work, and don't give yourself the slightest uneasiness about that. You may do whatever you like, if you only succeed in unmasking this dear marquis, and Coralth, his worthy acolyte. Show me up in whatever light you choose. Who will you be in Valorsay's eyes? Why, Maumejan, one of my business agents, and I can always throw the blame on you." And as if to prove that he had divined even the details of the scheme devised by his young friend, he added: "Besides, every one knows that a millionaire's business agent is anything but a pleasant person to deal with. A millionaire, who is not a fool, must always smile, and no matter how absurd the demands upon him may be, he must always answer: 'Yes, certainly, certainly—I should be only too happy!' But then he adds: 'You must arrange the matter with my agent. Confer with him.' And it is the unlucky agent who must object, declare that his employer has no money at his disposal just now, and finally say, 'No.'"

Pascal was still disposed to insist, but the baron was obdurate. "Oh! enough, enough!" he exclaimed. "Don't waste precious time in idle discussion. The days are only twenty-four hours long: and as you see, I'm very busy, so busy that I've not touched a card since the day before yesterday. I am preparing a delightful surprise for Madame Trigault, my daughter, and my son-in-law. It has been rather a delicate operation, but I flatter myself that I have succeeded finely." And he laughed a laugh that was not pleasant to hear. "You see, I've had enough of paying several hundred thousand francs a year for the privilege of being sneered at by my wife, scorned by my daughter, swindled by my son-in-law, and vilified and anathematized by all three of them. I am still willing to go on paying, but only on conditions that they give me in return for my money, if not the reality, at least a show of love, affection, and respect. I'm determined to have the semblance of these things; I'm quite resolved on that. Yes, I will have myself treated with deference. I'll be petted and coddled and made much of, or else I'll suspend payment. It was one of my old friends, a *parvenu* like myself—a man whose domestic happiness I have envied for many years—who gave me this receipt: 'At home,' said he, 'with my wife, my daughters, and my sons-in-law, I'm like a peer of England at an hotel. I order first-class happiness at so much a month. If I get it I pay for it; if I don't get it, I cut off the supplies. When I get extras I pay for them cheerfully, without haggling. Follow my example, my old friend, and you'll have a comfortable life.' And I shall follow his advice, M. Ferailleur, for I am convinced that his theory is sound and practicable. I have led this life long enough. I'll spend my last days in peace, or, as God hears me, I'll let my family die of starvation!"

His face was purple, and the veins on his forehead stood out like whipcords, but not so much from anger as from the constraint he imposed upon himself by speaking in a whisper. He drew a long breath, and then in a calmer tone, resumed: "But you must make haste and succeed, M. Ferailleur, if you don't want the young girl you love to be deprived of her rightful heritage. You do not know into what unworthy hands the Chalusse property is about to fall." He was on the point of telling Pascal the story of Madame d'Argelès and M. Wilkie, when he was interrupted by the sound of a lively controversy in the hall.

"Who's taking such liberty in my house?" the baron began. But the next instant he heard some one fling open the door of the large room adjoining, and then a coarse, guttural voice called out: "What! he isn't here! This is too much!"

The baron made an angry gesture. "That's Kami-Bey," said he, "the Turk whom I am playing that great game of cards with. The devil take him! He will be sure to force his way in here—so we may as well join him, M. Ferailleur."

On reëntering the adjoining apartment Pascal beheld a very corpulent man, with a very red face, a straggling beard, a flat nose, small, beadlike eyes, and sensual lips. He was clad in a black frock-coat, buttoned tight to the throat, and he wore a fez. This costume gave him the appearance of a chunky bottle, sealed with red wax. Such, indeed, was Kami-Bey, a specimen of those semi-barbarians, loaded with gold, who are not attracted to Paris by its splendors and glories, but rather by its corruption—people who come there persuaded that money will purchase anything and everything, and who often return home with the same conviction. Kami was no doubt more impudent, more cynical and more arrogant than others of his class. As he was more wealthy, he had more followers; he had been more toadied and flattered, and victimized to a greater extent by the host of female intriguers, who look upon every foreigner as their rightful prey.

He spoke French passably well, but with an abominable accent. " Here you are at last! " he exclaimed, as the baron entered the room. " I was becoming very anxious."

" About what, prince? "

Why Kami-Bey was called prince no one knew, not even the man himself. Perhaps it was because the lackey who opened his carriage door on his arrival at the Grand Hôtel had addressed him by that title.

" About what! " he repeated. " You have won more than three hundred thousand francs from me, and I was wondering if you intended to give me the slip."

The baron frowned, and this time he omitted the title of prince altogether. " It seems to me, sir, that according to our agreement, we were to play until one of us had won five hundred thousand francs," he said haughtily.

" That's true—but we ought to play every day."

" Possibly : but I'm very busy just now. I wrote to you explaining this, did I not? If you are at all uneasy, tear up the book in which the results of our games are noted, and that shall be the end of it. You will gain considerably by the operation."

Kami-Bey felt that the baron would not tolerate his arrogance, and so with more moderation he exclaimed: " It isn't strange that I've become suspicious. I'm so victimized on every side. Because I'm a foreigner and immensely rich, everybody fancies he has a right to plunder me. Men, women, hotel-keepers and merchants, all unite in defrauding me. If I buy pictures, they sell me vile daubs at fabulous prices. They ask ridiculous amounts for horses, and then give me worthless, worn-out animals. Everybody borrows money

from me—and I'm never repaid. I shall be ruined if
this sort of thing goes on much longer."

He had taken a seat, and the baron saw that he was
not likely to get rid of his guest very soon; so approaching Pascal he whispered: "You had better go
off, or you may miss Valorsay. And be careful, mind;
for he is exceedingly shrewd. Courage and good
luck!"

Courage! It was not necessary to recommend that
to Pascal. He who had triumphed over his despair in
the terrible hours, when he had reason to suppose that
Marguerite believed him guilty and had abandoned
him, could scarcely lack courage. While he was condemned to inaction, his mind had no doubt been assailed
by countless doubts and fears; but now that he knew
whom he was to attack—now that the decisive moment
had come, he was endowed with indomitable energy;
he had turned to bronze, and he felt sure that nothing
could disconcert or even trouble him in future. The
weapons he had to use were not at all to his taste, but
he had not been allowed a choice in the matter; and
since his enemies had decided on a warfare of duplicity,
he was resolved to surpass them in cunning, and vanquish them by deception.

So, while hastening to the Marquis de Valorsay's
residence, he took stock of his chances, and recapitu-
lated his resources, striving to foresee and remember
everything. Thus if he failed—for he admitted the
possibility of defeat, without believing in it—he would
have no cause to reproach himself. Only fools find
consolation in saying: "Who could have foreseen
that?" Great minds do foresee. And Pascal felt almost certain that he was fully prepared for any
emergency.

That morning, before leaving home, he had dressed with extreme care, realizing that the shabby clothes he had worn on his first visit to the Trigault mansion would not be appropriate on such an occasion as this. The baron's agent could scarcely have a poverty-stricken appearance, for contact with millionaires is supposed to procure wealth as surely as proximity to fire insures warmth. So he arrayed himself in a suit of black, which was neither too elegant nor too much worn, and donned a broad white necktie. He could see only one immediate, decisive chance against him. M. de Valorsay might possibly recognize him. He thought not, but he was not sure; and anxious on this account, he at first decided to disguise himself. However, on reflection, he concluded not to do so. An imperfect disguise would attract attention and awaken suspicion; and could he really disguise his physiognomy? He was certain he could not. Very few men are capable of doing so successfully, even after long experience. Only two or three detectives and half a dozen actors possess the art of really changing their lineaments. Thus after weighing the pros and cons, Pascal determined to present himself as he was at the marquis's house.

On approaching M. de Valorsay's residence in the Avenue des Champs Elysées, he slackened his pace. The mansion, which stood between a courtyard and a garden, was very large and handsome. The stables and carriage-house—really elegant structures—stood on either side of the courtyard, near the half-open gate of which five or six servants were amusing themselves by teasing a large dog. Pascal was just saying to himself that the coast was clear, and that he should incur no danger by going in, when he saw the servants step aside, the gate swing back, and M. de Coralth emerged, accompanied by a young, fair-haired man, whose mustaches were waxed and turned up in the most audacious fashion. They were arm in arm, and turned in the direction of the Arc de Triomphe. Pascal's heart thrilled with joy. " Fate favors me!" he said to himself. " If it hadn't been for Kami-Bey, who detained me a full quarter of an hour at Baron Trigault's, I should have found myself face to face with that miserable viscount, and then all would have been lost. But now I'm safe!"

It was with this encouraging thought that he approached the house.

"The marquis is very busy this morning," said the servant to whom Pascal addressed himself at the gate. "I doubt if he can see you." But when Pascal handed him one of his visiting cards, bearing the name of Maumejan, with this addition in pencil: " Who calls as the representative of Baron Trigault," the valet's face changed as if by enchantment. " Oh!" said he, "that's quite a different matter. If you come from Baron Trigault, you will be received with all the respect due to the Messiah. Come in. I will announce you myself."

Everything in M. de Valorsay's house, as at the baron's residence, indicated great wealth, and yet a close observer would have detected a difference. The luxury of the Rue de la Ville-l'Evéque was of a real and substantial character, which one did not find in the Avenue des Champs Elysées. Everything in the marquis's abode bore marks of the haste which mars the merest trifle produced at the present age. " Take a seat here, and I will see where the marquis is," said the servant, as he ushered Pascal into a large drawing-room. The apartment was elegantly furnished, but had somewhat lost its freshness; the carpet, which had once been a marvel of beauty, was stained in several places, and as the servants had not always been careful to keep the shutters closed, the sunlight had perceptibly faded the curtains. The attention of visitors was at once attracted by the number of gold and silver cups, vases, and statuettes scattered about on side-tables and chef-foniers. Each of these objects bore an inscription, setting forth that it had been won at such a race, in such a year, by such a horse, belonging to the Marquis de Valorsay. These were indeed the marquis's chief claims to glory, and had cost him at least half of the immense fortune he had inherited. However, Pascal did not take much interest in these trophies, so the time of waiting seemed long. " Valorsay is playing the diplomat," he thought. " He doesn't wish to appear to be anxious. Unfortunately, his servant has betrayed him."

At last the valet returned. "The marquis will see you now, monsieur," said he.

This summons affected Pascal's heart like the first roll of a drum beating the charge. But his coolness did not desert him. " Now is the decisive moment," he thought. " Heaven grant that he may not recognize me! " And with a firm step he followed the valet.

M. de Valorsay was seated in the apartment he usually occupied when he remained at home—a little smoking-room connected with his bedroom. He was to all intents busily engaged in examining some sporting journals. A bottle of Madeira and a partially filled glass stood near him. As the servant announced " Monsieur Mauméjan! " he looked up and his eyes met Pascal's. But his glance did not waver; not a muscle of his face moved; his countenance retained its usually cold and disdainful expression. Evidently he had not the slightest suspicion that the man he had tried to ruin—his mortal enemy—was standing there before him.

" M. Mauméjan," said he, "Baron Trigault's agent?"

" Yes, monsieur——"

" Pray be seated. I am just finishing here; I shall be at leisure in a moment."

Pascal took a chair. He had feared that he might not be able to retain his self-control when he found himself in the presence of the scoundrel who, after destroying his happiness, ruining his future, and depriving him of his honor—dearer than life itself—was at that moment endeavoring, by the most infamous manœuvres, to rob him of the woman he loved. " If my blood mounted to my brain," he had thought, " I should spring upon him and strangle him!" But no. His arteries did not throb more quickly; it was with perfect calmness—the calmness of a strong nature— that he stealthily watched M. de Valorsay. If he had seen him a week before he would have been startled by the change which the past few days had wrought in this brilliant nobleman's appearance. He was little more than a shadow of his former self. And seen at this hour, before placing himself in his valet's hands, before his premature decrepitude had been concealed by the artifices of the toilet, he was really frightful. His face was haggard, and his red and swollen eyelids betrayed a long-continued want of sleep.

The fact is, he had suffered terribly during the past week. A man may be a scapegrace and a spendthrift and may boast of it; he may have no principle and no conscience; he may be immoral, he may defy God and the devil, but it is nevertheless true that he suffers fearful anguish of mind when he is guilty, for the first time, of a positive crime, forbidden by the laws and punishable with the galleys. And who can say how many crimes the Marquis de Valorsay had committed since the day he provided his accomplice, the Viscount de Coralth, with those fatal cards? And apart from this there was something extremely appalling in the position of this ruined millionaire, who was contending desperately against his creditors for the vain appearance of splendor, with the despairing energy of a ship-wrecked mariner struggling for the possession of a floating spar. Had he not confessed to M. Fortunat that he had suffered the tortures of the damned in his struggle to maintain a show of wealth, while he was often without a penny in his pocket, and was ever subject to the pitiless surveillance of thirty servants? His agony, when he thought of his precarious condition, could only be compared to that of a miner, who, while ascending from the bowels of the earth, finds that the rope, upon which his life depends, is slowly parting strand by strand, and who asks himself, in terror, if the few threads that still remain unsevered will be strong enough to raise him to the mouth of the pit.

However, the moment which M. de Valorsay had asked for had lengthened into a quarter of an hour, and he had not yet finished his work. "What the devil is he doing?" wondered Pascal, who was following his enemy's slightest movement with eager curiosity.

Countless sporting newspapers were strewn over the table, the chairs, and the floor around the marquis, who took them up one after another, glanced rapidly through their columns, and threw them on the floor again, or placed them on a pile before him, first marking certain passages with a red pencil. At last, probably fearing that Pascal was growing impatient, he looked up and said:

"I am really very sorry to keep you waiting so long, but some one is waiting for this work to be completed."

"Oh! pray continue, Monsieur le Marquis," interrupted Pascal. "Strange to say, I have a little leisure at my command just now."

The marquis seemed to feel that it was necessary to make some remark in acknowledgment of this courtesy on his visitor's part, and so, as he continued his work, he condescended to explain its purpose. "I am playing the part of a commentator," he remarked. "I sold seven of my horses a few days ago, and the purchaser, before paying the stipulated price, naturally required an exact and authentic statement of each animal's performances. However, even this does not seem to have satisfied the gentleman, for he has now taken it into his head to ask for such copies of the sporting journals as record the victories or defeats of the animals he has purchased. A gentleman is not so exacting generally. It is true, however, that I have a foreigner to deal with —one of those half-civilized nabobs who come here every year to astonish the Parisians with their wealth and display, and who, by their idiotic prodigality, have so increased the price of everything that life has become well-nigh an impossibility to such of us as don't care to squander an entire fortune in a couple of years. These folks are the curse of Paris, for, with but few exceptions, they only use their millions to enrich notorious women, scoundrels, hotel-keepers, and jockeys."

Pascal at once thought of the foreigner, Kami-Bey, whom he had met at Baron Trigault's half an hour before, and who had complained so bitterly of having had worthless scrubs palmed off upon him when he fancied he had purchased valuable animals. " Kami-Bey must be this exacting purchaser," thought Pascal, " and it's probable that the marquis, desperately strait-ened as he is, has committed one of those frauds which lead their perpetrator to prison?" The surmise was by no means far-fetched, for in sporting matters, at least, there was cause to suspect Valorsay of great elasticity of conscience. Had he not already been ac-cused of defrauding Domingo's champions by a con-spiracy?

At last the marquis heaved a sigh of relief. " I've finished," he muttered, as he tied up the bundle of papers he had laid aside, and after ringing the bell, he said to the servant who answered the summons : " Here, take this package to Prince Kami at the Grand Hôtel."

Pascal's presentiments had not deceived him, and he said to himself : " This is a good thing to know. Before this evening I shall look into this affair a little."

A storm was decidedly gathering over the Marquis de Valorsay's head. Did he know it? Certainly he must have expected it. Still he had sworn to stand fast until the end. Besides, he would not concede that all was lost; and, like most great gamblers, he told himself that since he had so much at stake, he might reasonably hope to succeed. He rose, stretched him-self, as a man is apt to do after the conclusion of a tiresome task, and then, leaning against the mantel-shelf, he exclaimed : " Now, Monsieur Maumêjan, let us speak of the business that brings you here." His negligent attitude and his careless tone were admirably assumed, but a shrewd observer would not have been deceived by them, or by the indifferent manner in which he added: "You bring me some money from Baron Trigault?"

Pascal shook his head, as he replied: "I regret to say that I don't, Monsieur le Marquis."

This response had the same effect as a heavy rock falling upon M. de Valorsay's bald pate. He turned whiter than his linen, and even tottered, as if his lame leg, which was so much affected by sudden changes in the weather, had utterly refused all service. "What! you haven't—this is undoubtedly a joke."

"It is only too serious!"

"But I had the baron's word."

"Oh! his word!"

"I had his solemn promise."

"It is sometimes impossible to keep one's promises, sir."

The consequences of this disappointment must have been terrible, for the marquis could not maintain his self-control. Still he strove valiantly to conceal his emotion. He thought to himself that if he allowed this man to see what a terrible blow this really was, he would virtually confess his absolute ruin, and have to renounce the struggle, and own himself vanquished and lost. So, summoning all his energy, he mastered his emotion in some degree, and, instead of appearing desperate, succeeded in looking only irritated and annoyed. "In short," he resumed, angrily, "you have brought no money! I counted on a hundred thousand francs this morning. Nothing! This is kind on the baron's part! But probably he doesn't understand the embarrassing position in which he places me."

"Excuse me, Monsieur le Marquis, he understands it so well that, instead of informing you by a simple note, he sent me to acquaint you with his sincere regret.

When I left him an hour ago, he was really disconsolate. He was particularly anxious I should tell you
that it was not his fault. He counted upon the payment
of two very large amounts, and both of these have
failed him."

The marquis had now recovered a little from the
shock, though he was still very pale. He looked at
Pascal with evident distrust, for he knew with what
sweet excuses well-bred people envelope their refusals.
" So the baron is disconsolate," he remarked, in a tone
of perceptible irony.

" He is indeed ! "

" Poor baron ! Ah ! I pity him—pity him deeply."

As cold and as unmoved as a statue, Pascal seemed
quite unconscious of the effect of the message he had
brought—quite unconscious of Valorsay's sufferings
and self-constraint. " You think I am jesting, monsieur," he said, quietly, " but I assure you that the
baron is very short of money just now."

" Nonsense ! a man worth seven or eight millions of
francs."

" I should say ten millions, at least."

" Then the excuse is all the more absurd."

Pascal shrugged his shoulders disdainfully. " It
astonishes me, Monsieur le Marquis, to hear you speak
in this way. It is not the magnitude of a man's income
that constitutes affluence, but rather the way in which
that income is spent. In this foolish age, almost all
rich people are in arrears. What income does the
baron derive from his ten millions of francs? Not
more than five hundred thousand. A very handsome
fortune, no doubt, and I should be more than content
with it. But the baron gambles, and the baroness is
the most elegant—in other words, the most extravagant

—woman in Paris. They both of them love luxury, and their establishment is kept up in princely style. What are five hundred thousand francs under such circumstances as those? Their situation must be something like that of several millionaires of my acquaintance, who are obliged to take their silver to the pawnbroker's while waiting for their rents to fall due."

This excuse might not be true, but it was certainly a very plausible one. Had not a recent lawsuit revealed the fact that certain rich folks, who had an income of more than a hundred thousand francs a year, had kept a thieving coachman for six months, simply because, in all that time, they were not able to raise the eight hundred francs they owed him, and which must be paid before he was dismissed? M. de Valorsay knew this, but a terrible disquietude seized him. Had people begun to suspect *his* embarrassment? Had any rumor of it reached Baron Trigault's ears? This was what he wished to ascertain. "Let us understand each other, Monsieur Maumejan," said he; "the baron was unable to procure this money he had promised me to-day—but when will he let me have it?"

Pascal opened his eyes in pretended astonishment, and it was with an air of the utmost simplicity that he replied, "I concluded the baron would take no further action in the matter. I judged so from his parting words: 'It consoles me a little,' he said, 'to think that the Marquis de Valorsay is very rich and very well known, and that he has a dozen friends who will be delighted to do him this trifling service.'"

Until now, M. de Valorsay had cherished a hope that the loan was only delayed, and the certainty that the decision was final, crushed him. "My ruin's known," he thought, and feeling that his strength was deserting him, he poured out a brimming glass of Madeira, which he emptied at a single draught. The wine lent him fictitious energy. Fury mounted to his brain; he lost all control over himself, and springing up, with his face purple with rage, he exclaimed: " It's a shame! an infamous shame! and Trigault deserves to be severely punished. He has no business to keep a man in hot water for three days about such a trifle. If he had said 'No' in the first place, I should have made other arrangements, and I shouldn't now find myself in a dilemma from which I see no possible way of escape. No gentleman would have been guilty of such a contemptible act—no one but a shopkeeper or a thief would have stooped to such meanness! This is the result of admitting these ridiculous *parvenus* into society, just because they happen to have money."

It certainly hurt Pascal to hear these insults heaped upon the baron, and it hurt him all the more since they were entirely due to the course he had personally adopted.

However, a gesture, even a frown, might endanger the success of his undertaking, so he preserved an impassive countenance. "I must say that I don't understand your indignation, Monsieur le Marquis," he said, coldly. "I can see why you might feel annoyed, but why you should fly into a passion——"

"Ah! you don't know——" began M. de Valorsay, but he stopped short. It was time. The truth had almost escaped his lips.

"Know what?" inquired Pascal.

But the marquis was again upon his guard. "I have a debt that must be paid this evening, at all hazards— a sacred obligation—in short, a debt of honor."

"A debt of one hundred thousand francs?"

" No, it is only twenty-five thousand."

" Is it possible that a rich man like you can be troubled about such a trifling sum, which any one would lend you? "

M. de Valorsay interrupted him with a contemptuous sneer. " Didn't you just tell me that we were living in an age when no one has any money except those who are in business? The richest of my friends have only enough for themselves, even if they have enough. The time of old stockings, stuffed full of savings, is past! Shall I apply to a banker? He would ask two days for reflection, and he would require the names of two or three of my friends on the note. If I go to my notary, there will be endless forms to be gone through, and remonstrances without number."

For a moment or more already, Pascal had been moving about uneasily on his chair, like a man who is waiting for an opportunity to make a suggestion, and as soon as M. de Valorsay paused to take breath, he exclaimed: " Upon my word! if I dared——"

" Well? "

" I would offer to obtain you these twenty-five thousand francs."

" You? "

" Yes, I."

" Before six o'clock this evening? "

" Certainly."

A glass of ice-water presented to a parched traveller while journeying over the desert sands of Sahara could not impart greater relief and delight than the marquis experienced on hearing Pascal's offer. He literally felt that he was restored to life.

For ruin was inevitable if he did not succeed in obtaining twenty-five thousand francs that day. If he could procure that amount he might obtain a momentary respite, and to gain time was the main thing. Moreover, the offer was a sufficient proof that his financial difficulties were not known. " Ah! I have had a fortunate escape," he thought. " What if I had revealed the truth ! "

But he was careful to conceal the secret joy that filled his heart. He feared lest he might say " Yes " too quickly, so betray his secret, and place himself at the mercy of the baron's envoy. " I would willingly accept your offer," he exclaimed, " if——"

" If what? "

" Would it be proper for me, after the baron has treated me in such a contemptible manner, to have any dealings with one of his subordinates? "

Pascal protested vigorously. " Allow me to say," he exclaimed, " that I am not any one's subordinate. Trigault is my client, like thirty or forty others—nothing more. He employs me in certain difficult and delicate negotiations, which I conduct to the best of my ability. He pays me, and we are each of us perfectly independent of the other."

From the look which Valorsay gave Pascal, one would have sworn that he suspected who his visitor really was. But such was not the case. It was simply this: a strange, but by no means impossible, idea had flashed through the marquis's mind—" Oh! " thought he, " this unknown party with whom Maumejan offers to negotiate the loan, is probably none other than the baron himself. That worthy gambler has invented this ingenious method of obliging me so as to extort a rate of interest which he would not dare to demand openly. And why not? There have been plenty of such instances. Isn't it a well-known fact that the N——

Brothers, the most rigidly honest financiers in the world, have never under any circumstances directly obliged one of their friends? If their own father, of whom they always speak with the greatest veneration, asked them to lend him fifty francs for a month, they would say to him as they do to every one else: 'We are rather cramped just now; but see that rascal B——.' And that rascal B——, who is the most pliable tool in existence, will, providing father N—— offers unquestionable security, lend the old gentleman his son's money at from twelve to fifteen per cent. interest, plus a small commission."

These ideas and recollections were of considerable assistance in restoring Valorsay's composure. "Enough said, then," he answered, lightly. "I accept with pleasure. But——"

"Ah! so there is a but!"

"There is always one. I must warn you that it will be difficult for me to repay this loan in less than two months."

This, then, was the time he thought necessary for the accomplishment of his designs.

"That does not matter," replied Pascal, "and even if you desire a longer delay——"

"That will be unnecessary, thank you! But there is one thing more."

"What is that?"

"What will this negotiation cost me?"

Pascal had expected this question, and he had prepared a reply which was in perfect keeping with the spirit of the *rôle* he had assumed. "I shall charge you the ordinary rates," he answered, "six per cent. interest, plus one-and-a-half per cent. commission."

"Bah!"

" Plus the remuneration for my trouble and services."

" And what remuneration will satisfy you? "

" One thousand francs. Is it too much? "

If the marquis had retained the shadow of a doubt, it vanished now. " Ah! " he sneered, " that strikes me as a very liberal compensation for your services! "

But he would gladly have recalled the sneer when he saw how the agent received it. Pascal drew up his head with a deeply injured air, and remarked in the chilling tone of a person who is strongly tempted to retract his word, " Then there is nothing more to be said, M. le Marquis; and since you find the conditions onerous——"

" I did not say so," interrupted M. de Valorsay, quickly—" I did not even think it! "

This gave Pascal an opportunity to present his programme, and he availed himself of it. " Others may pretend to oblige people merely from motives of friendship," he remarked. " But I am more honest. If I do anything in the way of business, I expect to be paid for it; and I vary my terms according to my clients' need. It would be impossible to have a fixed price for services like mine. When, on two different occasions, I saved a gentleman of your acquaintance from bankruptcy, I asked ten thousand francs the first time, and fifteen thousand the second. Was that an exaggerated estimate of my services? I might boast with truth that I once assured the marriage of a brilliant viscount by keeping his creditors quiet while his courtship was in progress. The day after the wedding he paid me twenty thousand francs. Didn't he owe them to me? If, instead of being a trifle short of money, you happened to be ruined, I should not ask you merely for a thousand francs. I should study your position, and fix my terms according to the magnitude of the peril from which I rescued you."

There was not a sentence, not a word of this cynical explanation which had not been carefully studied beforehand. There was not an expression which was not a tempting bait to the marquis's evil instincts. But M de Valorsay made no sign. "I see that you are a shrewd man, Monsieur Mauméjan," said he, "and if I am ever in difficulty I shall apply to you."

Pascal bowed with an air of assumed modesty; but he was inwardly jubilant, for he felt that his enemy would certainly fall into the trap which had been set for him. "And now, when shall I have this money?" inquired the marquis.

"By four o'clock."

"And I need fear no disappointment as in the baron's case?"

"Certainly not. What interest would M. Trigault have in lending you a hundred thousand francs? None whatever. With me it is quite a different thing. The profit I'm to realize is your security. In business matters distrust your friends. Apply to usurers rather than to them. Question people who are in difficulties, and ninety-five out of a hundred will tell you that their worst troubles have been caused by those who called themselves their best friends."

He had risen to take leave, when the door of the smoking-room opened, and a servant appeared and said in an undertone: "Madame Léon is in the drawing-room with Dr. Jodon. They wish to see you, monsieur."

Though Pascal had armed himself well against any unexpected mischance, he changed color on hearing the name of the worthy housekeeper. "All is lost if this creature sees and recognizes me!" he thought.

Fortunately the marquis was too much engrossed in his own affairs to note the momentary agitation of Baron Trigault's envoy. " It is strange that I can't have five minutes' peace and quietness," he said. " I told you that I was at home to no one."

" But——"

" Enough! Let the lady and gentleman wait."

The servant withdrew.

The thought of passing out through the drawing-room filled Pascal with consternation. How could he hope to escape Madame Léon's keen eyes? Fortunately M. de Valorsay came to his relief, for as Pascal was about to open the same door by which he had entered, the marquis exclaimed: " Not that way! Pass out here —this is the shortest way."

And leading him through his bedroom the marquis conducted him to the staircase, where he even feigned to offer him his hand, saying: " A speedy return, dear M. Mauméjan."

It is not at the moment of peril that people endure the worst agony; it is afterward, when they have escaped it. As he went down the staircase, Pascal wiped the cold sweat from his forehead. " Ah! it was a narrow escape! " he exclaimed, under his breath.

He felt proud of the manner in which he had sustained a part so repugnant to his nature. He was amazed to find that he could utter falsehoods with such a calm, unblushing face—he was astonished at his own audacity. And what a success he had achieved! He felt certain that he had just slipped round M. de Valorsay's neck the noose which would strangle him later on. Still he was considerably disturbed by Madame Léon's visit to the marquis. " What is she doing here

with this physician? " he asked himself again and again.
" Who is this man? What new piece of infamy are
they plotting to require his services? " One of those
presentiments which are prompted by the logic of
events, told him that this physician had been, or would
be, one of the actors in the vile conspiracy of which he
and Mademoiselle Marguerite were the victims. But
he had no leisure to devote to the solution of this
enigma. Time was flying, and before returning to the
marquis's house he must find out what had aroused the
suspicions of the purchaser of those horses, the biog-
raphies of which had been so rigidly exacted. Through
the baron, he might hope to obtain an interview with
Kami-Bey—and so it was to the baron's house that
Pascal directed his steps.

After the more than cordial reception which the
baron had granted him that morning, it was quite natural that the servants should receive him as a friend
of the household. They would scarcely allow him to
explain what he desired. It was the pompous head
valet in person who ushered him into one of the small
reception-rooms, exclaiming: " The baron's engaged,
but I'm sure he would be annoyed if he failed to see
you; and I will inform him at once."

A moment later, the baron entered quite breathless
from his hurried descent of the staircase. " Ah! you
have been successful," he exclaimed, on seeing Pascal's
face.

" Everything is progressing as favorably as I could
wish, Monsieur le Baron, but I must speak with that
foreigner whom I met here this morning."

" Kami-Bey? "

" Yes." And in a few words, Pascal explained the
situation.

"Providence is certainly on our side," said the baron, thoughtfully. "Kami is still here."

"Is it possible?"

"It's a fact. Did you think it would be easy to get rid of this confounded Turk! He invited himself to breakfast without the slightest ceremony, and would give me no peace until I promised to play with him for two hours. I was closeted with him, cards in hand, when they told me you were here. Come, we'll go and question him."

They found the interesting foreigner in a savage mood. He had been winning when the servant came for the baron, and he feared that an interruption would change the luck. "What the devil took you away?" he exclaimed, with that coarseness of manner which was habitual with him, and which the flatterers around him styled "form." "A man should no more be disturbed when he's playing than when he's eating."

"Come, come, prince," said the baron, good-naturedly, "don't be angry, and I'll give you three hours instead of two. But I have a favor to ask of you."

The foreigner at once thrust his hand into his pocket, with such a natural gesture, that neither the baron nor Pascal could repress a smile, and he himself understanding the cause of their merriment broke into a hearty laugh. "It's purely from force of habit," said he. "Ah! since I've been in Paris—— But what do you wish?"

The baron sat down, and gravely replied: "You told us scarcely an hour ago that you had been cheated in the purchase of some horses."

"Cheated! it was worse than highway robbery."

"Would it be indiscreet to ask you by whom you have been defrauded?"

Kami-Bey's purple cheeks became a trifle pale. " Hum ! " said he, in an altered tone of voice, " that is a delicate question. My defrauder appears to be a dangerous fellow—a duellist—and if I disclose his knavery, he is quite capable of picking a quarrel with me—not that I am afraid of him, I assure you, but my principles don't allow me to fight. When a man has an income of a million, he doesn't care to expose himself to the dangers of a duel."

" But, prince, in France folks don't do a scoundrel the honor to cross swords with him."

" That's just what my steward, who is a Frenchman, told me; but no matter. Besides, I am not sufficiently sure of the man's guilt to noise it abroad. I have no positive proofs as yet."

He was evidently terribly frightened, and the first thing to be done was to reassure him. " Come," insisted the baron, " tell us the man's name. This gentleman here "—pointing to Pascal—" is one of my most esteemed friends. I will answer for him as I would for myself; and we will swear upon our honor not to reveal the secret we ask you for, without your permission."

" Truly ? "

" You have our word of honor," replied both the baron and Pascal in a breath.

After casting a half-frightened glance around him, the worthy Turk seemed to gather courage. But no ! He deliberated some time, and then rejoined: " Really, I'm not sufficiently convinced of the accuracy of my suspicions to incur the risk of accusing a man who belongs in the very best society; a man who is very rich and very highly respected, and who would tolerate no imputations upon his character."

It was plain that he would not speak. The baron shrugged his shoulders, but Pascal stepped bravely forward. "Then I will tell you, prince," he said, "the name that you are determined to hide from us."

"Oh!"

"But you must allow me to remark that the baron and myself retract the promise we made you just now."

"Naturally."

"Then, your defrauder is the Marquis de Valorsay!"

If Kami-Bey had seen an emissary of his sovereign enter the room carrying the fatal bow-string he would not have seemed more terror-stricken. He sprang nervously on to his short, fat legs, his eyes wildly dilating and his hands fluttering despairingly. "Don't speak so loud! don't speak so loud!" he exclaimed, imploringly.

As he did not even attempt to deny it, the truth of the assertion might be taken for granted. But Pascal was not content with this. "Now that we know the fact, I hope, Prince, that you will be sufficiently obliging to tell us how it all happened," he remarked.

Poor Kami. He was in despair. "Alas!" he replied, reluctantly, "nothing could be more simple. I wanted to set up a racing stable. Not that I care much for sport. I can scarcely distinguish a horse from a mule—but morning and evening, everybody says to me: 'Prince, a man like you ought to make your name celebrated on the turf.' Besides I never open a paper without reading: 'Such a man ought to be a patron of the noblest of sports.' At last, I said to myself: 'Yes, they are right. I ought to take part in racing.' So I began to look about for some horses. I had purchased several, when the Marquis de Valorsay proposed to sell me some of his, some that were very well known, and that had—so he assured me—won at least ten times the amount they had cost him. I accepted his offer, and visited his stables, where I selected seven of his best horses and paid for them; and I paid a good round price, I assure you. Now comes the knavery. He has not given me the horses I purchased. The real animals, the valuable ones—have been sold in England under false names, and although the horses sent to me may be like the others in appearance, they are really only common animals, wanting both in blood and speed."

Pascal and the baron exchanged astonished glances. It must be confessed that frauds of every description are common enough in the racing world, and a great deal of dishonest manœuvring results from greed for gain united with the fever of gambling. But never before had any one been accused of such an audacious and impudent piece of rascality as that which Kami-Bey imputed to Valorsay.

"How did you fail to discover this at the outset, prince?" inquired Pascal in an incredulous tone.

"Because my time was so much occupied."

"But your servants?"

"Ah! that's another thing. I shouldn't be at all surprised if it were proved that the man who has charge of my stables had been bribed by the marquis."

"Then, how were your suspicions aroused?"

"It was only by the merest chance. A jockey whom I thought of employing had often ridden one of the animals which I fancied myself the owner of. Naturally, I showed him the horse, but he had no sooner set eyes on it than he exclaimed: 'That the horse! Never! You've been cheated, prince!' Then we examined the others, and the fraud became apparent."

Knowing Kami's character better than Pascal, the baron had good reason to distrust the accuracy of these statements. For the Turkish millionaire's superb contempt of money was only affected. Vanity alone unloosed his purse-strings. He was quite capable of presenting Jenny Fancy with a necklace costing five-and-twenty thousand francs for the sake of seeing his generosity recorded in the *Gaulois* or the *Figaro* the next day; but he would refuse to give a trifle to the mother of a starving family. Besides, it was his ambition to be regarded as the most swindled man in Europe. But though he was shamefully imposed upon, it was not voluntarily—for there was a strong dose of Arabian avarice and distrust in his composition.

"Frankly, prince," said the baron, "your story sounds like one of the wild legends of your native land. Valorsay is certainly no fool. How is it possible that he could have been guilty of so gross a fraud—a fraud which might be, which could not fail to be discovered in twenty-four hours—and which, once proven, would dishonor him forever?"

"Before perpetrating such a piece of deception upon any one else, he would have thought twice; but upon me it's different. Isn't it an established fact that a person incurs no risk in robbing Kami-Bey?"

"Had I been in your place I should have quietly instituted an investigation."

"What good would that have done? Besides, the sale was only conditional, and took place under the seal of secrecy. The marquis reserved the right to take his horses back on payment of a stipulated sum, and the time he was to have for consideration only expired on the day before yesterday."

"Eh! why didn't you tell us that at first?" cried the baron.

The marquis's rascality was now easily explained. Finding himself in a desperate strait, and feeling that his salvation was certain if he could only gain a little time, he had yielded to temptation, saying to himself, like unfaithful cashiers when they first appropriate their employers' money: "I will pay it back, and no one will ever know it!" However, when the day of settlement came he had found himself in as deplorable a plight as on the day of the robbery, and he had been compelled to yield to the force of circumstances.

"And what do you intend to do, prince?" asked Pascal.

"Ah! I am still in doubt. I have compelled the marquis to give me the papers in which the exploits of these horses are recorded. These statements will be of service in case of a law-suit. But shall I or shall I not enter a complaint against him? If it were a mere question of money I should let the matter drop; but he has defrauded and deceived me so outrageously that it annoys me. On the other hand, to confess that he has cheated me in this fashion would cover me with ridicule. Besides, the man is a dangerous enemy. And what would become of me if I happened to side against him? I should be compelled to leave Paris. Ah! I'd give ten thousand francs to any one who'd settle this cursed affair for me!"

His perplexity was so great, and his anger so intense, for that once he tore off his eternal fez and flung it on to the table, swearing like a drayman. However, controlling himself at last, he exclaimed in a tone of assumed indifference: "No matter, there's been enough said on this subject for one day—I'm here to play—

so let us begin, baron. For we are wasting precious time, as you so often remark."

Pascal had nothing more to learn; so he shook hands with the baron, made an appointment with him for the same evening, and went away.

It was only half-past two; a good hour and a half remained at his disposal. "I will profit by this opportunity to eat something," he thought; a sudden faintness reminding him that he had taken nothing but a cup of chocolate that day. Thereupon perceiving a *café* near by, he entered it, ordered breakfast, and lingered there until it was time to return to the Marquis de Valorsay's. He would have gone there before the appointed time if he had merely listened to the promptings of his impatience, so thoroughly was he persuaded that this second interview would be decisive. But prudence advised him not to expose himself to the danger of an encounter with Madame Léon and Dr. Jodon.

"Well! Monsieur Mauméjan," cried the marquis, as soon as Pascal made his appearance. He had been counting the seconds with intense anxiety, as his tone of voice unmistakably revealed.

In reply Pascal gravely drew from his pocket twenty-four bank-notes, of a thousand francs each, and he placed them upon the table, saying: "Here is the amount, Monsieur le Marquis. I have, of course, deducted my commission. Now, if you will write and sign a note for twenty-five thousand francs, payable to my order two months hence, our business for to-day will be concluded."

M. de Valorsay's hand trembled nervously as he penned the desired note, for, until the very last moment, he had doubted the promises of this unknown agent who had made his appearance so opportunely. Then, when the document was signed, he carelessly slipped the money into a drawer and exclaimed: "So here's the needful to pay my debt of honor; but my embarrassment is none the less great. These twenty-four thousand francs won't take the place of the hundred thousand which Baron Trigault promised me."

And, as Pascal made no reply, the marquis began a desultory tramp up and down the smoking-room. He was very pale, his brows were knit; he looked like a man who was meditating a decisive step, and who was calculating the consequences. But having no time to waste in hesitation, he soon paused in front of Pascal, and exclaimed: "Since you have just lent me twenty-four thousand francs, why won't you lend me the rest?"

But Pascal shook his head. "One risks nothing by advancing twenty-five thousand francs to a person in your position, Monsieur le Marquis. Whatever happens, such a sum as that can always be gathered from the wreck. But double or triple the amount! The deuce! that requires reflection, and I must understand the situation thoroughly."

"And if I told you that I am—almost ruined, what would you reply?"

"I shouldn't be so very much surprised."

M. de Valorsay had now gone too far to draw back. "Ah, well!" he resumed, "the truth is this—my affairs are terribly involved."

"The devil! You should have told me that sooner."

"Wait; I am about to retrieve my fortune—to make it even larger than it has ever been. I am on the point of contracting a marriage which will make me one of the richest men in Paris; but I must have a little time to bring the affair to a successful termination, and I need money—and my creditors are pressing me unmercifully. You told me this morning that you once assisted a man who was in a similar position. Will you help me? You can set your own price on your services."

More easily overcome by joy than by sorrow, Pascal almost betrayed himself. He had attained his object. Still, he succeeded in conquering his emotion, and it was in a perfectly calm voice that he replied: " I can promise nothing until I understand the situation, Monsieur le Marquis. Will you explain it to me? I am listening."

XIV.

IT was nearly midnight when M. Wilkie left the Hôtel d'Argelès after the terrible scene in which he had revealed his true character. On seeing him pass out with haggard eyes, colorless lips, and disordered clothing, the servants gathered in the vestibule took him at first for another of those ruined gamblers who not unfrequently left the house with despair in their hearts.

"Another fellow who's had bad luck!" they remarked sneeringly to one another.

"No doubt about that. He is pretty effectually used up, judging from appearances," one of them remarked.

It was not until some moments later that they learned a portion of the truth through the servants who had been on duty upstairs, and who now ran down in great terror, crying that Madame d'Argelès was dying, and that a physician must be summoned at once.

M. Wilkie was already far away, hastening up the

boulevard with an agile step. Any one else would have been overcome with shame and sorrow—would have been frightened by the thought of what he had done, and have striven to find some way to conceal his disgrace; but he, not in the least. In this frightful crisis, he was only conscious of one fact—that just as he raised his hand to strike Madame Lia d'Argelès, his mother, a big, burly individual had burst into the room, like a bombshell, caught him by the throat, forced him upon his knees, and compelled him to ask the lady's pardon. He, Wilkie, to be humiliated in this style! He would never endure that. This was an affront he could not swallow, one of those insults that cry out for vengeance and for blood. "Ah! the great brute shall pay for it," he repeated, again and again, grinding his teeth. And if he hastened up the boulevard, it was only because he hoped to meet his two chosen friends, M. Costard and the Viscount de Serpillon, the co-proprietors of Pompier de Nanterre.

For he intended to place his outraged honor in their care. They should be his seconds, and present his demand for satisfaction to the man who had insulted him. A duel was the only thing that could appease his furious anger and heal his wounded pride. And a great scandal, which he would be the hero of, was not without a certain charm for him. What a glorious chance to win notoriety at an epoch when newspapers have become public laundries, in which every one washes his soiled linen and dries it in the glare of publicity! He saw his already remarkable reputation enhanced by the interest that always attaches to people who are talked about, and he could hear in advance the flattering whisper which would greet his appearance everywhere: "You see that young man?—he is the hero of that famous adventure," etc. Moreover, he was already twisting and turning the terms of the notice which his seconds must have inserted in the *Figaro*, hesitating between two or three equally startling beginnings: "Another famous duel," or "Yesterday, after a scandalous scene, an encounter," etc., etc.

Unfortunately, he did not meet either M. Costard or the Viscount de Serpillon. Strange to say, they were not in any of the *cafés*, where the flower of French chivalry usually congregates, in the company of golden-haired young women, from nine in the evening until one o'clock in the morning. This disappointment grieved M. Wilkie sorely, although he derived some benefit from it, for his disordered attire attracted attention at each place he entered, and acquaintances eagerly inquired: "Where have you come from, and what has happened to you?" Whereupon he replied with an air of profound secrecy: "Pray don't speak of it. A shocking affair! If it were noised abroad I should be inconsolable."

At last the *cafés* began to close, and promenaders became rare. M. Wilkie, much to his regret, was obliged to go home. When he had locked his door and donned his dressing-gown, he sat down to think over the events of the day, and collect his scattered wits. What most troubled and disquieted him was not the condition in which he had left Madame Lia d'Argelès, his mother, who was, perhaps, dying, through his fault! It was not the terrible sacrifice that this poor woman had made for him in a transport of maternal love! It was not the thought of the source from which the money he had squandered for so many years had been derived. No, M. Wilkie was quite above such paltry considerations—good enough for commonplace and antiquated people.

"He was too clever for that. Ah! yes. He had a stronger stomach, and was up with the times!" If he were sorely vexed in spirit it was because he thought that the immense property which he had believed his own had slipped, perhaps for ever, from his grasp. For rising threateningly between the Chalusse millions and himself, he pictured the form of his father, this man whom he did not know, but whose very name had made Madame d'Argelès shudder.

M. Wilkie was seized with terror when he looked his actual situation in the face. What was to become of him? He was certain that Madame d'Argelès would not give him another sou. She could not—he recognized that fact. His intelligence was equal to that. On the other hand, if he ever obtained anything from the count's estate, which was more than doubtful, would he not be obliged to wait a long time for it? Yes, in all probability such would be the case. Then how should he live, how would he be able to obtain food in the meantime? His despair was so poignant that tears came to his eyes; and he bitterly deplored the step he had taken. Yes, he actually sighed for the past; he longed to live over again the very years in which he had so often complained of his destiny. Then, though not a millionaire by any means, he at least wanted for nothing. Every quarter-day a very considerable allowance was promptly paid him, and, in great emergencies, he could apply to Mr. Patterson, who always sent a favorable answer if not drawn upon too heavily. Yes, he sighed for that time! Ah! if he had only then realized how fortunate he was! Had he not been one of the most opulent members of the society in which he moved? Had he not been flattered and admired more than any of his companions? Had he not found the most exquisite happiness in his part ownership of Pompier de Nanterre!

Now, what remained? Nothing, save anxiety concerning the future, and all sorts of uncertainties and terrors! What a mistake! What a blunder he had made! Ah! if he could only begin again. He sincerely wished that the great adversary of mankind had the Viscount de Coralth in his clutches. For, in his despair, it was the once dear viscount that he blamed, accused, and cursed.

He was in this ungrateful frame of mind when a loud, almost savage, ring came at his door. As his servant slept in an attic upstairs, Wilkie was quite alone in his rooms, so he took the lamp and went to open the door himself. At this hour of the night, the visitor could only be M. Costard or the Viscount de Serpillon, or perhaps both of them. "They have heard that I was looking for them, and so they have hastened here," he thought.

But he was mistaken. The visitor was neither of these gentlemen, but M. Ferdinand de Coralth in person. Prudence had compelled the viscount to leave Madame d'Argelès's card-party one of the last, but as soon as he was out of the house he had rushed to the Marquis de Valorsay's to hold a conference with him, far from suspecting that he was followed, and that an auxiliary of Pascal Ferailleur and Mademoiselle Marguerite was even then waiting for him below— an enemy as formidable as he was humble—Victor Chupin.

At sight of the man who had so long been his model —the friend who had advised what he styled his blunder—Wilkie was so surprised that he almost dropped his lamp. Then as his wrath kindled, "Ah! so it's you!" he exclaimed, angrily, "You come at a good time!"

But M. de Coralth was too much exasperated to notice Wilkie's strange greeting. Seizing him roughly by the arm, and closing the door with a kick, he dragged Wilkie back into the little drawing-room. "Yes, it's I," he said, curtly. "It's I—come to inquire if you have gone mad?"

"Viscount!"

"I can find no other explanation of your conduct! What! You choose Madame d'Argelès's reception day, and an hour when there are fifty guests in her drawing-room to present yourself!"

"Ah, well! it wasn't from choice. I had been there twice before, and had the doors shut in my face."

"You ought to have gone back ten times, a hundred times, a thousand times, rather than have accomplished such an idiotic prank as this."

"Excuse me."

"What did I recommend? Prudence, calmness and moderation, persuasive gentleness, sentiments of the loftiest nature, tenderness, a shower of tears——"

"Possibly, but——"

"But instead of that, you fall upon this woman like a thunderbolt, and set the whole household in the wildest commotion. What could you be thinking of, to make such an absurd and frightful scene? For you howled and shrieked like a street hawker, and we could hear you in the drawing-room. If all is not irretrievably lost, there must be a special Providence for the benefit of fools!"

In his dismay, Wilkie endeavored to falter some excuses, but he was only able to begin a few sentences which died away, uncompleted in his throat. The vio-

lence shown by M. de Coralth, who was usually as cold
and as polished as marble, quieted his own wrath.
Still toward the last he felt disposed to rebel against
the insults that were being heaped upon him. "Do
you know, viscount, that I begin to think this very
strange," he exclaimed. "If any one else had led me
into such a scrape, I should have called him to account
in double-quick time."

M. de Coralth shrugged his shoulders with an air
of contempt, and threateningly replied: "Understand,
once for all, that you had better not attempt to bully
me! Now, tell me what passed between your mother
and yourself?"

"First I should like——"

"Dash it all! Do you suppose that I intend to remain here all night? Tell me what occurred, and be
quick about it. And try to speak the truth."

It was one of M. Wilkie's greatest boasts that he
had an indomitable will—an iron nature. But the viscount exercised powerful influence over him, and, to
tell the truth, inspired him with a form of emotion
which was nearly akin to fear. Moreover, a glimmer
of reason had at last penetrated his befogged brain:
he saw that M. de Coralth was right—that he had
acted like a fool, and that, if he hoped to escape from
the dangers that threatened him, he must take the advice of more experienced men than himself. So, ceas-
ing his recriminations, he began to describe what he
styled his explanation with Madame d'Argelès. All
went well at first; for he dared not misrepresent the
facts.

But when he came to the intervention of the man
who had prevented him from striking his mother, he
turned crimson, and rage again filled his heart. "I'm

sorry I let myself get into such a mess!" he exclaimed.
"You should have seen my condition. My shirt-collar
was torn, and my cravat hung in tatters. He was much
stronger than I—the contemptible scoundrel!—ah! if it
hadn't been for that—— But I shall have my revenge.
Yes, he shall learn that he can't trample a man under
foot with impunity. To-morrow two of my friends
will call upon him; and if he refuses to apologize or
to give me satisfaction, I'll cane him."

It was evident enough that M. de Coralth had to exercise considerable constraint to listen to these fine
projects. "I must warn you that you ought to speak
in other terms of an honorable and honored gentleman,"
he interrupted, at last.

"Eh! what! You know him then?"

"Yes, Madame d'Argelès's defender is Baron
Trigault."

M. Wilkie's heart bounded with joy, as he heard this
name. "Ah! this is capital!" he exclaimed. "What!
So it was Baron Trigault—the noted gambler—who
owns such a magnificent house in the Rue de la Ville
l'Evéque, the husband of that extremely stylish lady,
that notorious *cocotte*——"

The viscount sprang from his chair, and interrupting
M. Wilkie: "I advise you, for the sake of your own
safety," he said, measuring his words to give them
greater weight, "never to mention the Baroness
Trigault's name except in terms of the most profound
respect."

There was no misunderstanding M. de Coralth's tone,
and his glance said plainly that he would not allow
much time to pass before putting his threat into execution. Having always lived in a lower circle to that
in which the baroness sparkled with such lively bril-

liancy, M. Wilkie was ignorant of the reasons that induced his distinguished friend to defend her so warmly; but he *did* understand that it would be highly imprudent to insist, or even to discuss the matter. So, in his most persuasive manner, he resumed: "Let us say no more about the wife, but give our attention to the husband. So it was the baron who insulted me! A duel with him—what good luck! Well! he may sleep in peace to-night, but as soon as he is up in the morning he will find Costard and Serpillon on hand. Serpillon has not an equal as a second. First, he knows the best places for a meeting; then he lends the combatants weapons when they have none; he procures a physician; and he is on excellent terms with the journalists, who publish reports of these encounters."

The viscount had never had a very exalted opinion of Wilkie's intelligence, but now he was amazed to see how greatly he had overestimated it. "Enough of such foolishness," he interrupted, curtly. "This duel will never take place."

"I should like to know who will prevent it?"

"I will, if you persist in such an absurd idea. You ought to have sense enough to know that the baron would kick Serpillon out of the house, and that you would only cover yourself with ridicule. So, between your duel and my help make your choice, and quickly."

The prospect of sending his seconds to demand satisfaction from Baron Trigault was certainly a very attractive one. But, on the other hand, Wilkie could not afford to dispense with M. de Coralth's services. "But the baron has insulted me," he urged.

"Well, you can demand satisfaction when you obtain possession of your property; but the least scandal now would spoil your last chances."

"I will abandon the project, then," sighed Wilkie, despondently; "but pray advise me. What do you think of my situation?"

M. de Coralth seemed to consider a moment, and then gravely replied: "I think that, *unassisted,* you have no chance whatever. You have no standing, no influential connections, no position—you are not even a Frenchman."

"Alas! that is precisely what I have said to myself."

"Still, I am convinced that with some assistance you might overcome your mother's resistance, and even your father's pretentions."

"Yes, but where could I find protectors?"

The viscount's gravity seemed to increase. "Listen to me," said he; "I will do for you what I would not do for any one else. I will endeavor to interest in your cause one of my friends, who is all powerful by reason of his name, his fortune, and his connections—the Marquis de Valorsay, in fact."

"The one who is so well known upon the turf?"

"The same."

"And you will introduce me to him?"

"Yes. Be ready to-morrow at eleven o'clock, and I will call for you and take you to his house. If he interests himself in your cause, it is as good as gained." And as his companion overwhelmed him with thanks, he rose, and said: "I must go now. No more foolishness, and be ready to-morrow at the appointed time."

Thanks to the surprising mutability of temper which was the most striking characteristic of his nature, M. Wilkie was already consoled for his blunder.

He had received M. de Coralth as an enemy; but he now escorted him to the door with every obsequious attention—in fact, just as if he looked upon him as his preserver. A word which the viscount had dropped during the conversation had considerably helped to bring about this sudden revulsion of feelings. "You cannot fail to understand that if the Marquis de Valorsay espouses your cause, you will want for nothing. And if a lawsuit is unavoidable, he will be perfectly willing to advance the necessary funds." How could M. Wilkie lack confidence after that? The brightest hopes, the most ecstatic visions had succeeded the gloomy forebodings of a few hours before. The mere thought of being presented to M. de Valorsay, a noble-man celebrated for his adventures, his horses, and his fortune, more than sufficed to make him forget his troubles. What rapture to become that illustrious nobleman's acquaintance, perhaps his friend! To move in the same orbit as this star of the first magnitude which would inevitably cast some of its lustre upon him! Now he would be a somebody in the world. He felt that he had grown a head taller, and Heaven only knows with what disdain poor Costard and Serpillon would have been received had they chanced to present themselves at that moment.

It is needless to say that Wilkie dressed with infinite care on the following morning, no doubt in the hope of making a conquest of the marquis at first sight. He tried his best to solve the problem of appearing at the same time most *recherché* but at ease, excessively elegant and yet unostentatious; and he devoted himself to the task so unreservedly that he lost all conception of the flight of time: so that on seeing M. de Coralth enter his rooms, he exclaimed in unfeigned astonish-ment: "You here already?"

It seemed to him that barely five minutes had elapsed since he took his place before the looking-glass to study attitudes and gestures, with a new and elegant mode of bowing and sitting down, like an actor practising the effects which are to win him applause.

"Why do you say ' already?' " replied the viscount. "I am a quarter of an hour behind time. Are you not ready? "

"Yes, certainly."

"Let us start at once, then; my brougham is outside."

The drive was a silent one. M. Ferdinand de Coralth, whose smooth white skin would ordinarily have excited the envy of a young girl, did not look like himself. His face was swollen and covered with blotches, and there were dark blue circles round his eyes. He seemed, moreover, to be in a most savage humor. "He hasn't had sleep enough," thought M. Wilkie, with his usual discernment; "he hasn't a bronze constitution like myself."

M. Wilkie himself was insensible to fatigue, and although he had not closed his eyes the previous night, he only felt that nervous trepidation which invariably attacks *débutants,* and makes the throat so marvellously dry. For the first, and probably the last time in his life, M. Wilkie distrusted his own powers, and feared that he was not "quite up to the mark," as he elegantly expressed it.

The sight of the Marquis de Valorsay's handsome mansion was not likely to restore his assurance. When he entered the courtyard, where the master's mail-phaeton stood in waiting; when through the open doors of the handsome stables he espied the many valuable horses neighing in their stalls, and the numerous carriages shrouded in linen covers; when he counted the valets on duty in the vestibule, and when he ascended the staircase behind a lackey attired in a black dress-coat, and as serious in mien as a notary; when he passed through the handsome drawing-rooms, filled to overflowing with pictures, armor, statuary, and all the trophies gained by the marquis's horses upon the turf, M. Wilkie mentally acknowledged that he knew nothing of high life, and that what he had considered luxury was scarcely the shadow of the reality. He felt actually ashamed of his own ignorance. This feeling of inferiority became so powerful that he was almost tempted to turn and fly, when the man clothed in black opened the door and announced, in a clear voice: " M. le Vicomte de Coralth !—M. Wilkie."

With a most gracious and dignified air—the air of a true *grand* seigneur—the only portion of his inheritance which he had preserved intact, the marquis rose to his feet, and, offering his hand to M. de Coralth, exclaimed: " You are most welcome, viscount. This gentleman is undoubtedly the young friend you spoke of in the note I received from you this morning? "

" The same; and really he stands greatly in need of your kindness. He finds himself in an extremely delicate position, and knows no one who can lend him a helping hand."

" Ah, well, I will lend him one with pleasure, since he is your friend. But I must know the circumstances before I can act. Sit down, gentlemen, and enlighten me."

M. Wilkie had prepared his story in advance, a touching and witty narrative; but when the moment came to begin it, he found himself unable to speak. He opened his mouth, but no sound issued from his lips, and it seemed as if he had been stricken dumb. Accordingly it was M. de Coralth who made a statement of the case, and he did it well.   The narrative thus gained considerably in clearness and precision; and even M. Wilkie noticed that his friend understood how to present the events in their most favorable light, and how to omit them altogether when his heartless conduct would have appeared too odious.   He also noticed—and he considered it an excellent omen—that M. de Valorsay was listening with the closest attention.

Worthy marquis! if his own interests had been in jeopardy he could not have appeared more deeply concerned.   When the viscount had concluded his story, he gravely exclaimed: " Your young friend is indeed in a most critical position, a position from which he cannot escape without being terribly victimized, if he's left dependent on his own resources."

" But it is understood that you will help him, is it not?"

M. de Valorsay reflected for a little, and then, addressing M. Wilkie, replied: " Yes, I consent to assist you, monsieur.   First, because your cause seems to me just, and, also, because you are M. de Coralth's friend. I promise you my aid on one condition—that you will follow my advice implicitly."

The interesting young man lifted his hand, and, by dint of a powerful effort, he succeeded in articulating: "Anything you wish!—upon my sacred word!"

" You must understand that when I engage in an enterprise, it must not fail.   The eye of the public is upon me, and I have my *prestige* to maintain.   I have given you a great mark of confidence, for in lending you my influence I become, in some measure at least, your sponsor.   But I cannot accept this great responsibility unless I am allowed absolute control of the affair."

" Of course."

" And I think that we ought to begin operations this very day. The main thing is to circumvent your father, the terrible man with whom your mother has threatened you."

" Ah! but how?"

" I shall dress at once and go to the Hôtel de Chalusse, in order to ascertain what has occurred there. You on your side must hasten to Madame d'Argelès and request her politely, but firmly, to furnish you with the necessary proofs to assert your rights. If she consents, well and good! If she refuses, we will consult some lawyer as to the next step. In any case, call here again at four o'clock."

But the thought of meeting Madame d'Argelès again was anything but pleasing to Wilkie. " I would willingly yield that undertaking to some one else," said he. " Cannot some one else go in my place?"

Fortunately M. de Coralth knew how to encourage him. " What! are you afraid?" he asked.

Afraid! he?—never! It was easy to see that by the way he settled his hat on his head and went off, slamming the door noisily behind him.

" What an idiot!" muttered M. de Coralth. " And to think that there are ten thousand in Paris built upon the very same plan!"

M. de Valorsay gravely shook his head. " Let us thank fortune that he is as he is. No youth who possessed either heart or intelligence would play the part that I intend for him, and enable me to obtain proud Marguerite and her millions. But I fear he won't go to Madame d'Argelès's house. You noticed his repugnance!"

" Oh, you needn't trouble yourself in the least on that account—he'll go. He would go to the devil if the noble Marquis de Valorsay ordered him to do so."

M. de Coralth understood Wilkie perfectly. The fear of being considered a coward by a nobleman like the Marquis de Valorsay was more than sufficient, not only to divest him of all his scruples, but even to induce him to commit any act of folly, or actually a crime. For if he had looked upon M. de Coralth as an oracle, he considered the marquis to be a perfect god.

Accordingly, as he hastened toward Madame d'Argelès's residence, he said to himself: "Why shouldn't I go to her house? I've done her no injury. Besides, she won't eat me." And remembering that he should be obliged to render a report of this interview, he resolved to assert his superiority and to remain cool and unmoved, as he had seen M. de Coralth do so often.

However, the unusual aspect of the house excited his surprise, and puzzled him not a little. Three huge furniture vans, heavily laden, were standing outside the gate. In the courtyard there were two more vehicles of the same description, which a dozen men or so were busily engaged in loading. "Ah, ha!" muttered M. Wilkie, "it was fortunate that I came—very fortunate; so she was going to run away!" Thereupon, approaching a group of servants who were in close conference in the hall, he demanded, in his most imperious manner: "Madame d'Argelès!"

The servants remembered the visitor perfectly; they now knew who he really was, and they could not understand how he could have the impudence and audacity to come there again so soon after the shameful scene of the previous evening. "Madame is at home," replied one of the men, in anything but a polite tone; "and I will go and see if she will consent to see you. Wait here."

He went off, leaving M. Wilkie in the vestibule to settle his collar and twirl his puny mustaches, with affected indifference; but in reality he was far from comfortable. For the servants did not hesitate to stare at him, and it was quite impossible not to read their contempt in their glances. They even sneered audibly and pointed at him; and he heard five or six epithets more expressive than elegant which could only have been meant for himself. "The fools!" thought he, boiling with anger. "The scoundrels! Ah! if I dared—— If a gentleman like myself was allowed to notice such blackguards, how I'd chastise them!"

But the valet who had gone to warn Madame d'Argelès soon reappeared and put an end to his sufferings. "Madame will see you," said the man, impudently. "Ah! if I were in her place——"

"Come, make haste," rejoined Wilkie, indignantly, and following the servant, he was ushered into a room which had already been divested of its hangings, curtains, and furniture. He here found Madame d'Argelès engaged in packing a large trunk with household linen and sundry articles of clothing.

By a sort of miracle the unfortunate woman had survived the terrible shock which had at first threatened to have an immediately fatal effect. Still she had none the less received her death-blow. It was only necessary to look at her to be assured of that. She was so greatly changed that when M. Wilkie's eyes first fell on her, he asked himself if this were really the same person whom he had met on the previous evening. Henceforth she would be an old woman. You would have taken her for over fifty, so terrible had been the sufferings caused her by the shameful conduct of her son. In this sad-eyed, haggard-faced woman, clad in black, no one would have recognized the notorious Lia d'Argelès, who, only the evening before, had driven round the lake, reclining on the cushions of her victoria, and eclipsing all the women around her by the splendor of her toilette. Nothing now remained of the gay worldling but the golden hair which she was condemned to see always the same, since its tint had been fixed by dyes as indelible as the stains upon her past.

She rose with difficulty when M. Wilkie entered, and in the expressionless voice of those who are without hope, she asked: "What do you wish of me?"

As usual, when the time came to carry out his happiest conceptions, his courage failed him. "I came to talk about our affairs, you know," he replied, "and I find you moving."

"I am not moving."

"Nonsense! you can't make me believe that! What's the meaning of these carts in the courtyard?"

"They are here to convey all the furniture in the house to the auction-rooms."

Wilkie was struck dumb for a moment, but eventually recovering himself a little, he exclaimed: "What! you are going to sell everything?"

"Yes."

"Astonishing, upon my honor! But afterward?"

"I shall leave Paris."

"Bah! and where are you going?"

With a gesture of utter indifference, she gently replied: "I don't know; I shall go where no one will know me, and where it will be possible for me to hide my shame."

A terrible disquietude seized hold of Wilkie. This sudden change of residence, this departure which so strongly resembled flight, this cold greeting when he expected passionate reproaches, seemed to indicate that Madame d'Argelès's resolution would successfully resist any amount of entreaty on his part. "The devil," he remarked, "I don't think this at all pleasant! What is to become of *me?* How am I to obtain possession of the Count de Chalusse's estate? That's what I am after! It's rightfully mine, and I'm determined to have it, as I told you once before. And when I've once taken anything into my head——"

He paused, for he could no longer face the scornful glances that Madame d'Argelès was giving him. "Don't be alarmed," she replied bitterly, "I shall leave you the means of asserting your right to my parents' estate."

"Ah—so——"

"Your threats obliged me to decide contrary to my own wishes. I felt that no amount of slander or disgrace would daunt you."

"Of course not, when so many millions are at stake."

"I reflected, and I saw that nothing would arrest you upon your downward path except a large fortune. If you were poor and compelled to earn your daily bread—a task which you are probably incapable of performing—who can tell what depths of degradation you might descend to? With your instincts and your vices, who knows what crime you wouldn't commit to obtain money? It wouldn't be long before you were in the dock, and I should hear of you only through your disgrace. But, on the other hand, if you were rich, you would probably lead an honest life, like many others, who, wanting for nothing, are not tempted to do wrong, who, in fact, show virtue in which there is nothing worthy of praise. For real virtue implies temptation—a struggle and victory."

Although he did not understand these remarks very well, M. Wilkie evinced a desire to offer some objections; but Madame d'Argelès had already resumed: " So I went to my notary this morning. I told him everything; and by this time my renunciation of my rights to the estate of the Count de Chalusse is already recorded."

" What! your renunciation. Oh! no."

" Allow me to finish since you don't understand me. As soon as I renounce the inheritance it becomes yours."

" Truly?"

" I have no wish to deceive you. I only desire that the name of Lia d'Argelès should not be mentioned. I will give you the necessary proofs to establish your identity; my marriage contract and your certificate of birth."

It was joy that made M. Wilkie speechless now. " And when will you give me these documents?" he faltered, after a short pause.

" You shall have them before you leave this house; but first of all I must talk with you."

XV.

AGITATED and excited though he was, M. Wilkie had not once ceased to think of M. de Coralth and the Marquis de Valorsay. What would they do in such a position, and how should he act to conform himself to the probable example of these models of deportment? Manifestly he ought to assume that stolid and insolent air of boredom which is considered a sure indication of birth and breeding. Convinced of this, and seized with

a laudable desire to emulate such distinguished ex-
amples, he had perched himself upon a trunk, where he
still sat with his legs crossed. He now pretended to
suppress a yawn, as he growled, "What! some more
long phrases—and another melodramatic display?"

Absorbed in the memories she had invoked, Madame
d'Argelès paid no heed to Wilkie's impertinence. "Yes,
I must talk with you," she said, "and more for your
sake than for my own. I must tell you who I am, and
through what strange vicissitudes I have passed. You
know what family I belong to. I will tell you, however—for you may be ignorant of the fact—that our
house is the equal of any in France in lineage, splendor
of alliance, and fortune. When I was a child, my
parents lived at the Hôtel de Chalusse, in the Faubourg
Saint Germain, a perfect palace, surrounded by one
of those immense gardens, which are no longer seen
in Paris—a real park, shaded with century-old trees.
Certainly everything that money could procure, or vanity desire, was within my reach; and yet my youth was
wretchedly unhappy. I scarcely knew my father, who
was devoured by ambition, and had thrown himself
body and soul into the vortex of politics. Either my
mother did not love me, or thought it beneath her dignity to make any display of sensibility; but at all events
her reserve had raised a wall of ice between herself
and me. As for my brother he was too much engrossed
in pleasure to think of a mere child. So I lived quite
alone, too proud to accept the love and friendship of
my inferiors—abandoned to the dangerous inspirations
of solitude, and with no other consolation than my
books—books which had been chosen for me by my
mother's confessor, and which were calculated to fill
my imagination with visionary and romantic fancies.

The only conversation I heard dealt with the means of leaving all the family fortune to my brother, so that he might uphold the splendor of the name, and with the necessity of marrying me to some superannuated nobleman who would take me without a dowry, or of compelling me to enter one of those aristocratic convents, which are the refuge, and often the prison, of poor girls of noble birth.

"I do not pretend to justify my fault, I am only explaining it. I thought myself the most unfortunate being in the world—and such I really was, since I honestly believed it—when I happened to meet Arthur Gordon, your father. I saw him for the first time at a *fête* given at the house of the Comte de Commarin. How he, a mere adventurer, had succeeded in forcing his way into the most exclusive society in the world, is a point which I have never been able to explain. But, alas! it is only too true that when our glances met for the first time, my heart was stirred to its inmost depths; I felt that it was no longer mine—that I was no longer free! Ah! why does not God allow a man's face to reflect at least something of his nature? This man, who was a corrupt and audacious hypocrite, had that air of apparent nobility and frankness which inspires you with unlimited confidence, and the melancholy expression on his features seemed to indicate that he had known sorrow, and had good cause to rail at destiny. In his whole appearance there was certainly a mysterious and fatal charm. I afterward learned that this was only a natural result of the wild life he had led. He was only twenty-six, and he had already been the commander of a slave ship, and had fought in Mexico at the head of one of those guerilla bands which make politics an excuse for pillage and murder. He divined only too well the impression he had made upon my heart. I met him twice afterward in society. He did not speak to me; he even pretended to avoid me, but standing a little on one side, he watched my every movement with burning eyes in which I fancied I could read a passion as absorbing as my own. At last he ventured to write to me. The moment a letter addressed to me in an unknown hand was covertly handed me by my maid, I divined that it came from him. I was frightened, and my first impulse was to take it, not to my mother—whom I regarded as my natural enemy—but to my father. However, he chanced to be absent; I kept the letter, I read it, I answered it—and he wrote again.

"Alas! from that moment my conduct was inexcusable. I knew that it was worse than a fault to continue this clandestine correspondence. I knew my parents would never give my hand in marriage to a man who was not of noble birth. I knew that I was risking my reputation, the spotless honor of our house, my happiness, and life! Still I persisted—I was possessed with a strange madness that made me ready to brave every danger. Besides, he gave me no time to breathe, or reflect. Everywhere, constantly, every instant, he compelled me to think of him. By some miracle of address and audacity, he had discovered a means of intruding upon my presence, even in my father's house. For instance, every morning I found the vases in my room full of choice flowers, though I was never able to discover what hands had placed them there. Ah! how can one help believing in an omnipresent passion which one inhales with the very air one breathes! How can one resist it?

"I only discovered Arthur Gordon's object when it

was too late. He had come to Paris with the fixed determination of trapping some rich heiress, and forcing her family to give her to him with a large dowry, after one of those disgraceful scandals which render a marriage inevitable. At the very same time he was pursuing two other rich young girls, persuaded that one of the three would certainly become his victim.

"I was the first to yield. One of those unforeseen events which are the work of Providence, was destined to decide my fate. Several times, already, in compliance with Arthur's urgent entreaties, I had met him at night time in a little pavilion in our garden. This pavilion contained a billiard-room and a spacious gallery in which my brother practised fencing and pistol shooting with his masters and friends. There, thanks to the liberty I enjoyed, we thought ourselves perfectly secure from observation, and we were imprudent enough to light the candles. One night when I had just joined Arthur in the pavilion, I thought I heard the sound of hoarse, heavy breathing behind me. I turned round in a fright and saw my brother standing on the threshold. Oh! then I realized how guilty I had been! I felt that one or the other of these two men—my lover or my brother—would not leave that room alive.

"I tried to speak, to throw myself between them, but I found I could neither speak nor move; it was as if I had been turned to stone. Nor did they exchange a word at first. But at last my brother drew two swords from their scabbards, and throwing one at Arthur's feet, exclaimed: 'I have no wish to assassinate you. Defend yourself, and save your life if you can!' And as Arthur hesitated, and seemed to be trying to gain time instead of picking up the weapon that was lying on the floor near him, my brother struck him in the face with the flat side of his sword, and cried: 'Now will you fight, you coward!' In an instant it was all over. Arthur caught up the sword, and springing upon my brother, disarmed him, and wounded him in the breast. I saw this. I saw the blood spurt out upon my lover's hands. I saw my brother stagger, beat the air wildly with his hands, and fall apparently lifeless to the floor. Then I, too, lost consciousness and fell!"

Any one who had seen Madame d'Argelès as she stood there recoiling in horror, with her features contracted, and her eyes dilated, would have realized that by strength of will she had dispelled the mists enshrouding the past, and distinctly beheld the scene she was describing. She seemed to experience anew the same agony of terror she had felt twenty years before; and this lent such poignant intensity to the interest of her narrative that if M. Wilkie's heart was not exactly touched, he was, as he afterward confessed, at least rather interested. But Madame d'Argelès seemed to have forgotten his existence. She wiped away the foam-flecked blood which had risen to her lips, and in the same mournful voice resumed her story.

"When I regained my senses it was morning, and I was lying, still dressed, on a bed in a strange room. Arthur Gordon was standing at the foot of the bed anxiously watching my movements. He did not give me time to question him. 'You are in my house,' said he. 'Your brother is dead!' Almighty God! I thought I should die as well. I hoped so. I prayed for death. But, in spite of my sobs, he pitilessly continued: 'It is a terrible misfortune which I shall never cease to regret. And yet, it was his own fault. You, who witnessed the scene, know that it was so. You can still see on my face the mark of the blow he dealt me. I only defended myself and you.' I was ignorant then of the accepted code of duelling. I did not know that by throwing himself upon my brother before he was on guard, Arthur Gordon had virtually assassinated him. He relied upon my ignorance for the success of the sinister farce he was playing. ' When I saw your brother fall,' he continued, ' I was wild with terror; and not knowing what I did, I caught you up in my arms and brought you here. But don't tremble, I know that you are not in my house of your own free will. A carriage is below and awaits your orders to convey you to your parents' home. It will be easy to find an explanation for last night's catastrophe. Slander will not venture to attack such a family as yours.' He spoke in the constrained tone, and with that air which a brave man, condemned to death, would assume in giving utterance to his last wishes. I felt as if I were going mad. ' And you!' I exclaimed, ' you! What will become of you?' He shook his head, and with a look of anguish, replied: ' Me! What does it matter about me! I am ruined undoubtedly. So much the better. Nothing matters now that I must live apart from you'! Ah! he knew my heart. He knew his power! Swayed by an emotion which was madness rather than heroism, I sprang toward him, and clasped him in my arms: ' Then I, too, am lost!' I cried. ' Since fate united us, nothing but death shall separate us. I love you. I am your accomplice. Let the curse fall upon both!'

"A keen observer would certainly have detected a gleam of fiendish joy in his eyes. But he protested, or pretended to protest. With feigned energy he refused to accept such a sacrifice. He could not link my des-

tiny to his, for misery had ever been his lot; and now
that this last and most terrible misfortune had over-
taken him, he was more than ever convinced that there
was a curse hanging over him! He would not suffer
me to bring misery upon myself, and eternal remorse
upon him. But the more he repulsed me, the more
obstinately I clung to him. The more forcibly he
showed the horror of the sacrifice, the more I was convinced that my honor compelled me to make it. So at
last he yielded, or seemed to yield, with transports of
gratitude and love. 'Well! yes, I accept your sacrifice,
my darling!' he exclaimed. 'I accept it; and before
the God who is looking down upon us, I swear that I
will do all that is in human power to repay such sublime
and marvellous devotion.' And, bending over me, he
printed a kiss upon my forehead. 'But we must fly!'
he resumed, quickly. 'I have my happiness to defend
now! I will not suffer any one to discover us and separate us now. We must start at once, without losing a
moment, and gain my native land, America. There, we
shall be safe. For rest assured they will search for us.
Who knows but even now the officers of the law are
upon our track? Your family is all-powerful—I am a
mere nobody—we should be crushed if they discover
us. They would bury you in a gloomy cloister, and I
should be tried as a common thief, or as a vile assassin.'
My only answer was: 'Let us go! Let us go at once!'

"It had been easy for him to foresee what the result
of this interview would be. A vehicle was indeed waiting at the door, but not for the purpose of conveying
me to the Hôtel de Chalusse—as was proved conclusively by the fact that his trunks were already strapped
upon it. Besides, the coachman must have received his
instructions in advance, for he drove us straight to the

Hâvre Railway station without a word. It was not until some months afterward that these trifles, which entirely escaped my notice at the time, opened my eyes to the truth. When we reached the station we found a train ready to start, and we took our places in it. I tried to quiet my conscience with miserable sophistries. Remembering that God has said to woman: To follow thy husband thou shalt abandon all else, native land, paternal home, parents and friends, I told myself that this was the husband whom my heart had instinctively chosen, and that it was my duty to follow him and share his destiny. And thus I fled with him, although I thought I left a corpse behind me—the corpse of my only brother."

M. Wilkie was actually so much interested that he forgot his anxiety concerning his attitude, and no longer thought of M. de Coralth and the Marquis de Valorsay. He even sprang up, and exclaimed: " Amazing ! "

But Madame d'Argelès had already resumed: " Such was my great, inexcusable, irreparable fault. I have told you the whole truth, without trying either to conceal or justify anything. Listen to my chastisement! On our arrival at Le Hâvre the next day, Arthur confessed that he was greatly embarrassed financially. Owing to our precipitate flight, he had not had time to realize the property he possessed—at least so he told me—a banker, on whom he had depended, had moreover failed him, and he had not sufficient money to pay our passage to New York. This amazed me. My education had been absurd, like that of most young girls in my station. I knew nothing of real life, of its requirements and difficulties. I knew, of course, that there were rich people and poor people, that money was a necessity, and that those who did not possess it would stoop to any meanness to obtain it. But all this was not very clear in my mind, and I never suspected that a few francs more or less would be a matter of vital importance. So I was not in the least prepared for the request to which this confession served as preface, and Arthur Gordon was obliged to ask me point-blank if I did not happen to have some money about me, or some jewelry which could be converted into money. I gave him all I had, my purse containing a few louis, a ring and a necklace, with a handsome diamond cross attached to it. However, the total value was comparatively small, and such was Arthur's disappointment that he made a remark which frightened me even then, though I did not fully understand its shameful meaning until afterward: 'A woman who repairs to a *rendezvous* should always have all the valuables she possesses about her. One never knows what may happen.'

"Want of money was keeping us prisoners at Le Hâvre, when Arthur Gordon chanced to meet an old acquaintance, who was the captain of an American sailing vessel. He confided his embarrassment to his friend, and the latter, whose vessel was to sail at the end of the same week, kindly offered us a free passage. The voyage was one long torture to me, for it was then that I first served my apprenticeship in shame and disgrace. By the captain's offensive gallantry, the lower officers' familiarity of manner, and the sailors' ironical glances whenever I appeared on deck, I saw that my position was a secret for no one. Everybody knew that I was the mistress and not the wife of the man whom I called my husband; and, without being really conscious of it, perhaps, they made me cruelly expiate my fault. Moreover, reason had regained its ascendency, my eyes were gradually opening to the truth, and I was beginning to learn the real character of the scoundrel for whom I had sacrificed all that makes life desirable.

"Not that he had wholly ceased to practise dissimulation. But after the evening meal he often lingered at table smoking and drinking with his friend the captain, and when he joined me afterward, heated with alcohol, he shocked me by advocating theories which were both novel and repulsive to me. Once, after drinking more than usual, he entirely forgot his assumed part, and revealed himself in his true character. He declared he bitterly regretted that our love affair had ended so disastrously. It was deplorable to think that so happily conceived and so skilfully conducted a scheme should have terminated in bloodshed. And the blow had fallen just as he fancied he had reached the goal; just as he thought he would reap the reward of his labor. In a few weeks' more time he would undoubtedly have gained sufficient influence over me to persuade me to elope with him. This would, of course, have caused a great scandal; the next day there would have been a family conclave; a compromise would have been effected, and finally, a marriage arranged with a large dowry, to hush up the affair. 'And I should now be a rich man,' he added, 'a very rich man—I should be rolling through the streets of Paris in my carriage, instead of being on board this cursed ship, eating salt cod twice a day, and living on charity.'

"Ah! it was no longer possible to doubt. The truth was as clear as daylight. I had never been loved, not even an hour, not even a moment. The loving letters which had blinded me, the protestations of affection which had deceived me, had been addressed to my

father's millions, not to myself. And not unfrequently
I saw Arthur Gordon's face darken, as he talked with
evident anxiety about what he could do to earn a living
for himself and me in America. ' I have had trouble
enough to get on alone,' he grumbled. ' What will it
be now? To burden myself with a penniless wife!
What egregious folly! And yet I couldn't have acted
differently—I was compelled to do it.' Why had he
been ιcompelled to do it? why had he not acted differently?—that was what I vainly puzzled my brain to
explain. However, his gloomy fears of poverty were
not realized. A delightful surprise awaited him at New
York. A relative had recently died, leaving him a
legacy of fifty thousand dollars—a small fortune. I
hoped that he would now cease his constant complaints,
but he seemed even more displeased than before.
' Such is the irony of fate,' he repeated again and
again. ' With this money, I might easily have married
a wife worth a hundred thousand dollars, and then I
should be rich at last!' After that, I had good reason
to expect that I should soon be forsaken—but no,
shortly after our arrival, he married me. Had he done
so out of respect for his word? I believed so. But,
alas! this marriage was the result of calculation, like
everything else he did.

"We were living in New York, when one evening
he came home, looking very pale and agitated. He
had a French nawspaper in his hand. ' Read this,' he
said, handing it to me. I took the paper as he bade
me, and read that my brother had not been killed, that
he was improving, and that his recovery was now certain. And as I fell on my knees, bursting into tears,
and thanking God for freeing me from such terrible
remorse, he exclaimed: ' We are in a nice fix! I advise

you to congratulate yourself!' From that time forward, I noticed he displayed the feverish anxiety of a
man who feels that he is constantly threatened with
some great danger. A few days afterward, he said to
me: 'I cannot endure this! Have our trunks ready to-
morrow, and we will start South. Instead of calling ourselves Gordon, we'll travel under the name of Grant.' I
did not venture to question him. He had quite mastered me by his cruel tyranny, and I was accustomed
to obey him like a slave in terror of the lash. However,
during our long journey, I learned the cause of our
flight and change of name.

"'Your brother, d——n him,' he said, one day, 'is
hunting for me everywhere! He wants to kill me or
to deliver me up to justice, I don't know which. He
pretends that I tried to murder him!' It was strange;
but Arthur Gordon, who was bravery personified, and
who exposed himself again and again to the most
frightful dangers, felt a wild, unreasoning, inconceiv-
able fear of my brother. It was this dread that had
decided him to burden himself with me. He feared
that if he left me, lying unconscious beside my brother's
lifeless form, I might on recovering my senses reveal
the truth, and unconsciously act as his accuser. You
were born in Richmond, Wilkie, where we remained
nearly a month, during which time I saw but little of
your father. He had formed the acquaintance of several rich planters, and spent his time hunting and gambling with them. Unfortunately, fifty thousand dollars
could not last long at this rate; and, in spite of his
skill as a gambler, he returned home one morning
ruined. A fortnight later when he had sold our effects,
and borrowed all the money he could, we embarked
again for France. It was not until we reached Paris

that I discovered the reasons that had influenced him in returning to Europe. He had heard of my father and mother's death, and intended to compel me to claim my share of the property. He dared not appear in person on account of my brother. At last the hour of my vengeance had arrived; for I had taken a solemn oath that this scoundrel who had ruined me should never enjoy the fortune which had been his only object in seducing me. I had sworn to die inch by inch and by the most frightful tortures rather than give him one penny of the Chalusse millions. And I kept my word.

" When I told him that I was resolved not to assert my rights, he seemed utterly confounded. He could not understand how the down-trodden slave dared to revolt against him. And when he found that my decision was irrevocable, I thought he would have an attack of apoplexy. It made him wild with rage to think that he was only separated from this immense fortune—the dream of his life—by a single word of mine, and to find that he had not the power to extort that word from me. Then began a struggle between us, which became more and more frightful as the money he possessed gradually dwindled away. But it was in vain that he resorted to brutal treatment; in vain that he struck me, tortured me, and dragged me about the floor by the hair of my head! The thought that I was avenged, that his sufferings equalled mine, increased my courage a hundredfold, and made me almost insensible to physical pain. He would certainly have been the first to grow weary of the struggle, if a fiendish plan had not occurred to him. He said to himself that if he could not conquer the wife, he *could* conquer the mother, and he threatened to turn his bru-

tality to you, Wilkie. To save you—for I knew what
he was capable of—I pretended to waver, and I asked
twenty-four hours for reflection. He granted them.
But the next day I left him forever, flying from him
with you in my arms."

M. Wilkie turned white, and a cold chill crept up
his spine. However, it was not pity for his mother's
sufferings, nor shame for his father's infamy that agitated him, but ever the same terrible fear of incurring
the enmity of this dangerous coveter of the Chalusse
millions. Would he be able to hold his father at bay
even with the assistance of M. de Coralth and the
Marquis de Valorsay? A thousand questions rose to
his lips, for he was eager to hear the particulars of his
mother's flight; but Madame d'Argelès hurried on with
her story as if she feared her strength would fail before
she reached the end.

"I was alone with you, Wilkie, in this great city,"
she resumed. "A hundred francs was all that I possessed. My first care was to find a place of shelter.
For sixteen francs a month, which I was compelled to
pay in advance, I found a small, meagrely furnished
room in the Faubourg Saint Martin. It was badly
ventilated and miserably lighted, but still it was shelter.
I said to myself that we could live there together by
my work, Wilkie. I was a proficient in feminine ac-
complishments; I was an excellent musician, and I
thought I should have no difficulty in earning the four
or five francs a day which I considered absolutely
necessary for our subsistence. Alas! I discovered only
too soon what chimerical hopes I had cherished. To
give music lessons it is necessary to obtain pupils.
Where should I find them? I had no one to recommend
me, and I scarcely dared show myself in the streets,

so great was my fear that your father would discover
our hiding-place. At last, I decided to try to find
some employment in needlework, and timidly offered
my services at several shops. Alas! it is only those
who have gone about from door to door soliciting work
who know the misery of the thing. To ask alms would
be scarcely more humiliating. People sneered at me,
and replied (when they deigned to reply at all) that
' there was no business doing, and they had all the help
they wanted.' My evident inexperience was probably
the cause of many of these refusals, as well as my
attire, for I still had the appearance of being a rich
woman. Who knows what they took me for? Stiil
the thought of you sustained me, Wilkie, and nothing
daunted me.

"I finally succeeded in obtaining some bands of
muslin to embroider, and some pieces of tapestry work
to fill in. Unremunerative employment, no doubt, especially to one ignorant of the art of working quickly,
rather than well. By rising with daylight, and working
until late at night, I scarcely succeeded in earning
twenty sous a day. And it was not long before even
this scanty resource failed me. Winter came, and the
cold weather with it. One morning I changed my last
five-franc piece—it lasted us a week. Then I pawned
and sold everything that was not absolutely indispensable until nothing was left me but my patched dress
and a single skirt. And soon an evening came when
the owner of our miserable den turned us into the
street because I could no longer pay the rent.

"This was the final blow! I tottered away, clinging
to the walls for support; too weak from lack of food
to carry you. The rain was falling, and chilled us to
the bones. You were crying bitterly. And all that

night and all the next day, aimless and hopeless, we wandered about the streets. I must either die of want or return to your father. I preferred death. Toward evening—instinct having led me to the Seine—I sat down on one of the stone benches of the Point-Neuf, holding you on my knees and watching the flow of the dark river below. There was a strange fascination— a promise of peace in its depths—that impelled me almost irresistibly to plunge into the flood. If I had been alone in the world, I should not have stopped to consider a second, but on your account, Wilkie, I hesitated."

Moved by the thought of the danger he had escaped, M. Wilkie shuddered. "*B-r-r-r!*" he growled. "You did well to hesitate."

She did not even hear him, but continued: "I at last decided that it was best to put an end to this misery, and rising with difficulty, I was approaching the parapet, when a gruff voice beside us exclaimed: 'What are you doing there?' I turned, thinking some police officer had spoken, but I was mistaken. By the light of the street lamp, I perceived a man who looked some thirty years of age, and had a frank and rather genial face. Why this stranger instantly inspired me with unlimited confidence I don't know. Perhaps it was an unconscious horror of death that made me long for any token of human sympathy. However it may have been, I told him my story, but not without changing the names, and omitting many particulars. He had taken a seat beside me on the bench, and I saw big tears roll down his cheeks as I proceeded with my narrative. 'It is ever so! it is ever so!' he muttered. 'To love is to incur the risk of martyrdom. It is to offer one's self as a victim to every perfidy, to the

basest treason and ingratitude.' The man who spoke
in this fashion was Baron Trigault. He did not allow
me to finish my story. 'Enough!' he suddenly exclaimed, 'follow me!' A cab was passing, he made
us get in, and an hour later we were in a comfortable
room, beside a blazing fire, with a generously spread
table before us. The next day, moreover, we were installed in a pleasant home. Alas! why wasn't the baron
generous to the last? You were saved, Wilkie, but at
what a price!"

She paused for a moment, her face redder than fire;
but soon mastering her agitation, she resumed: " There
was one great cause of dissension between the baron
and myself. I wished you to be educated, Wilkie, like
the son of a noble family, while he desired you should
receive the practical training suited to a youth who
would have to make his own way in the world, and
win position, fortune, and even name for himself. Ah!
he was a thousand times right, as events have since
proved only too well! But maternal love blinded me,
and, after an angry discussion, he went away, declaring
he would not see me again until I became more reasonable. He thought that reflection would cure me of
my folly. Unfortunately, he was not acquainted with
the fatal obstinacy which is the distinguishing characteristic of the Chalusse family. While I was wondering how I could find the means of carrying the plans
I had formed for you into execution, two of the baron's
acquaintances presented themselves, with the following
proposal: Aware of the enormous profits derived by
clandestine gambling dens, they had conceived the project of opening a public establishment on a large scale,
where any Parisian or foreigner, if he seemed to be a
gentleman, and possessed of means, would find no diffi-

culty in obtaining admission. By taking certain precautions, and by establishing this gambling den in a
private drawing-room, they believed the scheme practicable, and came to suggest that I should keep the
drawing-room in question, and be their partner in the
enterprise. Scarcely knowing what I pledged myself
to, I accepted their offer, influenced—I should rather
say decided—by the exalted positions which both these
gentlemen occupied, by the public consideration they
enjoyed, and the honored names they bore. And that
same week this house was rented and furnished, and I
was installed in it under the name of Lia d'Argelès.

"But this was not all. There still remained the task
of creating for myself one of those scandalous reputa-
tions that attract public attention. This proved an easy
task, thanks to the assistance of my silent partners, and
the innocent simplicity of several of their friends and
certain journalists. As for myself, I did my best to
insure the success of the horrible farce which was to
lend infamous notoriety to the name of Lia d'Argelès.
I had magnificent equipages and superb dresses, and I
made myself conspicuous at the theatres and all places
of public resort. As is generally the case when one
is acting contrary to conscience, I called the most absurd sophistries to my assistance. I tried to convince
myself that appearances are nothing, that reality is
everything, and that it did not matter if I were known
as a courtesan since rumor lied, and my life *was* really
chaste. When the baron hastened to me and tried to
rescue me from the abyss into which I had flung myself,
it was too late. I had discovered that the business
would prove successful; and for your sake, I longed
for money as passionately, as madly, as any miser.
Last year my gaming-room yielded more than one hun-

dred and fifty thousand francs clear profit, and I received as my share the thirty-five thousand francs which you squandered. Now you know me as I really am. My associates, my partners, the men whose secret I have faithfully kept, walk the streets with their heads erect. They boast of their unsullied honor, and they are respected by every one. Such is the truth, and I have no reason to make their disgrace known. Besides, if I proclaimed it from the house-tops, no one would believe me. But you are my son, and I owe you the truth, the whole truth!"

In any age but the present, Madame d'Argelès's story would have seemed absolutely incredible. Nowadays, however, such episodes are by no means rare. Two men—two men of exalted rank and highly respected, to use a common expression—associate in opening a gaming-house under the very eyes of the police, and in coining money out of a woman's supposed disgrace. 'Tis after all but an everyday occurrence.

The unhappy woman had told her story with apparent coldness, and yet, in her secret heart, she perhaps hoped that by disclosing her terrible sacrifice and long martyrdom, she would draw a burst of gratitude and tenderness from her son, calculated to repay her for all her sufferings. But the hope was vain. It would have been easier to draw water from a solid rock than to extract a sympathetic tear from Wilkie's eyes. He was only alive to the practical side of this narrative, and what impressed him most was the impudent assurance of Madame d'Argelès's business associates. "Not a bad idea; not bad at all," he exclaimed. And, boiling over with curiosity, he continued: "I would give something handsome to know those men's names. Really you ought to tell me. It would be worth one's while to know."

Any other person than this interesting young man would have been crushed by the look his mother gave him—a look embodying the deepest disappointment and contempt. "I think you must be mad," she remarked coldly. And as he sprang up, astonished that any one should doubt his abundant supply of good sense, "Let us put an end to this," she sternly added.

Thereupon she hastily went into the adjoining room, reappearing a moment later with a roll of papers in her hand. "Here," she remarked, "is my marriage certificate, your certificate of birth, and a copy of my renunciation—a perfectly valid document, since the court has authorized it, owing to my husband's absence. All these proofs I am ready and willing to place at your disposal, but on one condition."

This last word fell like a cold shower-bath upon Wilkie's exultant joy. "What is this condition?" he anxiously inquired.

"It is that you should sign this deed, which has been drawn up by my notary—a deed by which you pledge yourself to hand me the sum of two million francs on the day you come into possession of the Chalusse property."

Two millions! The immensity of the sum struck Wilkie dumb with consternation. Nor did he forget that he would be compelled to give the Viscount de Coralth the large reward he had promised him—a reward promised in writing, unfortunately. "I shall have nothing left," he began, piteously.

But with a disdainful gesture Madame d'Argelès interrupted him. "Set your mind at rest," said she. "You will still be immensely rich. All the estimates which have been made are far below the mark. When I was a girl I often heard my father say that his income amounted to more than eight hundred thousand francs a year. My brother inherited the whole property, and I would be willing to swear that he never spent more than half of his income."

Wilkie's nerves had never been subjected to so severe a shock. He tottered and his brain whirled. "Oh! oh!" he stammered. This was all he could say.

"Only I must warn you of a more than probable deception," pursued Madame d'Argelès. "As my brother was firmly resolved to deprive me even of my rightful portion of the estate, he concealed his fortune in every possible way. It will undoubtedly require considerable time and trouble to gain possession of the whole. However I know a man, formerly the Count de Chalusse's confidential agent, who might aid you in this task."

"And this man's name?"

"Is Isidore Fortunat. I saved his card for you. Here it is."

M. Wilkie took it up, placed it carefully in his pocket, and then exclaimed: "That being the case, I consent to sign, but after this you need not complain. Two millions at five per cent. ought to greatly alleviate one's sufferings."

Madame d'Argelès did not deign to notice this delicate irony. "I will tell you in advance to what purpose I intend to apply this sum," she said.

"Ah!"

"I intend one of these two millions to serve as the dowry of a young girl who would have been the Count de Chalusse's sole legatee, if his death had not been so sudden and so unexpected."

"And the other one?"

"The other I intend to invest for you in such a way that you can only touch the interest of it, so that you will not want for bread after you have squandered your inheritance, even to the very last penny."

This wise precaution could not fail to shock such a brilliant young man as M. Wilkie. "Do you take me for a fool?" he exclaimed. "I may appear very generous, but I am shrewd enough, never you fear."

"Sign," interrupted Madame d'Argelès, coldly.

But he attempted to prove that he was no fool by reading and re-reading the contract before he would consent to append his name to it. At last, however, he did so, and stowed away the proofs which insured him the much-coveted property.

"Now," said Madame d'Argelès, "I have one request to make of you. Whenever your father makes his appearance and lays claim to this fortune, I entreat you to avoid a lawsuit, which would only make your mother's shame and the disgrace attached to the hitherto stainless name of Chalusse still more widely known. Compromise with him. You will be rich enough to satisfy his greed without feeling it."

M. Wilkie remained silent for a moment, as if he were deliberating upon the course he ought to pursue. "If my father is reasonable, I will be the same," he said at last. "I will choose as an arbiter between us one of my friends—a man who acts on the square, like myself—the Marquis de Valorsay."

"My God! do you know him?"

"He is one of my most intimate friends."

Madame d'Argelès had become very pale. "Wretched boy!" she exclaimed. "You don't know that it's the marquis——" She paused abruptly. One word more and she would have betrayed Pascal Ferailleur's secret plans, with which she had been made acquainted by Baron Trigault. Had she a right to do this, even to put her son on his guard against a man whom she considered the greatest villain in the world?

"Well?" insisted M. Wilkie, in surprise.

But Madame d'Argelès had recovered her self-possession. "I only wished to warn you against too close a connection with the Marquis de Valorsay. He has an excellent position in society, but yours will be far more brilliant. His star is on the wane; yours is just rising. All that he is regretting, you have a right to hope for. Perhaps even now he is jealous of you, and wishes to persuade you to take some false step."

"Ah! you little know him!"

"I have warned you."

M. Wilkie took up his hat, but, though he was longing to depart, embarrassment kept him to the spot. He vaguely felt that he ought not to leave his mother in this style. "I hope I shall soon have some good news to bring you," he began.

"Before night I shall have left this house," she answered.

"Of course. But you are going to give me your new address."

"No."

"What?—No!"

She shook her head sadly, and in a scarcely audible voice responded: "It is not likely that we shall meet again."

"And the two millions that I am to turn over to you?"

"Mr. Patterson will collect the money. As for me, say to yourself that I'm dead. You have broken the

only link that bound me to life, by proving the futility
of the most terrible sacrifices. However, I am a
mother, and I forgive you." Then as he did not move,
and as she felt that her strength was deserting her,
she dragged herself from the room, murmuring,
" Farewell! "

XVI.

STUPEFIED with astonishment, M. Wilkie stood for a
moment silent and motionless. " Allow me," he faltered at last; " allow me—I wish to explain." But
Madame d'Argelès did not even turn her head; the door
closed behind her and he was left alone.

However strong a man's nature may be, he always
has certain moments of weakness. For instance, at
the present moment Wilkie was completely at a loss
what to do. Not that he repented, he was incapable
of that; but there are hours when the most hardened
conscience is touched, and when long dormant instincts
at last assert their rights. If he had obeyed his first
impulse, he would have darted after his mother and
thrown himself on his knees before her. But reflection,
remembrance of the Viscount de Coralth, and the Marquis de Valorsay, made him silent the noblest voice that
had spoken in his soul for many a long day. So, with
his head proudly erect, he went off, twirling his mustaches and followed by the whispers of the servants—
whispers which were ready to change into hisses at any
moment.

But what did he care for the opinion of these plebeians! Before he was a hundred paces from the house
his emotion had vanished, and he was thinking how he

could most agreeably spend the time until the hour
appointed for his second interview with M. de Valorsay. He had not breakfasted, but "his stomach was
out of sorts," as he said to himself, and it would really
have been impossible for him to swallow a morsel.
Thus not caring to return home, he started in quest of
one of his former intimates, with the generous intention
of overpowering him with the great news. Unfortunately he failed to find this friend, and eager to vent
the pride that was suffocating him, in some way or
other, he entered the shop of an engraver, whom he
crushed by his importance, and ordered some visiting
cards bearing the inscription W. de Gordon-Chalusse,
with a count's coronet in one of the corners.

Thus occupied, time flew by so quickly that he was a
trifle late in keeping his appointment with his dear
friend the marquis. Wilkie found M. de Valorsay as
he had left him—in his smoking-room, talking with the
Viscount de Coralth. Not that the marquis had been
idle, but it had barely taken him an hour to set in
motion the machinery which he had had in complete
readiness since the evening before. "Victory!" cried
Wilkie, as he appeared on the threshold. "It was a
hard battle, but I asserted my rights. I am the acknowledged heir! the millions are mine!" And without
giving his friends time to congratulate him, he began
to describe his interview with Madame d'Argelès, presenting his conduct in the most odious light possible,
pretending he had indulged in all sorts of harsh re-
joinders, and making himself out to be "a man of
bronze," or "a block of marble," as he said.

"You are certainly more courageous than I fancied,"
said M. de Valorsay gravely, when the narrative was
ended.

" Is that really so? "

" It is, indeed. Now the world is before you. Let
your story be noised abroad—and it will be noised
abroad—and you will become a hero. Imagine the
amazement of Paris when it learns that Lia d'Argelès
was a virtuous woman, who sacrificed her reputation
for the sake of her son—a martyr, whose disgrace was
only a shameful falsehood invented by two men of rank
to increase the attractions of their gambling-den! It
will take the newspapers a month to digest this strange
romance. And whom will all this notoriety fall upon?
Upon you, my dear sir; and as your millions will lend
an additional charm to the romance, you will become
the lion of the season."

M. Wilkie was really too much overwhelmed to
feel elated. " Upon my word, you overpower me,
my dear marquis—you quite overpower me," he stammered.

" I too have been at work," resumed the marquis.
" And I have made numerous inquiries, in accordance
with my promise. I almost regret it, for what I have
discovered is—very singular, to say the least. I was
just saying so to Coralth when you came in. What I
have learned makes it extremely unpleasant for me, to
find myself mixed up in the affair; accordingly, I have
requested the persons who gave me this information to
call here. You shall hear their story, and then you
must decide for yourself." So saying, he rang the bell,
and as soon as a servant answered the summons, he
exclaimed: " Show M. Casimir in."

When the lackey had retired to carry out this order,
the marquis remarked: " Casimir was the deceased
count's valet. He is a clever fellow, honest, intelligent,
and well up in his business—such a man as you will

need, in fact, and I won't try to conceal the fact that the hope of entering your service has aided considerably in unloosening his tongue."

M. Casimir, who was irreproachably clad in black, with a white cambric tie round his neck, entered the room at this very moment, smiling and bowing obsequiously. "This gentleman, my good fellow," said M. de Valorsay, pointing to Wilkie, "is your former master's only heir. A proof of devotion might induce him to keep you with him. What you told me a little while ago is of great importance to him; see if you can repeat it now for his benefit."

In his anxiety to secure a good situation, M. Casimir had ventured to apply to the Marquis de Valorsay; he had talked a good deal, and the marquis had conceived the plan of making him an unsuspecting accomplice. "I never deny my words," replied the valet, "and since monsieur is the heir to the property, I won't hesitate to tell him that immense sums have been stolen from the late count's estate."

M. Wilkie bounded from his chair. "Immense sums!" he exclaimed. "Is it possible!"

"Monsieur shall judge. On the morning preceding his death, the count had more than two millions in bank-notes and bonds stowed away in his escritoire, but when the justice of the peace came to take the inventory, the money could not be found. We servants were terribly alarmed, for we feared that suspicion would fall upon us."

Ah! if Wilkie had only been alone he would have given vent to his true feelings. But here, under the eyes of the marquis and M. de Coralth, he felt that he must maintain an air of stoical indifference. He *almost* succeeded in doing so, and in a tolerably firm voice he remarked: "This is not very pleasant news. Two millions! that's a good haul. Tell me, my friend, have you any clue to the thief?"

The valet's troubled glance betrayed an uneasy conscience, but he had gone too far to draw back. "I shouldn't like to accuse an innocent person," he replied, "but there was some one who constantly had access to that escritoire."

"And who was that?"

"Mademoiselle Marguerite."

"I don't know the lady."

"She's a young girl who is—at least people say—the count's illegitimate daughter. Her word was law in the house."

"What has become of her?"

"She has gone to live with General de Fondège, one of the count's friends. She wouldn't take her jewels and diamonds away with her, which seemed very strange, for they are worth more than a hundred thousand francs. Even Bourigeau said to me: 'That's unnatural, M. Casimir.' Borigeau is the concierge of the house, a very worthy man. Monsieur will not find his equal."

Unfortunately, this tribute to the merits of the valet's friend was interrupted by the arrival of a footman, who, after tapping respectfully at the door, entered the room and exclaimed: "The doctor is here, and desires to speak with Monsieur le Marquis."

"Very well," replied M. de Valorsay, "ask him to wait. When I ring, you can usher him in." Then addressing M. Casimir, he added:

"You may retire for the present, but don't leave the house. M. Wilkie will acquaint you with his intentions by and by."

The valet thereupon backed out of the room, bowing profoundly.

" There is a story for you ! " exclaimed M. Wilkie as soon as the door was closed. " A robbery of two millions ! "

The marquis shook his head, and remarked, gravely : " That's a mere nothing. I suspect something far more terrible."

" What, pray? Upon my word ! you frighten me."

" Wait ! I may be mistaken. Even the doctor may be deceived. But you shall judge for yourself." As he spoke, he pulled the bell-rope, and an instant after, the servant announced : " Dr. Jodon."

It was, indeed, the same physician who had annoyed Mademoiselle Marguerite by his persistent curiosity and impertinent questions, at the Count de Chalusse's bedside; the same crafty and ambitious man, constantly tormented by covetousness, and ready to do anything to gratify it—the man of the period, in short, who sacrificed everything to the display by which he hoped to deceive other people, and who was almost starving in the midst of his mock splendor.

M. Casimir was an innocent accomplice, but the doctor knew what he was doing. Interviewed on behalf of the Marquis de Valorsay by Madame Léon, he had fathomed the whole mystery at once. These two crafty natures had read and understood each other. No definite words had passed between them—they were both too shrewd for that; and yet, a compact had been concluded by which each had tacitly agreed to serve the other according to his need.

As soon as the physician appeared, M. de Valorsay rose and shook hands with him; then, offering him an arm-chair, he remarked : " I will not conceal from you, doctor, that I have in some measure prepared this gentleman "—designating M. Wilkie—" for your terrible revelation."

By the doctor's attitude, a keen observer might have divined the secret trepidation that always precedes a bad action which has been conceived and decided upon in cold blood.

" To tell the truth," he began, speaking slowly, and with some difficulty, " now that the moment for speaking has come, I almost hesitate. Our profession has painful exigencies. Perhaps it is now too late. If there had been any of the count's relatives in the house, or even an heir at the time, I should have insisted upon an autopsy. But now——"

On hearing the word " autopsy," M. Wilkie looked round with startled eyes. He opened his lips to interrupt the speaker, but the physician had already resumed his narrative. " Besides, I had only suspicions," he said, " suspicions based, it is true, upon strange and alarming circumstances. I am a man, that is to say, I am liable to error. In the kingdom of science it would be unpardonable temerity on my part to affirm——"

" To affirm what? " interrupted M. Wilkie.

The physician did not seem to hear him, but continued in the same dogmatic tone. " The count apparently died from an attack of apoplexy, but certain poisons produce similar and even identical symptoms which are apt to deceive the most experienced medical men. The persistent efforts of the count's intellect, his muscular rigidity alternating with utter relaxation, the dilation of the pupils of his eyes, and more than aught else the violence of his last convulsions, have led me to ask myself if some criminal had not hastened his end."

Whiter than his shirt, and trembling like a leaf, M. Wilkie sprang from his chair. "I understand!" he exclaimed. "The count was murdered—poisoned."

But the physician replied with an energetic protest. "Oh, not so fast!" said he. "Don't mistake my conjectures for assertions. Still, I ought not to conceal the circumstances which awakened my suspicions. On the morning preceding his attack, the count took two spoonfuls of the contents of a vial which the people in charge could not or would not produce. When I asked what this vial contained, the answer was: 'A medicine to prevent apoplexy.' I don't say that this is false, but prove it. As for the motive that led to the crime, it is apparent at once. The escritoire contained two millions of francs, and the money has disappeared. Show me the vial, find the money, and I will admit that I am wrong. But until then, I shall have my suspicions."

He did not speak like a physician but like an examining magistrate, and his alarming deductions found their way even to M. Wilkie's dull brain. "Who could have committed the crime?" he asked.

"It could only have been the person likely to profit by it; and only one person besides the count knew that the money was in the house, and had possession of the key of this escritoire."

"And this person?"

"Is the count's illegitimate daughter, who lived in the house with him—Mademoiselle Marguerite."

M. Wilkie sank into his chair again, completely overwhelmed. The coincidence between the doctor's deposition and M. Casimir's testimony was too remarkable to pass unnoticed. Further doubt seemed impossible. "Ah! this is most unfortunate!" faltered Wilkie.

"What a pity! Such difficulties never assail any one but me! What am I to do?" And in his distress he glanced from the doctor to the Marquis de Valorsay, and then at M. de Coralth, as if seeking inspiration from each of them.

"My profession forbids my acting as an adviser in such cases," replied the physician, "but these gentlemen have not the same reasons for keeping silent."

"Excuse me," interrupted the marquis quickly; "but this is one of those cases in which a man must be left to his own inspirations. The most I can do, is to say what course I should pursue if I were one of the deceased count's relatives or heirs."

"Pray tell me, my dear marquis," sighed Wilkie. "You would render me an immense service by doing so."

M. de Valorsay seemed to reflect for a moment; and then he solemnly exclaimed: "I should feel that my honor required me to investigate every circumstance connected with this mysterious affair. Before receiving a man's estate, one must know the cause of his death, so as to avenge him if he has been foully murdered."

For M. Wilkie the oracle had spoken. "Such is my opinion exactly," he declared. "But what course would you pursue, my dear marquis? How would you set about solving this mystery?"

"I should appeal to the authorities."

"Ah!"

"And this very day, this very hour, without losing a second, I should address a communication to the public prosecutor, informing him of the robbery which is patent to any one, and referring to the possibility of foul play."

"Yes, that would be an excellent idea; but there is

one slight drawback—I don't know how to draw up such a communication."

"I know no more about it than you do yourself; but any lawyer or notary will give you the necessary information. Are you acquainted with any such person? Would you like me to give you the address of my business man? He is a very clever fellow, who has almost all the members of my club as his clients."

This last reason was more than sufficient to fix M. Wilkie's choice. "Where can I find him?" he inquired.

"At his house—he is always there at this hour. Come! here is a scrap of paper and a pencil. You had better make a note of his address. Write: 'Maumèjan, Route de la Révolte.' Tell him that I sent you, and he will treat you with the same consideration as he would show to me. He lives a long way off, but my brougham is standing in the courtyard; so take it, and when your consultation is over, come back and dine with me."

"Ah! you are too kind!" exclaimed M. Wilkie. "You overpower me, my dear marquis, you do, upon my word! I shall fly and be back in a moment."

He went off looking radiant; and a moment later the carriage which was to take him to M. Maumèjan's was heard rolling out of the courtyard.

The doctor had already taken up his hat and cane. "You will excuse me for leaving you so abruptly, Monsieur le Marquis," said he, "but I have an engagement to discuss a business matter."

"Indeed!"

"I am negotiating for the purchase of a dentist's establishment."

"What, you?"

"Yes, I. You may tell me that this is a downfall, but I will answer, ' It will give me a living.' Medicine is becoming a more and more unremunerative profession. However hard a physician may work, he can scarcely pay for the water he uses in washing his hands. I have an opportunity of purchasing the business of a well-established and well-known dentist, in an excellent neighborhood. Why not avail myself of it? Only one thing worries me—the lack of funds."

The marquis had expected the doctor would require remuneration for his services. Before compromising himself any further, M. Jodon wished to know what compensation he was to receive. The marquis was so sure of this, that he quickly exclaimed: " Ah, my dear doctor, if you have need of twenty thousand francs, I shall be only too happy to offer them to you."

" Really? "

" Upon my honor! "

" And when can you let me have the money? "

" In three or four days' time."

The bargain was concluded. The doctor was now ready to find traces of any poison whatsoever in the Count de Chalusse's exhumed remains. He pressed the marquis's hand and then went off, exclaiming: " Whatever happens you can count upon me."

Left alone with the Viscount de Coralth, and consequently freed from all restraint, M. de Valorsay rose with a long-drawn sigh of relief. " What an interminable *séance!*" he growled. And, approaching his acolyte, who was sitting silent and motionless in an arm-chair, he slapped him on the shoulder, exclaiming: " Are you ill that you sit there like that, as still as a mummy? "

The viscount turned as if he had been suddenly

aroused from slumber. "I'm well enough," he answered somewhat roughly. "I was only thinking."

"Your thoughts are not very pleasant, to judge from the look on your face."

"No. I was thinking of the fate that you are preparing for us."

"Oh! A truce to disagreeable prophecies, please! Besides, it's too late to draw back, or to even think of retreat. The Rubicon is passed."

"Alas! that is the cause of my anxiety. If it hadn't been for my wretched past, which you have threatened me with like a dagger, I should long ago have left you to incur this danger alone. You were useful to me in times past, I admit. You presented me to the Baroness Trigault, to whose patronage I owe my present means, but I am paying too dearly for your services in allowing myself to be made the instrument of your dangerous schemes. Who aided you in defrauding Kami-Bey? Who bet for you against your own horse Domingo? Who risked his life in slipping those cards in the pack which Pascal Ferailleur held? It was Coralth, always Coralth."

A gesture of anger escaped the marquis, but resolving to restrain himself, he made no rejoinder. It was not until after he had walked five or six times round the smoking-room and grown more calm that he returned to the viscount's side. "Really, I don't recognize you," he began. "Is it really you who have turned coward? And at what a moment, pray? Why, on the very eve of success."

"I wish I could believe you."

"Facts shall convince you. This morning I might have doubted, but now, thanks to that vain idiot who goes by the name of Wilkie, I am sure, perfectly,

mathematically sure of success. Maumèjan, who is entirely devoted to me, and who is the greediest, most
avaricious scoundrel alive, will draw up such a complaint that Marguerite will sleep in prison. Moreover,
other witnesses will be summoned. By what Casimir
has said, you can judge what the other servants will
say. This testimony will be sufficient to convict her of
the robbery. As for the poisoning, you heard Dr.
Jodon. Can I depend upon him? Evidently, if I pay
without haggling. Very well; I shall pay."

But all this did not reassure M. de Coralth. "The
accusation will fall to the ground," said he, "as soon
as the famous vial from which M. de Chalusse took two
spoonfuls is found."

"Excuse me; it won't be found."

"But why?"

"Because I know where it is, my dear friend. It is
in the count's escritoire, but it won't be there any longer
on the day after to-morrow."

"Who will remove it?"

"A skilful fellow whom Madame Léon has found for
me. Everything has been carefully arranged. To-
morrow night at the latest Madame Léon will let this
man into the Hôtel de Chalusse by the garden gate,
which she has kept the key of. Vantrasson, as the man
is called, knows the management of the house, and he
will break open the escritoire and take the vial away.
You may say that there are seals upon the furniture,
placed there by the justice of the peace. That's true,
but this man tells me that he can remove and replace
them in such a way as to defy detection; and as the
lock has been forced once already—the day after the
count's death—a second attempt to break the escritoire open will not be detected."

The viscount remarked, with an ironical air: "All that is perfect; but the autopsy will reveal the falseness of the accusation."

"Naturally—but an autopsy will require time, and that will suit my plans admirably. After eight or ten days' solitary confinement and several rigid examinations, Mademoiselle Marguerite's energy and courage will flag. What do you think she will reply to the man who says to her: ' I love you, and for your sake I will attempt the impossible. Swear to become my wife and I will establish your innocence?' "

"I think she will say: 'Save me and I will marry you!' "

M. de Valorsay clapped his hands. " Bravo! " he exclaimed; "you have spoken the truth. Remember, now, that your dark forebodings are only chimeras! Yes, she will swear it, and I know she is the woman to keep her vow, even if she died of sorrow. And the very next day I will go to the examining magistrate and say to him: 'Marguerite a thief! Ah, what a frightful mistake. A robbery has been committed, it's true; but I know the real culprit—a scoundrel who fancied that by destroying a single letter he would annihilate all traces of the breach of fidelity he had committed. Fortunately, the Count de Chalusse distrusted this man, and proof of his breach of trust is in existence. I have this proof in my hands.' And I will show a letter establishing the truth of my assertion."

No forebodings clouded the marquis's joy; he saw no obstacles; it seemed to him as if he had already triumphed. "And the day following," he resumed, "when Marguerite becomes my wife, I shall take from a certain drawer a certain document, given to me by M. de Chalusse when I was on the point of becoming his son-in-law, and in which he recognizes Marguerite as his daughter, and makes her his sole legatee. And this document is perfectly *en règle*, and unattackable. Maumejan, who has examined it, guarantees that the value of the count's estate cannot be less than ten millions. Five will go to Madame d'Argelès, or her son Wilkie, as their share of the property. The remaining five will be mine. Come, confess that the plan is admirable!"

"Admirable, undoubtedly; but terribly complicated. When there are so many wheels within wheels, one of them is always sure to get out of order."

"Nonsense!"

"Besides, you have I don't know how many accomplices—Maumejan, the doctor, Madame Léon, and Vantrasson, not counting myself. Will all these people perform their duties satisfactorily?"

"Each of them is as much interested in my success as I am myself."

"But we have enemies—Madame d'Argelès, Fortunat——"

"Madame d'Argelès is about to leave Paris. If Fortunat is troublesome I will purchase his silence; Maumejan has promised me money."

But M. de Coralth had kept his strongest argument until the last. "And Pascal Ferailleur?" said he. "You have forgotten him."

No; M. de Valorsay had not forgotten him. You do not forget the man you have ruined and dishonored. Still, it was in a careless tone that ill accorded with his state of mind that the marquis replied: "The poor devil must be *en route* for America by this time."

The viscount shook his head. "That's what I've in vain been trying to convince myself of," said he. "Do you know that Pascal was virtually expelled from the Palais de Justice, and that his name has been struck off the list of advocates? If he hasn't blown his brains out, it is only because he hopes to prove his innocence. Ah! if you knew him as well as I do, you wouldn't be so tranquil in mind!"

He stopped short for the door had suddenly opened. The interruption made the marquis frown, but anger gave way to anxiety when he perceived Madame Léon, who entered the room out of breath and extremely red in the face.

"There wasn't a cab to be had!" she groaned. "Just my luck. I came on foot, and ran the whole way. I'm utterly exhausted;" and so saying, she sank into an arm-chair.

M. de Valorsay had turned very pale. "Defer your complaints until another time," he said, harshly. "What has happened? Tell me."

The estimable woman raised her hands to heaven, as she plaintively replied: "There is so much to tell? First, Mademoiselle Marguerite has written two letters, but I have failed to discover to whom they were sent. Secondly, she remained for more than an hour yesterday evening in the drawing-room with the General's son, Lieutenant Gustave, and, on parting, they shook hands like a couple of friends, and said, 'It is agreed.'"

"And is that all?"

"One moment and you'll see. This morning Mademoiselle went out with Madame de Fondège to call on the Baroness Trigault. I do not know what took place there, but there must have been a terrible scene; for they brought Mademoiselle Marguerite back unconscious, in one of the baron's carriages."

"Do you hear that, viscount?" exclaimed M. de Valorsay.

"Yes! You shall have the explanation to-morrow," answered M. de Coralth.

"And last, but not least," resumed Madame Léon, "on returning home this evening at about five o'clock, I fancied I saw Mademoiselle Marguerite leave the house and go up the Rue Pigalle. I had thought she was ill and in bed, and I said to myself, ' This is very strange.' So I hastened after her. It was indeed she. Of course, I followed her. And what did I see? Why, Mademoiselle paused to talk with a vagabond, clad in a blouse. They exchanged notes, and Mademoiselle Marguerite returned home. And here I am. She must certainly suspect something. What is to be done? "

If M. de Valorsay were frightened, he did not show it. "Many thanks for your zeal, my dear lady," he replied, " but all this is a mere nothing. Return home at once; you will receive my instructions to-morrow."

XVII.

MADEMOISELLE MARGUERITE had been greatly surprised on the occasion of her visit to M. Fortunat when she saw Victor Chupin suddenly step forward and eagerly exclaim: "I shall be unworthy of the name I bear if I do not find M. Ferailleur for you in less than a fortnight."

It is true that M. Fortunat's clerk did not appear to the best advantage on this occasion. In order to watch M. de Coralth, he had again arrayed himself in his cast-off clothes, and with his blouse and his worn-out shoes, his " knockers " and his glazed cap, he looked the vagabond to perfection. Still, strange as it may seem, Mademoiselle Marguerite did not once doubt the devotion of this strange auxiliary. Without an instant's hesitation she replied, " I accept your services, monsieur."

Chupin felt at least a head taller as he heard this beautiful young girl speak to him in a voice as clear and as sonorous as crystal. " Ah! you are right to trust me," he rejoined, striking his chest with his clinched hand, " for I have a heart—but——".

" But what, monsieur? "

" I am wondering if you would consent to do what I wish. It would be a very good plan, but if it displeases you, we will say no more about it."

" And what do you wish? "

" To see you every day, so as to tell you what I've done, and to obtain such directions as I may require. I'm well aware that I can't go to M. de Fondège's door and ask to speak to you; but there are other ways of seeing each other. For instance, every evening at five o'clock precisely, I might pass along the Rue Pigalle, and warn you of my presence by such a signal as this: ' Pi-ouit!' " So saying he gave vent to the peculiar call, half whistle, half ejaculation, which is familiar to the Parisian working-classes. " Then," he resumed, " you might come down and I would tell you the news; besides, I might often help you by doing errands."

Mademoiselle Marguerite reflected for a moment, and then bowing her head, she replied:

" What you suggest is quite practicable. On and after to-morrow evening I will watch for you; and if I don't come down at the end of half an hour, you will know that I am unavoidably detained."

Chupin ought to have been satisfied. But no, he had still another request to make; and instinct, supplying

the lack of education, told him that it was a delicate
one. Indeed, he dared not present his petition; but his
embarrassment was so evident, and he twisted his poor
cap so despairingly, that at last the young girl gently
asked him: "Is there anything more?"

He still hesitated, but eventually, mustering all his
courage, he replied: "Well, yes, mademoiselle. I've
never seen Monsieur Ferailleur. Is he tall or short,
light or dark, stout or thin? I do not know. I might
stand face to face with him without being able to say,
'It's he.' But it would be quite a different thing if I
only had a photograph of him."

A crimson flush spread over Mademoiselle Marguerite's face. Still she answered, unaffectedly, "I will
give you M. Ferailleur's photograph to-morrow, monsieur."

"Then I shall be all right!" exclaimed Chupin.
"Have no fears, mademoiselle, we shall outwit these
scoundrels!"

So far a silent witness of this scene, M. Fortunat
now felt it his duty to interfere. He was not particularly pleased by his clerk's suddenly increased importance; and yet it mattered little to him, for his only
object was to revenge himself on Valorsay. "Victor is
a capable and trustworthy young fellow, mademoiselle,"
he declared; "he has grown up under my training, and
I think you will find him a faithful servant."

A "have you finished, you old liar?" rose to Chupin's
lips, but respect for Mademoiselle Marguerite prevented him from uttering the words. "Then everything is decided," she said, pleasantly. And with a
smile she offered her hand to Chupin as one does in
concluding a bargain.

If he had yielded to his first impulse he would have

thrown himself on his knees and kissed this hand of
hers, the whitest and most beautiful he had ever seen.
As it was, he only ventured to touch it with his finger-
tips, and yet he changed color two or three times.
"What a woman!" he exclaimed, when she had left
them. "A perfect queen! A man would willingly
allow himself to be chopped in pieces for her sake; and
she's as good and as clever as she's handsome. Did you
notice, monsieur, that she did not offer to pay me. She
understood that I offered to work for her for my own
pleasure, for my own satisfaction and honor. Heavens!
how I should have chafed if she had offered me money.
How provoked I should have been!"

Chupin was so fascinated that he wished no reward
for his toil! This was so astonishing that M. Fortunat
remained for a moment speechless with surprise. "Have
you gone mad, Victor?" he inquired at last.

"Mad! I?—not at all; I'm only becoming——" He
stopped short. He was going to add: "an honest
man." But it is scarcely proper to talk about the rope
in the hangman's house, and there are certain words
which should never be pronounced in the presence of
certain people. Chupin knew this, and so he quickly
resumed: "When I become rich, when I'm a great
banker, and have a host of clerks who spend their time
in counting my gold behind a grating, I should like to
have a wife of my own like that. But I must be
off about my business now, so till we meet again,
monsieur."

The foregoing conversation will explain how it happened that Madame Léon chanced to surprise her dear
young lady in close conversation with a vagabond clad
in a blouse. Victor Chupin was not a person to make
promises and then leave them unfulfilled. Though he

was usually unimpressionable, like all who lead a precarious existence, still, when his emotions were once aroused, they did not spend themselves in empty protestations. It became his fixed determination to find Pascal Ferailleur, and the difficulties of the task in no wise weakened his resolution. His starting point was that Pascal had lived in the Rue d'Ulm, and had suddenly gone off with his mother, with the apparent intention of sailing for America. This was all he knew positively, and everything else was mere conjecture. Still Mademoiselle Marguerite had convinced him that instead of leaving Paris, Pascal was really still there, only waiting for an opportunity to establish his innocence, and to wreak his vengeance upon M. de Coralth and the Marquis de Valorsay. On the other hand, with such a slight basis to depend upon, was it not almost madness to hope to discover a man who had such strong reasons for concealing himself? Chupin did not think so; in fact, when he declared his determination to perform this feat, his plan was already perfected.

On leaving M. Fortunat's office, he hastened straight to the Rue d'Ulm, at the top of his speed. The concierge of the house where Pascal had formerly resided was by no means a polite individual. He was the very same man who had answered Mademoiselle Marguerite's questions so rudely; but Chupin had a way of conciliating even the most crabbish doorkeeper, and of drawing from him such information as he desired. He learned that at nine o'clock on the sixteenth of October Madame Ferailleur, after seeing her trunks securely strapped on to a cab, had entered the vehicle, ordering the driver to take her to the Railway Station in the Place du Hâvre! Chupin wished to ascertain the number of the cab, but the concierge could not give it·

He mentioned, however, that this cab had been procured by Madame Ferailleur's servant-woman, who
lived only a few steps from the house. A moment later
Chupin was knocking at this woman's door. She was
a very worthy person, and bitterly regretted the misfortunes which had befallen her former employers. She
confirmed the doorkeeper's story, but unfortunately she,
too, had quite forgotten the number of the vehicle. All
she could say was that she had hired it at the cab stand
in the Rue Soufflot, and that the driver was a portly,
pleasant-faced man.

Chupin repaired at once to the Rue Soufflot, where
he found the man in charge of the stand in the most
savage mood imaginable. He began by asking Chupin
what right he had to question him, why he wished to
do so, and if he took him for a spy. He added that his
duty only consisted in noting the arrivals and depart-
ures of the drivers, and that he could give no information whatever. There was evidently nothing to be
gained from this ferocious personage; and yet Chupin
bowed none the less politely as he left the little office.
"This is bad," he growled, as he walked away, for he
was really at a loss what to do next; and if not discouraged, he was at least extremely disconcerted and
perplexed. Ah! if he had only had a card from the
prefecture of police in his pocket, or if he had been
more imposing in appearance, he would have encoun-
tered no obstacles; he might then have tracked this cab
through the streets of Paris as easily as he could have
followed a man bearing a lighted lantern through the
darkness. But poor and humble, without letters of
recommendation, and with no other auxiliaries than his
own shrewdness and experience, he had a great deal to
contend against. Pausing in his walk, he had taken off

his cap and was scratching his head furiously, when
suddenly he exclaimed: "What an ass I am!" in so
loud a tone that several passers-by turned to see who
was applying this unflattering epithet to himself.

Chupin had just remembered one of M. Isidore Fortunat's debtors, a man whom he often visited in the
hope of extorting some trifling amount from him, and
who was employed in the Central office of the Paris
Cab Company. "If any one can help me out of this
difficulty, it must be that fellow," he said to himself.
"I hope I shall find him at his desk! Come, Victor,
my boy, you must look alive!"

However, he could not present himself at the office
in the garb he then wore, and so, much against his will,
he went home and changed his clothes. Then he took
a cab at his own expense, and drove with all possible
speed to the main office of the Cab Company, in the
Avenue de Ségur. Nevertheless it was already ten
o'clock when he arrived there. He was more fortunate
than he had dared to hope. The man he wanted had
charge of a certain department, and was compelled to
return to the office every evening after dinner. He was
there now.

He was a poor devil who, while receiving a salary
of fifteen hundred francs a year, spent a couple of
thousand, and utilized his wits in defending his meagre
salary from his creditors. On perceiving Chupin, he
made a wrathful gesture, and his first words were: "I
haven't got a penny."

But Chupin smiled his most genial smile. "What!"
said he, "do you fancy I've come to collect money from
you here, and at this hour? You don't know me. I
merely came to ask a favor of you."

The clerk's clouded face brightened. "Since that is

the case, pray take a seat, and tell me how I can serve you," he replied.

"Very well. At nine o'clock in the evening, on the sixteenth of October, a lady living in the Rue d'Ulm sent to the stand in the Rue Soufflot for a cab. Her baggage was placed upon it, and she went away no one knows where. However, this lady is a relative of my employer, and he so much wishes to find her that he would willingly give a hundred francs over and above the amount you owe him, to ascertain the number of the vehicle. He pretends that you can give him this number if you choose; and it isn't an impossibility, is it?"

"On the contrary, nothing could be easier," replied the clerk, glad of an opportunity to explain the ingenious mechanism of the office to an outsider. "Have you ten minutes to spare?"

"Ten days, if necessary," rejoined Chupin.

"Then you shall see." So saying the clerk rose and went into the adjoining room, whence a moment later he returned carrying a large green box. "This contains the October reports sent in every evening by the branch offices," he remarked in explanation. He next opened the box, glanced over the documents it contained, and joyfully exclaimed: "Here we have it. This is the report sent in by the superintendent of the cab-stand in the Rue Soufflot on the 16th October. Here is a list of the vehicles that arrived or left from a quarter to nine o'clock till a quarter past nine. Five cabs came in, but we need not trouble ourselves about them. Three went out bearing the numbers 1781, 3025, and 2140. One of these three must have taken your employer's relative."

"Then I must question the three drivers."

The clerk shrugged his shoulders. "What is the

use of doing that?" he said, disdainfully. "Ah! you don't understand the way in which we manage our business! The drivers are artful, but the company isn't a fool. By expending a hundred and fifty thousand francs on its detective force every year, it knows what each cab is doing at each hour of the day. I will now look for the reports sent in respecting these three drivers. One of the three will give us the desired information."

This time the search was a considerably longer one, and Chupin was beginning to grow impatient, when the clerk waved a soiled and crumpled sheet of paper triumphantly in the air, and cried: "What did I tell you? This is the report concerning the driver of No. 2140. Listen: Friday, at ten minutes past nine, sent to the Rue d'Ulm—— What do you think of that?"

"It's astonishing! But where can I find this driver?"

"I can't say, just at this moment; he's on duty now. But as he belongs to this division he will be back sooner or later, so you had better wait."

"I will wait then; only as I've had no dinner, I'll go out and get a mouthful to eat. I can promise you that M. Fortunat will send you back your note cancelled."

Chupin was really very hungry, and so he rushed off to a little eating-house which he had remarked on his way to the office. There for eighteen sous he dined, or rather supped, like a prince; and as he subsequently treated himself to a cup of coffee and a glass of brandy, as a reward for his toil, some little time had elapsed when he returned to the office. However, No. 2140 had not returned in his absence, so he stationed himself at the door to wait for it.

His patience was severely tried, for it was past midnight when Chupin saw the long-looked-for vehicle enter the courtyard. The driver slowly descended from his box and then went into the cashier's office to pay over his day's earnings, and hand in his report. Then he came out again evidently bound for home. As the servant-woman had said, he was a stout, jovial-faced man, and he did not hesitate to accept a glass of "no matter what" in a wine-shop that was still open. Whether he believed the story that Chupin told to excuse his questions or not, at all events he answered them very readily. He perfectly remembered having been sent to the Rue d'Ulm, and spoke of his " fare " as a respectable-looking old lady, enumerated the number of her trunks, boxes, and packages, and even described their form. He had taken her to the railway station, stopping at the entrance in the Rue d'Amsterdam; and when the porters inquired, as usual, " Where is this baggage to go? " the old lady had answered, " To London."

Chupin felt decidedly crestfallen on hearing this. He had fancied that Madame Ferailleur had merely announced her intention of driving to the Hâvre railway station so as to set possible spies on the wrong track, and he would have willingly wagered anything, that after going a short distance she had given the cabman different instructions. Not so, however, he had taken her straight to the station. Was Mademoiselle Marguerite deceived then? Had Pascal really fled from his enemies without an attempt at resistance? Such a course seemed impossible on his part. Thinking over all this, Chupin slept but little that night, and the next morning, before five o'clock, he was wandering about the Rue d'Amsterdam peering into the wine-shops in search of some railway porter. It did not take him

long to find one, and having done so, he made him
the best of friends in less than no time. Although this
porter knew nothing about the matter himself, he took
Chupin to a comrade who remembered handling the
baggage of an old lady bound for London, on the evening of the sixteenth. However, this baggage was not
put into the train after all; the old lady had left it in
the cloak-room, and the next day a fat woman of un-
prepossessing appearance had called for the things, and
had taken them away, after paying the charges for
storage. This circumstance had been impressed on the
porter's mind by the fact that the woman had not given
him a farthing gratuity, although he had been much
more obliging than the regulations required. However,
when she went off, she remarked in a honeyed voice,
but with an exceedingly impudent air: " I'll repay you
for your kindness, my lad. I keep a wine-shop on the
Route d'Asnières, and if you ever happen to pass that
way with one of your comrades, come in, and I'll reward you with a famous drink! "

What had exasperated the porter almost beyond endurance, was the certainty he felt that she was mocking him. " For she didn't give me her name or address, the old witch! " he growled. " She had better
look out, if I ever get hold of her again! "

But Chupin had already gone off, unmoved by his
informant's grievances. Now that he had discovered
the stratagem which Madame Ferailleur had employed
to elude her pursuers, his conjectures were changed into
certainties. This information proved that Pascal *was*
concealed somewhere in Paris; but where? If he could
only find out this woman who had called for the trunks,
it would lead to the discovery of Madame Ferailleur
and her son, but how was he to ascertain the woman's

whereabouts? She had said that she kept a wine-shop on the Route d'Asnières. Was this true? Was it not more likely that this vague direction was only a fresh precaution?

This much was certain: Chupin, who knew every wine-shop on the Route d'Asnières, did not remember any such powerful matron as the porter had described. He had not forgotten Madame Vantrasson. But to imagine any bond of interest between Pascal and such a woman as she was, seemed absurd in the extreme. However, as he found himself in such a plight and could not afford to let any chance escape, he repaired merely for form's sake to the Vantrasson establishment. It had not changed in the least since the evening he visited it in company with M. Fortunat—but seen in the full light of day, it appeared even more dingy and dilapidated. Madame Vantrasson was not in her accustomed place, behind the counter, between her black cat—her latest idol—and the bottles from which she prepared her ratafia, now her supreme consolation here below. There was no one in the shop but the landlord. Seated at a table, with a lighted candle near him, he was engaged in an occupation which would have set Chupin's mind working if he had noticed it. Vantrasson had taken some wax from a sealed bottle, and, after melting it at the flame of the candle, he let it drop slowly on to the table. He then pressed a sou upon it, and when the wax had become sufficiently cool and stiff, he removed it from the table without destroying the impression, by means of a thin bladed knife similar to those which glaziers use. However, Chupin did not remark this singular employment. He was engaged in mentally ejaculating, "Good! the old woman isn't here." And as his plan of campaign was already prepared, he entered without further hesitation.

As Vantrasson heard the door turn upon its hinges, he rose so awkwardly, or rather so skilfully, as to let all his implements, wax, knife, and impressions, fall on the floor behind the counter. " What can I do to serve you? " he asked, in a husky voice.

" Nothing. I wished to speak with your wife."

" She has gone out. She works for a family in the morning."

This was a gleam of light. Chupin had not thought of the only hypothesis that could explain what seemed inexplicable to him. However, he knew how to conceal his satisfaction, and so with an air of disappointment, he remarked: " That's too bad! I shall be obliged to call again."

" So you have a secret to tell my wife? "

" Not at all."

" Won't I do as well, then? "

" I'll tell you how it is. I'm employed in the baggage room of the western railway station, and I wanted to know if your wife didn't call there a few days ago for some trunks? "

The landlord's features betrayed the vague perturbation of a person who can count the days by his mistakes, and it was with evident hesitation that he replied:

" Yes, my wife went to the Hâvre station for some baggage last Sunday."

" I thought so. Well, this is my errand: either the clerk forgot to ask her for her receipt, or else he lost it. He can't find it anywhere. I came to ask your wife if she hadn't kept it. When she returns, please deliver my message; and if she has the receipt, pray send it to me through the post."

The ruse was not particularly clever, but it was sufficiently so to deceive Vantrasson. "To whom am I to
send this receipt?" he asked.

"To me, Victor Chupin, Faubourg Saint Denis," was
the reply.

Imprudent youth! alas, he little suspected what a
liberty M. Fortunat had taken with his name on the
evening he visited the Vantrassons. But on his side
the landlord of the Model Lodging House had not forgotten the name mentioned by the agent. He turned
pale with anger on beholding his supposed creditor, and
quickly slipping between the visitor and the door, he
said: "So your name is Victor Chupin?"

"Yes, certainly."

"And you are in the employment of the Railway
Company?"

"As I just told you."

"That doesn't prevent you from acting as a col-
lector, does it?"

Chupin instinctively recoiled, convinced that he had
betrayed himself by some blunder, but unable to discover in what he had erred. "I did do something in
that line formerly," he faltered.

Vantrasson doubted no longer. "So you confess
that you are a vile scoundrel!" he exclaimed. "You
confess that you purchased an old promissory note of
mine for fourpence, and then sent a man here to seize
my goods! Ah! you'd like to trample the poor under
foot, would you! Very well. I have you now, and I'll
settle your account! Take that!" And so saying, he
dealt his supposed creditor a terrible blow with his
clinched fist that sent him reeling to the other end of
the shop.

Fortunately, Chupin was very nimble. He did not

lose his footing, but sprung over a table and used it as
a rampart to shield himself from his dangerous assail-
ant. In the open field, he could easily have protected
himself; but here in this narrow space, and hemmed
in a corner, he felt that despite this barrier he was lost.
"What a devil of a mess!" he thought, as with wonderful agility he avoided Vantrasson's fist, a fist that
would have felled an ox. He had an idea of calling
for assistance. But would any one hear him? Would
any one reply? And if help came, would not the police
be sure to hear of the broil? And if they did, would
there not be an investigation which would perhaps disturb Pascal's plans? Fearing to injure those whom he
wished to serve, he resolved to let himself be hacked
to pieces rather than allow a cry to escape him; but
he changed his tactics, and instead of attempting to
parry the blows as he had done before, he now only
thought of gaining the door, inch by inch.

He had almost reached it, not without suffering considerable injury, when it suddenly opened, and a young
man clad in black, with a smooth shaven face, entered the
shop, and sternly exclaimed: "Why! what's all this?"

The sight of the newcomer seemed to stupefy Vantrasson. "Ah! it is you, Monsieur Mauméjan?" he
faltered, with a crestfallen air. "It's nothing; we were
only in fun."

M. Mauméjan seemed perfectly satisfied with this
explanation; and in the indifferent tone of a man who
is delivering a message, the meaning of which he
scarcely understood, he said: "A person who knows
that your wife is in my employ requested me to ask you
if you would be ready to attend to that little matter
she spoke of."

"Certainly. I was preparing for it a moment ago."

Chupin heard no more. He had hurried out, his clothes in disorder, and himself not a little hurt; but his delight made him lose all thought of his injuries. "That's M. Ferailleur," he muttered, "I'm sure of it, and I'm going to prove it." So saying he hid himself in the doorway of a vacant house a few paces distant from the Vantrassons', and waited.

Then as soon as M. Mauméjan emerged from the Model Lodging House, he followed him. The young man with the clean shaven face walked up the Route d'Asnières, turned to the right into the Route de la Révolte, and at last paused before a house of humble aspect. At that moment Chupin darted toward him, and softly called, "M'sieur Ferailleur!"

The young man turned instinctively. Then seeing his mistake, and feeling that he had betrayed himself, he sprang upon Chupin, and caught him by the wrists: "Scoundrel! who are you?" he exclaimed. "Who has hired you to follow me! What do you want of me?"

"Not so fast, m'sieur! Don't be so rough! You hurt me. I'm sent by Mademoiselle Marguerite!"

XVIII.

"O GOD! send Pascal to my aid," prayed Mademoiselle Marguerite, as she left M. Fortunat's house. Now she understood the intrigue she had been the victim of; but, instead of reassuring her the agent had frightened her, by revealing the Marquis de Valorsay's desperate plight. She realized what frenzied rage must fill this man's heart as he felt himself gradually slipping from the heights of opulence, down into the depths of pov-

erty and crime. What might he not dare, in order to
preserve even the semblance of grandeur for a year,
or a month, or a day longer! Had they measured the
extent of his villainy? Would he even hesitate at murder? And the poor girl asked herself with a shudder
if Pascal were still living; and a vision of his bleeding
corpse, lying lifeless in some deserted street, rose before
her. And who could tell what dangers threatened her
personally? For, though she knew the past, she could
not read the future. What did M. de Valorsay's letter
mean? and what was the fate that he held in reserve
for her, and that made him so sanguine of success?
The impression produced upon her mind was so terrible that for a moment she thought of hastening to the
old justice of the peace to ask for his protection and a
refuge. But this weakness did not last long. Should
she lose her energy? Should her will fail her at the
decisive moment? "No, a thousand times no!" she
said to herself again and again. "I will die if needs
be, but I will die fighting!" And the nearer she approached the Rue Pigalle, the more energetically she
drove away her apprehension, and sought for an excuse calculated to satisfy any one who might have
noticed her long absence.

An unnecessary precaution. She found the house as
when she left it, abandoned to the mercy of the servants—the strangers sent the evening before from the
employment office. Important matters still kept the
General and his wife from home. The husband had to
show his horses; and the wife was intent upon shopping. As for Madame Léon, most of her time seemed
to be taken up by the family of relatives she had so
suddenly discovered. Alone, free from all *espionage*,
and wishing to ward off despondency by occupation,

Mademoiselle Marguerite was just beginning a letter to her friend the old magistrate, when a servant entered and announced that her dressmaker was there and wished to speak with her. " Let her come in," replied Marguerite, with unusual vivacity. " Let her come in at once."

A lady who looked some forty years of age, plainly dressed, but of distinguished appearance, was thereupon ushered into the room. Like any well-bred modiste, she bowed respectfully while the servant was present, but as soon as he had left the room she approached Mademoiselle Marguerite and took hold of her hands: " My dear young lady," said she, " I am the sister-in-law of your old friend, the magistrate. Having an important message to send to you, he was trying to find a person whom he could trust to play the part of a dressmaker, as had been agreed upon between you, when I offered my services, thinking he could find no one more trusty than myself."

Tears glittered in Mademoiselle Marguerite's eyes. The slightest token of sympathy is so sweet to the heart of the lonely and unfortunate! " How can I ever thank you, madame? " she faltered.

" By not attempting to thank me at all, and by reading this letter as soon as possible."

The note she now produced ran as follows:

" MY DEAR CHILD—At last I am on the track of the thieves. By conferring with the people from whom M. de Chalusse received the money a couple of days before his death, I have been fortunate enough to obtain from them some minute details respecting the missing bonds, as well as the numbers of the bank-notes which were deposited in the escritoire. With this information, we cannot fail to prove the guilt of the culprits sooner or later. You write me word that the Fondèges are spending money lavishly; try and find out the names of the people they deal with, and communicate them to me. Once more, I tell you that I am sure of success. Courage ! "

"Well ! " said the spurious dressmaker, when she saw that Marguerite had finished reading the letter. " What answer shall I take my brother-in-law ? "

" Tell him that he shall certainly have the information he requires to-morrow. To-day, I can only give him the name of the carriage builder, from whom M. de Fondège has purchased his new carriages."

" Give it to me in writing, it is much the safest way."

Mademoiselle Marguerite did so, and her visitor who, as a woman, was delighted to find herself mixed up in an intrigue, then went off repeating the old magistrate's advice : " Courage ! "

But it was no longer necessary to encourage Mademoiselle Marguerite. The assurance of being so effectually helped, had already increased her courage an hundredfold. The future that had seemed so gloomy only a moment before, had now suddenly brightened. By means of the negative in the keeping of the photographer, Carjat, she had the Marquis de Valorsay in her power ; and the magistrate, thanks to the numbers of the bank-notes, could soon prove the guilt of the Fondèges. The protection of Providence was made evident in an unmistakable manner. Thus it was with a placid and almost smiling face that she successively greeted Madame Léon, who returned home quite played out, then Madame de Fondège, who made her appearance attended by two shop-boys overladen with packages, and finally the General, who brought his son, Lieutenant Gustave, with him to dinner.

The lieutenant was a good-looking fellow of twenty-seven, or thereabouts, with laughing eyes and a heavy mustache. He made a great clanking with his spurs, and wore the somewhat theatrical uniform of the 13th Hussars rather ostentatiously. He bowed to Mademoiselle Marguerite with a smile that was too becoming to be displeasing; and he offered her his arm with an air of triumph to lead her to the dining-room, as soon as the servant came to announce that " Madame la Comtesse was served."

Seated opposite to him at table, the young girl could not refrain from furtively watching the man whom they wished to compel her to marry. Never had she seen such intense self-complacency coupled with such utter mediocrity. It was evident that he was doing his best to produce a favorable impression; but as the dinner progressed, his conversation became rather venturesome. He gradually grew extremely animated; and three or four adventures of garrison life which he persisted in relating despite his mother's frowns, were calculated to convince his hearers that he was a great favorite with the fair sex. It was the good cheer that loosened his tongue. There could be no possible doubt on that score; and, indeed, while drinking a glass of the Château Laroze, to which Madame Léon had taken such a liking, he was indiscreet enough to declare that if his mother had always kept house in this fashion, he should have been inclined to ask for more frequent leaves of absence.

However, strange to say, after the coffee was served, the conversation languished till at last it died out almost entirely. Madame de Fondège was the first to disappear on the pretext that some domestic affairs required her attention. The General was the next to

rise and go out, in order to smoke a cigar; and finally
Madame Léon made her escape without saying a word.
So Mademoiselle Marguerite was left quite alone with
Lieutenant Gustave. It was evident enough to the
young girl that this had been preconcerted; and she
asked herself what kind of an opinion M. and Madame
de Fondège could have of her delicacy. The proceeding made her so indignant that she was on the point of
rising from the table and of retiring like the others,
when reason restrained her. She said to herself that
perhaps she might gain some useful information from
this young man, and so she remained.

His face was crimson, and he seemed by far the more
embarrassed of the two. He sat with one elbow resting on the table, and with his gaze persistently fixed
upon a tiny glass half full of brandy which he held in
his hand, as if he hoped to gain some sublime inspiration from it. At last, after an interval of irksome
silence, he ventured to exclaim: " Mademoiselle, should
you like to be an officer's wife? "

" I don't know," answered Marguerite.

" Really! But at least you understand my motive in
asking this question? "

" No."

Any one but the complacent lieutenant would have
been disconcerted by Mademoiselle Marguerite's dry
tone; but he did not even notice it. The effort that he
was making in his intense desire to be eloquent and
persuasive absorbed the attention of all his faculties.
"Then permit me to explain, mademoiselle," he resumed. " We meet this evening for the first time, but
our acquaintance is not the affair of a day. For I know
not how long my father and mother have continually
been chanting your praises. ' Mademoiselle Marguerite

does this; Mademoiselle Marguerite does that.' They never cease talking of you, declaring that heart, wit, talent, beauty, all womanly charms are united in your person. And they have never wearied of telling me that the man whom you honored with your preference would be the happiest of mortals. However, so far I had no desire to marry, and I distrusted them. In fact, I had conceived a most violent prejudice against you. Yes, upon my honor! I felt sure that I should dislike you; but I have seen you and all is changed. As soon as my eyes fell upon you, I experienced a powerful revulsion of feeling. I was never so smitten in my life—and I said to myself, ' Lieutenant, it is all over— you are caught at last!'"

Pale with anger, astonished and humiliated beyond measure, the young girl listened with her head lowered, vainly trying to find words to express the feelings which disturbed her; but M. Gustave, misunderstanding her silence, and congratulating himself upon the effect he had produced, grew bolder, and with the tenderest and most impassioned inflection he could impart to his voice, continued: " Who could fail to be impressed as I have been? How could one behold, without rapturous admiration, such beautiful eyes, such glorious black hair, such smiling lips, such a graceful mien, such wonderful charms of person and of mind? How would it be possible to listen, unmoved, to a voice which is clearer and purer than crystal? Ah! my mother's descriptions fell far short of the truth. But how can one describe the perfections of an angel? To any one who has the happiness or the misfortune of knowing you, there can only be one woman in the world!"

He had gradually approached her chair, and now extended his hand to take hold of Marguerite's, and prob·

ably raise it to his lips. But she shrank from the contact as from red-hot iron, and rising hurriedly, with her eyes flashing, and her voice quivering with indignation: "Monsieur!" she exclaimed, "Monsieur!"

He was so surprised that he stood as if petrified, with his eyes wide open and his hand still extended. "Permit me—allow me to explain," he stammered. But she declined to listen. "Who has told you that you could address such words to me with impunity?" she continued. "Your parents, I suppose; I daresay they told you to be bold. And that is why they have left us, and why no servant has appeared. Ah! they make me pay dearly for the hospitality they have given me!" As she spoke the tears started from her eyes and glistened on her long lashes. "Whom did you fancy you were speaking to?" she added. "Would you have been so audacious if I had a father or a brother to resent your insults?"

The lieutenant started as if he had been lashed with a whip. "Ah! you are severe!" he exclaimed.

And a happy inspiration entering his mind, he continued: "A man does not insult a woman, mademoiselle, when, while telling her that he loves her and thinks her beautiful, he offers her his name and life."

Mademoiselle Marguerite shrugged her shoulders ironically, and remained for a moment silent. She was very proud, and her pride had been cruelly wounded; but reason told her that a continuation of this scene would render a prolonged sojourn in the General's house impossible; and where could she go, without exciting malevolent remarks? Whom could she ask an asylum of? Still this consideration alone would not have sufficed to silence her. But she remembered that a quarrel and a rupture with the Fondèges would certainly imperil the success of her plans. "So I will swallow even this affront," she said to herself; and then in a tone of melancholy bitterness, she remarked, aloud: "A man cannot set a very high value on his name when he offers it to a woman whom he knows absolutely nothing about."

"Excuse me—you forget that my mother——"

"Your mother has only known me for a week."

An expression of intense surprise appeared on the lieutenant's face. "Is it possible?" he murmured.

"Your father has met me five or six times at the table of the Count de Chalusse, who was his friend—but what does he know of me?" resumed Mademoiselle Marguerite. "That I came to the Hôtel de Chalusse a year ago, and that the count treated me like a daughter—that is all! Who I am, where I was reared, and how, and what my past life has been, these are matters that M. de Fondège knows nothing whatever about."

"My parents told me that you were the daughter of the Count de Chalusse, mademoiselle."

"What proof have they of it? They ought to have told you that I was an unfortunate foundling, with no other name than that of Marguerite."

"Oh!"

"They ought to have told you that I am poor, very poor, and that I should probably have been reduced to the necessity of toiling for my daily bread, if it had not been for them."

An incredulous smile curved the lieutenant's lips. He fancied that Mademoiselle Marguerite only wished to prove his disinterestedness, and this thought restored his assurance. "Perhaps you are exaggerating a little, mademoiselle," he replied.

"I am not exaggerating—I possess but ten thousand

francs in the world—I swear it by all that I hold sacred."

" That would not even be the dowry required of an officer's wife by law," muttered the lieutenant.

Was his incredulity sincere or affected? What had his parents really told him? Had they confided everything to him, and was he their accomplice? or had they told him nothing? All these questions flashed rapidly through Marguerite's mind. " You suppose that I am rich, monsieur," she resumed at last. " I understand that only too well. If I was, you ought to shun me as you would shun a criminal, for I could only be wealthy through a crime."

" Mademoiselle——"

" Yes, through a crime. After M. de Chalusse's death, two million francs that had been placed in his escritoire for safe keeping, could not be found. Who stole the money? I myself have been accused of the theft. Your father must have told you of this, as well as of the cloud of suspicion that is still hanging over me."

She paused, for the lieutenant had become whiter than his shirt. " Good God!" he exclaimed in a tone of horror, as if a terrible light had suddenly broken upon his mind. He made a movement as if to leave the room, but suddenly changing his mind, he bowed low before Mademoiselle Marguerite, and said, in a husky voice: " Forgive me, mademoiselle, I did not know what I was doing. I have been misinformed. I have been beguiled by false hopes. I entreat you to say that you forgive me."

" I forgive you, monsieur."

But still he lingered. " I am only a poor devil of a lieutenant," he resumed, " with no other fortune than my epaulettes, no other prospects than an uncertain advancement. I have been foolish and thoughtless. I have committed many acts of folly; but there is nothing in my past life for which I have cause to blush." He looked fixedly at Mademoiselle Marguerite, as if he were striving to read her inmost soul; and in a solemn tone, that contrasted strangely with his usual levity of manner, he added: "If the name I bear should ever be compromised, my prospects would be blighted forever! The only course left for me would be to tender my resignation. I will leave nothing undone to preserve my honor in the eyes of the world, and to right those who have been wronged. Promise me not to interfere with my plans."

Mademoiselle Marguerite trembled like a leaf. She now realized her terrible imprudence. He had divined everything. As she remained silent, he continued wildly: "I entreat you. Do you wish me to beg you at your feet?"

Ah! it was a terrible sacrifice that he demanded of her. But how could she remain obdurate in the presence of such intense anguish? "I will remain neutral," she replied, "that is all I can promise. Providence shall decide."

"Thank you," he said, sadly, suspecting that perhaps it was already too late—"thank you." Then he turned to go, and, in fact, he had already opened the door, when a forlorn hope brought him back to Mademoiselle Marguerite, whose hand he took, timidly faltering, "We are friends, are we not?"

She did not withdraw her icy hand, and in a scarcely audible voice, she repeated: "We are friends?"

Convinced that he could obtain nothing more from her than her promised neutrality, the lieutenant thereupon hastily left the room, and she sank back in her chair more dead than alive. " Great God! what is coming now? " she murmured.

She thought she could understand the unfortunate young man's intentions, and she listened with a throbbing heart, expecting to hear a stormy explanation between his parents and himself. In point of fact, she almost immediately afterward heard the lieutenant inquire in a stern, imperious voice: " Where is my father? "

" The General has just gone to his club."

" And my mother? "

" A friend of hers called a few moments ago to take her to the opera."

" What madness! "

That was all. The outer door opened and closed again with extreme violence, and then Marguerite heard nothing save the sneering remarks of the servants.

It was, indeed, madness on the part of M. and Madame de Fondège not to have waited to learn the result of this interview, planned by themselves, and upon which their very lives depended. But delirium seemed to have seized them since, thanks to a still inexplicable crime, they had suddenly found themselves in possession of an immense fortune. Perhaps in this wild pursuit of pleasure, in the haste they displayed to satisfy their covetous longings, they hoped to forget or silence the threatening voice of conscience. Such was Mademoiselle Marguerite's conclusion; but she was not long left to undisturbed meditation. By the lieutenant's departure the restrictions which had been placed upon the servants' movements had evidently been removed, for they came in to clear the table.

Having with some little difficulty obtained a candle

from one of these model servants, Mademoiselle Marguerite now retired to her own room. In her anxiety, she forgot Madame Léon, but the latter had not forgotten her; she was even now listening at the drawing-room door, inconsolable to think that she had not succeeded in hearing at least part of the conversation between the lieutenant and her dear young lady. Marguerite had no wish to reflect over what had occurred. As she was determined to keep the promise which Lieutenant Gustave had wrung from her, it mattered little whether she had committed a great mistake in allowing him to discover her knowledge of his parent's guilt, and in listening to his entreaties. A secret presentiment warned her that the punishment which would overtake the General and his wife would be none the less terrible, despite her own forbearance, and that they would find their son more inexorable than the severest judge.

The essential thing was to warn the old magistrate; and so in a couple of pages she summarized the scene of the evening, feeling sure that she would find an opportunity to post her letter on the following day. This duty accomplished, she took a book and went to bed, hoping to drive away her gloomy thoughts by reading. But the hope was vain. Her eyes read the words, followed the lines and crossed the pages, but her mind utterly refused to obey her will, and in spite of all her efforts persisted in turning to the shrewd youth who had solemnly sworn to find Pascal for her. A little after midnight Madame de Fondège returned from the opera, and at once proceeded to reprimand her maid for not having lighted a fire. The General returned some time afterward, and he was evidently in the best of spirits.

"They have not seen their son," said Mademoiselle Marguerite to herself, and this anxiety, combined with many others, tortured her so cruelly, that she did not fall asleep until near daybreak. Even then she did not slumber long. It was scarcely half-past seven when she was aroused by a strange commotion and a loud sound of hammering. She was trying to imagine the cause of all this uproar, when Madame de Fondège, already arrayed in a marvellous robe composed of three skirts and an enormous puff, entered the room. "I have come to take you away, my dear child," she exclaimed. "The owner of the house has decided to make some repairs, and the workmen have already invaded our apartments. The General has taken flight, let us follow his example—so make yourself beautiful and we'll go at once."

Without a word, the young girl hastened to obey, while Madame de Fondège expatiated on the delightful drive they would take together in the wonderful brougham which the General had purchased a couple of days before. As for Lieutenant Gustave, she did not even mention his name.

Accustomed to the superb equipages of the Chalusse establishment, Mademoiselle Marguerite did not consider the much-lauded brougham at all remarkable. At the most, it was very showy, having apparently been selected with a view to attracting as much attention as possible. Madame de Fondège was not in a mood to consider this an objection that morning. She was evidently in a nervous state of mind, extremely restless and excited, indeed, it seemed impossible for her to keep still. In default of something better to do, she visited at least a dozen shops, asking to see everything, finding everything frightful, and purchasing without

regard to price. It might have been fancied that she
wished to buy all Paris. About ten o'clock she dragged
Marguerite to Van Klopen's. Received as a *habituée*
of the establishment, thanks to the numerous orders she
had given within the past few days, she was even allowed to enter the mysterious saloon in which the illustrious ruler of Fashion served such of his clients as had
a predilection for absinthe or madeira. On leaving the
place, and before entering the carriage again, Madame
de Fondège turned to Marguerite and inquired:
"Where shall we go now? I have given the servants
an 'outing' on account of the workmen, and we cannot
breakfast at home. Why can't we go to a restaurant,
we two? Many of the most distinguished ladies are in
the habit of doing so. You will see how people will
look at us! I am sure it will amuse you immensely."

"Ah! madame, you forget that it is not a fortnight
since the count's death!"

Madame de Fondège was about to make an impatient
reply, but she mastered the impulse, and in a tone of
hypocritical compassion, exclaimed: "Poor child! poor,
dear child! that's true. I had forgotten. Well, such
being the case, we'll go and ask Baroness Trigault to
give us our breakfast. You will see a lovely woman."
And addressing the coachman she instructed him to
drive to the Trigault mansion in the Rue de la Ville
l'Evêque.

When Madame de Fondège's brougham drew up before the door, the baron was standing in the courtyard
with a cigar between his teeth, examining a pair of
horses which had been sent him on approbation. He
did not like his wife's friend, and he usually avoided
her. But precisely because he was acquainted with the
General's crime and Pascal's plans, he thought it politic

to seem amiable. So, on recognizing Madame de Fondège through the carriage window, he hastened forward with outstretched hand to assist her in alighting.
" Did you come to take breakfast with us?" he asked.
" That would be a most delightful——"

The remainder of the sentence died unuttered upon
his lips. His face became crimson, and the cigar he
was holding slipped from his fingers. He had just
perceived Mademoiselle Marguerite, and his consternation was so apparent that Madame de Fondège could
not fail to remark it; however, she attributed it to the
girl's remarkable beauty. " This is Mademoiselle de
Chalusse, my dear baron," said she, " the daughter of
the noble and esteemed friend whom we so bitterly
lament."

Ah! it was not necessary to tell the baron who this
young girl was; he knew it only too well. He was not
overcome for long; a thought of vengeance speedily
flashed through his mind. It seemed to him that Providence itself offered him the means of putting an end
to an intolerable situation. Regaining his self-control
by a powerful effort, he preceded Madame de Fondège
through the magnificent apartments of the mansion,
lightly saying: " My wife is in her *boudoir*. She will
be delighted to see you. But first of all, I have a good
secret to confide to you. So let me take this young lady
to the baroness, and you and I can join them in a
moment!" Thereupon, without waiting for any rejoinder, he took Marguerite's arm and led her toward
the end of the hall. Then opening a door, he exclaimed
in a mocking voice: " Madame Trigault, allow me to
present to you the daughter of the Count de Chalusse."
And adding in a whisper: " This is your mother, young
girl," he pushed the astonished Marguerite into the

room, closed the door, and returned to Madame de Fondège.

Paler than her white muslin wrapper, the Baroness Trigault sprang from her chair. This was the woman who, while her husband was braving death to win fortune for her, had been dazzled by the Count de Chalusse's wealth, and who, later in life, when she was the richest of the rich, had sunk into the very depths of degradation—had stooped, indeed, to a Coralth! The baroness had once been marvellously beautiful, and even now, many murmurs of admiration greeted her when she dashed through the Champs Elysées in her magnificent equipage, attired in one of those eccentric costumes which she alone dared to wear. She was a type of the wife created by the customs of fashionable society; the woman who feels elated when her name appears in the newspapers and in the chronicles of Parisian " high life "; who has no thought of her deserted fireside, but is ever tormented by a terrible thirst for bustle and excitement; whose head is empty, and whose heart is dry—the woman who only exists for the world; and who is devoured by unappeasable covetousness, and who, at times, envies an actress's liberty, and the notoriety of the leaders of the *demi-monde;* the woman who is always in quest of fresh excitement, and fails to find it; the woman who is *blasé,* and prematurely old in mind and body, and who yet still clings despairingly to her fleeting youth.

Inaccessible to any emotion but vanity, the baroness had never shed a tear over her husband's sufferings. She was sure of her absolute power over him. What did the rest matter? She even gloried in her knowledge that she could make this man—who loved her in spite of everything—at one moment furious with rage or wild with grief, and then an instant afterward plunge him into the rapture of a senseless ecstasy by a word, a smile, or a caress. For such was her power, and she often exercised it mercilessly. Even after the frightful scene that Pascal had witnessed, she had made another appeal to the baron, and he had been weak enough to give her the thirty thousand francs which M. de Coralth needed to purchase his wife's silence.

However, this time the baroness trembled. Her usual shrewdness had not deserted her, and she perfectly understood all that Marguerite's presence in that house portended. Since her husband brought this young girl—her daughter—to her, he must know everything, and have taken some fatal resolution. Had she, indeed, exhausted the patience which she had fancied inexhaustible? She was not ignorant of the fact that her husband had disposed of his immense fortune in a way that would enable him to say and prove that he was insolvent whenever occasion required; and if he found courage to apply for a legal separation, what could she hope to obtain from the courts? A bare living, almost nothing. In such a case, how could she exist? She would be compelled to spend her last years in the same poverty that had made her youth so wretched. She saw herself—ah! what a frightful misfortune—turned out of her princely home, and reduced to furnished apartments rented for five hundred francs a year!

Mademoiselle Marguerite was no less startled and horror-stricken than Madame Trigault, and she stood rooted to the spot, exactly where the baron had left her. Silent and motionless, they confronted each other for a moment which seemed a century to both of them. The resemblance which had astonished Pascal could not fail to strike them, for it was still more noticeable

now that they stood face to face. But anything was
preferable to this torturing suspense, and so, summoning all her courage, the baroness broke the silence by
saying: "You are the daughter of the Count de
Chalusse?"

"I think so, but I have no proofs of it."

"And—your mother?"

"I do not know her, madame, and I have no desire
to know her."

Disconcerted by this brief but implacable reply,
Madame Trigault hung her head.

"What could I have to say to my mother?" continued Marguerite. "That I hate her? My courage
would fail me to do so. And yet, how can I think without bitterness of the woman who, after abandoning me
herself, endeavored to deprive me of my father's love
and protection? I could have forgiven anything but
that. Ah! I have not always been so patient and resigned! The laws of our country do not forbid illegitimate children to search for their parents, and more than
once I have said to myself that I would discover my
mother, and have my revenge."

"But you have no means of discovering her?"

"In this you are greatly mistaken, madame. After
the Count de Chalusse's death, a package of letters, a
glove, and some withered flowers were found in one
of the drawers of his escritoire."

The baroness started back as if a yawning chasm had
suddenly opened at her feet. "My letters!" she exclaimed. "Ah! wretched woman that I am, he kept
them! It is all over! I am lost, for of course, they have
been read."

"The ribbon securing them together has not even
been untied."

"Is that true? Don't deceive me! Where are they, then—where are they?"

"Under the protection of the seals affixed by the justice of the peace."

Madame Trigault tottered, as if she were about to fall. "Then it is only a reprieve," she moaned, "and I am none the less ruined. Those cursed letters will necessarily be read, and all will be discovered. They will see——" The thought of what they would see endowed her with the energy of despair, and clutching hold of Marguerite's wrists: "Listen!" said she, approaching so near that her hot breath scorched the girl's cheeks, "no one must be allowed to see those letters! —it must not be! I will tell you what they contain. I hated my husband; I loved the Count de Chalusse madly, and he had sworn that he would marry me if ever I became a widow. Do you understand now? The name of the poison I obtained—how I proposed to administer it, and what its effects would be—all this is plainly written in my own handwriting and signed— yes, signed—with my own name. The plot failed, but it was none the less real, positive, palpable—and those letters are a proof of it. But they shall never be read —no—not if I am obliged to set fire to the Hôtel de Chalusse with my own hand."

Now the count's constant terror, the fear with which this woman had inspired him, were explained. He was an accomplice—he also had written no doubt, and she had preserved his letters as he had preserved hers. Crime had bound them indissolubly together.

Horrified beyond expression, Marguerite freed herself from Madame Trigault's grasp. "I swear to you, madame, that everything any human being can do to save your letters shall be done by me," she exclaimed.

"And have you any hope of success?"

"Yes," replied the girl, remembering her friend, the magistrate.

Moved by a far more powerful emotion than any she had ever known before, the baroness uttered an exclamation of joy. "Ah! how good you are!" she exclaimed—"how generous! how noble! You take your revenge in giving me back life, honor, everything —for you are my daughter; do you not know it? Did they not tell you, before bringing you here, that I was the hated and unnatural mother who abandoned you?"

She advanced with tearful eyes and outstretched arms, but Marguerite sternly waved her back. "Spare yourself, madame, and spare me, the humiliation of an unnecessary explanation."

"Marguerite! Good God! you repulse me. After all you have promised to do for me, will you not forgive me?"

"I will try to forget, madame," replied the girl and she was already stepping toward the door when the baroness threw herself at her feet, crying, in a heart-rending tone: "Have pity, Marguerite, I am your mother. One has no right to deny one's own mother."

But the young girl passed on. "My mother is dead, madame; I do not know you!" And she left the room without even turning her head, without even glancing at the baroness, who had fallen upon the floor in a deep swoon.

XIX.

BARON TRIGAULT still held Madame de Fondège a prisoner in the hall. What did he say to her in justification of the expedient he had improvised? His own
agitation was so great that he himself scarcely knew,
and it mattered but little after all, for the good lady did
not even pretend to listen to his apologies. Although
by no means overshrewd, she suspected some great
mystery, some choice bit of scandal, perhaps, and her
eyes never once wandered from the door leading to the
boudoir. At last this door opened again, and Mademoiselle Marguerite reappeared. "Great Heavens!"
exclaimed Madame de Fondège; "what has happened
to my poor child?"

For the unfortunate girl advanced with an automatic
tread, her eyes fixed on vacancy, and her hands outstretched, as if feeling her way. It indeed seemed to
her as if the floor swayed to and fro under her feet,
as if the walls tottered, as if the ceiling were about to
fall upon her and crush her.

Madame de Fondège sprang forward. "What is the
matter, my dearest?"

Alas! the poor girl was utterly overcome. "It is but
a trifle," she faltered. But her eyes closed, her hands
clutched wildly for some support, and she would have
fallen to the ground if the baron had not caught her
in his arms and carried her to a sofa. "Help!" cried
Madame de Fondège, "help, she is dying!—a physician!"

But there was no need of a physician. One of the
maids came with some fresh water and a bottle of

smelling salts, and Marguerite soon recovered sufficiently to sit up, and cast a frightened glance around
her, while she mechanically passed her hand again and
again over her cold forehead. "Do you feel better,
my darling?" inquired Madame de Fondège at last.

"Yes."

"Ah! you gave me a terrible fright; see how I
tremble." But the worthy lady's fright was as nothing
in comparison with the curiosity that tortured her. It
was so powerful, indeed, that she could not control it.
"What has happened?" she asked.

"Nothing, madame, nothing."

"But——"

"I am subject to such attacks. I was very cold, and
the heat of the room made me feel faint."

Although she could only speak with the greatest difficulty, the baron realized by her tone that she would
never reveal what had taken place, and his gratitude
and relief knew no bounds. "Don't tire the poor child,"
he said to Madame de Fondège. "The best thing you
can do would be to take her home and put her to bed."

"I agree with you; but, unfortunately, I have sent
away my brougham with orders not to return for me
until one o'clock."

"Is that the only difficulty? If so, you shall have a
carriage at once, my dear madame." So saying, the
baron made a sign to one of the servants, and the man
started on his mission at once.

Madame de Fondège was silent but furious. "He is
actually putting me out of doors," she thought. "This
is a little too much! And why doesn't the baroness
make her appearance—she must certainly have heard
my voice? What does it all mean? However, I'm
sure Marguerite will tell me when we are alone."

But Madame de Fondège was wrong, for she vainly plied the girl with questions all the way from the Rue de la Ville l'Evêque to the Rue Pigalle. She could only obtain this unvarying and obstinate reply: "Nothing has happened. What do you suppose could have happened?"

Never in her whole life had Madame de Fondège been so incensed. "The blockhead!" she mentally exclaimed. "Who ever saw such obstinacy! Hateful creature!—I could beat her!"

She did not beat her, but on reaching the house she eagerly asked: "Do you feel strong enough to go up stairs alone?"

"Yes, madame."

"Then I will leave you. You know Van Klopen expects me again at one o'clock precisely; and I have not breakfasted yet. Remember that my servants are at your disposal, and don't hesitate to call them. You are at home, recollect."

It was not without considerable difficulty—not without being compelled to stop and rest several times on her way up stairs—that Mademoiselle Marguerite succeeded in reaching the apartments of the Fondège family. "Where is madame?" inquired the servant who opened the door.

"She is still out."

"Will she return to dinner?"

"I don't know."

"M. Gustave has been here three times already; he was very angry when he found that there was no one at home—he went on terribly. Besides, the workmen have turned everything topsy-turvy."

However, Marguerite had already reached her own room, and thrown herself on the bed. She was suffering terribly. Her brave spirit still retained its energy; but the flesh had succumbed. Every vein and artery throbbed with violence, and while a chill seemed to come to her heart, her head burned as if it had been on fire. " My Lord," she thought, " am I going to fall ill at the last moment, just when I have most need of all my strength? "

She tried to sleep, but was unable to do so. How could she free herself from the thought that haunted her? Her mother! To think that such a woman was her mother! Was it not enough to make her die of sorrow and shame? And yet this woman must be saved —the proofs of her crime must be annihilated with her letters. Marguerite asked herself whether the old magistrate would have it in his power to help her in this respect. Perhaps not, and then what could she do? She asked herself if she had not been too cruel, too severe. Guilty or not, the baroness was still her mother. Had she the right to be pitiless, when by stretching out her hand she might, perhaps, have rescued the wretched woman from her terrible life.

Thus thinking, the young girl sat alone and forgotten in her little room. The hours went by, and daylight had begun to wane, when suddenly a shrill whistle resounded in the street, under her windows. " Pi-ouit." It came upon her like an electric shock, and with a bound she sprang to her feet. For this cry was the signal that had been agreed upon between herself and the young man who had so abruptly offered to help her on the occasion of her visit to M. Fortunat's office. Was she mistaken? No—for on listening she heard the cry resound a second time, even more shrill and prolonged than before.

This was no time for hesitation, and so she went

down stairs at once. Hope sent new blood coursing through her veins and endowed her with invincible energy. On reaching the street-door, she paused and looked around her. At a short distance off she perceived a young fellow clad in a blouse, who was apparently engaged in examining the goods displayed in a shop window. Despite his position, he saw her also, for coming nearer, he hurriedly exclaimed: " Follow me at a little distance in the rear until I stop."

Marguerite obeyed him in breathless suspense. The young fellow was our friend Victor Chupin, now somewhat the worse for his encounter with Vantrasson that same morning. His face was considerably disfigured, and one of his eyes was black and swollen ; nevertheless he was in a state of ecstatic happiness. Happy, and yet anxious ; for, as he preceded Mademoiselle Marguerite, he said to himself: " How shall I tell her that I have succeeded? There must be no folly. If I tell her the news suddenly, she will most likely faint, so I must break the news gently."

On reaching the Rue Boursault, he turned the corner, and paused, waiting for Mademoiselle Marguerite to join him. " What is the news? " she anxiously asked.

"Everything is progressing finely—slowly, but finely."

"You know something, monsieur! Speak! Don't you see how anxious I am? "

He did see it only too well; and his embarrassment increased to such a pitch that he began to scratch his head furiously. At last he decided on a plan. " First of all, mademoiselle, brace yourself against the wall, and now stand firm. Yes, like that. Now, are you all right? Well, I have found M. Ferailleur!"

Chupin's precaution was a wise one, for Marguerite

tottered. Such a success, so quickly gained, was indeed
astounding. "Is it possible?" she murmured.

"So possible that I have a letter for you from M.
Ferailleur in my pocket, mademoiselle. Here it is—
I am to wait for an answer."

She took the note he handed her, broke the seal with
trembling hand, and read as follows:

"We are approaching the end, my dearest. One step
more and we shall triumph. But I must see you to-day
at any risk. Leave the house this evening at eight
o'clock. My mother will be waiting for you in a cab,
at the corner of the Rue Pigalle and the Rue Boursault.
Come, and let no fear of arousing the suspicions of the
Fondèges deter you. They are henceforth powerless to
injure you.   PASCAL."

"I will go!" replied Marguerite at once, careless of
the obstacles that might impede the fulfilment of her
promise. For it was quite possible that serious difficulties might arise. Madame Léon, who had been in-
visible since the morning, might suddenly reappear, or
the General and his wife might return to dinner. And
what could Marguerite answer if they asked her where
she wanted to go alone, and at such an hour of the
evening? And if they attempted to prevent her from
keeping her appointment, how could she resist? All
these were weighty questions and yet she did not hesitate. Pascal had spoken; that sufficed, and she was
determined to obey him implicitly, cost what it might.
If he advised such a step, it was because he deemed it
best and necessary; and she willingly submitted to the
instructions of the man in whom she felt such unbounded confidence.

Having told Chupin that she might be relied upon

for the evening, she was retracing her way home, when suddenly the thought occurred to her that she ought not to neglect this opportunity to place a decisive weapon in Pascal's hands. She was close to the Rue Notre Dame de Lorette and so without more ado she hurried to the establishment of Carjat the photographer. He was fortunately disengaged, and she at once obtained from him a proof of the compromising letter written by the Marquis de Valorsay to Madame Léon. She placed it carefully in her pocket, thanked the photographer, and then hurried back to the Rue Pigalle to wait for the hour appointed in Pascal's letter. Fortunately none of her unpleasant apprehensions were realized. The dinner-hour came and passed, and still the house remained deserted. The workmen had gone off and the laughter and chatter of the servants in the kitchen were the only sounds that broke the stillness. Faint for want of food—for she had taken no nourishment during the day—Marguerite had considerable difficulty in obtaining something to eat from the servants. At last, however, they gave her some soup and cold meat, served on a corner of the bare table in the dining-room. It was half-past seven when she finished this frugal meal. She waited a moment, and then fearing she might keep Madame Ferailleur waiting, she went down into the street.

A cab was waiting at the corner of the Rue Boursault, as indicated. Its windows were lowered, and in the shade one could discern the face and white hair of an elderly lady. Glancing behind her to assure herself that she had not been followed, Marguerite eagerly approached the vehicle, whereupon a kindly voice exclaimed: "Jump in quickly, mademoiselle."

Marguerite obeyed, and the door was scarcely closed

behind her before the driver had urged his horse into a gallop. He had evidently received his instructions in advance, as well as the promise of a magnificent gratuity.

Sitting side by side on the back seat, the old lady and the young girl remained silent, but this did not prevent them from casting stealthy glances at each other, and striving to distinguish one another's features whenever the vehicle passed in front of some brilliantly lighted shop. They had never met before, and their anxiety to become acquainted was intense, for they each felt that the other would exert a decisive influence upon her life. All of Madame Ferailleur's friends would undoubtedly have been surprised at the step she had taken, and yet it was quite in accordance with her character. As long as she had entertained any hope of preventing this marriage she had not hesitated to express and even exaggerate her objections and repugnance. But her point of view was entirely changed when conquered by the strength of her son's passion, she at last yielded a reluctant consent. The young girl who was destined to be her daughter-in-law at once became sacred in her eyes; and it seemed to her an act of duty to watch over Marguerite, and shield her reputation. Having considered the subject, she had decided that it was not proper for her son's betrothed to run about the streets alone in the evening. Might it not compromise her honor? and later on might it not furnish venomous Madame de Fondège with an opportunity to exercise her slanderous tongue? Thus the puritanical old lady had come to fetch Marguerite, so that whenever occasion required she might be able to say : " I was there ! "

As for Marguerite, after the trials of the day, she yielded without reserve to the feeling of rest and happi-

ness that now filled her heart. Again and again had
Pascal spoken of his mother's prejudices and the inflex-
ibility of her principles. But he had also spoken of her
dauntless energy, the nobility of her nature, and of her
love and devotion to him. With Marguerite, moreover,
one consideration—one which she would scarcely have
admitted, perhaps—outweighed all others: Madame
Ferailleur was Pascal's mother. For that reason alone,
if for no other, she was prepared to worship her. How
fervently she blessed this noble woman, who, a widow,
and ruined in fortune by an unprincipled scoundrel, had
bravely toiled to educate her son, making him the man
whom Marguerite had freely chosen from among all
others. She would have knelt before this grand but
simple-hearted mother had she dared; she would have
kissed her hands. And a poignant regret came to her
heart when she remembered her own mother, Baroness
Trigault, and compared her with this matchless woman.

Meanwhile the cab had passed the outer boulevards,
and was now whirling along the Route d'Asnières, as
fast as the horse could drag it. "We are almost
there," remarked Madame Ferailleur, speaking for the
first time.

Marguerite's response was inaudible; she was so
overcome with emotion. The driver had just turned
the corner of the Route de la Révolte; and it was not
long before he checked his panting horse. "Look,
mademoiselle," said Madame Ferailleur again, "this is
our home."

Upon the threshold, bareheaded, and breathless with
impatience and hope, stood a man who was counting
the seconds with the violent throbbings of his heart.
He did not wait for the cab to stop, but springing to
the door, he opened it; and then, catching Marguerite

in his arms, he carried her into the house with a cry of joy. She had not even time to look around her, ere he had placed her in an arm-chair, and fallen on his knees before her. "At last I see you again, my beloved Marguerite," he exclaimed. "You are mine—nothing shall part us again!"

They sobbed in each other's arms. They could bear adversity unmoved; but their composure deserted them in this excess of happiness; and standing in the doorway, Madame Ferailleur felt the tears come to her eyes as she stood watching them.

"How can I tell you all that I have suffered!" said Pascal, whose voice was hoarse with feeling. "The papers have told you all the details, I suppose. How I was accused of cheating at cards; how the vile epithet 'thief' was cast in my face; how they tried to search me; how my most intimate friends deserted me; how I was virtually expelled from the Palais de Justice. All this is terrible, is it not? Ah, well! it is nothing in comparison with the intense, unendurable anguish I experienced in thinking that you believed the infamous calumny which disgraced me."

Marguerite rose to her feet. "You thought that!" she exclaimed. "You believed that I doubted you? I! Like you, I have been accused of robbery myself. Do you believe me guilty?"

"Good God! I suspect you!"

"Then why——"

"I was mad, Marguerite, my only love, I was mad! But who would not have lost his senses under such circumstances? It was the very day after this atrocious conspiracy. I had seen Madame Léon, and had trusted her with a letter for you in which I entreated you to grant me five minutes' conversation."

"Alas! I never received it."

"I know that now; but then I was deceived. I went to the little garden gate to await your coming, but it was Madame Léon who appeared. She brought me a note written in pencil and signed with your name, bidding me an eternal farewell. And, fool that I was, I did not see that the note was a forgery!"

Mademoiselle Marguerite was amazed. The veil was now torn aside, and the truth revealed to her. Now she remembered Madame Léon's embarrassment when she met her returning from the garden on the night following the count's death. "Ah, well! Pascal," she said, "do you know what I was doing at almost the same moment? Alarmed at having received no news from you, I hastened to the Rue d'Ulm, where I learned that you had sold your furniture and started for America. Any other woman might have believed herself deserted under such circumstances, but not I. I felt sure that you had not fled in ignominious fashion. I was convinced that you had only concealed yourself for a time in order to strike your enemies more surely."

"Do not shame me, Marguerite. It is true that of us two I showed myself the weaker."

Lost in the rapture of the present moment, they had forgotten the past and the future, the agony they had endured, the dangers that still threatened them, and even the existence of their enemies.

But Madame Ferailleur was watching. She pointed to the clock, and earnestly exclaimed: "Time is passing, my son. Each moment that is wasted endangers our success. Should any suspicion bring Madame Vantrasson here, all would be lost."

"She cannot come upon us unawares, my dear mother. Chupin has promised not to lose sight of her. If she stirs from her shop, he will hasten here and throw a stone against the shutters to warn us."

But even this did not satisfy Madame Ferailleur.

" You forget, Pascal," she insisted, " that Mademoiselle Marguerite must be at home again by ten o'clock, if she consents to the ordeal you feel obliged to impose upon her."

This was the voice of duty recalling Pascal to the stern realities of life. He slowly rose, conquered his emotion, and, after reflecting for a moment, said: " First of all, Marguerite, I owe you the truth and an exact statement of our situation. Circumstances have compelled me to act without consulting you. Have I done right or wrong? You shall judge." And without stopping to listen to the girl's protestations, he rapidly explained how he had managed to win M. de Valorsay's confidence, discover his plans, and become his trusted accomplice. " This scoundrel's plan is very simple," he continued. " He is determined to marry you. Why? Because, though you are not aware of it, you are rich, and the sole heiress to the fortune of the Count de Chalusse, your father. This surprises you, does it not? Very well! listen to me. Deceived by the Marquis de Valorsay, the Count de Chalusse had promised him your hand. These arrangements were nearly completed, though you had not been informed of them. In fact, everything had been decided. At the outset, however, a grave difficulty had presented itself. The marquis wished your father to acknowledge you before your marriage, but this he refused to do. ' It would expose me to the most frightful dangers,' he declared. ' However, I will recognize Marguerite as my daughter in my will, and, at the same time, leave all my property to her.' But the marquis would not listen to this proposal.

'I don't doubt your good intentions, my dear count,'
said he, 'but suppose this will should be contested, your
property might pass into other hands.' This difficulty
put a stop to the proceedings for some time. The
marquis asked for guarantees; the other refused to give
them—until, at last, M. de Chalusse discovered an expedient which would satisfy both parties. He confided
to M. de Valorsay's keeping a will in which he recognized you as his daughter, and bequeathed you his entire fortune. This document, the validity of which is
unquestionable, has been carefully preserved by the
marquis. He has not spoken of its existence; and he
would destroy it rather than restore it to you at present.
But as soon as you became his wife, he intended to produce it and thus obtain possession of the count's
millions."

"Ah! the old justice of the peace was not mistaken,"
murmured Mademoiselle Marguerite.

Pascal did not hear her. All his faculties were absorbed in the attempt he was making to give a clear and
concise explanation, for he had much to say, and it was
growing late. "As for the enormous sum you have
been accused of taking," he continued, "I know what
has become of it; it is in the hands of M. de Fondège."

"I know that, Pascal—I'm sure of it; but the proof,
the proof!"

"The proof exists, and, like the will, it is in the hands
of the Marquis de Valorsay."

"Is it possible! Great Heavens! You are sure you
are not deceived?"

"I have seen the proof, and it is overpowering, irrefutable! I have touched it—I have held it in my hands.
And it explains everything which may have seemed
strange and incomprehensible to you. The letter which

M. de Chalusse received on the day of his death was
written by his sister. She asked in it for her share of
the family estate, threatening him with a terrible scandal if he refused to comply with her request. Had the
count decided to brave this scandal rather than yield?
We have good reason to suppose so. However, this
much is certain: he had a terrible hatred, not so much
for his sister, perhaps, as for the man who had seduced
her, and afterward married her, actuated by avaricious
motives alone. He had sworn thousands of times that
neither husband nor wife should ever have a penny of
the large fortune which really belonged to them. Believing that a lawsuit was now inevitable, and wishing
to conceal his wealth, he was greatly embarrassed by
the large amount of money he had on hand. What
should he do with it? Where could he hide it? He
finally decided to intrust it to the keeping of M. de
Fondège, who was known as an eccentric man, but
whose honesty seemed to be above suspicion. So, when
he left home, on the afternoon of his illness, he took
the package of bank-notes and bonds, which you had
noticed in the escritoire that morning, away with him.
We shall never know what passed between your father
and the General—we can only surmise. But what I
do know, and what I shall be able to prove, is that M.
de Fondège accepted the trust, and that he gave an
acknowledgment of it in the form of a letter, which
read as follows:

"'My Dear Count de Chalusse—I hereby acknowledge the receipt, on Thursday, October 15, 186—,
of the sum of two millions, two hundred and fifty thousand francs, which I shall deposit, in my name, at the
Bank of France, subject to the orders of Mademoiselle
Marguerite, your daughter, on the day she presents this

letter. And believe, my dear count, in the absolute devotion of your old comrade,
"GENERAL DE FONDÈGE.' "

Mademoiselle Marguerite was thunderstruck. "Who can have furnished you with these particulars?" she inquired.

"The Marquis de Valorsay, my dearest; and I will explain how he was enabled to do so. M. de Fondège wrote the address of his 'old comrade' on this letter, which was folded and sealed, but not enclosed in an envelope. M. de Chalusse proposed to post it himself, so that the official stamp might authenticate its date. But on reflection, he became uneasy. He felt that this tiny, perishable scrap of paper would be the only proof of the deposit which he had confided to M. de Fondège's honor. This scrap might be lost, burned, or stolen. Then what would happen? He had so often seen trustees betray the confidence of which they had seemed worthy. So M. de Chalusse racked his brains to discover a means of protection from an improbable but possible misfortune. He found it. Passing a stationer's shop, he went in, purchased one of those letter-presses which merchants use in their correspondence, and, under pretext of trying it, took a copy of M. de Fondège's letter. Having done this, he placed the copy in an envelope addressed to the Marquis de Valorsay, and, with his heart relieved of all anxiety, posted it at the same time as the original letter. A few moments later he got into the cab in which he was stricken down with apoplexy."

Extraordinary as Pascal's explanations must have seemed to her, Marguerite did not doubt their accuracy in the least. "Then it is the copy of this letter which you saw in the possession of the Marquis de Valorsay?"

"Yes."

"And the original?"

"M. de Fondège alone can tell what has become of that. It is evident that he has somehow succeeded in obtaining possession of it. Would he have dared to squander money as he has done if he had not been convinced that there was no proof of his guilt in existence? Perhaps on hearing of the count's sudden death he bribed the concierge at the Hôtel de Chalusse to watch for this letter and return it to him. But on this subject I have only conjectures to offer. If they wish you to marry their son, it is probably because it seems too hard that you should be left in abject poverty while they are enjoying the fortune they have stolen from you. The vilest scoundrels have their scruples. Besides, a marriage with their son would protect them against any possible mischance in the future."

He was silent for a moment, and then more slowly resumed: "You see, Marguerite, we have clear, palpable, and irrefutable proofs of *your* innocence; but in my efforts to clear my own name of disgrace, I have been far less fortunate. I have tried in vain to collect material proofs of the conspiracy against me. It is only by proving the guilt of the Marquis de Valorsay and the Viscount de Coralth that I can establish my innocence, and so far I am powerless to do so."

Mademoiselle Marguerite's face brightened with supreme joy. "Then I can serve you, in my turn, my only love," she exclaimed. "Ah! blessed be God who inspired me, and who thus rewards me for an hour of courage. My poor father's plan also occurred to me, Pascal. Was it not strange? The material proof of your innocence which you have sought for in vain, is in my possession, written and signed by the Marquis de Valorsay. Like M. de Fondège, he believes that the letter which proves his guilt is annihilated. He burned it himself, and yet it exists." So saying, she drew from her bosom one of the copies which she had received from Carjat the photographer, and handed it to Pascal, adding, " Look ! "

Pascal eagerly perused the marvellous fac-simile of the letter which the marquis had written to Madame Léon. "Ah! this is the scoundrel's death warrant," he exclaimed, exultantly. And approaching Madame Ferailleur, who still stood leaning against the door, silent and motionless : " Look, mother," he repeated, " look ! "

And he pointed to this paragraph which was so convincing and so explicit, that the most exacting jury would have asked for no further evidence. " I have formed a plan which will completely efface all remembrance of that cursed P. F., in case any one could condescend to think of him, after the disgrace we fastened upon him the other evening at the house of Madame d'A——."

" Nor is this all," resumed Mademoiselle Marguerite. " There are other letters which will prove that this plot was the marquis's work and which give the name of his accomplice, Coralth. And these letters are in the possession of a man of dubious integrity, who was once the marquis's ally, but who has now become his enemy. He is known as Isidore Fortunat, and lives in the Place de la Bourse."

Marguerite felt that Madame Ferailleur's keen glance was riveted upon her. She intuitively divined what was passing in the mind of the puritanical old lady, and realized that her whole future, and the happiness of her entire wedded life, depended upon her conduct at that moment. So, desirous of making a full confession, she hastily exclaimed: " My conduct may have seemed strange in a young girl, Pascal. A timid, inexperienced girl, who had been carefully kept from all knowledge of life and evil, would have been crushed by such a burden of disgrace, and could only have wept and prayed. I did weep and pray; but I also struggled and fought. In the hour of peril I found myself endowed with some of the courage and energy which distinguished the poor women of the people among whom I formerly earned my bread. The teachings and miseries of the past were not lost to me!" And as simply as if she were telling the most natural thing in the world, she described the struggle she had undertaken against the world, strong in her faith in Pascal and in his love.

"Ah, you are a noble and courageous girl!" exclaimed Madame Ferailleur. "You are worthy of my son, and you will proudly guard our honest name!"

For some little time already the obstinate old lady had been struggling against the sympathetic emotion that filled her heart, and big tears were coursing down her wrinkled cheeks.

Unable to restrain herself any longer, she now threw both arms around Marguerite's neck, and drew her toward her in a long embrace, murmuring: " Marguerite, my daughter! Ah! how unjust my prejudices were!"

It might be thought that Pascal was transported with joy on hearing this, but no; the lines of care on his forehead deepened, as he said: " Happiness is so near!

Why must a final test, another humiliation, separate us from it?"

But Marguerite now felt strong enough to meet even martyrdom with a smile. "Speak, Pascal!" said she, "don't you see that it is almost ten o'clock?"

He hesitated; there was grief in his eyes and his breath came quick and hard, as he resumed: "For your sake and mine, we must conquer, at any price. This is the only reason that can justify the horrible expedient I have to suggest. M. de Valorsay, as you know, has boasted of his power to overcome your resistance, and he really believes that he possesses this power. Why I have not killed him again and again when he has been at my mercy, I can scarcely understand. The only thing that gave me power to restrain myself was my desire for as sure, as terrible, and as public a revenge as the humiliation he inflicted on me. His plan for your ruin is such as only a scoundrel like himself could conceive. With the assistance of his vile tool, Coralth, he has formed a league, offensive and defensive, with the son of the Count de Chalusse's sister, who is the only acknowledged heir at this moment—a young man destitute of heart and intelligence, and inordinately vain, but neither better nor worse than many others who figure respectably in society. His name is Wilkie Gordon. The marquis has acquired great influence over him, and has persuaded him that it is his duty to denounce you to the authorities. He has, in short, accused you of defrauding the heirs of the Chalusse estate of two millions of francs and also of poisoning the count."

The girl shrugged her shoulders disdainfully. "As for the robbery, we have an answer to that," she answered, "and as regards the poisoning—really the accusation is too absurd!"

But Pascal still looked gloomy. "The matter is more serious than you suppose," he replied. "They have found a physician—a vile, cowardly scoundrel—who for a certain sum has consented to appear in support of the accusation."

"Dr. Jodon, I presume!"

"Yes; and this is not all. The count's escritoire contains the vial of medicine of which he drank a portion on the day of his death. Well, to-morrow night, Madame Léon will open the garden gate of the Hôtel de Chalusse and admit a rascal who will abstract the vial."

Marguerite shuddered. Now she understood the fiendish cunning of the plot. "It might ruin me!" she murmured.

Pascal nodded affirmatively. "M. de Valorsay wishes you to consider yourself as irretrievably lost, and then he intends to offer to save you on condition that you consent to marry him. I should say, however, that M. Wilkie is ignorant of the atrocious projects he is abetting. They are known only to the marquis and M. de Coralth; and it is I who, under the name of Maumejan, act as their adviser. It was to me that the marquis sent M. Wilkie for assistance in drawing up this accusation. I myself wrote out the denunciation, which was as terrible and as formidable as our bitterest enemy could possibly desire, combining, as it did, with perfidious art, the reports of the valets and the suspicions of the physician, and establishing the connection between the robbery and the murder. It finished by demanding a thorough investigation. And M. Wilkie copied and signed this document, and carried it to the prosecution office himself."

Mademoiselle Marguerite sank half-fainting into an arm-chair. "You have done this!" she faltered.

"It was necessary, my daughter," whispered Madame Ferailleur.

"Yes, it was necessary, absolutely necessary," repeated Pascal, "as you will see. Justice, which is a human institution, and limited in its powers, cannot fathom motives, read thoughts, or interfere with plans, however abominable they may be, or however near realization. Before it can interfere, the law must have material, tangible proof, convincing to the senses. Until you are arrested, the crimes committed by M. de Valorsay, and those associated with him, do not come within the reach of human justice; but as soon as you are in prison, I can hasten to our friend the justice of the peace, and we shall go at once to the investigating magistrate and explain everything. Now, when your innocence and the guilt of your accusers have been established, what do you fancy the authorities will do? They will wait until your enemies declare themselves, in order to capture them all at once, and prevent the escape of a single one. To-morrow night some clever detectives will watch the Hôtel de Chalusse, and just as Madame Léon and the wretch with her think themselves sure of success, they will be caught in the very act and arrested. When they are examined by a magistrate, who is conversant with the whole affair, can they deny their guilt? No; certainly not. Acting upon their confession, the authorities will force an entrance into Valorsay's house, where they will find your father's will and the receipt given by M. de Fondège— in a word, all the proofs of their guilt. And while this search is going on, all your enemies, reassured by your arrest, will be at a grand *soirée* given by Baron Trigault. I shall be there as well."

Mademoiselle Marguerite had mastered her momentary weakness. She rose to her feet, and in a firm voice exclaimed: "You have acted rightly."

"Ah! there was no other way. And yet I wished to see you, to learn if this course were too repugnant to you."

She interrupted him with a gesture. "When shall I be arrested?" she asked, quietly.

"This evening or to-morrow," was his answer.

"Very well! I have only one request to make. The Fondèges have a son who has no hand in the affair, but who will be more severely punished than his parents, if we do not spare them. Could you not——'

"I can do nothing, Marguerite. I am powerless now."

Everything was soon arranged. Marguerite raised her forehead to Pascal for his parting kiss, and went away accompanied by Madame Ferailleur, who escorted her to the corner of the Rue Boursault. The General and his wife had returned home in advance of Marguerite. She found them sitting in the drawing-room, with distorted faces and teeth chattering with fear. With them was a bearded man who, as soon as she appeared, exclaimed:

"You are Mademoiselle Marguerite, are you not? I arrest you in the name of the law. There is my warrant." And without more ado he led her away.

XX.

MONEY, which nowadays has taken the place of the good fairies of former times, had gratified M. Wilkie's every longing in a single night. Without any period of transition, dreamlike as it were, he had passed from what he called " straitened circumstances " to the splendid enjoyment of a princely fortune. Madame d'Argelès's renunciation had been so correctly drawn up, that as soon as he presented his claims and displayed his credentials he was placed in possession of the Chalusse estate. It is true that a few trifling difficulties presented themselves. For instance, the old justice of the peace who had affixed the seals refused to remove them from certain articles of furniture, especially from the late count's escritoire, without an order from the court, and several days were needed to obtain this. But what did that matter to M. Wilkie? The house, with its splendid reception-rooms, pictures, statuary and gardens, was at his disposal, and he installed himself therein at once. Twenty horses neighed and stamped in his stables; there were at least a dozen carriages in the coach-house. He devoted his attention exclusively to the horses and vehicles; but acting upon the advice of Casimir, who had become his valet and oracle, he retained all the former servants of the house, from Bourigeau the concierge down to the humblest scullery maid. Still, he gave them to understand that this was only a temporary arrangement. A man like himself, living in this progressive age, could scarcely be expected to content himself with what had satisfied the

Count de Chalusse. "For I have my plans," he re-marked to Casimir, "but let Paris wait awhile."

He repudiated his former friends. Costard and Ser-pillon, pretended viscounts though they were, were quite beneath the notice of a Gordon-Chalusse, as M. Wilkie styled himself on his visiting cards. However, he purchased their share of Pompier de Nanterre, feel-ing convinced that this remarkable steeplechaser had a brilliant future before him. He did not trouble himself to any great extent about his mother. Like every one else, he knew that she had disappeared, but nothing further. On the other hand, the thought of his father, the terrible *chevalier d'industrie,* hung over his joy like a pall; and each time the great entrance bell announced a visitor, he trembled, turned pale, and mut-tered: "Perhaps it's he!"

Tortured by this fear, he clung closely to the Mar-quis de Valorsay as if he felt that this distinguished friend was a powerful support. Besides, people of rank and distinction naturally exercised a powerful at-traction over him, and he fancied he grew several inches taller when, in some public place, in the street, or a restaurant, he was able to call out, "I say, Val-orsay, my good friend," or, "Upon my word! my dear marquis!"

M. de Valorsay received these effusions graciously enough, although, in point of fact, he was terribly bored by the platitudes of his new acquaintance. He intended to send him to Coventry later on, but just now M. Wilkie was too useful to be ignored. So he had intro-duced him to his club, and was seen with him every-where—in the Bois, at the restaurants, and the theatres. At times, some of his friends inquired: "Who is that queer little fellow?" with a touch of irony in their tone, but when the marquis carelessly answered: "A poor devil who has just come into possession of a property worth twenty millions!" they became serious, and requested the pleasure and honor of an introduction to this fortunate young man.

So M. de Valorsay had invited Gordon-Chalusse to accompany him to Baron Trigault's approaching *fête*. It was to be an entertainment for gentlemen only, a monster card-party; but every one knew the wealthy baron, and no doubt with a view of stimulating curiosity he had declared, and the *Figaro* had repeated, that he had a great surprise in store for his guests. Oh! such a surprise! They could have no idea what it was! This *fête* was to take place on the second day after Mademoiselle Marguerite's arrest; and on the appointed evening, between nine and ten o'clock, M. de Valorsay and his friend Coralth sat together in the former's smoking-room waiting for Wilkie to call for them, as had been agreed upon. They were both in the best of spirits. The viscount's apprehensions had been entirely dispelled; and the marquis had quite forgotten the twinges of pain in his injured limb. "Marguerite will only leave prison to marry me," said M. de Valorsay, triumphantly; and he added: "What a willing tool this Wilkie is! A single word sufficed to make him give all his servants leave of absence. The Hôtel de Chalusse will be deserted, and Madame Léon and Vantrasson can operate at their leisure."

It was ten o'clock when M. Wilkie made his appearance. "Come, my good friends!" said he, "my carriage is below."

They started off at once, and five minutes later they were ushered into the presence of Baron Trigault, who received M. Wilkie as if he had never seen him before.

There was quite a crowd already. At least three or four hundred people had assembled in the Baron's reception-rooms, and among them were several former *habitués* of Madame d'Argelès's house; one could also espy M. de Fondège ferociously twirling his mustaches as usual, together with Kami-Bey, who was conspicuous by reason of his portly form and eternal red fez. However, among these men, all noticeable for their studied elegance of attire and manner, and all of them known to M. de Valorsay, there moved numerous others of very different appearance. Their waistcoats were less open, and their clothes did not fit them as perfectly; on the other hand, there was something else than a look of idiotic self-complacency on their faces. "Who can these people be?" whispered the marquis to M. de Coralth. "They look like lawyers or magistrates." But although he said this he did not really believe it, and it was without the slightest feeling of anxiety that he strolled from group to group, shaking hands with his friends and introducing M. Wilkie.

A strange rumor was in circulation among the guests. Many of them declared—where could they have heard such a thing?—that in consequence of a quarrel with her husband, Madame Trigault had left Paris the evening before. They even went so far as to repeat her parting words to the Baron: "You will never see me again," she had said. "You are amply avenged. Farewell!" However, the best informed among the guests, the folks who were thoroughly acquainted with all the scandals of the day, declared the story false, and said that if the baroness had really fled, handsome Viscount de Coralth would not appear so calm and smiling.

The report *was* true, however. But M. de Coralth

did not trouble himself much about the baroness now.
Had he not got in his pocket M. Wilkie's signature
insuring him upward of half a million? Standing
near one of the windows in the main reception-room,
between the Marquis de Valorsay and M. Wilkie, the
brilliant viscount was gayly chatting with them, when
a footman, in a voice loud enough to interrupt all conversation, suddenly announced: "M. Mauméjan!"

It seemed such a perfectly natural thing to M. de
Valorsay that Mauméjan, as one of the baron's business agents, should be received at his house, that he
was not in the least disturbed. But M. de Coralth,
having heard the name, wished to see the man who had
aided and advised the marquius so effectually. He
abruptly turned, and as he did so the words he would
have spoken died upon his lips. He became livid, his
eyes seemed to start from their sockets, and it was
with difficulty that he ejaculated: "He!"

"Who?" inquired the astonished marquis.

"Look!"

M. de Valorsay did so, and to his utter amazement
he perceived a numerous party in the rear of the man
announced under the name of Mauméjan. First came
Mademoiselle Marguerite, leaning on the arm of the
white-haired magistrate, and then Madame Ferailleur;
next M. Isidore Fortunat, and finally Chupin—Victor
Chupin, resplendent in a handsome, bran-new, black
dress-suit.

The marquis could no longer fail to understand the
truth. He realized who Mauméjan really was, and the
audacious comedy he had been duped by. He was so
frightfully agitated that five or six persons sprang
forward exclaiming: "What is the matter, marquis?
Are you ill?" But he made no reply. He felt that he

was caught in a trap, and he glanced wildly around him seeking for some loophole of escape.

However, the word of command had evidently been given. Suddenly all the guests scattered about the various drawing-rooms poured into the main hall, and the doors were closed. Then, with a solemnity of manner which no one had ever seen him display before, Baron Trigault took the so-called Mauméjan by the hand and led him into the centre of the apartment opposite the lofty chimney-piece. " Gentlemen," he began, in a commanding tone, " this is M. Pascal Ferailleur, the honorable man who was falsely accused of cheating at cards at Madame d'Argelès's house. You owe him a hearing."

Pascal was greatly agitated. The strangeness of the situation, the certainty of speedy and startling rehabilitation, perhaps the joy of vengeance, the silence, which was so profound that he could hear his own panting breath, and the many eyes riveted upon him, all combined to unnerve him. But only for a moment. He swiftly conquered his weakness, and surveying his audience with flashing eyes, he explained, in a clear and ringing voice, the shameful conspiracy to obtain possession of the count's millions, and the abominable machinations by which Mademoiselle Marguerite and himself had been victimized. Then when he had finished his explanations he added, in a still more commanding voice, " Now look; you can read the culprits' guilt on their faces. One is the scoundrel known to you as the Viscount de Coralth, but Paul Violaine is his true name. He was formerly an accomplice of the notorious Mascarot; he is a cowardly villain, for he is married, and leaves his wife and children to die of starvation ! " The Viscount de Coralth fairly bellowed with

rage. But Pascal did not heed him. "The other criminal is the Marquis de Valorsay," he added, in the same
ringing tone. There was, moreover, a third culprit
who would have inspired mingled pity and disgust if
any one had noticed him shrinking into a corner, terrified and muttering: "It wasn't my fault, my wife compelled me to do it!" This was General de Fondège.

Pascal did not mention his name. But it was not
absolutely necessary he should do so, and besides, he
remembered Marguerite's entreaty respecting the son.

However, while the young lawyer was speaking, the
marquis had summoned all his energy and assurance
to his aid. Desperate as his plight might be, he would
not surrender. "This is an infamous conspiracy," he
exclaimed. "Baron, you shall atone for this. The
man's an impostor!—he lies!—all that he says is false!"

"Yes, it is false!" echoed M. de Coralth.

But a clamor arose, drowning these protestations, and
the most opprobrious epithets could be heard on every
side.

"How will you prove your assertion?" cried M. de
Valorsay.

"Don't try that dodge on us!" shouted Chupin.
"Vantrasson and mother Léon have confessed everything."

"Who defrauded us all with Domingo?" cried several people; and, loud above all the others, Kami-Bey
bawled out: "To say nothing of the fact that the sale
of your racing stud was a complete swindle!"

Meanwhile, Pascal's former friends and associates,
his brother advocates and the magistrates who had listened to his first efforts at the bar, crowded round him,
pressing his hands, embracing him almost to suffoca-
tion, censuring themselves for having suspected him,

the very soul of honor, and pleading in self-justification
the degenerate age in which we live—an age in which
we daily see those whom we had considered immaculate
suddenly yield to temptation. And a murmur of respectful admiration rose from the throng when the excitement had subsided a little, and the guests had an
opportunity to observe Mademoiselle Marguerite,
whose eyes sparkled more brightly than ever through
her happy tears; and whose beauty acquired an almost
sublime expression from her deep emotion.

The wretched Valorsay felt that all was over—that
he was irretrievably lost. Seized by a blind fury like
that which impels a hunted animal to turn and face the
hounds that pursue him, and bid them defiance, he confronted the throng with his face distorted with passion,
his eyes bloodshot, and foam upon his lips; he was
absolutely frightful in his cynicism, hatred, and scorn.
"Ah! well, yes!" he exclaimed—"yes, all that you
have just heard is true. I was sinking, and I tried to
save myself as best I could. Beggars cannot be choos-
ers; I staked my all upon a single die. If I had won,
you would have been at my feet; but I have lost and
you spurn me. Cowards! hypocrites! that you are,
insult me if you like, but tell me how many among you
all are sufficiently pure and upright to have a right to
despise me! Are there a hundred among you? are
there even fifty?"

A tempest of hisses momentarily drowned his voice,
but as soon as the uproar had ceased, he resumed,
sneeringly: "Ah! the truth wounds you, my dear
friends. Pray, don't pretend to be so distressingly virtuous! I was ruined—that is the long and short of it.
But what man of you is not embarrassed? Who among
you finds his income sufficient? Which one of you is

not encroaching upon his capital? And when you have
come to your last louis, you will do what I have done,
or something worse. Do not deny it, for not one
among you has a more uncompromising conscience,
more moral firmness, or more generous aspirations than
I once possessed. You are pursuing what I pursued.
You desire what I desired—a life of luxury, brief if it
must be, but happy—a life of gayety, wild excitement,
and dissipation. You, too, have a passion for pleasure
and gambling, race-horses, and notorious women, a
table always bountifully spread, glasses ever overflowing with wine, all the delights of luxury, and everything
that gratifies your vanity! But an abyss of shame
awaits you at the end of it all. I am in it now. I
await you there, for there you will surely, necessarily,
inevitably come. Ah, ha! you will not then think my
downfall so very strange. Let me pass! make way!
if you please."

He advanced with his head haughtily erect, and
would actually have made his escape if a frightened
servant had not at that moment appeared crying:
" Monsieur—Monsieur le Baron! a commissary of
police is downstairs. He is coming up. He has a
warrant! "

The marquis's frenzied assurance deserted him. He
turned even paler than he already was if that were
possible, and reeled like an ox but partially stunned by
the butcher's hammer. Suddenly a desperate resolution
could be read in his eyes, the resolution of the condemned criminal, who, knowing that he cannot escape
the scaffold, ascends it with a firm step.

He hastily approached Baron Trigault, and asked in
a husky voice: " Will you allow me to be arrested in
your house, baron? me—a Valorsay! "

It might have been supposed that the baron had expected this reproach, for without a word he led the marquis and M. de Coralth to a little room at the end of the hall, pushed them inside, and closed the door again.

It was time he did so, for the commissary of police was already upon the threshold. " Which of you gentlemen is the Marquis de Valorsay? " he asked. " Which of you is Paul Violaine, *alias* the Viscount de——."

The sharp report of firearms suddenly interrupted him. Every one at once rushed to the little room, where the wretched men had been conducted. There extended, face upward, on the floor, lay the Marquis de Valorsay, with his brains oozing from his fractured skull, and his right hand still clutching a revolver. He was dead. " And the other ! " cried the throng; " the other ! "

The open window, and a curtain rudely torn from its fastenings and secured to the balustrade, told how M. de Coralth had made his escape. It was not till later that people learned what precautions the baron had taken. On the table in that room he had laid two revolvers, and two packages containing ten thousand francs each. The viscount had not hesitated.

* .* * * *

Pascal Ferailleur and Mademoiselle Marguerite de Chalusse were married at the church of Saint Etienne du Mont, only a few steps from the Rue d'Ulm. Those who knew the mystery connected with the bride's parentage were greatly astonished when they saw Baron Trigault act as a witness on this occasion, in company with the venerable justice of the peace. But such was the fact, nevertheless. Treated more and more outrageously by his daughter and her husband, separated from his wife, who had nearly lost her reason, although her letters were saved, the baron has nowadays found affection and a home with Pascal and his wife. He plays cards but seldom now—only an occasional game of *piquet* with Madame Ferailleur, and he amuses himself by making her start when she is too long in discarding, by ejaculating, in a stentorian voice: "We are wasting precious time!" Sometimes they go out together, to the great astonishment of such as chance to meet the puritanical old lady leaning on the baron's arm. She often goes to visit and console the widow Gordon, formerly known as Lia d'Argelès, who now keeps an establishment near Montrouge, where she provides poor, betrayed and forsaken girls with a home and employment. She has yet to receive any token of remembrance from her son. As for her husband, she supposes he is dead or incarcerated in some prison.

It is to Madame Gordon that the Fondèges are often indebted for bread. Obliged to disgorge their plunder, and left with no resources save the fifty francs a month allowed them by their son, who has been promoted to the rank of captain, their poverty is necessarily extreme. Oh! those Fondèges! M. Fortunat only speaks of them with horror. But he is loud in his praises of Madame Marguerite, who repaid him the forty thousand francs he had advanced to M. de Valorsay. He speaks in the highest terms of Chupin also; but in this, he is scarcely sincere, for Victor, who has been set up in business by Pascal, told him very plainly that he was determined not to put his hand to any more dirty work, and that expression, "dirty work," rankles in M. Fortunat's heart.

Chupin's resolution did not, however, prevent him from attending the trial of Vantrasson and Madame Léon—the former of whom was sentenced to hard labor for life, and the latter to ten years' imprisonment. Nothing is known concerning M. de Coralth; but his wife has disappeared, to the great disappointment of M. Mouchon. As a dentist, Dr. Jodon is successful. As for M. Wilkie, you can learn anything you wish to know concerning him in the newspapers, for his sayings, doings, and movements, are constantly being chronicled. The reporters exhaust all the resources of their vocabulary in describing his horses, carriages, and stables, and the gorgeous liveries of his servants. His changes of residence are always mentioned; his brilliant sayings are quoted. He is a social success; he is admired, fondled, and flattered. He makes a great stir in the fashionable world—in fact, he reigns over it like a king. After all, assurance is the winning card in the game of life!

THE END.